STRONG WINE
RED AS BLOOD

Books by Robert Daley

Novels

STRONG WINE RED AS BLOOD

A PRIEST AND A GIRL

ONLY A GAME

THE WHOLE TRUTH

Nonfiction

TARGET BLUE

A STAR IN THE FAMILY

CARS AT SPEED

THE WORLD BENEATH THE CITY

Text and Photos

THE SWORDS OF SPAIN

THE CRUEL SPORT

THE BIZARRE WORLD OF EUROPEAN SPORT

CHATEAU CONDERIE

Grand Vin

GRAND CRU CLASSÉ 1855

MARGAUX

MÉDOC

Paul
Conderie

Propriétaire
Margaux

1961

MISE EN BOUTEILLES AU CHATEAU

STRONG WINE
RED AS BLOOD

Robert Daley

A novel

HARPER'S MAGAZINE PRESS
Published in Association with Harper & Row
New York

STRONG WINE RED AS BLOOD. Copyright © 1975 by Robert Daley. All rights reserved.
Printed in the United States of America. No part of this book may be used or reproduced
in any manner whatsoever without written permission except in the case of brief quota-
tions embodied in critical articles and reviews. For information address Harper & Row,
Publishers, Inc., 10 East 53rd Street, New York, N.Y. 10022. Published simultaneously in
Canada by Fitzhenry & Whiteside Limited, Toronto.

FIRST EDITION

Designed by C. Linda Dingler

Library of Congress Cataloging in Publication Data
Daley, Robert.
  Strong wine, red as blood.
  I. Title.
PZ4.D1415St [PS3554.A43]   813'.5'4   74-27300
ISBN 0-06-121875-8

75 76 77 78 79 10 9 8 7 6 5 4 3 2 1

This book is for Larry Freundlich

BOOK ONE

1

In the middle of the night, Édouard Bozon, wine merchant, waited in his Bordeaux waterfront office to receive a shipment of fraudulent wine. The truck was an hour overdue. Bozon's nerves were frayed. He wore a revolver in a shoulder holster.

He was a big man, forty years old, with thick black hair and mustache, and a powerful jaw; he showed sparkling white teeth when he smiled, which was not often. He was an important man and a bully, and his 200-year-old firm, Bozon, Fils & Frères, was the third-biggest wine shipper in Bordeaux, which meant the world. He had no partners. The profits were his. He was a rich man, but would be richer after tonight; for a shipment of cheap red wine would come in by tanker truck any minute, first of many such shipments. A few hours later it would go out in bottles labeled authentic high-priced Bordeaux, to be sold in obscure parts of the world to people who would not get what they paid for.

This was fraud, and punishable by prison under French law—which was why Bozon's pleasure and excitement had been so great during the weeks he had carefully and cautiously set the scheme up. If caught he would be ruined, of course, and possibly his business would be confiscated by the state. But there was no chance of being caught, he believed. The risk was merely titillating, not real. Although Bordeaux swarmed with government agents charged with safeguarding the integrity of the wine, they were not magicians. They needed evidence, and none would be found. Besides, he was too powerful. He had too much influence. No agent would dare investigate him except with extreme circumspection. If this should happen, which it would not, Bozon would have ample warning.

But tonight's truck was an hour overdue, and Bozon had grown increasingly nervous.

Pacing his office upstairs over the warehouse he found himself standing before the map of France on his wall. The wine regions were painted red. The biggest came two-thirds of the way down the Atlantic Coast, where it looked as if by some gigantic force an ax had been driven sixty miles deep into the ribs of the country. The gash was the mighty Gironde, seven miles wide where it met the ocean, a river that, according to the map, seemed to run blood red with wine. Inland from both banks sprawled vineyards that were like capillaries—they leaked wine down toward the river. The map showed that sixty miles upriver there at last were bridges, the gash had begun to scar itself over, and that was Bordeaux, population 300,000, capital of the southwest, sixth-biggest city in France, but a one-industry town: wine.

The wine supported lumbermills that cut oaks down into barrel staves, and coopers who made the barrels, not to mention all the men who made and sold the pumps and hoses, the carts and vats, the high, spindly vineyard tractors. The wine supported bottle makers and label printers, château owners and vineyard workers, of course, and the migrant pickers each autumn. It supported lawyers who wrote contracts, brokers who arranged deals, and shippers who sent the wine all over the world, one of them Édouard Bozon. It supported the law-enforcement officers who protected the industry against itself. It supported one man in five overall. Most of these categories of people earned a poor living, though wine could be lucrative. A few men had turned mighty profits lately, including Bozon, who had managed to expand his distribution network into countries never even considered by his father or grandfather or any of the ancestors who had owned this firm since 1732.

But past profits were minuscule compared with those opening up to Bozon beginning tonight.

What could be keeping that truck? Bozon studied the Bordeaux wine area on his map and thought:

It really does look like the vineyards bleed down into the Gironde; and why do I have blood on my mind tonight? Where is that truck? What could be keeping it?

Nervously he decided to wait downstairs.

His building was as narrow as the tenement it much resembled, but

4

it was three hundred yards deep, portions having been added over the centuries, and in it were stored millions of gallons of wine in various stages of growth and dress: stacks of ordinary wine in bottles on their sides, famous château wine in wooden cases of twelve, bulk wine aging in casks, new wine in great vats nearly two stories high. All the buildings along the waterfront belonged to wine shippers, all were as shabby outside as this one, and as deep and rich inside, and the ownership of such a building was, within the wine trade, a mark of distinction.

Bozon went downstairs on the waterfront side of his building and began walking toward the rear. It was like walking through a mine or subway tunnel, even to the tracks on the floor that were there to roll barrels along. The walls and high-vaulted ceiling were gluey with mold, and the place reeked of spilled wine. The walls were thick and there were no windows. A few widely spaced neon lights hung down from rafters that crossed high up, giving lateral support to the old walls. On either side of the corridor down which Bozon walked were barrels on their sides. They were stacked three barrels high, and the barrel ends were chalked with serial numbers. On the floor lay the poles used for running the third row of barrels up and down.

Beyond this barrel room, a new building started and the tunnel changed dimensions. This was the cooperage, where barrels were made, repaired, rebuilt. Stacks of staves and hoops lay about. Tools lay on the blacksmith's forge, where by day the hoops were hammered out by hand; the chimney flue went up through four stories and out.

In the next compartment were miniature sample bottles on shelves, each identified by numbers penned onto gummed labels, each corresponding to another number on a page in a ledger. For twenty yards Bozon walked past shelves of sample bottles, row after row after row, for Bozon was obliged by law to keep the samples a certain time, even though all the wine they represented might have been sold and drunk long ago, and this law Bozon obeyed, why not, for many men worked for him at menial tasks, and kept the samples and ledgers ready for government inspection at any time.

The configuration of the building changed again, narrowed, and on each side of the corridor were what appeared to be jail cells. One was a storeroom. Behind the bars of the other by Bozon's order a single dim bulb burned night and day; for this cell contained rare old bottles worth a great deal of money, and Bozon wanted to see at a glance if any of his treasures had been disturbed.

Bozon peered in through the bars. Withdrawing a heavy, rusty key, he opened the cell, stepped in on the dirt floor, and began to look over his bottles.

In 1855 some sixty of the greatest Bordeaux wines had been officially ranked into five categories. This cell contained at least one bottle of each of the top three categories from the vintage of 1858, the so-called Comet Year, reputed to be the greatest vintage of the last century. This was one of the rare collections of the world, though the one at Château Lafite was better, and in his safe upstairs Bozon had certificates of provenance attesting to the authenticity of each bottle.

The corners of the cell were festooned with cobwebs, as were the racks themselves, and the mold on the walls was like red glue. All the bottles were clotted with dust and dead spiders except one, for this single bottle was the rarest he owned and Bozon often handled it. He liked to read its label, which had nearly disintegrated; the faded words "Château Dubignon" could still be made out. Château Dubignon no longer existed.

The bottle of 1858 Dubignon reposed on the highest part of the rack and was always the last bottle Bozon would lift down whenever he sought to impress important buyers by showing the contents of this cell. He reached for the bottle now, but his tight-fitting blue blazer (he was impeccably dressed as always) constricted his movements and he was obliged to undo the buttons first. As he reached again his revolver rode across his chest almost to his heart.

What is keeping that truck?

Though he lifted the bottle down, cradling it like the brittle old man it was, it gave him no pleasure. It was rare. It was worth money. There was nothing more to say.

Bozon knew approximately what the wine inside would taste like. Its color would have gone off from ruby red toward the color of tea. Its taste and bouquet, though indubitably that of a fine old wine, would be fleeting—here one second, gone the next, only to reappear again, exquisitely tantalizing. Some people got pleasure from drinking such wines. Bozon did not. He did not desire to drink it, only to own it. Wine changed and aged in the bottle every day of its life, and eventually this bottle, like every bottle, would die. But by keeping it in this cell, by carefully changing the cork every twenty-five years, he could keep it alive almost indefinitely.

Since there was only one such bottle in the world, it would never be drunk.

Bozon lifted it back. Perhaps the truck had come in by now. He locked the cell.

In general Bozon sold two types of wine: everyday table wine that he bought, bottled, sold—and which was drunk—within a few months of fermentation; and the great château-bottled wines which arrived here already three years old, and not at their best until at least three years after that and preferably more. The château wines arrived already nailed into cases and went out the same way and were the smallest part of his business. His major profit was in bulk sales.

As for the third category of wine, the rare old treasures, such bottles were auctioned off for charity—though not by Bozon—a good deal more often than they were drunk. They were almost never drunk.

Bozon came out into his vatting room, which was serviced via the rear street. The building widened out here and the room was huge and high-ceilinged. Three Spanish laborers were gossiping idly under a light, surrounded by Bozon's great empty vats.

The truck had still not come in.

The gendarme stood in the road with his arm up. To Françoise the headlights seemed to bounce off the white of his helmet, and off his upraised white glove and gauntlet. In the glare she saw his eyes blink.

There was a squeal of brakes as the tanker truck slowed.

The gendarme moved to the cab. Françoise was scared. His flashlight played inside, first on the driver, then on her. She sensed his surprise and felt his flashlight beam, first on her face, then on her sweater.

"What's your cargo?" the gendarme demanded.

"Liquid gold," answered the smart-ass trucker, who then turned to leer at Françoise.

The gendarme's voice went hard. "License, registration, identity card, acquit," he snapped.

Documents began to be handed down by the suddenly voiceless trucker. Françoise stared out her window toward the dark forest, as if hoping the gendarme would forget she was there. But she felt his flashlight along the line of her jaw.

The flashlight flicked back to the trucker. "Out of the truck," the gendarme ordered harshly.

I'm next, Françoise thought.

The gendarme was smooth-cheeked and not much older than

Françoise. He was interested in the truck, not her, but she didn't know that. She had begun, almost imperceptibly, to tremble.

The gendarme was two hours into his midnight to 8 A.M. tour of duty. He had a partner down the road who would signal by flashlight as wine trucks approached. Their only job tonight, barring emergencies, was to stop and check wine trucks, and this was the first they had seen and flagged down.

"Turn your pockets inside out," the gendarme ordered the trucker. "Now put your hands on the fender."

Françoise did not know what was happening to the trucker. The beam struck the back of her head. "You. Get down from the truck."

She slid across under the wheel and down to the road. Her knees felt weak.

"Papers," ordered the gendarme.

Reaching back inside, Françoise rummaged through her pack on the floor. She was so tense she could not find them.

"Hurry up."

She presented her identity card. "I didn't do anything," she said. "I just hitched a ride."

But the young gendarme, his gloved hand full of papers, walked over toward his motorcycle under the trees, where he spread the papers out on the seat. His partner had come up to shine a flashlight down on the papers, and the first gendarme, going through them, began to make notes in his memo book.

Like all wine trucks in France, this one carried a kind of passport whose pages showed seals, stamps, and signatures covering the many years that the truck had crisscrossed the country.

The most important document was the green acquit which related to this explicit shipment—ninety thousand liters of red wine en route from a warehouse in Marseilles to one in Bordeaux. It showed that internal excise taxes on the shipment had not been paid, meaning that the truck's hatches should be bonded, and the gendarme would check this in a moment. It also showed a kind of flight plan which the trucker had been obliged by law to file before setting out from Marseilles yesterday, and once his route was filed he was not allowed to deviate from it, but he had done so, the gendarme had observed at once. The gendarme now checked his watch. It was 2:10 A.M. and the truck at this moment was supposed to be on a parallel road ten kilometers south, and it should have reached this point, 114 kilometers east of Bordeaux, about an hour ago.

8

The gendarme noted all this down, then went back to the truck. "Hey, could I ask what's going on?" asked the trucker nervously. "Shut up."

There was an iron ladder up the side of the tank which the gendarme now climbed. He clomped along the top of the tank. There were three hatches. Straddling the tank, holding on by his calves and shins like a jockey on the neck of a horse, the gendarme began to spin the wheel of the number-one hatch cover.

"You're not supposed to open that hatch," suggested the cowed trucker. "Those hatches are bonded."

The second gendarme's flashlight beam swung hard as a blow onto the trucker. "I thought we told you to shut up."

Up there the seal snapped, and the cover clanged back. Françoise saw the gendarme's flashlight beam dip inside.

Wine. The most rigidly controlled commodity in France. More rigidly controlled inside France than almost any other commodity in any country in the world.

"Red," the gendarme called down. Françoise saw him reach down inside, then lick his fingers. "It's red all right."

He took some small sample bottles out of the side pocket of his uniform coat and filled one and corked it. With the heel of his hand he pushed the cork in all the way.

After screwing that hatch down, he moved along to open the other two.

"It's all red."

Françoise watched him reseal the hatches with official seals he took out of his pocket. He climbed down the ladder, dropping at last into the road.

"You're off your route," he accused the trucker.

He had four of the sample bottles filled and corked in his hand.

"So I'm off my route by four or five kilometers. There was a restaurant I wanted to stop at."

The second gendarme said harshly: "You should have put it down before you left Marseilles."

"France is a free country."

"You're late by over an hour," snapped the first gendarme.

"I stopped to eat," the trucker whined. "A man has a right to eat."

"You should have put it down."

Françoise's gaze flicked from one face to the other. She felt as terrified as a bird.

"And who is she?" the first gendarme demanded.

"I picked her up."

"You're not allowed to pick up hitchhikers when you're trucking wine."

On the fender of the truck, the gendarme began to write out summonses. No one had told him to write such summonses. On the other hand, no one had told him not to. He had no idea why he had been sent out here to check wine trucks, a job he had never been assigned before.

Light came from the truck's open door, from the second gendarme's flashlight, and from the headlights reflected off trees. The gendarme handed over two summonses.

"Why don't you give me one for the girl, too?"

"I'll overlook that," the gendarme said, and glanced at Françoise as if this might win him a smile. But it did not. She was too scared.

Under his breath the trucker began muttering. Françoise discerned something about fascist cops.

"What's that you're saying?"

The silent trucker climbed up into his cab.

"Here you are, mademoiselle," the gendarme said politely, handing back her identity card.

The truck engine coughed and began to rumble. Françoise climbed up on her side. It was over.

The first gendarme watched the truck's diminishing taillights. He was twenty-two years old and newly assigned to the motorcycle corps. He was proud of his uniform and of his powerful bike parked over there under the tree, and he was usually carefully polite to citizens, though not to smart-ass truck drivers who had broken the law. A miner's son from Roubaix in the north, he knew nothing about wine except that one drank it with meals. He supposed that tonight's sample bottles would go to laboratories for testing, but he did not know which laboratories or what they would test for.

The truck rumbled west toward Bordeaux. Gradually Françoise's heartbeat began to slow down. She had hitchhiked before, but never alone and never at night. She had been scared for hours, scared from the moment she first forced herself to climb up into this truck, thinking: If you're going to get home you have to accept rides. Being nineteen, she considered herself a mature young woman with, therefore, nothing to fear, but the trucker, a big rough man who stared at her sweater, had left the main road almost at once. She had crouched silent in her corner

10

for over a hundred kilometers until the gendarmes stopped the truck. She had been even more scared, if possible, of the gendarmes.

Now she heard the trucker, staring out over his headlights, begin muttering under his breath.

Françoise, who was the daughter of Jean Gorr, the cellar master at Château Conderie, heard him say: "When the Party comes to power you'll see. Heads will roll."

Françoise found she could talk again.

"What party?"

"The Party," answered the trucker.

It was a relief to talk. "Oh, you mean that party."

"You're too young to understand. When the Nazis were here, the Party saved France."

"They taught us in school that De Gaulle saved France."

"De Gaulle was a fascist."

The truck rumbled up onto the great suspension bridge over the Garonne River. Françoise was nearly home now, nearly safe. From high up the river was black, and she could see the glow of Bordeaux to the south. Home was in the Médoc, a few kilometers to the north.

On the other side of the river, the girl, who was on her way home from the university at Toulouse, got down from the cab. She was the first member of her family ever to go past secondary education and she trudged north under her heavy pack along a narrow country road. It was dark. No cars passed.

The truck driver, Armand Picot, wearing a thirty-six-hour growth of beard, teeth flashing angrily as he muttered to himself, continued south toward the increasing glow of the city. He had picked the girl up in the middle of the night for company, thinking she was a boy. When he saw that bosom his plans changed. The trucker had turned onto a dark secondary road, but the gendarmes—fascist state cops to Armand —stopped him. What were they looking for? They had their informants, he knew. Probably some stool pigeon had informed on his truck, which meant that his load was in some way fraudulent. This did not surprise him. Lately he had made several of these trips timed to reach Bordeaux between 3 and 4 A.M., which was not normal. He got paid a bit extra for such trips, which was suspicious in itself.

His truck rolled along the waterfront. The divided boulevard was lit by lampposts down the middle. On one side he could see cargo ships with solitary lights burning on deck. On the other rose the narrow waterfront buildings, each owned by one or another of the great wine

11

shippers. Delivery entrances were in the back.

There were double iron doors in the wall. A Spaniard answered Armand's knock, and two other Spaniards came out dragging hoses, which they hooked up to the truck. Armand wanted his papers signed, and to go home, but none of the Spaniards spoke French, so he went inside looking for a boss. In a lighted office he came upon the owner of the firm, Édouard Bozon himself, who immediately began shouting at him for being late and for entering this building at all.

"Get out," Bozon shouted. "At once."

Bozon was marching forward, a brute of a man. Armand had to back up or Bozon would have walked over him.

"I just delivered you ninety thousand liters of red," Armand offered.

"Out, I said. Out." Bozon was shoving him. "Wait in the truck."

"It will take you three hours to empty that truck," Armand whined. "I want to go home to bed. I've been on the road since early yesterday."

Bozon shouted: "You will drive that truck away from my door the minute it is empty."

"But—"

"Now get out of my place."

The cowed Armand backed out past the row of great vats, past the three Spaniards working to join hoses. A pump began going. A hose on the floor thicker than Armand's arm moved with the weight of the wine as he stepped over it. He saw it suddenly thicken and swell.

Once safe on the dark street Armand thought: The Party will see to this guy. I'll see to this guy personally.

Down the street Armand stood at a bar drinking wine.

The barman, known as Le Grand Jo, was a fat man with pudgy hands.

"Something's going on across the street," Armand muttered. He pushed his glass forward for a refill.

Jo looked interested.

"What are you talking about?" he asked.

"I'm no stool pigeon," said Armand.

The barman waited.

"They got gendarmes out tonight. They're out stopping wine trucks. I just came in from Marseilles." Armand nodded his head. "You understand me?"

"What's that got to do with across the street?"

"Not a thing, pal."

12

The fat barman walked away from him. Armand watched him polishing glasses at the other end of the bar. For all Armand knew, Le Grand Jo was a police informer. Armand understood that the cops paid off everybody who worked in the neighborhood of the wine houses.

Le Grand Jo came back to Armand's end of the bar. "I've seen you in here a lot," said the fat barman conversationally. "I don't remember your name."

"Joan of Arc," said Armand. He pushed his empty wine glass forward. "Give me another glass of pinard."

When Armand went back to the warehouse the hoses still reached from his truck under the steel door. Armand had drunk enough wine to feel truculent. He tried to get in the door but it was locked, and when he banged on it no one came. He watched the hoses surging as if they were alive. He climbed up into his truck, pulled his beret down over his eyes, and fell asleep.

One of the Spaniards woke him up, standing on the running board to reach inside the cab, shaking him. Armand looked up at the sky, which had turned gray with faint pink clouds. The Spaniard handed over the papers from the shipment. Armand turned the key and the engine rumbled.

Steering his brother-in-law's truck toward the yard, Armand thought: I bet Bozon would like to know about that police control I went through tonight. That's why I'm not telling him. Screw him.

Back in the warehouse Édouard Bozon paid off the three Spaniards and brusquely herded them out. They were laborers hired for one night only. He closed and bolted the iron doors behind them. The vast room he was standing in was crowded with twenty great oak vats, each of which could hold twelve thousand liters of wine. The contents of Armand's truck had just been emptied into eight of these vats, and with a piece of chalk Bozon now marked each vat with the date and the number of the shipment. He chalked the wood out of habit. He wasn't likely to forget what wine this was.

Tomorrow was Saturday. He had another force of Spanish day laborers coming in at 9 A.M. Barring a breakdown in one of his machines, all this wine would be bottled and labeled by noon Sunday, and by Sunday night it would be sailing down the Gironde toward the open sea, 10,000 cases, 120,000 bottles nonstop to the other side of the ocean. The profit to Bozon over and above his normal markup would be about one American dollar per bottle. Once the ship cast off, once there was one meter of river running between its side and the pilings, then there was no further risk for Bozon. The risk between now and Sunday night was practically nonexistent also, for he had thought out all details, and the newly arrived wine was now covered by a magnificent set of forged papers. Bozon was in a good mood. He was about to add 120,000 American dollars to one of his Swiss accounts. For one night's risk.

Taking out his revolver, the grinning Bozon walked along the row of newly filled vats, tapping them. The wood was stained purple from generations of vintages. Banging the wood, he listened to the dull, heavy thunk that came back. The noise had a substantial solidity to it. It sounded of money. At the end of the row Bozon tapped an empty vat, then the full one next to it. By then he was giggling. Plunging the revolver back into its holster, he opened wide his arms as if to embrace something, and began laughing hard. The room filled up with Bozon's strident laughter. But presently his laughter stopped, and his arms dropped. He stood contemplating his oaken vats, then switched off the lights and went upstairs to his sumptuous apartment on the top floor, where he locked the revolver in his safe, put a silk dressing gown on over his underwear, and fell asleep on his bed. He could afford only a few hours' sleep. He himself would open to the new gang of Spaniards in the morning.

Françoise Gorr, sleeping against a tree, awakened because of the dawn cold. At least now it felt safe to hitchhike. Hoping that a car would come by soon, she began walking down the narrow country road into the Médoc. There was forest on both sides of her. Ahead there was sunlight, the forest opened up and the vineyards stretched away on both sides. The girl was walking into the most famous wine country in the world, but she knew every building, every tree, and in addition she was only nineteen. The Médoc was not famous to her, it was—home.

She heard the car coming before she saw it, heard the heavy whine of expensive tires, and she stood part way into the road facing back the way she had come, thumbing.

The car that stopped was a new, black Mercedes, and behind the wheel sat Monsieur Conderie himself. Her family had been in the service of the Conderies for 150 years.

"Oh," she said, "it's you. Bonjour, monsieur."

"Françoise, what a delightful surprise."

She shook hands, for she had not been home or seen him in months. "You got a new car," she said, settling into it. "Nice."

14

"Yes, the Aston Martin was not really the car one wants to be seen driving this year."

She had dropped her pack over into the back seat. The car gathered speed.

"What time is it?" asked Françoise coolly. She knew Conderie had been out all night, either with a woman or gambling, and she wanted him to know she knew.

"Oh, about six o'clock in the morning, I should think," said Conderie.

Françoise, staring straight ahead, said nothing.

"I was with some friends in the city," Conderie explained. "I guess we lost track of time." After a moment he asked brightly, "Well, how is it you're home from the university so unexpectedly?"

"I felt like coming home."

Conderie waited for her to go on but she decided he would wait a long time.

"Hitchhiked all the way, did you?"

"I came most of the way on a truck," she said after a moment. "A wine truck, as it happens."

"I can't say I like the idea of young girls hitchhiking about the countryside. Anything could happen."

She had already forgotten last night's fear, and she didn't like lectures. She moved to cut this lecture off fast. "You mean a girl could lose her virginity or something?"

Conderie frowned. "I must seem out of date to you, Françoise, but you know I don't like to hear you talk that way. And I don't like to think of you alone in the middle of the night hitchhiking rides, either."

At Cantenac signs began pointing to the famous châteaux on either side of the road. It was like plunging headlong through the wine list of the greatest restaurant in the world. To the right, behind those high hedges, crouched Château d'Issan, according to the road sign. That lane to the left led up to Châteaux Brane-Cantenac, Cantenac-Brown, Kirwan, and Angludet, none of them visible from here. Ahead the turrets and towers of Château Palmer, flags flying, rose above the village. Château Margaux lay downhill and was approached via that alley of trees. A billboard rising above its vines announced Château Lascombes to the world. Châteaux Rausan-Ségla and Rauzan-Gassies, the signs declared, belonged to these fields of vines here, and that was Château Prieuré-Lichine half hidden there behind its priory and its wall.

15

Beyond Margaux they turned left onto a secondary road, and presently onto a dirt lane that led up to Château Conderie. The château itself was approached via an alley of sycamore trees. At the end of the alley was the arched gateway through the stone wall and beyond that was the château, part of which dated from the 1650s. Conderie drove into the gravel turn-around in front of the château, stopped, and faced Françoise.

"You really are turning into quite a lovely young woman, my dear. Every time I see you I'm surprised."

He put an affectionate hand on the knee of her blue jeans. She watched the hand on her knee until he became uncomfortable and took it off.

"How long do you think you'll be home? I have a good mind to take you into the city for dinner one of these nights, show everybody how proud of you I am."

Françoise looked at him. By now he needed a shave, of course. His hair was still black—maybe he dyed it—but in the morning light his stipple of beard showed gray or white, and the flesh of his face sagged. He must be over fifty, thought Françoise, who was too young to feel sympathy for the lines of age.

"Well, it certainly is a pleasure to me to be able to pay your way to the university," Conderie said brightly.

For the past week Françoise's boy friend had refused to let her out of their room except to go to the bathroom. For the moment she was fed up with college life altogether. She got out of the car.

Just then her father came around the side of the château.

The cellar master was sixty, but his face was so weathered that he looked older. He held the same job that his father and grandfather had held before him. He wore his workman's blues, and high rubber boots. He had taken off his beret as he approached. "Bonjour, monsieur," he said to his master, and waited respectfully several paces away. He did not shake hands with Conderie, or greet his daughter yet, but waited until his greeting had been acknowledged. Conderie, defeated by the daughter but still in charge here nonetheless, gave a nod, after which the cellar master moved to embrace Françoise.

The cellar master then turned back to Conderie, who was always hard to pin down and who was obviously about to slip away again.

"Monsieur, I was wondering if perhaps you had made any decision yet about spraying the vines against rot?"

"I told you I'd give my answer to that in good time."

16

"The first treatment should be done at once. I've been talking to some of the other régisseurs and cellar masters—"

Conderie stared out through the archway in the wall. The sun was now rising above the trees. His eyes seemed to go opaque. His face looked tired, Françoise thought—he was too old to stay up all night. After a moment Conderie turned back to his cellar master and said: "If you want to know the truth, I've decided against it. I make my wine according to the classical tradition. We never sprayed against rot two hundred years ago, did we? and I don't see why I should start now."

The cellar master stood with his cap in his hand. "Whatever you say, monsieur," he said glumly.

After a brusque nod at father and daughter both, Conderie crossed the gravel, stepped up the curving stone staircase with its wrought-iron railings, and they saw him disappear into the château.

The old cellar master stared pensively at the château.

"He doesn't have any money. That's why he doesn't want the treatment," said Françoise.

"I won't have you speaking that way against the patron," snapped her father.

"You still believe in the droit du seigneur, don't you?" said Françoise. "You still believe that just because he owns the château he's better than you are."

"That's enough."

"Where do you suppose he's been all night? How much do you suppose he has lost?"

"I won't stand for it."

Across from the château stood the back of one of the great stone aging sheds. Parked there was the little truck which the cellar master was allowed to use for personal transport. Françoise demanded the keys to this truck, and when her father handed them over, she threw her pack up onto the back, and drove the truck out through the arch and through the vines toward the stone cottage under the trees at the end of the lane, in which cottage her family had lived since the days when Napoleon was ruler of France.

Upstairs in his bedroom in the château, Paul Conderie rang for his housekeeper, who was also Gorr's wife and Françoise's mother, and when she came on the line he demanded café au lait and a basket of fresh crusty bread with butter and jam. Waiting for it, he paced the floor, and after it came he continued pacing, coffee cup in hand, so that, to his annoyance, the coffee overflowed and began to slosh around in

17

the saucer. Conderie was worried. He had spent the entire night playing baccarat in a cercle de jeu off the Cours de l'Intendance and he had
not done well. He had not done well at all.

Françoise, who had fallen immediately asleep on top of her bed in
the clothes she had journeyed in, became conscious of a hand stroking
her hair, and so stirred sensuously, as if urging it elsewhere. Then she
woke up. The hand belonged to her father. She saw from his face that
she had shocked him.

It was time he learned the facts of life, she thought.

He stood beside her bed in his stocking feet. The rubber boots that
he clomped about the vineyards in were no doubt parked as always
beside the back door, clotted with mud.

It annoyed her the way he padded about the house in stocking feet.

He sipped from a tumbler half filled with white wine. "Would you
like some wine?" he inquired.

The stone cottage was oak-paneled inside. Antique dealers in Paris
or New York would have paid fortunes for the paneling, but Françoise,
coming out into the main room, did not know this. The cottage dated
back nearly as far as the oldest part of the château. The paneling had
been made by hand, possibly by the same artisan who had done the
paneling in the château itself. He had worked there but lived here.

The cottage was small. The main room contained a fireplace ten
feet wide; it was so big there were benches to sit on inside it. The
impractical fireplace was no longer used. Instead a wood stove had been
set before it, the stove's flue connecting with the chimney flue. The
stove thus served the cottage both for cooking and as central heating.
Until Françoise was about nine years old there had been no bathroom
in the cottage. The "bathroom" had been out in the garden.

Her father handed her a tumbler of white wine.

"How did you get here?" asked her father.

She did not answer.

"I won't have you hitchhiking. It's too dangerous. How many times
do I have to tell you?"

Françoise made no jokes to her father about risking her virginity.

"So promise me you won't hitchhike ever again."

Françoise still said nothing. Her father could take her silence any
way at all. She knew he would want to take it as acquiescence on her
part, though she had agreed to nothing. Let him. After that she would
do what she wanted.

18

Françoise had learned that a person needed tricks to get through life, and this was the first she had mastered: when a man, your father or anyone else, wanted something from you, you gazed at him expressionlessly. He could read into your face whatever he wished.

Though she had peered at herself in mirrors often enough, Françoise did not see what men saw when they looked at her. They saw a very young, rather pretty face surrounded by dark hair, a face that looked already wounded by life.

"A man who picks you up, what is he to think? He thinks you're probably a street girl, that's what he thinks."

After a moment, Françoise said: "Papa, all the kids hitchhike."

"All he wants from you is your most precious possession."

Precious possession. Françoise almost laughed.

Jean Gorr kissed his daughter on the cheek. "I'm glad to have you home. I never wanted you to go away to that university anyway—"

Françoise said nothing.

"But Monsieur Conderie—" said Gorr.

At this hour Françoise's mother was probably up in the château preparing breakfast. They called her housekeeper, but she was the maid. The same thing would have become of me too, Françoise thought. It may still become of me.

"What does a beautiful young girl like you need with a university education? Pretty soon you'll be making some young man a fine wife."

Gorr smiled into his daughter's solemn, vulnerable face. "Nothing but Communists at that university anyway, so I am told," said the thick-fingered cellar master, pretending he was joking.

Françoise gazed at him expressionlessly.

"I wish you wouldn't wear pants all the time. You have some nice dresses too. So tell your old Papa that you'll put a dress on for dinner tonight."

Françoise wondered why she had come home. The university was at least looking outward, whereas this place looked down at the soil only. So why had she come home?

The only answer she could find was unacceptable to her: because she was very young, and had no place else to go.

2

New York.

Charles Stack wore vests he didn't like and horn-rimmed glasses he didn't need and always conservative suits cut in the style of three years ago. He was thirty-four, and although the personnel department knew this absolutely, and the company's other major executives vaguely, it was vital that all remained convinced by his appearance and demeanor that he was actually much older, and as thoroughly responsible as any other middle-aged man. Charles Stack's age was the only blot on his record. At thirty-four he was vice-president and, since Wilkinson died in March, chief operating officer of the Avco Drug Company and group vice-president of the conglomerate which owned Avco, and which was always spoken of inside as a "multinational company" ("conglomerate" being a newly dirty word) or simply as "The Company." Charles Stack had come very far very fast and meant to go further, faster. Since Wilkinson's death he had cut Avco's expenditures by eleven percent, principally by trimming the payroll, and had increased revenues by fourteen percent, principally by going nationwide with a new teenage pimple cream called Smoothness, which he himself had first sponsored three years ago, and which Wilkinson had been timidly, tentatively test marketing all the time since—until his death.

Charlie Stack was the youngest and most aggressive executive in The Company, and he knew that every executive on the level below was his enemy, and every executive on his own level, and also every executive on every level above. Those below envied him. All others feared him. It was a cutthroat conglomerate, as no one knew better than Charlie Stack. Charlie liked to joke that within The Company no one ever put his knife away, ever. Of course The Company also provided a living for hundreds of modest men and women. Charlie Stack scarcely knew these people existed.

The Company owned the seventh-biggest airline in the United

States, the fourth-biggest business-machine company, and a publishing company that produced movie magazines. It owned oil concessions in Libya and copper mines in three South American republics. It owned the ninth-biggest insurance company in America, and the world's largest firearm factory, which sold guns throughout the world to any nation or group of revolutionaries that paid cash money. Because the international sale of firearms was controlled in some areas by stringent laws, The Company five years ago had opened gun factories in Uruguay and Togo. That is, many of its operations were totally outside the control of any one country's laws. Recently it had been accused of subverting the government in Ghana, selling arms to both sides in Nigeria, and paying starvation wages to miners in Bolivia, Peru, and Ecuador.

The Company's publicity lately had been all bad, and so a message had arrived on the desks of all group vice-presidents marked "Top Secret Eyes Only," and signed by the chairman. The chairman had a name, Warren Endicott, but inside The Company he was referred to only as "The Chairman." The chairman's message was curt, as was the chairman himself most times. It pointed out that, in this world today, image was everything. A profitable business position could turn upside down overnight as a result of bad publicity. Consumer resistance and/or constricting legislation were realities best dealt with before they happened. Immediate steps must be taken therefore to uplift The Company's image world-wide. The way to uplift The Company's current image, which was perhaps somewhat less admired than heretofore (read: fallen to a miserable low state, thought Charlie Stack), was by a series of acquisitions of what the chairman termed leisure-time businesses. Ideally, for instance, The Company should acquire Walt Disney Studios. The Disney films were good clean fun everywhere in the world, and The Company, therefore, if it could buy Disney films, would in some measure be regarded as good clean fun as well. Of course, Disney Studios was obviously not for sale. But other fun companies might be. The chairman suggested a minimum of three acquisitions. Two should be of international character so that its new, good-clean-fun image should accrue to The Company world-wide. The third, since the biggest problem lay in the United States, might be of purely national import. The chairman suggested these fields of activity: candy, wine, sports. The type of thing he had in mind was the Nestlé Chocolate Company, a Swiss-based firm, he believed; Château Lafite-Rothschild wine; and, in the United States, the New York Yankees baseball team.

When Charlie Stack received this memo he laughed, and at the

21

Midtown Tennis Academy later he recounted the story to the pro who for the past hour had been trying to teach him a top-spin backhand. The pro had been born in Czechoslovakia, and had no idea what Charlie Stack was talking about. Stack said: "I'm surprised the old pirate didn't suggest that we buy the Vatican City and run it as a wholly owned subsidiary."

Charlie Stack thought he could afford to laugh. He thought the chairman's memo had nothing to do with him personally, for he was not even a member—not yet—of the executive committee, which would meet later to consider the chairman's ideas.

"You keep on good," said the Czech pro, "and you learn real good that top-spin backhand soon."

Charlie Stack shook his head, his mind filled not with tennis but with the arrogance of the chairman. Stack did not often discuss business with anyone, but had been unable to contain himself this time, and the pro was safe, almost the only contact Charlie Stack had who was safe, all others being either business associates or women, and most of Charlie Stack's women moved in the same circles he did. He did not like to waste time, and saw no reason not to combine sex and business.

Two days later came a budget meeting on the thirty-seventh floor of 660 Madison Avenue, The Company's international headquarters, which Charlie Stack attended, and at which he presented all of his accomplishments since the death of Wilkinson, also outlining his plans for the following year. To Stack's surprise the chairman was present at this meeting but, though he greeted Charlie warmly, he said nothing during Charlie's presentation. The meeting lasted four hours. The ten executives sat grouped around a long table shaped like the lid of a coffin, Charlie Stack thought, and polished to the same mahogany sheen. Legal pads and pencils lay in front of each executive, and as each made his presentation he withdrew the necessary papers and memos from a briefcase at his feet, replacing them in the briefcase the moment his turn ended—the chairman was known to like a neat table.

After Stack's presentation ended, the president of The Company's packaged-goods division, which included Stack's Avco Drug Company, questioned Stack carefully about past profits and planned future profits, but the questioning for once was in no way malicious, and Charlie Stack was surprised. These meetings were often as vicious as football games; you forced the ball forward, but you took your bruises doing it.

The president of the division, whose name was Johnston, had once held Stack's job himself, and Stack had once been his protégé. Stack was well aware that in Stack's place Johnston had failed to turn the profits Stack had turned. Johnston, fifty-two, had recently been promoted to division president and member of the board, and had been careful to hold the docile Wilkinson between himself and the fast-rising Stack. Now Wilkinson was dead, there was no buffer left, and Stack had looked for harder questioning than this from Johnston. Instead, toward the end of the questioning, Johnston, beaming, turned to the chairman and said: "What did I tell you? This guy's got it."

Stack was surprised, flattered, pleased, and afraid all at once. Keeping his face blank, he glanced at the other men around the table.

At lunchtime a Puerto Rican dressed in the white robe and toque of a master chef entered with a moving trolley containing tuna-fish sandwiches and coffee. One sandwich, one cup of coffee per man. As always, the chairman suggested that the meeting proceed, no need to interrupt it to eat a sandwich, any objections? Men munched silently while the presentations and the questioning continued.

Charlie Stack noted that two other executives of his rank were badgered more or less mercilessly by Johnston.

What did all this mean? Charlie Stack preferred to think that it meant he was about to be confirmed into Wilkinson's job and title.

When the conference ended at last, the chairman shook hands with everybody and strode from the room. Charlie Stack was on his way out the door when Johnston called him back: "Charlie, there's something I want to go over with you."

That's when Charlie Stack learned that someone else was to succeed to Wilkinson's job and title, and that Charles Stack was about to be named president and chief executive officer of The Company's thus far nonexistent wine division, with headquarters in Bordeaux, France. It would be Charlie Stack's job to fly over there, find and buy a famous château, and then begin producing profits within, say, two years, one year if possible.

When Charlie Stack got back into his own office he phoned the chairman. The chairman's secretary came on the line.

"Is he there?"

"Yes, he is."

But Charlie Stack's nerve failed him. "I'll tell you what I want. Tell him I have a court reserved for 8 P.M. if he'd like to play."

In a moment the girl came back on the line. "He said he'll meet you there."

"Fine," said Charlie Stack. He put the phone back in the cradle, then banged both fists on the desk. There was still a small chance then. If he could get the chairman to overrule Johnston, if he could convince the chairman of the idiocy of sending Charlie Stack, expert in drug marketing, to find and buy and run a wine château in some dumpy city at the end of the world—if he could make the chairman see that Johnston was merely trying to cut Charlie Stack's balls off . . .

If at that moment Charlie Stack could have destroyed the whole goddamn company he would have done it. But the only person within his power to destroy was Charlie Stack.

3

"I was sent over there as general manager for marketing, Europe and Africa, almost six years ago," said Carter. "Of course things might have changed since then."

Stack nodded.

"I was, you might say, asked to volunteer for the job. How about another?"

Charlie Stack put his hand over his glass. In an hour he would have to play the toughest kind of tennis there is, and he did not want to be muddled. The bar was dark and crowded, and he stared at himself in the dim mirror above the bottles.

"I think I'll have another," said Carter. Charlie Stack noticed that Carter's hand trembled slightly as he raised his glass to catch the barman's attention. Carter's hair had got very gray in the past year, Stack observed. Carter was in the drug business too, and the two men were what passed for friends inside the New York business community.

"Hell, all that's ancient history now," said Carter. "What did you bring it up for, anyway?"

"I've just been offered a hell of an opportunity," said Charlie Stack enthusiastically. "I can't tell you very much about it, but it involves the presidency of one of our divisions in Europe."

"Say, Charlie, that's great. I'm really happy for you."

"You've been over there, and I just wondered how it had turned out for you. A lot of guys that go over there, it's usually a three-year deal, and they get a lot of money and save on taxes, but I hear the re-entry problem is really difficult."

Stack watched the slightly trembling glass during its voyage to and from Carter's lips.

"Well, I could have left my firm," said Carter. "There were a number of other firms after me at the time, but, well, I had twelve years invested in them, and them in me, and I thought that going over there would be best for the company. I knew the drug business, and I knew marketing, and marketing is the same all over the world, right? Okay, so I didn't speak French. But all the middle-management guys anywhere in Europe speak English, you'll find. That's why European middle management of American companies is so mediocre, as a matter of fact. Most American companies hire middle managers on the basis not of how good they are, but of how well they speak English.

"So my wife and I had about two weeks between the time the job was offered and my due date in the Paris Profit Center. It wasn't really enough as far as selling the house went, and taking the kids out of school and all that, but we made it. I had a three-year contract."

"You mean a written contract?" asked Stack.

"No, a handshake deal. The president and the chairman both assured me that at the end of three years I'd come back to a job at least one rank higher than I had left, and if I really did well over there, then the sky would be the limit."

Stack stared at his hands on the bar. He had already read accurately between the lines: a power struggle within the company which Carter lost. His choice became dismissal or exile. He had chosen exile. Or, more correctly, he had had no choice at all.

As, at this moment, Charlie Stack had no choice at all. The difference was that Charlie Stack did not mean to accept exile without a fight, and if defeat took effect anyway, he did not mean to complain about it, not now, and not nearly six years later like Carter, either. Not ever.

"So, before I accept this opportunity, if I accept it, and believe me it's a major opportunity," said Charlie Stack, "I want to hear both the best and the worst from such an experienced, successful executive as yourself."

After Carter ordered a third martini his spirits rallied, and he began to describe his own marketing successes in Europe—during his second, third, and fourth years abroad, the company had shown profits of up to

25

twelve percent in five out of its six profit centers, showing a deficit only in Scandinavia.

"I thought your contract was for only three years," said Charlie Stack.

"Well, yes, but my company decided I was so effective that I was asked to stay on for a fourth year."

"How did this sit with your wife and kids?"

As a matter of fact, Carter's wife and kids had already returned to America at the end of the third year. His wife had found a house in the same suburb as before and had contracted to buy it—before Carter was informed that at the moment there was no job open for him in New York on the level he deserved. If he would stay on in Europe one more year, perhaps at the end of that time there might be. So during the fourth year Carter lived in Paris while his family lived in New York.

Under questioning by Charlie Stack, Carter admitted that, during his period in Europe, three other jobs he coveted had become vacant in New York. All were filled by promotions from within the New York office. Each time Carter had learned of one of these promotions he'd gone out to a bar to get drunk, Charlie Stack supposed.

Carter had been at that time, Charlie Stack knew, an extremely competent, aggressive, fast-rising executive. He was not that now. His European exile had smothered his career; perhaps he and it would never recover.

Stack was not particularly sympathetic.

Carter was still sharp enough over the next twenty minutes to describe in some detail his many successes in Europe, the number of servants he had employed there, the amount of money he had saved each year on income taxes, his vacations to Corfu and the Canary Islands—two or even three short vacations each year—the conferences in Scandinavia, Athens, Nairobi, to which often enough his wife had been able to accompany him because their children could be left in the care of servants. During this period Carter had driven a big black Mercedes and had lived in a villa in Versailles.

Nonetheless, his four-year exile in Europe had ruined him.

"Another advantage of such a job," said Carter, "is that you get to be on intimate personal terms with the very highest executives in your company. They're always flying over for this conference or that, the old tax write-off, you know. What would happen, I'd send a car and a chauffeur out to the airport to meet them, and then it would be up to me to act as a sort of tour guide. I'd have to set up reservations in all

26

the best restaurants, and at the golf courses and so on. My wife did the same for their wives. You're still not married, Charlie?"

"No."

Carter ordered another drink.

"What about re-entry?" asked Charlie Stack.

At the end of the fourth year, Carter had had to return to his old job at the same pay under the same executive who had driven him out in the first place.

"After about three months," said Carter, "I decided that the best thing for me to do was to move on to another firm." Carter now described how two cosmetic firms had "fought" over him, and he had chosen the bigger of the two, at a "substantial" though undisclosed salary, but at the end of three months he had become convinced that he had made a mistake, and had thereupon moved on to the other one. He began to describe his many triumphs in this, his third job in less than two years, and Stack waited patiently until these lies would come to an end.

"You hear all the executives talking about this re-entry problem," said Carter, "but in my case, as you can see, there really wasn't any re-entry problem."

Stack nodded, and signaled the barman for the check. Stack thought: Somebody ruined you, and we both know it, and now somebody's trying to do the same thing to me, but you don't know it and nobody is going to know it.

Out in the street, Stack shook hands with Carter.

"So don't be a stranger," said Carter.

"If I decide to take this opportunity," said Charlie Stack, "I'll send you a postcard with an exotic stamp on it."

Crowds on the sidewalk were thin now. Stack strode alone down Lexington Avenue toward what he thought of as the most important tennis match of his life—tonight's match with the chairman. He began to decide how he would play his shots, both on the court and off. The basic structure of big business was clear to him and always had been. Careers were built as much on internal politics as on sales reports. Once out of New York, he would not be able to get back in. If he did well in Europe, New York would not open ranks to readmit a powerful rival, and of course if he flopped he would have no credentials with which to seek readmittance. Of course he could seek another job from his European power base. The trouble was, no one would notice what he was doing so far away, there would be no offers, and if he went seeking a job then he would be dealing from weakness, not strength. Once he was over there he was lost. He must seek at all costs to get the chairman to countermand the order. That meant tonight's tennis game. As far as Charlie Stack was concerned, his career rode on tonight's tennis game.

The Midtown Tennis Club was in a huge, drafty old armory on Thirty-third Street. You could drive a lob high up into the darkness, and you would lose sight of it, and it would come down again into the lights without striking the roof. The armory was so vast that it was, in winter, virtually impossible to heat, and players played in a fifty-degree chill. The locker room was small and primitive. In other words this was the shabbiest tennis club Charlie Stack had ever known, but New York's mayor played there—his city Cadillac, with his detective-chauffeur seated at the wheel and the engine running, was often seen parked in the bus stop outside—as did both U.S. senators, certain film stars when in town, and numerous other celebrities big and small. This was the popular, the "in" tennis club in New York, and so it was where Charlie Stack would want to belong, whether or not the chairman also belonged, which he did. Charlie Stack aggressively sought out whatever were the in people, the in places, the in things this year, and changed them again next year as necessary, for one did not move ahead in life by following one's own mood and whim. Let artists and such freaks live on some lofty plane of their own. Charlie Stack meant to get down in the pit and slug it out with the best of the competition. Charlie Stack meant to move inexorably to the top. He meant to head this company at forty. The secret of life, as Charlie Stack saw it, was to get down there in the mud with everybody else who was trying to sell out. That's where the competition was. There was no competition up among the artists and philosophers who were refusing to play in the game at all.

Tonight as Charlie Stack entered the locker room, he passed the chairman seated on a bench, already dressed in tennis whites, slipping sweatbands onto both wrists.

"Hey, Warren," said Charlie Stack.

"Charlie," said the chairman. "How's your top-spin backhand coming?"

"Not good, Warren, not good," said Charlie Stack, thinking, Surely this is the only society in the world where one is advised to address the god figure in one's life as God behind his back but by his first name when face to face. "I'll be with you in a minute, Warren."

His own locker was in another row, and he began whistling a tune as he got undressed. So far as he knew, he and the chairman were the only men in the locker room at the moment, and he wanted to keep his own presence there at the top of the chairman's mind. So Stack, stepping into his jock and shorts, whistled. Barefoot and bare-chested, he stepped around the row of lockers and said to the chairman with a big grin: "Say, Warren, have you heard about my new assignment?"

"Oh," said the chairman, "Yes, I have."

Charlie ducked back in front of his own locker and began tugging on his sneakers. "It sounds like a great opportunity," Charlie called across the top of the lockers. "I sure want to thank you."

That was enough for the moment, Charlie Stack reflected. A hint to the chairman, as if the chairman had had any doubts, that more on this subject would be forthcoming. But in what way and for what purpose? For the moment, the chairman would remain in doubt.

Fully dressed, and hefting his tennis racket, Charlie Stack came around the row of lockers. "As for my top-spin backhand," he said, "you don't have to worry about that tonight. I just don't have any confidence in it yet."

The two men walked out of the locker room and onto an empty court.

"Well, Rosewall had no top-spin backhand," commented the chairman.

"That's right, and he did okay, didn't he?"

The ball began spinning back and forth across the net. The chairman was fifty-four and had once been a fine college tennis player. Charlie Stack was twenty years younger and played every single day during lunch hour. He was six feet two and weighed 195 pounds. In college at Ohio State he had played on the tennis team and had been conference champion as a junior. He had even considered turning pro, but had opted for a business career because competition was what he loved, and the competition was stiffer there. He had taken care of his body religiously then and since, and even now was probably as fit as most professional athletes. Stack was proud of his body, proud of the way women responded to it, and convinced that rival businessmen responded to it too, acceding to his will as much because he was fitter and stronger as because of his grasp of profit and loss. Charlie Stack used his body whenever possible to intimidate people, male as well as female.

The chairman, Stack knew, was vain about his tennis, and no doubt was one of the best fifty-four-year-old tennis players in the world. Having lost much of his youthful power, he attempted to compensate for it with a bewildering assortment of slices and spins, any one of which

Charlie Stack could have driven back down his throat had he so chosen. In addition the chairman had no backhand volley to speak of, and of course no speed of foot. On the other hand, his forehand drives were amazingly accurate. Give him a two-foot alley down the line, and he would pass you every time.

Stack had now played the chairman about five times during the past year, beating him approximately 6–4, 6–4 each time. The chairman did not really expect to beat a player of Stack's youth and class, and it would have been a major mistake to throw the game completely, Stack knew. The chairman was vain, but not an idiot. The problem in the past, and tonight too, was to return the ball always to the chairman's strength, to give him the two-foot alley whenever possible, and absolutely never, once the chairman had rushed the net, to return him the type of high backhand volley that would tie him in knots. Playing the chairman was delicate tennis, for Stack had to smother all his normal, aggressive instincts, to place the ball each time into a zone that his instincts screamed at him to avoid, and, in addition, this entire pattern must be totally disguised. The chairman must not guess what was happening to him.

And so the game began with Stack serving. He hammered in three high, hard serves, and the ball came up off the court so fast that the chairman scarcely got his racket back at all. Leading 40–love, Stack deliberately drove his first serve into the net, then aimed his second serve toward the chairman's forehand, and rushed the net. Predictably, the chairman drove the ball past him. Now Charlie hammered his first serve in, but he had taken something off it, enough so that the chairman drove it back, a twisting shot that landed at Charlie's feet at the service line. He scooped it up, a soft looping shot that carried into the forehand corner, so that the chairman was able to drive another winner past him.

Enough, thought Charlie Stack, and he drove his first service into the backhand corner, and the chairman never saw it go by.

Now the chairman served. His serves had very little steam, but a lot of high, bouncing kick to them, and Charlie drove the first one back into the forehand corner, and they rallied from the baseline, Charlie hitting the ball flat and deep, the chairman alternately slicing the ball to Charlie's backhand, and hitting top-spin drives to Charlie's forehand. As soon as a ball landed short, Charlie rushed the net, and the chairman drove the ball by him. Following his next service, the chairman rushed the net and put away a sharply angled volley. After that they again rallied from the baseline. Charlie's concentration was off. He was think-

30

ing about the more important of the games he was playing here tonight, which was not tennis.

As they each held service, Charlie's concentration began to come on sharp. One game at a time, he told himself, and the game right now is tennis. In the tenth game, he at last broke the chairman's service, letting the score go several times to deuce, before hammering a passing shot into the backhand corner.

First set to Charlie Stack, 6–4.

The two men sat on the bench with their backs toward the stone wall of the armory.

"I wasn't sharp there at all at first," said Charlie Stack. "I kept missing the lines."

The chairman wiped his sweaty face with a towel.

"You're sharp as hell tonight, though," said Charlie Stack.

"I always play well against you, Charlie."

"Those spins of yours give me a lot of trouble."

The chairman stood up. "Maybe I can take you in this second set."

"I found myself thinking of my new European assignment out there," said Charlie Stack. "The wine thing. That's no way to play tennis."

"We'll talk about it later. Let's play tennis," said the chairman.

The second set was a repeat of the first, except sharper and faster. Charlie Stack chased all thoughts of wine, France and exile from his mind, and slashed each shot directly into the chairman's strength. It was returned hard, and Charlie slashed it back again to the same place. Some rallies lasted six strokes or more, and each time they changed over the chairman would plop down on the bench and wipe his face with a towel, breathing hard but beaming. The score was 5–5, and Charlie decided to let the game go on, but at 6–6 the chairman began to run out of breath and energy, and though Charlie widened the alley down the sideline, the chairman no longer had enough left to aim the ball accurately, or hit it hard enough for Charlie to lunge but miss.

When the game ended, the chairman was exhausted, and no longer beaming. Damn, thought Charlie Stack, I may have let the game go on too long.

"You didn't hit me three backhand volleys all night," gasped the chairman.

Look out, thought Charlie Stack. "I tried to, but you put so god-damn much spin on the ball that I couldn't control it."

The chairman gave him a tired smile. "Don't snow me, Charlie. I

31

started to wonder out there why I always played so well against you. No one else hits me as many forehands as you do. Am I on to something, Charlie?"

Charlie Stack, pretending exhaustion, pretending also to have missed the import of the chairman's remark, stared at the floor and muttered, "It's those goddamn slices and spins of yours. I'm a power player. I play much better against power players."

The chairman got up off the bench and walked toward the locker room. After a moment, Charlie Stack trailed after him. Charlie Stack thought: He's going to see through anything I say. That's why he's chairman.

In the locker room the chairman sat slumped on the bench, his head almost between his knees. Standing over him, Stack said: "I don't know whose idea it was to put me at the head of the new wine division, whether it was yourself or another, but I know that you all considered my liabilities as well as my assets. Yes sir." Charlie Stack gave a confident laugh. "On the one hand, you saw how I turned Avco completely around, and brought in a profit picture that hadn't been possible before. On the other hand, you must have thought for a long time over the fact that I don't speak French, that I've never been to France except on vacation, and that I don't have any experience in the wine business."

Charlie Stack, one foot up on the bench, waited.

The chairman, looking up, patted Charlie on the calf, saying, "France is a backward country, Charlie. With your experience in the drug business, you'll eat them alive over there."

"I'm really looking forward to it," lied Stack. "—Even though I'm not sure, given those handicaps I just mentioned which I'll be starting out with, that choosing me was absolutely the best thing as far as The Company is concerned. If you or anyone else was to have second thoughts, I certainly could understand it, and you certainly know that Avco is my first love. If you decided that that's where I should stay, well, fine." It was a rather long speech, and sounded clumsier than Charlie had hoped, so now he gave a large laugh and remarked: "I saw your original memo, by the way, and I was rather hoping I'd be the one you chose to buy the Yankees."

There was a somewhat long silence. It did not end.

"Well," said Charlie Stack. "That shower is sure going to feel good."

Charlie stood under the shower. The stream struck him directly on top of the head and spilled down over his face, so that he could neither see nor hear. After a while he turned the shower off, toweled himself dry, dressed, put on the goddamn horn rims, and he was combing his hair in front of the mirror when the chairman appeared beside him to do the same. They strolled outside into the night together. The chairman's limousine was waiting at the curb. It was as long as the mayor's limousine, and of course in salary the chairman earned about fifteen times what the mayor earned, nearly a million dollars in salary and bonuses last year.

"Can I drop you anywhere, Charlie?"

"No thanks, Warren."

The chairman patted Charlie Stack on the back. "Start with Château Lafite-Rothschild. I don't suppose the Rothschilds want to sell, though. Get something with a tennis court, and I'll come over there and play you and you can groove another five hundred shots into my power. Night, Charlie."

Shit.

Charlie Stack, stuffing the horn rims into his breast pocket, hailed a cab. He knew a divorcee who would be glad to see him. He could work off his frustration on her still-elegant body. After that he would get ready to go to Bordeaux—where he would buy them a château to make their eyes bug out. He judged he had made two mistakes. The first was to report a fourteen percent increase in profits since Wilkinson died. That was about eight percentage points too much. Six percent extra profit would have branded him a competent, dependable new executive. Fourteen terrified everyone. No one's job was safe from a man who could turn fourteen percent.

The second mistake was to think he could con the chairman at tennis.

Shit.

4

Paul Conderie awakened in the great bedroom of his château at noon. Opening French doors, he stepped onto his small balcony and stood blinking into the noon sunlight. Then he reentered the room and stared at his telephone.

Perhaps it had already rung. Perhaps the maid had not dared to wake him.

He moved to the phone. "Any calls?"

"No, monsieur."

"Bring me my breakfast."

"Oui, monsieur."

Slipping on his dressing gown, Conderie paced his room.

Preceded by a timid knock, Madame Gorr entered bearing a breakfast tray. She was a thick-legged, middle-aged peasant woman with red hands.

The Médoc was a poor country except for the wine, which was only now being rediscovered. It was possible that Madame Gorr scarcely knew how to read and write—very few of these peasants had had more than three or four years of schooling. Conderie lifted a croissant from the basket on the tray: "They're cold."

The woman snatched up the basket. "I'll heat them for you, monsieur."

"Put the basket down."

"Oui, monsieur."

"Now leave me."

"Oui, monsieur."

When the door closed, Conderie stared at the telephone that refused to ring, then turned toward his breakfast tray. It held a folded newspaper, steaming café au lait in a double-sized cup of English bone china so fine it was almost transparent, the basket of croissants, and a single perfect rose standing in a slim vase of etched crystal. An embroidered napkin served the tray as a tablecloth. Flowers were important to these peasants, Conderie had once been surprised to learn, and a rose bush grew at either end of every row of vines belonging to his château, and most others. The stem of the rose that decorated his tray had been, today as always, stripped of its thorns before being offered to him.

Conderie nibbled a croissant and stared at his telephone. He was not hungry.

At last he went to the telephone and made the call he had been afraid to make. "Hello, Eddie? This is Paul."

Conderie spoke in English—deliberately.

"I told you not to call me here," Édouard Bozon snapped.

Conderie gave a nervous laugh. "I say, old man, there's no reason why a prominent château owner can't talk on the telephone to a prominent shipper."

"I can't talk to you now."

Conderie tried to keep his voice relaxed. "Well, when can you talk to me? I expected your call by now."

"As I told you, when I have something to report, I'll report it."

Conderie did not know who might be listening in, and the majority of people involved in the wine trade spoke at least some English. But desperation got the better of him. "I was just wondering when I might realize something from our—" He had started to say "transaction" but the word suddenly sounded incriminating. "—From the fruits of our efforts," Conderie said.

"Not yet."

"I'm in a bit of a bind," said Conderie, trying to keep the urgency out of his voice. He needed money. He had notes to meet.

"I'll call you when I have something, and not before," said Bozon rudely and hung up.

Conderie had ground his cigarette out while speaking. He lit another, and paced his room, smoking.

Where were the enormous profits Bozon had promised him? When Conderie had handed over the cash, Bozon had signed nothing—to protect Conderie if anything went wrong, Bozon had explained. Maybe the shipper's scheme—Conderie had asked no questions—had from the very start included the swindling of Paul Conderie too. Maybe there would never be any profits. Maybe Conderie would never get his investment back.

From his balcony, Conderie flicked the nub of his cigarette down into the garden. His view was almost entirely of vines. About a mile away ran the road that joined all the Médoc villages together and, even as he watched, a high red tourist bus went by, slashing through the blanketing vines, like a surgeon's scalpel producing sudden gouts of blood. All of the vines between the road and the château belonged to Paul Conderie. The vines on the other side belonged in part to Château Margaux, and in part to Château Palmer.

Conderie turned back into his bedroom. From its fourteen-foot ceiling hung a great crystal chandelier dating from the reign of Marie Antoinette. Conderie much preferred his modern apartment in Paris, though that was lost to him for the time being, for he had recently loaned it to the Swedish ambassador, whom he scarcely knew. It had been a grand and hilarious gesture in the midst of a grand and hilarious party. The gesture had given Conderie great pleasure at the time, and he had been choking off regret ever since. He made it a policy never to regret gestures afterward. A gesture was the greatest luxury of all, a luxury given only to a few men like himself, and the elation of the moment was its own reward.

"The ability to make the grand gesture is what separates the men from the cows," Conderie had whispered to some friends, as he handed over his door keys to the surprised Swede. Everyone had laughed, and then applauded, and they had toasted him in champagne.

Still, he thought, pulling on a new cigarette, if he could somehow wedge that ambassador out into the street, he could sell the apartment, or mortgage it, and so raise some money. But how, without the people who had applauded him finding out about it?

Smoking, he looked out over his vines. He could not see any grapes, but he knew that now in September each vine was heavily weighted. Each vine was as heavy and portentous as a pregnant woman; each wore its thick, broad leaves like clothing that concealed both its swollen promise and its incredible vulnerability.

There was a wind today, he saw. The fields seemed to swell and subside and swell again. The wind seemed to pass over the vines like a hand smoothing the hair of a young girl.

It was a peaceful view, but Conderie was not at peace. In a week the harvest would begin. Soon Conderie would have something to sell. He might be able to sell a few futures almost at once.

An hour later, wearing a blue blazer, an ascot stuffed elegantly into his open shirt, Conderie came into the courtyard formed on three sides by the long stone chais, the sheds in which the wine was aged, and on the fourth by the cuverie, the building in which the wine was actually made. The cuverie contained the machinery for processing the grapes, and the great oak vats in which fermentation took place each October. Standing in the center of the courtyard awaiting him were the first of that day's visitors, four men and a woman. With a smile, Conderie introduced himself. One of the men was the head of the Kansas City Wine and Food Society, whatever that was, and the woman was his wife. Two of the other men owned a liquor store in New York, and the third was a member of the Quebec Liquor Board of Control. Conderie did not know if these people were important or not, and so was obliged to treat them as if they were. He wished that the wine syndicate in Bordeaux would exercise a bit more care before sending such visitors out here.

"Well, would you like to see how we make wine here at the château?" Conderie asked with a big smile.

Of course they would, why else were they here? They were also hoping, no doubt, for a taste of last year's wine, which was still aging in the barrels, and possibly for a taste of the two-year-old wine which had just been bottled. In the old days when few visitors came, châteaux could afford to give a taste to everybody. Now hordes came, relatively speaking, and in a year could empty a barrel or two of very valuable wine. So today only lesser châteaux still offered tastings. Their wine was worth less.

In the cuverie, Conderie pointed out the Bosnian oak vats, each of which held 3,300 gallons, all twenty-four of which had just been descaled and scrubbed clean with a ten percent solution of carbonate of soda, after which they had been rinsed with clear water. The new grapes would be thrown in there beginning next week.

This information brought sighs of wonder from the woman, and Conderie smiled.

"Wine is more delicate than people think," said Conderie. "You don't make fine wine just by stomping barefoot on the grapes, you know." He wagged a finger at them and got back an appreciative chuckle.

The machinery which ripped the grapes from their stems and pumped them up into the vats was of little interest to this group, so Conderie led them across the courtyard into the aging shed for new wines. Throwing open the chai's double oak doors, he exposed the view —six rows of neatly aligned barrels stretching into the dim distance.

The far wall was nearly a hundred yards away.

The shed was lit by electric candles held in wrought-iron wall fixtures. The only other wall decorations were ancient, gnarled wine roots, the outstretched arms of each achieving a spread of six feet or more.

"This shed holds last year's wine," said Conderie. "There are about six hundred barrels in this one room, and each barrel will fill about three hundred bottles."

He pointed toward the vine roots on the wall. "What you see there is that portion of each vine which was above ground. Each of those roots was about one hundred years old when ripped out. Vines begin to give usable grapes at four years old—in fact, it's against the law for us to make wine from a plant until after it has given leaves four times. The young roots give the most grapes, but the old ones give the best. By the time the roots that you see on the wall there were pulled out, they probably gave only a few grapes each year, but those few I can assure you provided juice that was pure nectar."

The people were so attentive, so grateful at having met an actual owner, that Conderie began to feel better.

There were questions. The casks were oak, Conderie explained expansively, and were used only once before being sold to lesser châteaux, which would use them many times. But the great châteaux absorbed the expense of new casks every year, because the oak was believed to impart additional tannin and it was tannin that accounted for the longevity of the wine. It depended upon the year and the château, of course, but the great wines of the Médoc would live longer than any other wines in the world, would live as long as a man or longer. Most would improve in the bottle for twenty years or more, and would hold the same voluptuous taste until they were well past fifty. Occasionally a rare and carefully made wine might live to be over a hundred. Wine was truly alive, Conderie said.

Conderie's audience was so appreciative that he resolved to offer a taste of his new wine after all, and he sent a workman for glasses and a pipette. The workman returned carrying thin crystal wine glasses upside down among the fingers of his hands, and a slim glass tube—the pipette. At the nearest barrel, Conderie removed the glass bung, which, as he pointed out to his guests, was merely laid in there loosely, for at this state of its development the new wine needed to breathe. Inserting the pipette up to his knuckles, he stoppered its top hole with his thumb, and withdrew the pipette from the barrel. The pipette was now two-thirds full of wine. Holding it over the first glass, Conderie removed his thumb, and the wine ran out the other end into the glass. Conderie filled each of the glasses in turn in the same manner. The workman had returned with a tray of cubes of cheeses, which Conderie passed around, saying: "There's an old saying in the wine business. If you're selling wine, serve cheese. If you're buying wine, eat apples."

"That's right," the woman said. "Wine is at its best with cheese."

Conderie passed the glasses around. "Note how the wine is still hard, still rather acidic, almost unpleasant."

After gargling a mouthful, Conderie spat it down into the sand-filled stone spittoon on the floor. The wine which was left he poured back into the cask, wishing his guests would do the same, but guests, especially Americans, almost never did. Americans thought spitting rude, and not only swallowed the first mouthful but, for fear of offending the owner, usually drained the glass. Few ever returned wine to the barrel, and a group this large could, in a few seconds, guzzle the equivalent of a full bottle of château wine, which, on a table five years from now, would be worth a good deal in terms of both pleasure and money.

Out in the sunshine, Conderie bade them goodbye. His smiles and jokes boosted them into their rented cars. But, once they were gone, Conderie began to worry about money again.

Gorr stood talking to him, wanting a decision of some kind—Gorr in his workman's blues and rubber boots, beret twisting in his thick, dirty fingers, his manner abject. Why didn't Gorr just do what needed to be done? Gorr knew more about wine than Conderie did. But Gorr was as ill at ease with decisions as with men who outranked him. Gorr was not a decision maker. Neither was Paul Conderie. Conderie should have hired a new general manager after the last one quit, but had been short of money; he and Gorr could handle it, he had decided.

Gorr wanted to know how many pickers to hire and at what price. But Conderie put off the decision by changing the subject to Gorr's daughter, Françoise.

"Lovely girl, lovely," said Conderie. "I'm as proud of her as of my own daughter." He was waiting till the next visitors should appear. According to the wine syndicate in Bordeaux, he could expect a pair of American journalists any minute.

There they were now, entering the courtyard, one with cameras strung around his neck.

"I'm Paul Conderie. Welcome to my château."

The man with the cameras was big. He had a way of leaning forward aggressively and his grip was hard.

"Charlie Stack," the man said.

"Welcome, Mr. Stack, welcome. And what publication do you represent?"

It was important to know that detail in advance. Then you knew whether to go through the entire performance of showing off the château and its wines.

"I'm writing a book about wine," said Stack.

Conderie said cheerfully: "Not another wine book. I hope you have a new angle at least."

Stack gave a rather engaging grin. "I think I do, but I'd rather not talk about it as yet." Conderie shook hands with the second man. "This is my friend Aino Saar from Paris," said Stack. "I brought him along as my interpreter, but I find you don't really need one in Bordeaux."

"Don't be so surprised," said Paul Conderie. "Bordeaux was an English province for hundreds of years, and even after that Bordeaux always shipped most of its wine to England. The English were not only our best clients, they also moved down here and became our biggest shippers and brokers. Come, let me show you my chais and cellars."

It was a relief to Conderie to get away from Gorr, and from the need to make decisions.

"Did you go to school in England?" Stack asked.

He was obviously a persistent journalist. Conderie did not like journalists of any nationality.

"I did go to school in England," conceded Conderie. "So did my father, and my grandfather, and my daughter. You'll find that's true of a great many château owners here."

Conderie threw open the great doors to the chai, and they stepped inside. Though he seemed unimpressed, Stack promptly withdrew a notebook. Conderie began talking about the vine roots on the wall that so amazed other tourists, but Stack interrupted him.

"How many barrels would this chai hold?"

"About six hundred, I should think," said Paul Conderie.

"Don't you know for sure?"

"When I want a detail like that, I ask one of my employees."

"I see."

Conderie resolved to offer no tasting of the new wine to these two.

Stack was making notes. "Do you still put your new wine into brand-new casks?"

"Of course."

"All the new wine?"

"All the new wine. Why do you ask?"

"Because new barrels cost eight hundred francs—that's nearly two hundred dollars in our money—and some owners seem to be having second thoughts about using new barrels every year."

Conderie was one such, and a third of the wine in this chai was aging in old barrels. He had decided that this percentage, once the wine was all blended together prior to bottling, would not lower the quality by a perceptible amount. Whereas savings would be both perceptible and important.

"The wine at my château is made according to traditions dating back well into the last century."

The journalist persisted with his questions. "Tell me about your two-year-old wine. Is all of it sold?"

"If I had twice as much I could sell that too." Conderie watched Stack scribble in his notebook. Conderie had never approved of Americans. Unfortunately America had become a major part of the market. Not that Americans knew wine. Americans bought names. If you had a big name, as Conderie did, but were cutting corners a bit in the way your wine was made, Americans would not notice.

"How about giving us a taste of the new wine?" said Stack.

Conderie considered himself too well bred to refuse.

"Of course," Conderie said suavely, and called out to a workman, "Fetch some glasses." When the worker had come up with glasses and pipette, Conderie offered his visitors cheese.

"There's an old saying in the wine business that when you're selling wine, serve cheese. When you're buying wine, eat apples." Conderie gave a laugh, but the American did not join in.

Conderie passed around glasses containing an inch of wine. He himself gargled a mouthful, then spit down into the sand. Not unexpectedly the American swallowed his, and afterward drained the entire glass.

"I'm getting to be an expert at this stuff," Stack said. "Yours is rather less astringent than most. That means it will be ready sooner, right?"

"Normally Château Conderie wine is ready sooner than, say, Château Margaux across the road. It's a more rounded wine normally. It has more finesse."

"This wine lingo drives me up the wall," said Stack with a smile. "Half the time I imagine you people are putting me on. What's a wine with finesse, for godsake?"

Five minutes from now this visit will be over, Conderie reflected. "It's just a way of trying to describe the way the wine tastes," said Conderie stiffly. "I thought you liked wine."

"I do. There's nothing better than wine, good food, a girl. I just don't like all the mystique that goes with it."

Conderie decided to smile. "Come along, I want to show you the cellars."

Downstairs they walked along the dim corridors between racks filled to the ceiling with dusty old bottles. Most visitors found this a romantic place, but Stack demanded only: "How much is this wine worth?"

Conderie put him down with a frosty answer: "I'm sure I have no idea. For the most part this is the personal cellar of the château, and it's no more for sale than the château is."

They came upstairs and out into the sunlight again, where Stack said unexpectedly: "I sure do thank you for showing us through your place," and an instant later both of them were gone, good riddance.

Paul Conderie, lighting a cigarette, thought immediately of Bozon. Bozon was doing something illegal with Conderie's money, and might not give it back.

And who was that lout who had just left? Conderie now realized that the friend from Paris had not spoken a single word, and that the lout himself had not taken a single photograph. Well, the ways of American journalists had always been a mystery to Paul Conderie.

Françoise Gorr took that moment to enter the courtyard, and Paul Conderie advanced to meet her, only to note an instant later that Stack had come back into the courtyard too and was staring at her rear. After shaking hands with Françoise, Conderie strode past her and approached Stack. "Yes?" he asked.

"Who's she?" asked Charlie Stack.

Conderie hesitated, then decided to say: "She's the daughter of my cellar master, and who exactly are you?"

Conderie felt as virtuous as if he had defended the honor of his own family.

The American appeared to have got the message at last. "Thank you again," he said, and strolled out the gate and was gone.

42

Conderie turned to watch Françoise Gorr walking across the court-yard to talk to her father. That girl knows how to wiggle her ass, he thought. But immediately he rebuked himself. Françoise was like a daughter to him, and to ogle her seemed almost an incestuous act. She was a good student, he knew. Whatever happened, her education must continue. He would find the money for that somewhere. Françoise's education came before any problems of his own.

5

Driving the rented car back toward Bordeaux, Charlie Stack said abruptly: "That's the château that's for sale."

Beside him, Saar, the company lawyer, said: "I beg your pardon, monsieur."

"You're going back to Paris tonight. We'll meet with that newspaper guy in an hour as scheduled. Immediately after that you'll catch a flight."

The lawyer had expected a major role in the purchase of a château for The Company. Instead he had been ordered to misrepresent Stack to a series of unsuspecting château owners, and had been consulted on nothing.

"And what do I tell this newspaper reporter when we get there?" inquired the lawyer coldly.

"The same fairy tale we've been telling everybody for ten days. You introduce me, and you translate my questions and his answers. You volunteer nothing."

Stack drove the rented car toward Bordeaux. The famous châteaux were passing one after another on either side of the road, but Stack ignored them. He was calculating hard.

The lawyer said: "I think you are mistaken about Conderie's châ-teau. That château has been in his family one hundred fifty years. No château in the entire Médoc has been in the same family that long. I think there is no chance he would sell."

"He'll sell," said Charlie Stack. He stopped the car. "You drive, I want to study my notes."

As Saar steered the car back into the road, upshifting, gathering speed, Stack turned slowly through the pages, reliving the last ten days, searching through his notes and his mind.

Where had Stack first picked up the rumor that the quality of Conderie's wine had fallen off? He had not even noted it down. Was it one of the real-estate agents? The second time he had heard it, bells had gone off all over his brain, and he had begun to ask specific questions. Why? No one exactly knew why. There was no specific reason. The soil was the same as always. Many of the vines were suitably old. But Conderie's general manager had quit some years before and had not been replaced. Conderie was acting as his own general manager. He was famous for his dinner parties, was seen in such night spots as Bordeaux offered, and was said to live in Paris during most of the year.

Upon his arrival in Bordeaux, Stack had wasted three days with real-estate agents, imagining that they could show him properties that were for sale. He had ordered the lawyer, Saar, to introduce him as a rich American, one of a group that wanted to buy a wine property. For three days Stack and Saar were shown rundown properties in unfashionable areas. The lawyer, repeatedly prodded by Stack, kept demanding to see properties in the category of Château Lafite-Rothschild, or Château Haut-Brion. The real-estate agents scarcely took these requests seriously, noting that such a property would be worth more than Stack could afford, adding that in any case none were for sale. On the fourth day Stack had ordered Saar to cancel all appointments with real-estate agents, and instead to seek introductions for him into as many of the great châteaux as possible. Saar was now to identify Stack as a famous journalist.

They had gone immediately to the wine syndicate, which saw no reason to disbelieve the lie, and whose policy it was to encourage all journalists. On Stack's behalf calls were made out into the country.

The Bordeaux area comprises five hundred square miles and some three thousand different châteaux, most small and obscure, most put there, it sometimes seemed, just to waste Charlie Stack's time. Stack had known what he was looking for—approximately—before he ever left New York; now he glanced impatiently at ten properties a day, able to discard most as possibilities after five minutes or less, thereafter wanting only to escape and get on to another. Most times he was barely able to contain rudeness, though making quick, copious notes nonetheless, for such notes would later become part of his report to the chairman. Reports were revered inside The Company and Charlie Stack knew how to make reports turn handsprings if he chose. This particular report would have to surround whatever château Stack would eventually buy like Christmas wrapping around a present. If the report stunned the chairman, then the purchase would.

Stack toured the Graves vineyards first, for they lay at the back door of Bordeaux proper, and were easiest to reach. He skipped Château Haut-Brion, which was wholly owned by the family of Douglas Dillon, former Secretary of the U.S. Treasury. Stack, who had made discreet inquiries in New York, had found no sign that the Dillon wealth was flagging or that the château was on the market.

Across the road was Château La Mission Haut-Brion, which Stack toured, notebook out, ballpoint scribbling. It too had a prosperous look, and the owner, a Parisian industrialist named Woltner, was on the scene, eagerly showing off his jewel of a property, an old man whose love for his château and for the wine it produced seemed absolutely unfeigned. No crack in this façade appeared, though Stack, hoping it might, persisted with his questions and his tour of the property for almost two hours. The old man was beaming as Stack left, no doubt confident Stack would give him a good write-up.

Stack toured other properties in the Graves region. The suburbs of Bordeaux appeared about to topple in on all of them. It was terribly crowded out there. To own one of those châteaux would be like trying to raise vines in Central Park.

Stack found he had wasted four more days touring the Graves. Into his notebook he had crammed two dozen pages of tightly scribbled notes, and he had learned a great deal about the making of wine and the running of a château, but he was no nearer to purchasing one than before. At night, alone in his room at the Hotel Splendide, he paced the floor and wondered how long his search would last, and whether there was any chance of ultimate success. If he failed to buy a château in Bordeaux, he could always try Burgundy, he supposed, although the vineyards there were all minuscule by comparison, and his mandate from The Company was to purchase a wine property that would be substantial, that would contribute both prestige and profit. Research before leaving New York had indicated precious little profit to be made in Burgundy. The wine might be high priced there, but no single owner made very much of it. If Stack failed in Bordeaux, failed in Burgundy too, there was perhaps the Champagne country to try, though that was an aristocrat's drink and not what the chairman had in mind. There were nights when Stack saw himself condemned to wander the vineyards of France for a year or more, each day, each week forced to proclaim additional failures to the board of directors in New York. Stack saw his career with The Company in ruins. Unless he could come up with some perfect purchase here, his career would never recover.

Each night with a pad and a pencil Stack reduced his problem to three essentials: (1) He had to buy a name château, one already famous. He discarded in advance the idea of buying a second-rate property and lifting it to prominence by himself. He needed an instant success, not success five years from now. He needed to bring home a huge and brilliant diamond, not a raw chunk of rock that would require many years' polishing. (2) The property must be large, capable of delivering at least 200,000 bottles a year, meaning big profits, not small ones. (3) Although The Company had stipulated no ceiling on purchase price, it was clear that he must search out a relative bargain. He must find the cripple. He must find the guy who had to sell, and sell fast, for he could not afford negotiations that could drag out and perhaps fail in the end.

Stack awarded the St. Émilion region two days of his precious time, trudging from château to château, asking the same hard questions: what is the size of your property; what is your approximate annual production; how many people do you employ; and even—provided answers to the first questions were satisfactory—what is the condition of your machinery? These were not a journalist's normal questions in St. Émilion or any other wine-growing area, but none of the owners protested. All seemed eager for the publicity they thought Stack could bring them.

The walled village itself was handsome, most of it dating from the Middle Ages. It crouched on top of a steep hill, with narrow cobblestone streets and precipitous staircases diving straight down between some of the buildings. There was a church which had been cut into the solid limestone of the hill a thousand or more years ago, its vaults lit now by dim lights, one of the stone sepulchers said to contain the remains of Saint Émilion himself, who had stopped here looking for a clear spring a dozen centuries ago. According to legend, the spring he finally found had gushed forth St. Émilion wine. Many of these wine villages, Stack noted in his notebook, boasted old superstitions and legends which could be useful in publicity when marketing The Company's eventual wine.

Stack visited Château Ausone, the most dramatic place he had seen

46

yet, or was to see. Instead of storing its casks and newly bottled wine in the long, low aging sheds above ground as elsewhere, Château Ausone stored its precious stock in limestone caves, which, beginning in the seventh century, had been hollowed out of the hillside beneath the vineyards themselves. The roots from the vines came down through one foot of soil and six feet of solid limestone ceiling, and snaked along under the ceiling of the caves themselves, tangling themselves here and there among the electric-light wires. The caves of Château Ausone, and also the view from the hilltop château itself, were indeed stunning, and for a time Stack wondered if his search had come to an end—he could always make an offer so outstanding that it could not be refused. The château name was famous enough too, and its prices were as high as the best growths anywhere else. But finally Stack concluded that it was simply too small, less than twenty-five acres under vines. He needed more; he had to have more.

The best wines of St. Émilion, so the connoisseurs claimed, were equal in taste to the best wines from anywhere. They simply were not quite as famous as those of the great châteaux of the Médoc across the river, and so, at the end of two days, Stack concluded his search there and crossed back over the bridge. That night in his hotel room he again studied his maps. He discarded the Pomerol region. Some of its wines were great but it was even less known than St. Émilion. He discarded the Sauternes vineyards to the south, for although they were famous and expensive, the sweet white wines they produced were out of fashion right now. To buy a Sauternes vineyard would bring less than maximum prestige to The Company, less than maximum profit.

And so it had to be the Médoc. Stack would find his château there or nowhere. The furthest of the great châteaux were, he noted, forty miles north of Bordeaux, and the nearest were fifteen miles north of Bordeaux. He would start at the bitter end and work in. Over the next few days he drove Saar hard, for it was Saar's job not only to make the appointments, but to engage managers and cellar masters in idle conversation, leaving Stack free to deal with owners.

The days passed relentlessly while Stack and Saar plodded doggedly from château to château, Stack asking the same stubborn questions over and over again, asking also now which châteaux might draw what type of selling price presuming that they were on the market, which of course everyone knew they were not.

The answer Stack got at Château Palmer was repeated everywhere: "Ah, monsieur, if you only knew how many syndicates have tried lately to buy a great château here in the Médoc. Nothing is for sale. Only a month ago a Japanese syndicate was forced to buy on the other side of the river, in the unfashionable Premières Côtes de Bordeaux region. They paid a fantastic price."

Now Saar, driving away from Conderie's château, began to advise Stack that their quest was hopeless. "Conderie will never sell," said Saar.

Stack ignored him and stared at his notes. What was it that made him imagine Conderie would sell?

Principally it was the rumor that quality had fallen off. In business the quality of a profitable property fell off because the man in charge was incompetent, or had no great personal interest in the property, or because he lacked capital and therefore could not afford expenditures essential to keep his property on top. And so, arriving at Château Conderie, Stack had been prepared to observe minor details which might otherwise have passed by him.

First he had stopped his car beside the road, and walked down several of the alleyways through Conderie's vines. He noticed a great many gaps in the rows. He had seen enough vineyards by now to realize that some gaps were inevitable—vines got bruised by the plow and died. Or one vine, during a hailstorm, got shelled rather more than others, and later died. So every vineyard had gaps, and some owners preferred not to replace individual vines immediately, so as to keep all of the vines in an individual parcel the same age. That way, at the age of, say, forty, every vine in the parcel could be ripped out, and the parcel allowed to lie fallow for eight or ten years. There was no point planting a new vine in a gap when the new vine would not give usable grapes at all until four years of age, and possibly get ripped out altogether in seven or eight years, when the whole field was taken out of production. New vines were expensive. Ever since the phylloxera louse had attacked and killed every vine in the Bordeaux growing area in the late nineteenth century, each new French vine had had to be grafted onto an American root stock, the American root stocks being immune to the parasite. Even now, though there had been no new outbreak of phylloxera since the turn of the century, every vine in every vineyard in France was a graft. The grafting was a delicate and expensive process, as was the training of the new vine along the wires.

But, if some gaps in the rows were normal, Conderie's vineyards contained too many gaps. Also, even where the rows were full, they did not seem as neat to Charlie Stack as rows of vines in other people's fields. Nor did the heavy bunches of grapes seem as copious or as plump as the grapes across the road that belonged to Château Margaux. Stack could not be sure. He had never seen vineyards in his life before this month. He walked back and forth across the road, comparing Conderie's vines to those belonging to Margaux and to Palmer.

If Conderie's vineyards were not as carefully tended as those across the road, then this meant either that Conderie employed too few workers, or else did not oversee them carefully enough. The one explanation indicated a lack of money, and the other a lack of interest.

Driving up the dirt lane, he saw that the château's elegance had become rather shabby. It was of course a building of great age. But that seemed to Stack no reason not to paint the shutters, not to polish the great brass front-door handle. Inside the chais Stack had noticed at once that some of the barrels were not new. Also the place had not been adequately swept out in a long time.

Their car was entering Bordeaux now, plunging into the heavy traffic that swirled around the Boulevard Extérieur. Every afternoon when returning from the so far fruitless search Stack had felt them poured into this turgid glut of traffic, and each day he had wished they might have stayed in a hotel out in the Médoc. But there was no such hotel, not one, and Stack had already begun to think of expanding his mandate to include the building of a major resort hotel. The Médoc was sparsely populated. The biggest town was Pauillac, population under six thousand, and the population of Margaux was under fifteen hundred. Important visitors to any château stayed overnight at the château itself, and the locals returned to their hovels, having no need of hotels. Yet, Stack had begun to reason, hundreds of tourists, now that the great wines had exploded into popularity once again, visited the Médoc each week. A great hotel would attract more. And Charlie Stack's wine division, if it owned a great hotel too, would accede to a higher level of importance within The Company.

Their car hovered, immobilized in traffic. Charlie Stack hated traffic jams. He hated waiting for anyone. In life, as Charlie Stack saw life, time was everything, the only tool and also the only luxury a man had. To waste time made Charlie Stack feel like vomiting.

Glancing up, staring into the backs of unmoving cars, he fretted. He forced himself to return to his notes.

Inside Conderie's shed, a brass plaque underneath the oldest and most gnarled of the ancient vine roots had carried that particular root's dates: 1820–1928. Below, a second plaque had borne the following lines:

49

Que trois paires sont placés auprès du rang suprême
Qu'ils sont seul reconnus premier prince de sang
Et c'est vous Conderie, Mouton et Rausan
D'autres peuvent jeter une flamme aussi belle
Mais elle n'a qu'un jour, la vôtre est éternelle.

They were moving again. Stack's eyes dropped back to the poetry in his lap. "What do these lines mean?" Stack asked Saar, and read them off with what was no doubt an execrable accent. Stack had studied French in college for two years, but had retained almost none of it.

Saar laughed.

"What's so funny?"

"Your rape of the French language."

"Just translate me the goddamn lines."

Saar did so: " 'Three wines are placed near the highest rank, next to those which alone are recognized as first princes of the blood; I'm speaking of you, Conderie, Mouton, and Rausan. Others can throw a flame as beautiful as yours, but their flame lasts only a day, yours is eternal.'

"I didn't know you were interested in poetry," said Saar.

The plaque gave the poet's name and poem's date: 1850.

"Look up this poet for me," Stack ordered. "Is he well known, or what?" A new poem, any new poem, was worthless, as were poets, Stack believed. But an old poem could be worth money in an ad, if the poet was important. The poem could constitute a kind of seal of approval for the wine: Our wine is so glorious, The Company ads could proclaim, that it once provoked this lyric outburst from a great poet more than a hundred years dead. Those old vines might be worked into the ads too.

In size and reputation Château Conderie matched what Stack was looking for.

The problem became how to make Conderie turn over the door keys to the château that had been in his family 150 years, to sell out to an American conglomerate with a reputation for absolute rapaciousness, and then to get himself the hell out.

Stack closed his notebook. The problem had become to find Conderie's weaknesses. What was Conderie ashamed of? What did he fear? What was he hiding? Every man had committed indiscretions, and a good many at one time or another had broken the law. Usually it did not take very much evidence to extort a man's signature on a bill of sale. With a little evidence in hand, plus a little quiet bluffing over lunch in a restaurant, plus a lot of fear on the part of the subject, the acquisition

50

could be made. Any acquisition could be made. Previously Charlie Stack had acquired two smaller drug companies in exactly this way.

Now he meant to acquire Château Conderie.

Who would know some dirt about Paul Conderie? And be willing to tell it to a perfect stranger named Charlie Stack? The Bordeaux newspaper was the place to start.

6

The *Étoile* of Bordeaux was perhaps a profitable newspaper, but no one knew for sure except its owners, who each year claimed minimal profits on income-tax returns and paid minimal taxes. Each year investigators from the tax office went over the paper's books, and assessed higher taxes which were still not very substantial, given the scope of the paper. Each day the *Étoile* published twenty-three regional editions, and blanketed one-fourth of France with its headlines. In France there were a few national papers published in Paris, most of which reached the provinces a day late, and in each corner of the country there was an *Étoile* or its equivalent, with its regional editions and its vast profits. The *Étoile*'s printing plant was modern, many of the machines having been imported from America, and its distribution network was excellent. But its editorial department operated on a shoestring. There were fewer than a dozen reporters, who were paid derisory salaries; each of them each working day wrote thousands of words of copy and, since they were paid according to length, they padded every story as much as possible, and spent very little time running down facts. While a man was running down facts he could not be gainfully employed writing long-winded, padded stories.

One of the reporters for the *Étoile* was named Fernand Front. Front was a small middle-aged man who wore shabby suits in winter, and loud sports shirts in summer, and his specialties were crime, wine, and politics. These were also the specialties of every other reporter on the *Étoile*. It was Front's habit to rush to crime scenes to interview

51

witnesses. On the whole, policemen would not speak to journalists in France. Hardly anyone would speak to journalists in France. Journalists, Front had long ago realized, were members of a despised profession. But witnesses to gory deeds were usually eager to talk, and Front knew how to interrogate such witnesses for lurid details. Front liked crime, the gorier the better, especially those crimes so unusual that he could send reports off to other regional papers, phoning such reports in to Nice, to Perpignan, to Lyon, writing and phoning in five different padded versions of the same story in an hour, for the other papers paid him by length too, though only a fraction of what his own paper paid him, which was not very much.

Irregularly, Front also wrote a wine column for the *Étoile*, usually containing information he collected over the telephone. The weather bureau was always good for a few hundred words on the subject of last month's weather, and next month's. The Station Oenologue could be depended upon to rate the probable size and quality of the current harvest. Sometimes there were public auctions of old wine, or new. And often enough château owners were fined for infractions of the strict and enormously complicated rules which governed the growing and making of wine, which rules were rigidly enforced by the government. Whenever Front had such an item, he invariably phoned the château owner, who invariably refused to speak to him at first. When this happened, Front would browbeat the cellar master, or secretary, or whoever took the call, threatening to blacken the château's name if the owner didn't come on the wire. Once the owner did come on the wire, Front's voice would become syrupy. He would explain that he was in possession of information about the infraction and the fine, and suggest that it might be in the owner's interest if the item wound up in the wastebasket.

Usually the owner in question, after a moment, convinced Fernand Front that it would be in the interests of everyone if the item did not appear, and the next day, either in the mail or by messenger, Fernand Front would receive an envelope containing money. Not very much money. Fernand Front was for sale for twenty francs, and up. In any case, Front got by. He drove a small secondhand car, and he owned two suits, one of them new.

Of course he worked very hard. He was a stringer also for *France Dimanche*, a scandalous weekly printed in Paris. *France Dimanche* paid best for scandals of a sexual nature, and when film stars such as Brigitte Bardot came to Bordeaux, Front and a photographer friend

52

might trail the star half the night, hoping to come upon an indiscretion. The indiscretion might be no more than having dinner with some other film star's husband or wife. That was reason enough for Front and the photographer to burst into the restaurant, flash bulbs exploding. However innocent the raided dinner party might have been, the appearance of Fernand Front and the photographer invariably provoked a brawl of some kind and made for fine photos and lurid text—padded, of course. But Fernand Front valued his good name, and his stories in *France Dimanche* appeared under the name Marcel Eugène Picard.

The best single story that Fernand Front had ever fallen upon involved a wine fraud almost twenty years ago. A grower of ordinary white wine was lacing his stuff with sugar, and planning to sell it as Sauternes. Front had been tipped off, and had gone to the grower with his information. The envelope which changed hands was fat—the equivalent of two weeks' pay for Front—but Front had then gone to the Fraud Brigade, and informed anonymously on the grower, collecting a second fee.

At this point in his career, Front had rather more prestige than any of the paper's other reporters, based primarily on his irregular wine column. It was Front that foreign journalists, particularly Americans, usually asked to interview—there was another American journalist coming in today to see him.

The girl at the reception desk signaled Front that two men waited to see him, so he went down the narrow wooden staircase and along the shabby corridor and came out into the spacious marble lobby. The receptionist pointed the two men out to him, and Front went over and shook hands. He suggested they go across the street to a café.

As soon as their drinks had come, the American journalist said something to his French friend, who handed an envelope across to Fernand Front.

The Frenchman said: "Mr. Stack asks you to accept that. His publication is accustomed to paying for information, and he knows your time is valuable."

Front was accustomed to accepting envelopes, though never before from fellow journalists. Reaching for this one, he was careful to let no surprise show. He glanced inside as always, for it was important to know how much of his experience and expertise was being bought. Fifty American dollars. To Front, an extraordinary sum. Fifty. Christ.

But over the next few minutes, almost imperceptibly, so much money as this made Front swell with importance. His answers got as

long-winded as his prose, and each took on the weight of a pronounce-
ment.

Front's drink was gone, and with an imperious gesture he called
over the waiter. "Another round all around," he ordered.

"Mr. Stack asks what you know about Château Conderie," said
Saar.

Front was feeling very pleasant. "Château Conderie? One of our
finest châteaux. Mr. Conderie is one of the grands messieurs of the wine
industry."

Nodding his head pleasantly, Front waited for this to be translated.

"Mr. Stack has heard that the quality of the wine has fallen off and
wondered if you knew why."

"One hears such exaggerations all the time," said Fernand Front.
As this was being translated, Front noted that Stack's grin disappeared,
and his face took on a hard look.

"Mr. Stack says that he knows the rumor is true, and he has sought
the judgment of an expert such as yourself."

Fernand Front gave a weak laugh. "You know how it is when
you're talking to foreigners—you say what you feel to be in the best
interests of France."

"Then you know the rumor to be true?"

"Yes, of course."

Across the table Monsieur Stack leaned suddenly forward. "Why?"
he demanded. "Pourquoi?"

Front looked at the American in surprise. This had begun to seem
to Front a most strange interview. He was used to flattery from American journalists who called on him. Most asked only the names of people
in the wine business whom they should see. They fed Front's feeling of
self-importance, and went away. None previously had sought to intimidate him. None previously had paid him either.

"Monsieur Conderie has perhaps too many other interests apart
from his wine."

Stack and the Frenchman conferred. Then the Frenchman asked:
"Business interests?"

"Il adore les femmes," said Front. Looking directly at Stack, he
added in English: "He like the girls. Et le jeu." The last remark in
French was directed to Saar, but Front immediately added in English:
"And the games."

"The games?" said Charlie Stack.

54

Saar said to Stack: "Le jeu means gambling. He says our friend is a gambler."

Front understood the gist of this without understanding where the conversation was leading. A moment later Saar turned from Stack and asked: "And does he win?"

Fernand Front shrugged expressively. "Who do you know who wins?"

There was another conference across the table.

"Mr. Stack says that he does not know that such information would be of interest to his readers, or fit into his book in any way, but he asks you to be more specific."

"Bordeaux may be the sixth-biggest city in France, monsieur," said Fernand Front, "but it is also a village. Here everybody knows everything about everybody." Across the table, Stack watched him closely. Both men waited, so Front said: "In the summer sometimes he goes to the casino at Arcachon, where they say he plays baccarat in the private rooms. Those are the big-money rooms. He also belongs to a cercle de jeu here in the city.

"Where?" said Charlie Stack.

Surprised, Fernand Front gave an address and watched Stack copy it down.

"Mr. Stack would like to know if you have ever with your own eyes seen Conderie gambling."

"I am not a member of that cercle de jeu, but several times I have waited outside to photograph a celebrity who may have been there that night. Many of the celebrities who come to Bordeaux go there. They say that the stakes are sometimes enormous." Front now told of trailing one of France's most popular singers to the club. A bit later the wife of one of France's most famous movie directors, who was known to be carrying on with the singer, also entered. Front and his photographer waited in a car across the street for three hours until the pair came out together arm in arm. Whereupon Front and the photographer had rushed up, flash bulbs exploding, and Front had managed to get off a few specific questions which neither the singer nor the director's wife had answered. Front had then abused both of them, with the result that the singer lunged at him, grabbed him by the throat, and might have choked Front to death had not the girl jumped in and pried them apart. All this time the photographer was taking many excellent pictures. The ones that appeared in *France Dimanche* later showed Front being strangled, though you could not see his face; the faces of the male singer and the director's wife, both contorted, were very clear, however, and the caption described "Our intrepid correspondent Marcel Eugène Picard being attacked by the lovers for doing his job." With the profits from this one story, Front had been able to spend the weekend with his wife at a small hotel at the beach.

"My point is, monsieur," Fernand Front continued, "that Monsieur Conderie was there that night. We saw him go in during the period that we staked the place out, and later the commotion in the street brought him and several others out to see what was going on."

After a moment Saar turned back to Fernand Front. "Mr. Stack observes that you have no way of knowing whether Mr. Conderie loses heavily, if at all."

Fernand Front began to be irritated. Fifty American dollars did not give these men the right to push a Frenchman around in his own country. "Go there yourself, if you doubt me," Front said stiffly. "It is very easy for American journalists to get guest cards to that club, I believe."

"But not French journalists," observed Stack to Saar.

"Mr. Stack asks on what ground you base your claim that Mr. Conderie loses heavily."

"I know for a fact that he has borrowed money. A great deal of money. My wife's cousin is a cashier at the Bordeaux branch of the Banque Lyonnaise."

"Combien?" demanded Monsieur Stack.

Fernand Front said stiffly: "That is a private matter between a man and his bank."

"But it was a great deal?" asked Stack, in bad French.

"It would not be proper for me to say how much, even assuming that I knew," said Front, attempting to give the impression that he did know.

Across the table from him Stack said to Saar in English, "He doesn't have any idea how much. Let's get out of here. This bird has told us everything he knows."

Stack and Saar both stood up, so Fernand Front stood up too. Stack was grinning now and pumping Front's hand, though the grin looked as hard to Front as the handshake felt. Stack tapped Front on the breast pocket and to Saar said in English: "Tell him not to spend it all in one place."

Front guessed that Stack had said something friendly, so Front

56

smiled and said in English: "Thank you very much."

Saar looked from Stack, who was silent, back to Front, then said: "Mr. Stack has asked me to thank you most kindly for your graciousness in according us so much of your valuable time. He's asked me to tell you that you are a veritable fountain of information, and he considers himself fortunate to have been able to interview you."

Fernand Front beamed.

"Let's split," muttered Charlie Stack to Saar.

"Mr. Stack regrets that we must be on our way."

As Stack was paying the waiter, Front asked conversationally: "What did you say was the name of your publication?"

Saar translated the question. Stack, smiling at Front, replied in English: "Tell the slimy little bastard to screw himself."

Saar said to Front: "Actually Mr. Stack is free-lancing. This article will be for a publication you probably haven't heard of yet."

Front said: "Tell him that I admire anyone with the courage to free-lance. Tell him that journalism is indeed a hard profession."

"What did he say?" asked Charlie Stack.

"You wouldn't be interested, I'm afraid."

"How much tip should I leave?"

"About five francs, I should think."

Fernand Front looked from one to the other, wondering if they were talking about him.

Stack and Saar hurried to the Air France ticket office.

"Go in there and get yourself on the next plane to Paris," Stack instructed Saar. "I want you to look into Conderie's credit rating. I want to know everything. I don't suppose they have Dun and Bradstreet reports on businessmen in this country, do they?"

Saar said they did not. Because each Frenchman felt it his right to cheat on taxes, there was really no way to find out accurately how much a business was worth; everybody kept double books.

"You have the name of one bank where Conderie has borrowed heavily," said Stack. "Find out if there are others. Go to our banks. Have them find out. As I understand it, bankers talk to other bankers. Be discreet. But I want everything."

7

The club was up one flight and occupied the entire floor. It was like a small casino. There was one roulette table, Stack saw, several felt-top card tables, a baccarat table, a table for chemin de fer. There was a bar against one wall. A barman polished glasses. A number of people were crowded around the roulette table.

At the bar Stack nursed a Scotch whisky, listening to the click of the little ball falling into slots. He knew he was conspicuous. For two hours he waited, and spoke to no one. At one point he cashed a hundred-dollar traveler's check, bought chips, moved to the roulette table, stared down at the spinning wheel for ten minutes, did not bet, returned to the bar and ordered another drink. At midnight he abruptly paid his bar check and departed.

The next night Stack entered the club later, behaved in the same manner, and again left at midnight. Still no sign of Paul Conderie.

The third night Stack again took his place at the bar. Apparently he was accepted now, a gambler with weird habits, one who had not yet bet. All gamblers had weird habits. He was no longer conspicuous. Stack read all of this in the faces of the men around him. It amused him to see himself as these people no doubt saw him: mystery gambler.

On the fourth night in the doorway appeared Paul Conderie, wearing evening clothes, escorting a woman twenty years younger than himself, whose low-cut gown revealed most of a splendid bosom. Ignoring Conderie, Stack moved immediately to the roulette table and began to play. An hour later, apparently by chance, Stack took the empty chair next to Conderie at the baccarat table.

"Mr. Conderie," Stack said with feigned surprise. "So good to see you again. Charlie Stack. You remember me, of course."

Conderie looked up with a worried frown. "Yes, of course," he said unconvincingly.

The contact was made.

In front of Conderie's place Stack counted approximately a thousand dollars' worth of chips, which it took Conderie approximately one hour to lose. He pushed back his chair and stood up, saying: "Come along, my dear."

Stack rose to his feet at the same moment.

"I'm sorry you've had bad luck tonight, Mr. Conderie," said Stack with a broad smile. "I myself have had fabulous luck, and I'd very much like to invite you and the lady to celebrate with me. Can I offer you supper and champagne at La Trompette?"

Conderie looked at him abstractedly: "You're that journalist fellow."

"Tonight I wish you'd regard me just as a fellow gambler and a happy winner." Stack had turned his eyes onto the young woman. She had big eyes and nice teeth and that gleaming bosom. It was hard to keep his eyes from sinking downward. He gave her his best smile, speaking as much to her as to Conderie.

"Have pity," said Stack. "I've really been very successful, and you can't make me celebrate alone."

During the moment Conderie hesitated, Stack shot forth his hand and said to the young woman: "I'm Charlie Stack."

She gave an amused smile and said: "And I'm Mr. Conderie's daughter."

"What?"

"I thought that bit of information might surprise you," murmured the girl. "And who did you think I was? Tell the truth now."

Stack laughed and let go of her hand. "It's settled then," he said, ushering them forward. "I'm so pleased."

"Yes, well—" said Conderie doubtfully.

"I wouldn't mind some champagne," said his daughter.

Conderie bowed to the inevitable.

At the restaurant the girl ordered a dozen of the flat Marennes oysters and a bowl of onion soup. Stack said he would have the same. Conderie declared that champagne would be enough for him.

"And a magnum of Roederer champagne," said Stack to the waiter. "What's the oldest vintage you have in the house?"

When the waiter had gone, Stack confided: "I really know more about champagne than I do about Bordeaux wine."

"Do you know how much that magnum you just ordered is going to cost?" asked the girl.

"It doesn't matter, I'm a big winner tonight."

"Champagne is a good deal less expensive these days than my own wine," noted Conderie.

Stack gave Conderie a grin and said: "I'm aware of that."

He was aware of plenty. His luck so far seemed to him spectacular. Across the table he watched the girl scrape each flat, cold oyster from its shell, and lift it toward her lovely mouth. Then she drank the juice from the shell. Stack, smiling, sipped his champagne. When the girl's eyes met his, and she smiled back, Stack raised his glass to her.

Presently Stack learned that she lived in Paris, where she kept what was apparently a very expensive dress shop. She had come down here for the harvest, but could only stay through part of it, for it would last two weeks, and the winemaking after that would last two weeks more. But the start of the harvest was always so exciting, wasn't it?

The daughter's name was Aline. Stack guessed her age as twenty-six. She wore no wedding ring, and there was no mention of any husband. Break down her well-bred reserve and she might be the type who would bite and scratch.

Stack remarked that he would be out in the Médoc again tomorrow afternoon, and perhaps would stop by to say hello.

The girl took a swallow of champagne, then said: "If you're in the neighborhood, we'd be happy to see you, wouldn't we, Father?"

But later Stack lay in bed worrying. Suppose Conderie could not be budged?

Across the street from the back of the warehouse belonging to Édouard Bozon, a Fraud Brigade agent named Alexandre Dupont stood at the bar. His beer glass was full and had a head of foam. Dupont turned the glass in his fingers, waiting for Le Grand Jo to finish with customers at the other end. Presently Jo came down to Dupont's end.

"Well," said Dupont to Le Grand Jo, "what have you heard? Anything going on across the street?"

Le Grand Jo said: "That truck driver I told you about was in again."

"You still don't know his name?"

"No. I could probably get the plate number off his truck the next time he comes in. The trouble is I don't like to go out of the bar when there are people in here."

"Well, I don't know if it's important."

"Like I told you, he thinks something is going on."

"We think something is going on too. We just don't know what."

"Why don't you just bust in there? You have the right to bust in anywhere you want."

"It isn't as easy as that. Any time we go in a place, all their clients get suspicious. All of a sudden their wine doesn't taste so good any more. So before we go into a place we like to be sure."

"That trucker's got the wind up. I don't know why. It's not all that unusual for deliveries to be made in the middle of the night. That's why I stay open all night."

"What about the people handling the deliveries at that hour?"

"Spaniards. The other night some of them came in here after they finished. You should hear what they do to the French language. Jesus."

"It's no crime to speak French with a Spanish accent, is it?"

"It's never the same Spaniards though. That's the funny thing."

One of the workingmen was banging his glass again. "Hey, Jo, you want us to die of thirst down here?"

Dupont, who drank off the last of his beer, waited for Le Grand Jo to come back.

"If that trucker comes back, maybe you could get his name or his plate number."

"I'll try."

"It might make all the difference."

"Yes."

"—or no difference at all. You never know."

Dupont put money down on the counter. He added a two-franc tip.

"Merci, monsieur. Bon soir."

"Bon soir," said Dupont. Stepping back from the bar, he buttoned the jacket of his double-breasted suit, which was six years old and somewhat shiny in places. He was a small man, nearing sixty, with shiny false teeth. He had worked all of his life for the government, and never made much money at it. He was one of fifteen members of the Fraud Brigade assigned to the Bordeaux area. Fifteen men to police over three thousand châteaux. It's insane, Dupont often thought.

Still, one did what one could.

Dupont was not a policeman, but he had power of arrest. He was mild-mannered and thought himself ineffectual; so did certain forgers and swindlers who had come up against him, and they were in jail now. Dupont had a horror of being thought a policeman. He was not an enforcer, but he had the power to enter without warning any establishment in any way related to wine—any bar, warehouse, bottling plant, chai—and some of these he had entered at the head of a force of gendarmes or city police, after first ordering a door battered in. But such raids were rare and always upset him. He hated force. He was a functionary. He was at home with paperwork. When conducting an investigation he was painstaking. It took him too long to get things right, he thought. He documented everything not once but several times. He never moved until he was sure. Testifying in court was agony for him too—he could not bear to look the accused in the eye—and usually he read from his notes in a monotonous voice that should have put the jury to sleep but did not, because his details were always so fascinating. Juries listened open-mouthed, and usually voted to convict. Dupont took little credit for these convictions; the facts had done the job, not him, he always told himself. He hated to put someone in jail.

In the street Dupont yawned, for it had been a long day. He had been moving about the countryside since early morning, meeting informants. Those who worked nights had to be visited just as often as those who worked days, but it added up to many hours of asking his mild questions and not learning very much. As he got into his government-owned car he wondered if his wife had left anything out for him to eat. She would be long asleep, and he would be hungry. Well . . .

The streets were empty, and as he started his motor Dupont realized that he had forgotten to ask Le Grand Jo if the money had been reaching him. It wasn't very much money, but he supposed these fellows counted on it. He supposed they got used to being informants. This fellow Le Grand Jo had shown no shame.

Well, a man was what he was. Dupont himself was a government functionary and always had been. One did what one could.

As he drove past the entry driveway to Bozon's warehouse, Dupont noticed that lights were on inside.

At that very moment Armand's truck was approaching Bozon's warehouse. Fifteen minutes more and Agent Dupont would have seen it. Armand's truck pulled to a stop before the entryway. Armand did not go inside. He rang the bell and waited. Some Spaniards came out and hooked up hoses to the truck. The truck began to empty.

Tonight Armand considered killing the three hours in the bar, talking to the barman, whom he thought of as that fat slob Jo. However, this would eat up most of Armand's extra profit, and he decided instead to climb up into his cab, pull his beret down over his eyes, and go to sleep.

62

As dawn was breaking, one of the Spaniards woke him by opening the cab door and passed up the stamped documents and some money, and Armand started his truck and drove home through the still-empty streets of Bordeaux.

8

In the morning Stack phoned Saar in Paris.

"I've been to see our friends on the Place Vendôme," said Saar guardedly. One of The Company's principal banks had its Paris offices on the Place Vendôme. "They assure me they will be able to determine the amounts in question in Bordeaux, but it will take about a week."

Stack understood that the amount of Conderie's mortgage from the Bordeaux branch of the Banque Lyonnaise could be determined.

"What else?"

"They're doing a search of other possible sources."

So there were ways to determine which other banks might have lent Conderie money, and how much.

"They can promise definite results within about two weeks."

"I'm not interested in a loan to buy a car or something. I'm interested in big money."

"They understand that. That's what they think they are onto."

"Good," said Stack. "Hurry them along as much as you can. Let me know the moment you have something."

But, once he had hung up, the morning stretched interminably ahead of him. He knew no one in the city, and he did not speak French. He could buy a book and read, but he did not enjoy reading. He was sick of visiting châteaux, and the countryside with its interminable stretches of vines bored him. He could go shopping, buy some presents for one or two of the infrequent young women in his life. But he hated shopping.

He could not decently turn up at Conderie's château until midafternoon.

He went downstairs and through the lobby of the hotel onto the terrace. The September sun shone down through the trees. It was a fine morning. He ordered breakfast.

"And bring me a Paris *Herald Tribune*."

"Oui, monsieur."

The paper was yesterday's. Annoyed, Stack turned to the stock pages, and examined the figures. He read the front-page headlines, and every word on the sports pages, but not the political columns. The only politics that interested Stack was what went on on the thirty-seventh floor at corporate headquarters.

The fried eggs were fresh and delicious. Stack was beginning to be dimly aware that the food in this country was tastier than he was used to. Not that he was a man who ate for pleasure. Restaurants to Stack were refueling stations, and extensions to his office. Restaurants were excellent places in which to transact business.

When he had finished breakfast, Stack sat back in his wicker chair and gazed out into the small park in front of the hotel. He was remembering a number of successful business lunches: some of these suckers would drink three martinis and then try to deal with Charlie Stack, who had drunk nothing.

Stack was bored, and he missed New York. New York was where the action was. He wanted to get back there. It had occurred to him that if he could bring back Conderie's château swiftly at a relatively low price, then perhaps the chairman would agree to end his exile at once. The idea would have to come from the chairman. There must be no more heavy-handed tennis games. Still, it seemed reasonable. A great job by Stack in Bordeaux, a valuable property acquired. Wouldn't it make sense at that point to hire some famous wine guy to take over the property, and bring Stack back to New York? Sure it would. Stack would be happy just to get his old job back, although if he came home triumphant, a promotion might not be out of the question.

Now he was drumming his fingers on the table. He was bored.

Toward late afternoon, Stack parked his rented car on the gravel in front of Conderie's château, and strolled through the archway into the courtyard formed by the chais.

"Hello there," he said, walking toward Conderie with his hand outstretched.

"I came out to see your daughter," lied Stack.

"I think she's gone riding in the fields out behind the château," said Conderie, who had been talking to his cellar master.

64

When Conderie resumed his interrupted conversation, Stack strained hard to understand the French, for there might be a nugget there he could use.

But Conderie was nothing if not well bred. "I'm sorry," he said to Stack after a moment. "I didn't mean to ignore you. I was just giving instructions to my cellar master about the harvest. We are going to begin the vendange tomorrow."

Following Conderie's directions, Stack strolled around behind the château. Below a flagstone terrace, which evidently gave off the château's dining room, the land sloped down and away. There was a meadow in which two cows and a horse grazed, and below that were some trees through which, Stack judged, a stream must run. From the other side of the trees the land sloped up again, and was covered with vines. Stack knew that about three hundred acres belonged to the château, of which only about half was planted in vines.

As he looked off across the meadow, he saw a figure on horseback come out of the trees, and he waved. Aline Conderie waved back, and came toward him at a gallop. When she had reined in, he stepped forward to hold the reins, and she slipped off the horse. The sun was low and behind her, and, squinting, he saw that her face looked flushed and healthy.

"There's another horse. Do you ride?"

"No. Do you play tennis?"

She laughed. "No, I don't."

"There must be something we might enjoy doing together," said Stack. "If we think about it, maybe something will come to mind."

Instead of laughing she frowned.

She led the way up onto the terrace, a slim young woman in tight riding breeches.

"I like the way those breeches fit you," said Stack, with a confident smile. It was Stack's experience that women liked all compliments, particularly the mildly vulgar, though this one again seemed to frown.

"Yes, well, would you like a cup of tea or a bottle of beer or something?"

They sat in rattan chairs on the terrace.

Stack said: "What I'm really here for is to ask you to have dinner with me tonight. I'd like to take you to the nicest and most expensive restaurant in the Médoc."

"It happens that there are no expensive restaurants out here. There aren't even any that are particularly nice."

65

"Oh."

"The only place for miles around is the Savoie in Margaux. All the workingmen like it, anyway. I can't stand the place."

After a rather long silence, Aline Conderie wiped the sweat off her forehead with her sleeve. "You could have dinner here with us at the château, if you like."

Apparently the invitation had come with some reluctance, which Stack perceived clearly. She had felt obliged to extend country hospitality. A more sensitive man might therefore have declined. But Stack gave her another big grin and said: "I'd be delighted to have dinner with you here at the château."

"Come about eight then. Now, if you don't mind, I'm all sweaty, and I'd like to go bathe and change my clothes."

"I'll see you at eight then."

Stack watched the way her riding breeches moved as she went past him into the house. She wasn't very friendly, was she? Why?

Stack, as he walked around the outside of the château, felt restless. He wanted to work. He hated loafing. The only work he could think of now was to interrogate Conderie, perhaps find out something. But Conderie apparently had driven away in his car. It was ten after five. Three hours to kill. Stack didn't know what to do with himself.

As he strolled back to his car parked in front of the château, he glanced up at some of the tall windows on the second floor. Behind one of them at this moment Aline Conderie lay indolently in a hot tub. This was nice to contemplate, but got him nowhere. Stack climbed into his car and drove down into the village of Margaux. The Savoie, he saw, was more bar than restaurant. There were several round iron tables outside. He sat down on a plastic chair, and when the waiter came out ordered tea, which he sipped while going through his notebook again, restudying all he had learned so far. When the tea was gone he decided to order a bottle of beer, and much later he switched to Scotch. He had got the Paris *Herald Tribune* out of his car, and by 7 P.M. had read every word, and even done the crossword puzzle.

There were eleven at dinner. Count de Grenelle and his wife, who owned a neighboring château; Nathaniel Brown and his wife, Brown being president of a Bordeaux wine-shipping firm established by a London-born ancestor at the beginning of the last century; the president of the Kansas City Wine and Food Society and his wife, both of whom Stack had met at some previous château and had assumed to be tourists successfully freeloading their way through the wine country; and the owner of a prosperous Chicago liquor store and his wife.

Language was a problem. The Count de Grenelle spoke English fluently but with an accent; his wife's accent was so thick she was almost incomprehensible. Nathaniel Brown spoke English with an Oxford accent, but his wife, who was evidently Aline's great friend around here, spoke none at all. So the dinner-table conversation, to Stack's annoyance, was almost as much in French as in English. Once Aline even turned to him babbling in French, before realizing that Stack did not understand, at which point she switched effortlessly to English. It made Stack feel a bit of a fool, a feeling he didn't like.

It was soon clear to Stack that the Conderies, the Grenelles, and the Browns saw a great deal of each other, and also that all of them entertained foreigners such as tonight's batch more or less regularly, usually without any clear idea of the worth of the foreign guests, for the Bordeaux wine syndicate apparently provided introductions to almost anyone. Stack had seen through those freeloaders from Kansas City instantly, but it seemed they had dined at Grenelle's château two days ago, and at Brown's last week. The liquor-store owner and his wife were nice enough, though dull. Neither understood a word of French, and both seemed so worried about committing some heinous faux pas that they moved and spoke and even ate as little as possible.

The dining room was illuminated from silver wall fixtures, and there was a great silver and crystal chandelier hanging over the dining room table, which, however, was not lit. The walls were lined with portraits, apparently of Conderie's ancestors, all in heavy carved or gilded frames. These old paintings were no doubt valuable but gave the room a gloomy cast, Stack thought. The sideboard was heavy and old, walnut probably, its top waxed to a shine, its doors and drawers carved into diamonds, lozenges, and other shapes, and also polished to a shine. On top of this sideboard stood a number of decanters, all full as the meal commenced. Some of the decanters were of intricately cut crystal, others of thin clear crystal so delicately etched that one expected them to burst at any moment. Stack assumed, and it later proved true, that each gorgeous decanter contained a different gorgeous wine, treasure within treasure. There were candles on the table, and the tottering flames were caught by the decanters on the sideboard, so that white and ruby glints played upon the ceiling. A heap of jewelry lying on that sideboard would have been no more spectacular than those decanters.

The table was covered with a hand-embroidered white tablecloth, and the silver place settings were heavy and ornate. The china was from

Limoges, thin and delicate and bearing a subtle blue pattern which matched the drapes hanging beside the French doors and also the wallpaper throughout the room. In front of each plate stood four wine glasses of different sizes and designs.

Dinner was served by a middle-aged woman in a starched uniform who was referred to as Madame Gorr. Stack assumed this to be the wife of the cellar master. There were at least two other servants busy in the kitchen, Stack guessed, for he could hear movement there, the noise of dishes, and occasionally some girlish giggling.

The first course was a fresh vegetable soup which differed from what Stack might have expected in that the broth contained sherry, and the vegetables (leeks, diced carrots, string beans, and segments of tomatoes) had evidently been added to the broth late, for they were slightly undercooked and retained all their own flavor. The second course was a kind of mushroom tart: diced mushrooms in a cream sauce folded inside flaky pastry. The third course was a roast rack of lamb, the meat impregnated with pieces of garlic, and served slightly underdone, so that it was brown and crusty outside but pink on the inside. This came with fresh string beans, which had been cooked with slices of onion, and which again were served slightly underdone; and with fried potatoes, which were crisp outside but still firm inside. Then came a tray of cheeses, which filled the room, Stack considered, with too many too unsavory odors, though all the others seemed thrilled with the cheese tray. And lastly there was an apple tart, whose pastry was light and flaky, with the apples freshly picked and baked in a kind of caramel sauce to which cognac had been added.

Stack was not one to pay much attention to what he ate, but he did so tonight because the conversation throughout the meal was either about food itself, or else it took place in French, leaving Stack no choice. Evidently the fresh vegetables were grown in the garden out behind the aging sheds, and the whole concoction had been put together by Aline herself, who beamed and acted silly when praised at each course by others around the table.

Once Aline remarked: "It is a pleasure to come down here from Paris, and eat vegetables that are really fresh."

Stack grudgingly admitted that this was so. He could not remember eating vegetables this fresh since he was a child.

And of course the entire meal was accompanied by that symphony of wines.

The first and youngest to be served was a 1967 Château Lafite. This was greeted at the French end of the table with the explanation that only Lafite, among the great first growths, was normally light enough to be drunk so relatively young. Next came a 1952 Château Figeac from St. Émilion, followed by a Château Beychevelle of the same vintage, so that the guests could compare the two. After that came a 1950 Château Haut-Brion. The guests decided that the Château Beychevelle tasted more like the Haut-Brion than like the Figeac, Stack listening carefully but taking no part in the discussion to that point. The final wine, oldest of all, was a Château Conderie from the year that Paul Conderie had taken over the management of the château following the death of his father.

The conversation which introduced, accompanied, and followed each of these wines seemed to Stack idotic. He listened to people speak of the ampleur of the Château Lafite, which was rated a supple, elegant wine possessing both body and charm. But it was a short wine, compared to the Figeac, which was rated long, somewhat hard, but having a good deal of nose. The Beychevelle had started off a nervous wine, an austere wine, but a wine of breeding, and its great temperament had brought it through to what it was today. The oldest Conderie, or perhaps it was the Haut-Brion, had been precocious at first, but had turned into a robust wine with a beautiful robe, whatever that was. These people flung the words around like darts, as if hoping they'd stick somewhere, anywhere. Pretty soon the freeloader from Kansas City joined in, and after that even the mousy liquor-store owner from Chicago. It was all nonsense to Stack, and he would have thought it funny except that these people took themselves so seriously, and at last he decided to make the most outrageous remark he could think of. As he held his glass up, peering through the wine toward the candles, it seemed to him that everyone at the table leaned forward to hear what he would say. "This wine," said Stack, "has a bouquet that is almost— indiscreet."

Around the table everyone nodded, seeing nothing nonsensical in the nonsense Stack had just uttered. So Stack nodded too and added: "The last one had nose. This one has muscles."

He had thought that might get a laugh. There was no reaction whatsoever.

The party now withdrew to the drawing room. There was a fire in the stone fireplace, for the night had turned chilly. Stack stood with his back to the fire, glancing around. There were seventeenth-century paintings on two of the walls, and hanging tapestries that probably were even older on the other two.

Madame Gorr arrived bearing coffee on a tray. The tray was set down on another handsome antique sideboard, and Aline Conderie poured coffee out into demitasse cups. Handing the tiny cup to Stack she remarked in a low voice: "See if you find that this coffee has muscles."

Stack gave her his big grin, but she was already handing around other cups to other guests.

Conderie offered some fifty-year-old brandy to all who wanted any. Stack sipped his. It was good brandy.

The conversation had broken down now into two groups, the French and the English, and the Conderies were with their French friends, leaving Stack the choice either of silence or of listening to the fraud from Kansas City or the mouse from Chicago. Still, it had been a splendid dinner, and Stack wished only for a few minutes alone with Aline Conderie, for she might be important to his plans, and he had begun to feel that perhaps he had offended her.

At last the other guests began to depart until only Aline, her father, and Stack were left, and the fire was almost out on the hearth.

"More cognac?" asked Conderie.

"No, thank you," said Stack politely.

"I think I may have some more though."

"Muscles, indeed," said Aline to Stack. "Whoever heard of a wine with muscles?"

"I was being facetious."

"Nobody laughed."

"I know," said Stack ruefully. "But all that wine talk just doesn't make any sense." He added doubtfully: "Does it?"

"You're much more attractive when you're unsure of yourself," said Aline.

"Well, does it?"

Conderie said: "When you're in the business of making and selling wine, you have to be able to describe it to people who have not yet had the opportunity of tasting it. That's where all the jargon comes from, and it all means something to people who understand the jargon."

Stack persisted. "One of those wines you called feminine. How can a wine be feminine or masculine or anything else?"

70

"It just means that it's a softer, smoother, less robust, less acidic kind of wine."

"It seems to me it would make more sense," Stack said, "to talk about how many bottles you made that year, and how many you sold and at what price. That's hard information, and the rest is froth."

"Well, winemaking is an art, or pretends to be," said Conderie mildly. "This whole business of eating and drinking is an art. If music pleases the ear and a beautiful painting pleases the eye and a great wine pleases the palate, are they not all to be considered in the same terms? That is, in terms of art and of pleasure, rather than in terms of commerce."

"I'm more at home in commerce, I'm afraid."

Conderie smiled. "Stay with us in the Médoc long enough and you may change."

"That's just it. I'd like to live out here in the Médoc somewhere during the harvest. Can you recommend a hotel to me?"

Conderie shook his head. "No hotels out here at all, unfortunately. We could really use a good hotel."

"Because driving back and forth to Bordeaux each day really takes a lot of time. The traffic entering and leaving the city is incredible."

Stack had been hoping all evening for an opportunity to coax from the Conderies an invitation to move into their château, for he wanted to study his prey up close.

"I want to put in my book how a harvest is done at a typical château like this one," Stack lied.

Conderie and his daughter gazed at each other, and Stack watched silent messages flash back and forth between them.

"Since you've already been so cordial to me, I thought I would devote a good deal of space to Château Conderie. The publicity, I hope, would be of some use to you."

Conderie frowned, but Aline, whose gaze had shifted to Stack, missed this most important message so far. By the time she turned back to her father, presumably seeking another signal, Conderie had recovered, and his face was bland. Though Aline seemed to be seeking instructions from him, none came.

Stack realized that the invitation he coveted would be forthcoming. These people were so intent on being correct, so determined to display their so-called good breeding, that it now seemed to Stack laughably easy to manipulate them.

Aline said: "We could put you up here in the château, I suppose."

Stack showed no elation. "I hate to impose on you."

Conderie, who had turned away, appeared intent on a point half-way up one of the walls.

Aline said: "It's just that during the vendange we're all so busy that it might be impossible to look after you the way we might like."

Stack, expressing suitable gratitude, felt a twinge of guilt which he quickly switched to self-applause. This is a business deal, he thought grimly, in which there is no room for emotion of any kind.

Aline had turned to her father, as if seeking approval. Stack used the moment to eye her up and down, admiring her contours. Her bosom, to which all unknowing she had just pressed a viper—himself —looked especially tasty. Lucky viper. Unlucky bosom.

"The thing that did surprise me," said Stack at the door, "is that you serve such a variety of wine. How is it that you have wines from other châteaux?"

Conderie answered: "We always trade cases of our best vintages among ourselves. The great painters always did the same, I understand. Picasso and Matisse would exchange paintings the same way I would exchange wine with Baron Élie at Lafite, or with Manoncourt at Figeac. Wine really is more of an art than a business. That's what we like to believe, anyway."

When Stack's rented car had disappeared into the night, Conderie turned to his daughter. "I say, there was no need to invite the fellow to live with us."

Aline scuffed the gravel with her toe. "I thought that was what you wanted."

"What I wanted?" demanded Conderie incredulously.

"For the publicity and everything."

"My dear, he's not our kind at all. He's a—a journalist. Or so he says. He's got the manners of a tractor salesman."

Aline apologized. "It was such an awkward situation. I didn't see how to get out of it. I kept expecting you to say something."

In the light coming out the front door, father and daughter gazed at each other. "—But you didn't say a word." Her tone was mildly accusatory. "You simply stuck me with it."

After a moment Conderie said cheerfully: "Well, maybe something good will come out of it. Come, let's go up to bed."

9

The vendange began the next morning. A gang of migrant workers were driven up in a truck. They were poor Spaniards brought over from the north of Spain by the trainload each autumn. This year the châteaux had had a hard job finding enough Spaniards. Spain had become richer; Spanish peasants now could earn enough money in their own country. Next year there would be fewer Spaniards still.

To Stack Conderie explained the growing shortage of migrant workers. The châteaux close to Bordeaux hired students from Bordeaux University. They got all the pickers they needed. Up at the top end of the Médoc was the town of Pauillac, which was three or four times as big as Margaux. The châteaux up there hired local people to get their grapes in. But Margaux was too tiny and was at the mercy of migrants. Now the Spaniards were beginning to peter out.

Stack demanded: "Don't they have machines for picking grapes?"

This question amused Conderie. "You mean like a machine that picks corn?"

"I just thought that a machine might solve a lot of your problems."

"You believe in machines, do you?" inquired Conderie.

"Doesn't everybody?"

"But machines are blind, old man."

A machine did exist, Conderie explained. You pushed it along between two rows of vines. It was like a great vacuum cleaner: it sucked in everything, not only ripe grapes but also green grapes, rotten grapes, weeds, stones. "Such machines may be fine for making ordinary wine, not my wine," said Conderie.

Stack wondered how thoroughly such machines had been tested. The idea deserved to be looked into further.

In his notebook Stack jotted: Machines vs. snobbery.

Conderie did not bother to watch the start of the harvest, but Stack did. Along the rows of vines moved Spanish men, women, and kids. The clusters of tight purple grapes, nearly a foot in length, were snipped from the vine and dropped onto flat baskets. The porters, six of the strongest-looking men, each wore a two-foot-deep metal tub on his back. The tubs were black inside and a rich burgundy outside. The porters, moving down the rows, would crouch so the pickers could empty their flat baskets into the tubs. When each tub was filled, the porters trudged up the alley to where the wagon was parked behind a tractor. On top of the wagon rode four great wooden tubs called douils, each of which would hold a hundred gallons of grapes. Ladders led up to the top of the douils. The porters climbed the ladders, and at the top bent forward and, with a powerful shrugging motion, dumped the waterfall of grapes over their shoulders into the douils. In theory each picker could fill only a single hundred-gallon douil in an eight-hour day —and there were more than fifty thousand gallons of grapes to be picked.

My God, this is slow, Stack thought. The harvest would last fourteen days.

Above his head the sky was an unbroken sweep of blue. The leaves of the vines were beginning to turn autumn colors, and the trees at the end of the field were beginning to turn color too. Beyond those trees, Stack knew, the great river moved implacably toward the sea.

Where was Conderie? Why wasn't he overseeing all this?

Stack walked back to the chais and watched the douils being dumped into the stemming machine. It was like watching grapes dumped into the top of an enormous coffee grinder. With the rapidity of a machine gun the machine spit stems out into a pile in the yard. Meanwhile the destemmed grapes, together with the juices they leaked, were being pumped into a hose as thick as a man's leg. This hose led across the floor and then up the side and over the top of one of the great high vats. Stack could hear the new grapes bombarding the floor inside the vat.

Conderie came into the chai. Stack wanted to know where the presses were.

"We don't press the grapes, old man," Conderie said, surprised. As Conderie explained it, there was no need to. During the destemming and the pumping of the grapes into the vat, enough skins split, enough juice ran out, to start fermentation. The fermentation itself would break open any undamaged grapes. After a few days of fermentation every grape would have given up all its juice. There would be a layer of skins

74

and pits two feet thick floating on top of the juice. "We call that the chapeau, the hat," Conderie said.

The temperature of the fermenting wine would be checked constantly. Stack wanted to know why. Conderie explained that the yeast cells which collected naturally on the skins of the grapes on the vines were what caused the miracle of fermentation. These cells normally became active at about 65 degrees Fahrenheit, and died at about 100 degrees. It was absolutely essential to keep the temperature of the fermentation within those limits. Makers of fine wine felt the limit should be even narrower, somewhere between 70 and 86 degrees Fahrenheit. Sometimes, if the weather was very cold during harvest, the juice would have to be heated before it would start to ferment at all. Conversely, during excessively warm weather, the vats often had to be cooled, lest fermentation stop. Fermenting grape juice produced its own heat, and this heat could soar spontaneously to temperatures high enough to kill the yeast and stop the fermentation.

"Temperature in the making of wine is critical," Conderie said.

Stack tasted a sampling of the juice. It was sweet—so sweet it probably could not be sold as grape juice without being toned down. During fermentation it would burn up all its sugar, converting sugar into alcohol, and the resultant wine would be dry.

Stack had read a great many technical books before flying over here. Fermentation of grape juice into wine was indeed a miracle, and no one understood very much about it. It just happened. It had been happening more or less by itself since the beginning of time. The only difference was that here in the Médoc the fermentation was watched carefully and controlled to some extent.

At dinner that night, which Stack took with Conderie and his daughter, the three of them alone in the great dining room, Stack offered to pay for the cost of his food and lodging. To his surprise this offer appeared to offend the Conderies. "Well, this isn't a hotel, you know," said Conderie huffily.

"You Americans make rather much of money, don't you?" inquired Aline.

Stack decided to switch hurriedly to a safe subject. "What's this wine we're drinking now?" he asked.

Conderie and his daughter eyed each other.

Wine, the neutral ground.

"Our everyday wine is our vin de lie, or else vin de presse," explained Aline.

After fermentation had ended, the leftover pulps, pits, and skins were at last pressed. The juice they gave up was vin de presse, and in quality it was quite good enough to drink as ordinary table wine. Later, during the two years that the great wine would age in barrels, it would several times be poured off its dregs into clean barrels. The residue would then be filtered, and the wine it gave up was vin de lie, also an adequate table wine.

"Can't afford to drink vintage château wine with every meal," Conderie said. "Wouldn't want to even if you could. You'd soon lose your palate, I expect. Our everyday wine is the same wine we give our employees, and it's also the wine we serve these pickers."

"What is the overall expense of your harvest?" asked Stack, planning to imprint the figure in the notebook of his mind until he had a chance to write it down.

But Conderie answered: "I don't know. I never added it up."

Stack could hardly believe his ears. To Stack the idea of a manager who had never even calculated his expenses was preposterous.

"Last year," Conderie offered, "our food bill during the harvest was, let me see, the equivalent of about twenty-two hundred dollars American, or so the cook told me." The approximately fifty pickers earned about ten dollars per day per picker for fifteen days. The total cost of the harvest thus came to about ten thousand dollars.

"I've never had much of a head for figures," confessed Conderie.

The man's a dimwit, thought Stack, and has no right to own such a château.

When supper ended Conderie excused himself.

"Shall we have coffee in the living room?" Aline asked Stack.

But, as Stack and Aline were crossing the entrance hall, Conderie came down the curving staircase. "It's been a trying day," he told his daughter. "I think I'll go into the city for some relaxation."

Stack's true interest was the father, not the daughter. The daughter was a tidbit. The father was the whole meal. Stack, guessing Conderie's destination, said: "I'll go with you. I feel lucky tonight."

Conderie glanced up in surprise.

"Shall we take my car or yours?" asked Stack, but Conderie, obviously wanting to go alone, did not answer. Aline looked from one man to the other.

"I thought you were going to take coffee with me," said Aline, who seemed disappointed, almost pouting. "Coffee with—muscles," she suggested.

76

But Stack had his hand on Conderie's back and was half ushering him toward the door.

"Let's have that coffee when your father and I come back—if you're still up," he told Aline.

Conderie said stiffly: "Come along then."

As they drew up in the street in front of the club Conderie explained that he would be engaged in a bridge game for the next several hours.

"I trust you'll be able to amuse yourself that long, old chap?"

Stack concealed his annoyance at Conderie's condescension. "Would there be a seat for me in the game?"

"The stakes would be a bit high for you, I expect."

"Oh."

"Unless they pay journalists a good deal more in America than I had thought."

What does he suspect? Stack asked himself. Conderie was perhaps less a dimwit than Stack believed.

"Well, maybe I can kibitz then."

"Yes, you do that."

But the fourth member of Conderie's group had not yet arrived, and presently Stack, uninvited, sat down in the fourth chair. This caused raised eyebrows around the table, and Stack was not admitted to the conversation, which continued in French.

Stack had, of course, been introduced by Conderie to the two other men. Though unable to absorb the unfamiliar French names, he understood one man to be a marquis who owned a château in Sauternes, while the other was president of the wine brokers' syndicate. Stack attempted to break into the conversation in English, but no one responded. For a time, shuffling and reshuffling one of the decks of cards, he sat in bored silence.

He became aware that the subject of conversation was himself, and that the others were amused by him.

"Why don't we all speak English?" suggested Stack brightly.

All stared at him.

"I'm sure you all speak English," said Stack.

"You can try speaking English to the marquis," said Conderie, "but I'm not sure it will work, as he doesn't happen to speak any."

The broker gave a guffaw.

Stack said to the broker, "But you speak English, don't you?"

77

"I find English such a strain," the broker answered, and began again to speak in French.

"I don't quite understand the role of the brokers in the wine trade," said Stack. "I wonder if you would explain it to me."

"I'm afraid I never talk business in the club."

"I see."

The conversation resumed in French. Stack saw that he was again the subject.

"A journalist, you say?"

"A dealer in heavy machinery would be more like it."

"He's like all these Americans. No manners."

The tone—if not their words—was clear to Stack.

Conderie was enjoying himself. Secure among his peers, he took pleasure in putting the outsider in his place. The three Frenchmen were like schoolboys mocking the new kid.

Abruptly, Stack dealt out all the cards. "Why don't we play a few hands while you're waiting for your friend?" he suggested. "It will be like warming up."

The marquis picked up his hand, glanced at it, and turned the cards face up on the table.

"There's Georges," said Conderie, nodding toward the entrance hall.

In the hall a man had handed his topcoat to a lackey.

"That's Georges's chair you're sitting in," suggested Conderie to Stack.

Stack had dealt himself a hand of solitaire, and was playing it slowly. He looked up. "I'm afraid I was here first."

"But Georges owns that chair, old man. He bought it, you see. We all bought our chairs when we joined. If you look, you'll find Georges's nameplate on the backrest. So I'm afraid you'll have to give it to him."

Georges arrived at the table. Introduced to the American journalist, Georges accorded Stack a perfunctory handshake, no notice whatsoever, and dropped into his chair as if no one had been sitting there.

Pulling over a folding chair, Stack stationed himself at Conderie's elbow. He had a pile of chips in his hand, which he now, at irregular intervals, began clacking together.

Cards fell silently. Stack's chips clacked. Conderie, gathering up a hand, frowned. "I thought you'd be playing roulette or baccarat by now, old boy. I thought you felt lucky tonight."

"No hurry," answered Stack.

Conderie played bridge expertly, though with lapses that cost him money. He seemed thoroughly unsettled by Stack at his elbow, and obviously he felt responsible for having brought Stack into the club.

While Conderie attempted to concentrate on his cards, hard glances came toward Stack from the other players, but he ignored them, thinking: for all your pretensions you're a rude bunch of bastards, and I can be just as rude as you.

Conderie called over a lackey and whispered to him. This caused approving comments from the other players. A moment later the lackey appeared at Stack's elbow. "The manager would like a word with you, please, sir—"

Stack had no choice but to follow the lackey into a corner, where a man in evening dress waited.

"I'm sorry, sir, but I'll have to ask you not to sit close to the bridge games."

Stack stared at him.

"It tends to disturb the other players, sir."

The man was embarrassed, though not as embarrassed as Stack.

"If you'd care to play roulette or baccarat, sir—"

From Conderie's table, Stack heard smothered laughter. He felt their mocking eyes on his back.

Ears burning, Stack approached the roulette table, where he stared down at squares and numbers.

By the time Conderie moved to the baccarat table, Stack had recovered his poise. Conderie was alone now, and looked shaken. Presumably he had lost at bridge. Taking a chair across from Conderie, Stack studied the fall of the cards for a long time before placing a single small bet. After waiting three more hands, he bet again, this time heavily. Stack hated gambling almost as much as he hated being humiliated. A good businessman did not gamble and got humiliated rarely. A good businessman did a thorough investigation first, then brought all pressure to bear on the weakest point, and won automatically. Risks he kept at a minimum.

Conderie, conscious of Stack, appeared disconcerted. He seemed to follow a certain rigid pattern, betting three times against the bank, the same amount of money each time, never doubling his losses. Suddenly he would erupt from the pattern, plunging hard on the side of a streak which one of the other players seemed to be having.

Inexorably, Conderie lost money. Once he wrote out a check, then sent an attendant to the cashier's desk with it. The attendant returned with more chips. Conderie went on playing. Sweat, like raindrops on a windowpane, stood on his brow. Now he concentrated so intently on the cards that he seemed to have forgotten Stack across the table. Conderie, who was down about five thousand dollars now, as near as Stack could judge, suddenly pushed all his chips forward, betting on a single card. Only a two could save him, Stack saw. A wild bet.

Stack glanced at the faces around the table. All were intent on the next card about to be slipped out of the shoe. The dealer pressed it to the table, then flipped it up to face the anxious players.

The card turned up to the lights was a—two.

Beaming, almost laughing aloud, Conderie pushed back from the table. He had completely forgotten Stack and was listening to a song only he heard. He was rapturous. He strode from the table, leaving an attendant to scoop up his winnings and cash them in. Tipping attendants along the way, he walked straight out the door and downstairs to the street.

Stack had to hurry to keep up. "You didn't even count your winnings." Conderie had left some $10,000 worth of chips lying on the table.

"Oh, they'll take care of that for me," said Conderie.

The château owner had recouped all of tonight's staggering losses in one turn of the cards.

It was two-thirty in the morning. The streets were empty and wet —it must have rained while they were playing. They drove along the Quai des Chartrons. Ships moored at the docks showed under dim lights. On the other side of the street stood the dark, narrow buildings which housed the great wine-shipping firms.

Suddenly Conderie made a U-turn and parked directly in front of a building which showed lights on the second floor. He got out and rang.

The door opened. The man who stood in the light was about forty years old, and he wore a wide black mustache which turned down at the corners of his mouth. He was a big man, as big as Stack.

"I thought if I stopped you'd invite me in and offer me champagne," Stack heard Conderie say exuberantly.

"I'm busy," the man said rudely. He looked suspiciously across at Stack.

"Édouard Bozon, this is an acquaintance of mine, Charlie Stack," said Conderie. But his cheerfulness, and also perhaps his courage, were running down.

Stack moved forward, hand outstretched, forcing an encounter.

80

Their fingers barely touched before Bozon abruptly turned back to Conderie, spewing French.

"I thought you'd be glad to see me," said Conderie. "I just won a lot of money at the club. Why don't I ever hear from you?"

The conversation continued in French. Bozon, obviously angry, threw many suspicious glances at Stack. Conderie seemed increasingly apologetic. Stack, who understood only that the conversation concerned money, guessed, wrongly, that Conderie owed this Bozon money and was asking for time.

Abruptly Bozon stepped back inside and slammed the door in Conderie's face.

A nugget, thought Charlie Stack. Possibly useful later. You never knew.

Conderie was silent the rest of the way home. So was Stack beside him. Conderie's Mercedes rolled over the dark, empty roads of the Médoc, where the great wine châteaux brooded silently under the night.

10

Aline Conderie offered to drive Stack around to some of the châteaux that he had not yet visited. She was pretending to be nice to him but Stack guessed her true motive: She was suspicious. She distrusted him. She wanted to find out what his game was. At the same time, despite herself she was (Stack decided) powerfully attracted to him physically.

In each new château Aline was greeted warmly, and the owner or cellar master immediately went to fetch glasses in which to serve them a taste of last year's wine. Stack was amazed. These people repeatedly served tastes of last year's wine even to each other. It was as automatic as shaking hands, and evidently as obligatory. It had been the custom of the region for scores if not hundreds of years. But to Stack it seemed tremendously wasteful both of time and of wine, and he decided he would put a stop to it at his own château, as soon as he took charge there.

Some châteaux had almost finished picking. Others had just started. Those which had picked early feared the rainy weather which had been forecast for the next two weeks. Owners who had not started yet were counting on Indian-summer weather during the next two weeks; a single morning of hot sunshine could raise the sugar content of grapes on the vine by one entire degree, which meant an extra degree of alcohol and better wine.

In fermenting sheds, Stack found that some vats were oak similar to Paul Conderie's, but others were of thin stainless steel that gleamed like surgical instruments. Still others were lined with glass, and some were made of reinforced concrete. Speaking to owners through Aline Conderie, Stack found that each believed his own vats superior to all others.

On window sills in every fermenting shed instruments floated in test tubes filled with the new must.

One owner took Stack and Aline out into his fields and explained to Stack the difference between the principal types of grapes which went into the great wines of the Médoc. The Cabernet Sauvignon grapes grew in foot-long clusters. The Cabernet Franc clusters were very much tighter, the individual grapes pressed so tightly together that it was as if they had been magnetized to the stem. The Merlot grape was somewhat bigger than the other two varieties, and its leaves were twice as big. The Merlot grapes ripened first and were picked first. They were somewhat sweeter than the others, although all of these varieties were very sweet grapes. The Cabernet Sauvignon was the principal grape in all of the wines of Bordeaux, accounting for between fifty and ninety-five percent of the finished blend in each bottle, depending on the château.

At those châteaux where the vendange was being done by local villagers, these people were always returned to their homes at night by bus, taking with them in containers both their dinners and their breakfasts, for it was part of local tradition that every vendangeur was due three meals a day in addition to his pay. When the pickers were migrants—whether Spaniards or students—then sleeping quarters, however mean, also were provided. Stack saw mattresses laid out on floors of barns and garages. Spaniards presumably bedded down by families; as for students, no owner seemed to care how they bedded down. The students were having a fourteen-day party, almost a binge, and perhaps an orgy as well, for all Stack knew. Wherever there were students, there were cheerful refectories, cheerful dormitories, and much laughter and singing. Once Stack was brought into a dormitory in which a bunch of students sat around playing guitars. They had come in from the fields, and some had cleaned up by now though some had not, and when Stack was introduced as a writer preparing a book on wine, they crowded around laughing and bombarded him with questions.

When Stack and Aline were back in their car, Aline probed: "Exactly what kind of a book is it going to be?"

But Stack gave her his grin and refused to say. Aline insisted. Stack made a joke and still refused. Aline frowned.

They drove west, crossing the Médoc peninsula toward the ocean, and soon were beyond the thin strip of vineyards belonging to the great châteaux. Now vineyards began to be interspersed with apple orchards, and even forests. Instead of vast bands of pickers these small vineyards were being cleared by single families, often just mom and dad and one or two little kids, so that Stack said suddenly: "I wonder how their test tubes are reading."

Aline smiled at him. "You'd be surprised," she said. "They may be making wine in the backs of garages, but on the window sill they probably have the same test tubes and instruments that we have. It's wine like this that gets sold directly to the local restaurants, by the way. Perhaps it's very good wine. The restaurant will buy it in the barrel, and serve it under its own label, or even in carafes, and the customers will think they've made a real find, a lovely wine that only costs a dollar or something."

Stack looked at her. "You love this country, don't you?" he asked. He was surprised he had only realized this now. "I wonder why you moved away to Paris."

"Are you asking me why?"

"Yes."

After a moment Aline said: "I was married here. I was only twenty years old at the time." She fell silent.

"And—" Stack prompted.

After a moment she said: "I'm not married now. I haven't been married in over five years, and I'm much happier this way, thank you. Anyway, when I gave up the marriage I wanted to give up this place too."

"Who was he?"

"Nobody you know."

It was getting dark now, and they had passed beyond the area where wine was being made at all. Forests had closed in around them and the air had become scented with pine. Stack saw by the road signs that there would be no more villages until they reached the Atlantic Ocean.

Aline turned the car around. "Let's go home and have dinner, shall we?"

She did not speak after that. Stack watched her profile. They came back out of the forest country and into the country that was half orchard, half wine, and then into the country that was all wine, until at last Aline steered up the dirt road, through the tunnel of plane trees and onto the gravel in front of the château. There she got out of the car and went into the château without looking back.

At dinner her manner was distant, and afterward she shook hands with Stack and said, "I shall be going back to Paris very early in the morning. It's nice to have met you. I hope you write a fine book."

Stack said hurriedly: "Have a last drink with me first."

He gave her his best smile but her own face was expressionless. "If you'll excuse me, I must get on with my packing. Good night."

Stack watched her moving up the marble staircase. Again tonight she wore a gown which hid her from chin to shoes, and it made her body seem as enigmatic to him as her personality. When she had disappeared down the hallway, Stack shrugged. If he had once imagined seducing her, he had none the less devoted no energy whatsoever to the job, and basically he was just as glad she would be gone tomorrow. Soon the blood would flow here, and he did not need her in the way, either as an extra adversary to be slain, or as an innocent bystander to be wounded by some stray shot.

Again the next morning Stack drove to the Margaux post office and placed a call to Paris. Saar came on the phone speaking excitedly. Within ten minutes, Stack had all the facts he needed to make Conderie sell him the château.

Stack went looking for Conderie.

11

He stalked Conderie most of the day.

He found him first in the château's private cellar. This was a cellar off the cellar, a dim, vaulted room. A light bulb hung down on a wire. Cobwebs cloaked the room. The bottles were in iron racks, and from a single bottle in each rack hung a wooden signboard. On each board the vintage of that particular rack was marked in chalk. Conderie stood amidst his private stock.

"What are you doing down here," demanded Stack, "counting your money?"

Conderie turned one of the signboards toward the light. Though the chalk had faded, Stack made out the vintage: 1947. The ten or a dozen bottles left in that rack were worth perhaps a thousand dollars in all, perhaps more, Stack thought. Not enough to help Conderie much.

Conderie moved along the racks, occasionally brushing cobwebs out of his way, turning signboards toward the light.

One rack was marked 1914. This was the oldest vintage left in any quantity. Conderie carried a candle, which he now lit. Stack watched him withdraw several of the 1914 bottles part way out of the rack, holding the candle flame under the neck. In each of the bottles the level of wine ended two inches below the cork. Stack realized that the corks had dried out and rotted. The wine inside was probably ruined.

"Pity," commented Conderie. "I've been meaning to get the older bottles recorked for some years. Never got around to it."

"Why not?" Stack's voice was sharp and accusatory.

Conderie, surprised, said: "You have to call in a man who knows how to do it. Wine that old is delicate. The people who do this kind of work don't work cheap. Anyway, the whole business slipped my mind." Conderie gave Stack a grin. "A man can't think of everything."

"It's only money," said Stack.

"And what's money after all?" inquired Conderie cheerfully. He dipped his candle so that wet wax dripped onto a ledge. After blowing the candle out, he set it down in the wet wax. "I never did have a head for figures." He grinned at Stack. "The only figures that ever interested me were female figures."

Stack cut him off sharply. "I want to talk to you about some information that has come into my hands."

Conderie, Stack saw, became agitated at once. The fellow's as sensitive as a girl, thought Stack disgustedly.

"Well, I don't have time to talk to you now."

"When?" demanded Stack.

Conderie's voice had attained a high, artificial plane. "I'm going to be busy all day."

Stack trailed him up out of the cool cellar into the sunlight and across to the cuverie. By the time they got there the glaze of fear was gone from Conderie's face. He's been expecting the tap on the shoulder for weeks, Stack thought, but he's no longer sure this is it.

A ladder leaned against the wall of one of the great oak vats.

"Climb up that ladder," suggested Conderie, "and look down over the top."

Stack, after a moment's hesitation, climbed the ladder.

"Notice how the wine is bubbling as if it were boiling," called Conderie from below. "The surface looks literally like a boiling red soup, right?"

"That's right," Stack called down.

"What you're looking down on," called Conderie, "is the chapeau, the hat I told you about. In a vat of this size it's about as thick as the length of your arm. If you pushed your arm down through the chapeau you'd come to the pure juice from about your wrist to your fingertips. Our problem is to diffuse the elements contained in the chapeau down throughout the wine. There are various methods of doing this. We could punch holes in it two or three times a day, or insert a sort of chimney into it. The wine is bubbling around so much that it would bubble up over the top of the chimney and seep down through the chapeau again. Some cellar masters float a heavy wooden lid on top of the chapeau. This forces the chapeau down into the wine. What we do, and what most châteaux do, is simply to run the wine out of the bottom tap into a pump, and then pump it up over the top again so that it's continually circulating through that chapeau."

Stack climbed down the ladder. "When can we talk?"

86

Conderie's agitation instantly returned. "After about ten days or two weeks," Conderie continued, "we run the wine off into barrels from the bottom of the vat, and the chapeau sinks to the floor, and we have to fork it out of there. Hell of a nasty job. We lay it down outside in a kind of haystack, and a government inspector comes out here from the town and checks on it."

"The government checks up on the dregs?"

How quickly Conderie recovered. It was almost amusing; but he had control of his voice again. "Absolutely. The government controls everything that has anything to do with wine. With a big enough quantity of dregs chemists could concoct a false wine, wine that had never seen a grape; it might look like wine and even taste somewhat like wine, but it wouldn't be wine. I understand that in other countries scandals like that have in fact occurred." Conderie allowed himself a smug smile. "Never in France, of course."

"When do we talk?"

"That isn't all the government checks on by any means," Conderie said hastily. "In this country if you want to rip out vines, you have to file a declaration of intention to rip out vines one month in advance. Once the job is done you have to file a declaration of vines ripped out. The law specifies even which type vines you can plant and where."

They stood beside the great wooden tubs. They could hear the wine bubbling. The whole room was bubbling. Conderie said: "Wine is a very mysterious substance. Did you know that you can't ferment new wine too close to finished wine?" Conderie was nodding vigorously. "I didn't think you knew that. If you brought casks of last year's wine into this shed, the new wine fermenting in the vats would be likely to start last year's wine fermenting all over again."

Conderie nodded vigorously at Stack, who stared implacably back.

"I won't wait any longer. We need to talk now," said Stack.

"You want to interview me, is that it?" Conderie asked. His eyes frightened, he wet dry lips. His tongue flicked in and out. "I won't have time to accord you an interview today, I'm afraid."

"Not an interview."

"Not an interview? Oh?" Conderie's eyes cast wildly about. In the entrance to the chai visitors suddenly appeared, led by Gorr. Conderie rushed forward calling greetings and in a moment ushered his guests into the adjacent chai, where the year-old wine was aging. Stack, who followed, stood in the doorway. Glasses were sent for. The ritual began. "There's an old saying in the wine business," declaimed Conderie, his voice nearly normal, "that when you're selling wine, serve cheese—"

Conderie glanced across shoulders at the implacable Stack.

A crystal glass, half full of the new wine, toppled off the cask and smashed on the stone floor.

"Never mind the glass," cried Conderie, kicking pieces under the cask. "The glass can be replaced, can't it? And as for the wine, there's plenty more where that came from, isn't there?"

All right, thought Stack grimly, if he wants to sweat then let him sweat. The owner would work himself into a state where there would be no will to resist left in him. This was fine with Stack.

From then on Stack stalked Conderie at a distance. After greeting a second group of visitors, Conderie talked for a long time with a broker in the court, and later he conferred with Gorr. Several times, after glancing across at Stack, Conderie's voice cracked, and during the conversation with the broker the owner suddenly began to choke. This was followed by a coughing spasm which lasted until tears came to his eyes. Stack, leaning against a wall some distance away, neither moved nor spoke.

At first Stack had felt pity, thinking: The guy is like a butterfly pinned to the page; he knows he can't escape. But the pity did not last. I need a château, Stack thought grimly. It's you or me, pal. There was no need to torture the man. It was not a tactic Stack would deliberately have chosen. But it had its advantages—the owner would be a shell by nightfall. Stack was not displeased with it.

After dinner Conderie poured himself a stiff glass of cognac at the sideboard. Stack noticed that his hand was trembling.

"Let me tell you who I am," began Stack.

Conderie tossed down his cognac. "You're not a journalist. That's been clear to me for some time. Well, who are you then?" Conderie swallowed hard. "Are you the police?"

"I'm the man to whom you're about to sell your château," said Stack coldly.

"Château Conderie is not for sale," said Conderie.

Stack stared at him with what he hoped were the hardest eyes Conderie had ever looked into.

Conderie said hurriedly: "You're probably looking for a small château. You want to grow wine as a hobby, I expect. There's a doctor who has a villa down on the river. He calls it a château. Why don't you go talk to him? He has a lovely view of the river. Vines don't grow well

88

along the river, but behind his house he has a couple of acres of vines. Very nice wine. Entitled to the appellation contrôlée Margaux. That's probably the type of thing you're looking for." Conderie nodded his head. "Doctors are great drinkers of château-bottled wines, you'll find."

Stack studied him.

"You must admit that it's presumptuous of you, imagining the Château Conderie's for sale, imagining that you could afford to buy it."

"You got the Banque Lyonnaise to accord you an enormous mortgage."

"My financial affairs are no business of yours."

"After that you got an identical loan from the Chase Manhattan in Paris. You must have produced a double set of documents. That's forgery in my country. That's a felony. I don't imagine the law is very different in France. You've mortgaged this place up to the hilt, twice. I'll buy out and pay off both those mortgages. I'll pay you what the stock in the cellar is worth. The older bottles are not worth very much because you haven't been taking care of the corks. You have twelve hours to decide. I want your answer at breakfast."

Conderie had poured his cognac glass half full. A trembling hand lifted it to his lips. "And if I decline?"

"I imagine that the authorities would be interested to discover what I have discovered. The two banks might be interested, too."

"I've done nothing illegal. There was no forgery."

"Shall I press my inquiry a little further?"

Conderie swallowed involuntarily: "No—don't."

Stack smiled.

"Some people have a head for figures," Conderie said. "Some don't. One can't be blamed for that. You are what you are. You can't be what you're not."

Stack said nothing.

Conderie said: "If I refuse to sell you the château, you would make this information public?"

"Of course."

"You would ruin me at no gain to yourself?"

"Why not?" inquired Stack. "What are you to me?"

Conderie poured himself another cognac. "A share. Suppose I decided to sell you a share in my château?"

"All of it."

"Perhaps even a controlling interest."

"I said all."

Stack decided to add coolly: "Your arrangement with Bozon might be of interest to the police, also."

Stack was watching carefully to see where this not so random arrow might come down. He was prepared to notice the imperceptible tightening of Conderie's mouth, a single sudden blink. But the evidence, as Conderie's last resistance crumbled, was more blatant than that.

Conderie began to shiver as if from sudden, violent cold.

"Have you seen my tax returns, too?" he mumbled in a barely audible voice.

Stack said: "You have until breakfast," and strode from the room.

A half hour passed before Conderie went upstairs and looked into Aline's room. Once this room had been filled with stuffed animals and dolls. The little girl had had dolls in native costumes from every region in France. He had sent her to a private school in Bordeaux, because the local school was full of peasant brats. That was in the early days after Conderie's father had died, and Paul Conderie and his late wife had taken over the château. He had inherited race horses at that time, and also a yacht, but the yacht got too expensive. Later the race horses got too expensive too, but never the private school in Bordeaux. He would have sold the château first except that it was virtually worthless at that time. Wine had always been an up-and-down business. In the early 1800s there had been a boom, and in the middle of that century came another one. That's when the two branches of the Rothschild family came in. Then came the terrible phylloxera blight that wiped out every vine in the Médoc—in all of Europe, in fact—and some of the small growers literally starved. The next boom was ended by World War I. In the depression years there were a number of bad harvests in a row; besides, nobody had any money. Nothing sold. Then came another war. Conderie, when he first came here, found he couldn't sell the château's 1947 wine at all. It was a great vintage, too. You could probably get a hundred American dollars a bottle for that wine today, but at the time no one wanted it.

Aline had made her bed before leaving, or somebody had. He missed his daughter. He sat down on the coverlet and looked at the pillow where her head had lain. Funny, when they were both in Paris together he didn't see much of her. He supposed she had an active social life there. She wasn't a virgin any more.

After her divorce it was Conderie's idea to open a dress shop for her. He was able to make arrangements to get her haute couture mod-

90

els to sell, but that shop had never caught on. It was on a chic street, and the rent alone must be astronomical for her.

The dress shop was important to Aline. She had never said so, but Conderie was convinced it was important to her.

With a few good harvests in a row, he would have been out of difficulty. This year's harvest was good in quality, but small. Conderie realized he had been counting on three great harvests in a row beginning next year, and the weather was rarely that cooperative. Even two great harvests and a fair one would save him. Was that so unreasonable to hope for?

He had invested money with Bozon, and the shipper hadn't given him signed notes for it. Now Bozon wouldn't pay out any profits. He wouldn't even give the investment back, but had reinvested it, so he said, in some new and even more lucrative scheme. Conderie didn't want to know any details. All he wanted was to see his money again, but Bozon wouldn't give it to him.

Conderie walked through the château looking into empty rooms. He told himself he was lonely for his daughter. Was he not always lonely when she went away? If only his daughter were here he'd be all right.

That night Conderie lay awake in the dark. Across his ceiling the hours crawled like snakes. In the morning, when he came downstairs haggard, defeated, Stack waited there beside suitcases, ready to move out. Stack was clean shaven, combed, reeking of some disgusting after-shave lotion.

Conderie attempted to bargain. "I might be of use to you here. The château is in my name. You would not wish to change the name. I'll stay on here in the château. I should like my name on the board of directors. I should like a contract for ten years, and a salary commensurate with my stature."

Stack, who now believed that Conderie was involved in some illegal deal with Bozon, wanted to get rid of the owner altogether. But the illegal deal couldn't be very much—Conderie wouldn't have the guts —and the important thing was that Conderie agree to sell the château.

"Okay," said Stack, "you're chairman of the board. You're a figurehead, got that? The contract will be two years, not ten. We'll work out an appropriate salary. We'll take your wing of the château; you move in somewhere else. We have the right to use your name in any way we like."

Conderie bowed his head and said nothing.

Never mind that Conderie looked crushed. Stack felt terrifically

91

pleased with himself. Any man could learn the wine business. What you couldn't learn was to steal a guy's château. That you had to be born with.

Stack said, "Contact your lawyers. My lawyers will be down here today. I want the entire deal signed within a week. We'll announce it from New York. Not a word is to be mentioned here by you or anyone else. I'll be flying back to New York as soon as my lawyers arrive."

Standing amid his suitcases, Stack gave a huge grin, and stuck his hand out. Conderie stared at the hand, then into Stack's grin, then spun on his heel and went back up the marble staircase. Downstairs he heard the front door slam behind Charlie Stack.

12

To risk undermining confidence in the integrity of important figures in the wine industry was to risk undermining confidence in the integrity of the wine itself. One moved very, very slowly. It had taken Alexandre Dupont three weeks to learn the numbers off Armand Picot's truck, and then the truck proved to be owned not by Picot himself but by a firm. At that point Dupont still didn't have Picot's name, and another week of dogged questioning turned up only half of it: Armand. After mulling the situation over an entire day, Dupont decided to find and question this Armand himself.

It was 8 A.M. Low clouds hung over the city. Dupont, who feared rain, wore his thin raincoat. He was cold. One of the trucks was being refueled and the others were waiting their turn. A number of truck drivers stood in the yard. Dupont, having approached the group, asked mildly if Armand were around.

"Armand who?" asked the biggest of the truckers.

Suppose there were several? What did Dupont say then? "Is there more than one?" he asked mildly.

"No," said the big trucker. The other truckers laughed at such a witty answer.

This smart ass must be Armand, Dupont guessed. "May I speak to you a moment privately?"

Armand repeated Dupont's words in a girlish falsetto. The other truckers much appreciated his humor.

Dupont, annoyed, snapped, "It's important, and it's official. I'll have to ask you to step to one side."

At the authority in Dupont's voice the grins disappeared, and Armand followed meekly to the other side of the yard, where, feigning nonchalance, he leaned back against a parked car.

"So?" Armand demanded.

Dupont produced his credentials: "Alexandre Dupont de la Brigade de la Répression des Fraudes."

"Fraud Brigade, huh. What's that to me? I haven't done anything." But, as Armand took a cigarette package out of his windbreaker, Dupont noted that his hands trembled slightly. "I'm no stool pigeon," cried Armand nervously. "The trouble with France is that it's full of stool pigeons."

Dupont studied him, while Armand puffed hard on his cigarette. "If it's because I'm a member of the Party, I've a right. France is a free country."

Dupont rarely used a notebook when interrogating people, for notebooks tended to dry some people up, and they frightened nearly everybody. Dupont, who saw that Armand was frightened already, decided to keep him that way. He drew his notebook from his raincoat pocket: "Name, address, age, identity card."

Dupont laid Armand's papers out on the fender. "I want to know every job you've done in the last three months." As Armand began to talk, Dupont began noting down details.

"I've done nothing wrong," insisted Armand. "My papers are in order. The papers of my truck are in order. Everything's in order."

The mild Dupont knew how to play the tough role if necessary. "Just answer my questions."

The trucker took the package out of his pocket, and lit another cigarette off the butt of the one in his mouth.

"If we find anything illegal," warned Dupont, "you could lose your truck."

But this warning seemed only to give the trucker courage. "It's my brother-in-law's truck. The firm is him. You wanna confiscate the truck, confiscate it. That bastard is so rich he wouldn't know the difference."

Threatening the brother-in-law's truck had been a mild error, Dupont noted. Armand immediately felt better. His hated brother-in-law would have to come to his aid.

"We have informants. They are everywhere. Something funny happens in the wine trade, we know about it right away."

"Filthy stool pigeons," snarled Armand.

"We've had our eye on you, Picot. You go to a restaurant, the waiter works for us. You go to a bar, the barman works for us. You load the truck somewhere, the guy loading it works for us. We're all around you."

Dupont fixed the trucker with an intimidating stare. If only it were true, Dupont thought. We're fifteen men and a few informants. We don't have enough to do the job. "The success of the wine trade," Dupont said, "depends upon the integrity of the wine. If people fool around with the wine, that damages the whole industry. That's why I do the work I do. That's why," Dupont said in his coldest, hardest voice, "if we find out you've been fooling around, we'll throw your ass in jail."

Armand looked shaken.

"Now let's go over these jobs, one by one."

They went down the list.

Dupont said: "Somewhere in this list you were convinced you were involved in fraud. Don't lie to me. Our people heard you say it."

The trucker said, almost whining: "It was just a feeling I had. One night I got stopped out on the road."

"Tell me about that," purred Dupont.

As Armand recounted the story, Dupont took no notes.

"And you delivered that wine where?"

"Chez Bozon."

"What day was that?"

Armand found the date stamped on the papers to his truck.

"My brother-in-law paid the summons," whined Armand. "He took it out of my pay, the son of a bitch. You've got nothing on me."

"Let's get on to some of these other jobs," said Dupont.

"Is what I just told you important?"

"No," lied Dupont. "It's not even worth taking notes on."

"The next job after that one was—"

Out of the office building onto the platform came a man who shouted across at Armand: "Your truck's ready to go. If you want to gab, gab on your own time."

"My brother-in-law, the prick," explained Armand.

The brother-in-law came walking across the yard. When he reached them, Dupont flashed his credentials: "Alexandre Dupont de la Brigade de la Répression des Fraudes."

This stopped the brother-in-law in his tracks. "What's going on?"

"Routine," answered Dupont mildly. "I'm about finished now." Dupont glanced from the brother-in-law back to Armand. Dupont said: "Our little talk, Monsieur Armand Picot, is of course strictly confidential. You will not speak about it to anyone."

The baffled brother-in-law said: "This is my place, my truck, I have a right to know what's going on."

Armand was smirking at his brother-in-law: "You heard the man," Armand said. "I'm not allowed to say a goddamn thing."

When he got back to his office, Dupont sent a communication to the gendarmerie which had jurisdiction over the stretch of road where Armand Picot's truck had been stopped, demanding copies of the gendarme's report. Then he put out a tracer on the wine samples which the gendarmes presumably had taken, and which by now had no doubt been chemically analyzed and also tasted by a tasting panel.

A week passed before the gendarme's report came in, but the chemical analysis did not turn up for a month; for some reason the gendarmerie had misrouted the results to Paris. The samples themselves had afterward been sent to Bordeaux to go before the tasting panel, but Dupont could find no record that this had ever happened, and the samples themselves could not be located. They were no doubt on a shelf somewhere, and would turn up, but when? This tasting panel, composed of one shipper, one broker, and one grower, should have determined by taste what type wine it was, what type grapes it was made from, in approximately what region it was grown, and also its approximate age; and their judgment would have been official. It would stand up in court. It might then have been possible to prosecute Bozon for bringing no-account wine into his warehouse and sending it out labeled authentic Bordeaux. That's probably what he was doing—if he was doing anything. Forged documents might have turned up. Tax fraud might have been proven.

Instead two months had been lost, leaving Alexandre Dupont to conclude at length that the trail had gone cold, with his case still incomplete, and no new evidence coming in. And so he decided to close the investigation. This was a relief to him. Any prosecution involving a man as big as Bozon would have erupted into scandal, bad for the wine trade, bad for France, and very probably bad for Alexandre Dupont, whose case would have had to be airtight—and no case was airtight. Bozon's lawyers would have made Dupont look bad. Probably they would have got their client off. Probably Dupont would have been officially reprimanded, perhaps even suspended or dismissed.

He was glad he had not had to risk it.

And, in truth, was it not inconceivable that Bozon was involved in some illegal scheme? Why should he be? He was probably the richest shipper in Bordeaux. He owned apartment buildings in the town. It was said he might run for mayor. People would laugh at the idea of such a man trafficking in fraudulent wine.

Alexandre Dupont was glad he had not had to come up against a man as powerful as Bozon.

Nonetheless he decided to go around to question Armand one last time. The trucker this time was suitably servile. Dupont questioned him carefully. Armand must not suspect any special interest in deliveries to Bozon.

Armand had made none since Dupont's last visit.

Dupont checked with Le Grand Jo at the bar across from Bozon's warehouse. There had been no nighttime deliveries recently. The band of Spaniards no longer frequented Jo's bar. Whatever it was, if it was anything, it seemed over.

Back at his office, Dupont took the dossier marked "Bozon," inserted his latest few notes, slipped the dossier back into its alphabetical slot, and pushed the file drawer closed.

Investigations acquired implacable force. At the end each became like a kid on a tricycle rolling down hill with his feet off the pedals. The thing went faster and faster and when it bottomed there was cataclysm. But in its early stages an investigation was formless, an amorphous blob apparently heading nowhere. It was just a kind of police work. Police work was awfully slow, and was conducted by the most timorous of men. Cops always feared to offend men more powerful than they.

The case had petered out. Alexandre Dupont was really quite relieved.

The cold trail had left behind only a dossier—which, however, had a weight of its own. It was there, a presence. Left behind too was a nagging dissatisfaction in the mind of a mild functionary who was more tenacious than he realized. He himself believed that he might or might not try to add to this dossier, but in fact he would. His meticulousness would oblige him to.

13

"I gave the chairman a brief report as soon as I returned to the States," began Charlie Stack.

He was speaking to the board of directors in the major conference room on the thirty-seventh floor. All group vice-presidents also were present. Stack stood beside an easel holding display boards. The top board was blank. Let the suspense build up, Stack thought; this was show biz now, show biz being only one of the vital ingredients of success in big business. Big business embraced every technique, every type of judgment, which was why Charlie Stack loved it, why he had deliberately sought out the bloodiest parts of its bloody battlefield. A man could live safely for a lifetime at the edges of this battlefield, but near its core the turf was blood-soaked and any man who got careless there could lose his head or his balls in a second. That's right, Charlie Stack thought, his balls—be blunt. A woman only had to defend her life, but a man had to defend his manhood too, had to stay on the attack, as Charlie Stack was doing now. Charlie Stack was attacking hard. His troops in their various platoons awaited his signal: display boards on that easel, display material on the table in front of him, display slides in the projector, the pièce de résistance ready for display in the anteroom. Charlie Stack, having thought it all out in advance, felt himself invincible, and suddenly grinned.

His grin was rewarded by total attention. Thirty men leaned raptly forward, the chairman included. All earned more money than Charlie Stack, all were older.

"This is going to be quite an elaborate presentation," said Stack amiably, "for which you must forgive me. But I judge none of us are experts. The Company has decided to go into a new field and our goal is to be as much prestige as profits—perhaps prestige even more than profits. This was the chairman's idea, the chairman's decision, and there were those who felt it couldn't be done. I myself had serious doubts."

Dramatic pause. "But I've found, as we all have, that it doesn't pay to bet against the chairman."

Theatrical chuckle. "The chairman's track record is pretty good. Right, Warren?"

Stack chuckled again, everybody chuckled. The chairman, seated closest to Stack, said nothing.

The first display board showed France, the Bordeaux area in red. Stack, the friendly schoolteacher, gripped his disciplinary pointer. The second board showed Bordeaux exclusively, much enlarged. Arrows located the famous châteaux. Stack, pointer tapping, said: "Once the decision was made to add a wine division, then a choice had to be made. We could buy out Manischewitz, or we could open a factory in California to produce the equivalent of Gallo Mountain Red. But we wanted prestige, right? Once prestige became part of our goal, then our choice of country was limited to one: France. Within France we had three choices. Champagne, Burgundy, or Bordeaux. We discarded Champagne."

Dramatic pause again. "Champagne seemed too aristocratic. In addition wine is being made both in New York State and in California which goes by the name of champagne. Treaties exist among every other wine-producing nation in the world. According to these treaties champagne can be made only in Champagne. The United States is not party to that treaty, and ignores it. For our purposes, the marketing of New York and California champagne has seriously diluted the inherent prestige of the name."

Dramatic pause. "The next possibility was Burgundy. But during the French Revolution all the great estates of Burgundy were broken up into small holdings. They are still small holdings. No single person owns enough of any Burgundy vineyard to provide the type of acquisition we wanted to make. Take Chambertin, one of the greatest names in Burgundy. The Chambertin vineyards comprise only about seventy acres, and within this seventy acres there are more than two dozen different growers. In order to buy out Chambertin we'd have to make deals with two dozen people. Chances of success in such an undertaking would have been, it seems to me, small. You ask, why not some other Burgundy vineyard? But they're all small and cut up among many owners. Possibly the most expensive of the Burgundy wines is Romanée-Conti. Romanée-Conti is only four and a half acres. They put out only about six thousand bottles a year.

"So we turned our attention to Bordeaux," Stack said, tapping the

98

display board. "Bordeaux produces more great wine by far than any other region in the world. Many of the châteaux there are already famous, and prestige is what we're after, together with profits, of course. Now, within the Bordeaux area it might have been possible to buy properties here—" Stack tapped the Graves area—"or, we might have looked across the river in St. Émilion. But—" Stack dragged the pointer back across the river into the Médoc and there drew circles with it—"but the most prestigious wines in the world come from here. They come principally from two towns, Margaux and Pauillac. Pauillac might have certain advantages; the two Rothschild châteaux are out there, for instance. But you'll note that it's some forty miles from the center of Bordeaux. Margaux is twenty miles nearer. Margaux has one other advantage, which is that the name of the town is the same as the name of its greatest château. When you're selling a product you want to make buyer identification as simple as possible. Any wine made on specific land within the confines of Margaux is entitled to what the French call the controlled appellation of Margaux. You can put on the label not only the château's name but Margaux's name. It seemed to me, inasmuch as we're trying to build a market in America which is not knowledgeable about wines, that this simplification of buyer identification was important."

Stack removed the display board of the Bordeaux region. The one underneath was a blowup of the Margaux region with all of the Margaux châteaux identified. These display boards, and the other display material which still waited on the table, had been prepared for Stack by The Company's art department over the past ten days, and represented some $10,000 worth of man hours. Ten thousand dollars for one presentation before the board of directors.

"So here in Margaux we would have easier access and greater buyer identification. If it proved possible to buy a major property in Margaux, major in terms of prestige, acreage, and production, then my search—our search—would be ended."

Stack stepped away from the display board, moved to the head of the table, and said in a quiet voice, underplaying the big scene for maximum impact, "As you know, we are in the process of concluding the purchase of Château Conderie: three hundred acres of land, half of it currently under vines, the other half pasture and forest; plus the château itself, part of which dates from the seventeenth century; plus all of the sheds, cellars, and outbuildings."

At this moment an actor on stage would have bowed, accepting

99

applause. Stack gave a modest smile, and a certain modest hand clapping did ensue.

Johnston, president of the division which included Stack's Avco Drug Company, raised his hand: "Question. I understood the papers to be already signed. Are you saying the deal could yet fall through?"

The tactic of any good executive was to raise doubt about the performance of any other. In the guise of protecting the company's interests, one exposed where possible the defects of rivals.

"A document has already been signed," Stack said, "which our Paris lawyers tell me is legally binding. They're working out the final details now."

Johnston nodded. As he settled back in his chair, he looked like a man waiting to throw the next handful of sand into the works. Stack did not blame Johnston. If you loved the game, as Stack did, you had to accept the rules by which it was played. He would have done the same in Johnston's place.

"Let's hear the profit picture as you see it, Charlie," said the chairman.

A pile of brochures lay before Stack. He handed half to the chairman, half to Johnston at the other corner of the table, saying: "Pass these around, please." To the room at large he announced: "All of the numbers are in this brochure, as you will note. The production of the château this year will be about 150,000 bottles. There are ways to increase that harvest. With any kind of break from the weather we can get 200,000 bottles next year. As for quality, I don't know what this year's quality will be. We did not supervise the harvest. If this year's harvest proves to have been a good one, then we can claim it as the first year of our production. If not we can deny parentage."

Stack essayed a joke: "There are no paternity suits in the wine business."

An appreciative chuckle rippled around the table.

"I'm having an inventory made of stock in the château's cellar. Some of this is quite old wine. Some of it no doubt has gone bad. Some of it should be sound and if we use The Company's other assets and outlets each rare bottle can be made to enhance the prestige of our wine division. For instance, we should be able to get our wine served at the White House. We can have it served at various press banquets. We can get some into the hands of such people as the Rockefellers and the Fords."

"The profit picture, Charlie," said the chairman. "What are your

100

immediate and long-term projections?"

"Ten families live on the château property. Their lodging is provided. One of the old sheds has been divided into four apartments, for instance. These people are paid a pittance. Labor costs are not among our problems. I'm having studies made now of the cost of pesticides and fertilizers, and also the cost of replanting five percent of the vineyard each year. Only half the acreage is under vine. I would hope to increase that total. The laws are stringent as to what land can be planted in vines, but I'm told that inspectors can be induced to overlook vines that may sprawl a little too far in one direction or another. Methods can be found to force production up, and also to force up the retail price of the product."

One of Stack's assistants from the drug company had been standing by the door. Stack now signaled him.

"Speaking of the product," said Charlie Stack, "it's about time that all of you had a closer look at it."

A number of waiters now came through the door pushing a trolley which bore a dozen open bottles of Château Conderie wine and a carton of plastic wine glasses. Stack fell silent as the glasses were handed around and the wine was poured. Standing in front of his display board, Charlie Stack raised his glass in a toast: "To the newest division of The Company."

Wine was sipped, and there were smiles all around the table.

"As for profit," said Charlie Stack, "I think I can confidently predict that our new wine division will contribute a profit of one million dollars a year minimum."

A number of men whistled with surprise. The chairman looked pleased.

Johnston interjected: "Question, Charlie. Isn't Château Conderie what is called a second-category wine? You haven't mentioned that to us yet, Charlie." Johnston's hostility was being masked as good humor. "I imagine you're holding that back until what you judge to be the best moment. Any good salesman would do the same. But what I want to know is, Charlie, how do you square buying a second-category château? I mean, you're working for a first-class company, and how will that look?"

The young executive and the older one gazed at each other from hooded eyes. The mutual challenge was trumpeted across the void. Suddenly Stack smiled, a rash act. Prepared for stiffer opposition than this, he nodded his head vigorously. "I'm glad you asked that question.

101

Let me explain this category business." His next display board revealed the 1855 classification. "You'll note that in 1855 all the wines of the Médoc, strictly according to the price that they brought on the market at that time, were graded. Notice four wines in the first category, and that the second wine in the second category is ours. That makes ours in effect the sixth-best wine in the world. Out of some three thousand châteaux in the Bordeaux area, only about sixty were rated at all, and ours came in sixth. Now, I would have preferred to buy one of the top four. Unfortunately, none were for sale. In any case, second category here does not mean second class, as our advertising can make plain. In addition, there is a good deal of pressure in Bordeaux to upgrade and update this classification, and I'm confident that if this should occur—and I believe we can make it occur during the next year or two—then The Company will be able to exert enough pressure to move our wine into the top category." Stack added cockily: "Does that answer your question, Johnny?"

Stack and Johnston stared at each other. The challenge had been thrown back in Johnston's face. After a moment Johnston's smile came on, and he nodded, saying: "I'm satisfied."

Stack said: "I've arranged for a ceremonial signing of the papers by the chairman in Bordeaux. As I envisage the scene, we'll have a press conference, serve our own wine at the press conference, in effect going world-wide with the acquisition at that time."

"Why do you say ceremonial signing?" asked the chairman.

"Because a good many foreign syndicates have tried to buy châteaux lately, and the French have passed laws against this. Our château must be purchased by our French subsidiary, and the director of record, who must be a French citizen, will be, I assume, the general manager of our Paris Profit Center."

The chairman, obviously in a benevolent mood, said: "You seem to have thought of everything, Charlie."

"There is the possibility of some sort of outcry against us when the acquisition is announced," said Stack. "What I propose is that we announce our intent to build a luxury hotel in the Médoc next year. I've done some looking into this. There is no luxury hotel out there at all, and it's a region that will be visited more and more by tourists as the wine boom continues. As a matter of fact, we can keep the thing filled year round by sending tourists there via our own wholly-owned subsidiary, Comtours. I would propose either buying a château that overlooks the river—the river is several miles wide there—or else building a hotel

102

close to the river by buying up whatever land we need. The land around the hotel would be planted in vines. You will note that most of the land close to the river is not suitable for vines—" Stack's next display board showed a blowup of the Margaux river banks. "Any of this alluvial-silt area is too rich. Vines really grow best on extremely poor soil, and if you poured a bushel of our château soil through a sieve, you'd wind up with half a bushel of sandy dirt and half a bushel of round, flat stones. Anyway, the land down by the river should be cheap enough, and I would suggest buying up a good deal of it, and planting it in vines, and making from it a lesser wine which might carry on the label the name of our hotel. In this way we might eventually be marketing world-wide another quarter of a million bottles per year. The fame of the hotel would help sell the wine, and the fame of the wine would help keep the hotel full. What I'm suggesting is that we could make a wine worth perhaps only a dollar or two on the open market, but because of the label sell it for twice that."

What Stack was also suggesting was a wine division three or four times greater than had been envisioned by the chairman when the original proposal was made, and Stack now looked slowly around the table, meeting as many eyes as possible, trying to read the degree of approval. Not that anyone's approval mattered except the chairman's. However, the chairman was only human, and could be swayed. Several heads nodded, and Stack's gaze swept on, at last encountering that of the chairman, who said only: "Well, the idea certainly bears looking into."

Stack said: "Since the area needs a hotel so badly, we can use notice of our intent to build one as leverage over the local politicians, and the local press. We may find some opposition to a multinational company like ours moving in there. Our projected hotel should bring out just as many voices in our favor because, by upgrading the region, we upgrade the value of all their property."

Did Stack really believe all this? The Médoc was a sleepy kind of place, isolated, almost backward, and the chances were that most of the people who lived there wanted to keep it that way. But to those around this table Stack's reasoning sounded faultless. Around this table no one asked what Stack's plans would do to the region; he had not really expected anyone would.

Stack signaled his projectionist, and the lights were extinguished.

"Notice the photos of the château and its grounds now on the screen," suggested Stack.

Slides were shown. In the dark men murmured.

"Handsome old place, isn't it?"

"Looks something like Versailles, doesn't it?"

When the lights came on Johnston began thumbing through the brochure. He said: "That's a nice photo of the chairman you have on page three, Charlie, but you forgot to print his name under it."

Some imbecile of a printer had dropped the line, Stack realized. Stack was furious with this imbecile, whoever he might be, but his face betrayed nothing. An explanation, frantically sought, came to him just in time. "There's no need to belabor the obvious," Stack said coolly. "I mean, is there? The chairman's name is a household word. I felt there was simply no need to identify him. I would have felt the same if it were Rockefeller's picture, or Ford's." Stack and Johnston stared at each other. Stack thought: Score one for my side, and he smiled.

From opposite sides of the table, the chairman and Johnston nodded soberly.

Stack glanced around the table. "By all means, pour yourselves some more of our wine," he suggested.

The chairman was a teetotaler, and had barely touched his own. Wine in the boardroom was so incongruous that for a moment Stack felt like laughing. It was such a switch from the normal board meetings conducted around tuna-fish sandwiches and half-pint containers of coffee or milk.

"Any questions?" inquired Stack.

After a moment Johnston said: "You seem to have thought of everything, Charlie. We're real proud of you. You seem to have done an excellent job. But—I'm just playing the devil's advocate here, you understand—but my only reservation so far is that you seem to have found this château rather too fast. Maybe someone wanted you to find it."

Stack had worried about this possible argument. He had landed in Bordeaux, found the property, known instinctively it was the right property, and had bought it. But how could one defend instinct to a board of directors, even though every man present acted on his own instinct every day?

"It was not easy to find the Château Conderie," said Stack, "or to force the owner to sell. I was satisfied that I had made the correct decision, and I'm satisfied at this moment that time will prove me right."

Stack's gaze left Johnston's, and marched from face to face around the table. No one spoke. The chairman himself said nothing, in no way betrayed his feelings. Stack half expected Johnston to make some obsequious remark, to join what would obviously become the company viewpoint, the company decision, but instead Johnston said, "I hope you're right, Charlie. God knows I'm backing your judgment, as I've always backed it. But I must say that I'm still somewhat skeptical. I think we all should be skeptical at least a little while longer."

This shook Stack. Part of Johnston's strength within the company was due to his political connections—his brother was a congressman. Still, Johnston's position was in no way invulnerable, Stack believed, and he could safely have said nothing. Instead he had voiced skepticism publicly.

Stack, shaken, thought: Jesus, what have I overlooked?

The chairman rose to his feet: "Thank you, gentlemen, that will be all."

His performance over, Stack's muscles felt suddenly weak. His knees felt ready to bend both ways. He wanted to sit down, but couldn't yet.

Men came forward.

"That was a hell of a presentation, Charlie."

"You presented the hell out of it, Charlie."

Stack, grinning triumphantly, shook hand after hand.

The room emptied until only the chairman and Johnston were left. The chairman said: "Charlie. I think you've done exactly what we've asked you to do, whatever the skepticism of our friend here, Mr. Johnston."

"Thanks, Warren." Stack felt surging relief. Thanks, Warren old pal, thanks, Warren old buddy, Warren my brother, the only brother I have who could stab me in the back and sleep well that night.

"You and Johnny stop by my office tomorrow at noon," suggested the chairman. "We want to solidify our future plans for you."

"It'll be a pleasure," said Charlie Stack.

Johnston, nodding to Stack, followed the chairman out.

That night Stack attended a party in someone's glamorous duplex apartment in the United Nations Towers. The spectacular view was south over the UN building and the lights of the East River, one of the most spectacular views in the city. Most of those present were rich and powerful drug executives and their expensively dressed wives, and Stack was there not to socialize but to see and be seen by his peers. For two hours he flitted from glamorous group to glamorous group, imprinting himself and his achievements once again in all their minds, probing for information and weaknesses he might in some way someday use.

Late in the evening he became aware of a young woman, a big, meaty girl wearing a dress down to the floor, a dress that was rather tight from her ass on up. Garish colors being in vogue this year, her dress was a combination of reds, oranges, and purples, and she wore purple suede high-heeled, open-toed shoes which peeked out from beneath her dress from time to time. Her toenails were purple as well. She laughed a lot. Her laugh was as large as her bosom, which was substantial, and she stood in the group to which Stack was talking enthusiastically about drugs, listening apparently avidly, though the conversation could not have had much meaning for her. Stack had been too busy to notice her before, but he was not too busy now late in the evening, especially when she announced that it was late, she really must go, was anybody else heading uptown?

Was this an invitation to Stack, the only man in the room remotely her age?

A squat, middle-aged drug wholesaler announced himself a candidate for this ride. Stack, still feeling invincible, decided he would take this girl home to bed, and the odd threesome shook hands all around and left the apartment. Only in the hallway while waiting for the elevator did Stack notice that the girl had several teeth missing on the upper right side of her mouth. Well, whether or not she could chew meat had no bearing on Stack's plans for her.

Crossing First Avenue in search of a taxi, Stack took her gloved hand so as to protect her from nonexistent oncoming traffic or other danger, and once safe on the opposite curb he squeezed it. Not to his surprise, she squeezed back. He thought her gloved mitt fit well in his, and in the cab, while the middle-aged type prattled on, Stack affectionately massaged through her long dress the inside of her knee; she put her gloved hand over his and pressed.

He had still not touched her flesh, but was in the mood to find her gloves sexy. Like underwear, they seemed to reveal more than they concealed.

When they reached Stack's street, without bothering to clear it with the girl first, Stack announced that he and she would get out here, and stopped the cab. Throwing open the door, he pressed a five-dollar bill into the middle-aged drug creep's sweaty palm. This was double the price of the ride so far. It was like tipping a headwaiter for leading you to a table, Stack thought, all gluttony soon to be satisfied. Like any headwaiter, the wholesaler only lunged for the money.

106

Standing in the street with a girl whose name he did not even know, Stack watched the taillights diminish as the cab sped on uptown.

"I don't know what I'm doing standing here in the street with you," said the girl.

Stack, thinking fast and irresistibly, said, "I heard you say you had once looked for an apartment in my building. I thought you might like to see my apartment."

"Okay," she said cheerfully.

In the lobby Stack imagined that he could feel the weight of the elevator man's envious staring eyeballs; they overhung the man's cheeks like boobs in a bra. Stack's heart had begun to beat hard at the prospect of immediate sex. I need this, he told himself. As the cabin rose he turned and smiled at the girl and was reminded again, painfully, of her absent teeth. He would fix his gaze upon her eyes, which were quite lovely, he decided, rather than on the mouth he might soon have to kiss.

The elevator door slammed closed. Behind it the machine itself, not to mention the operator's eyeballs, sank all the way back where they had come from.

Stack took her hand and led her to his door. Inside, as he took her coat, he managed to give her shoulders a squeeze. But, despite the handholding in the cab, there was no response now. Stack made them each a drink, and sat down close to her on the sofa, but she promptly moved to the edge, all senses alert, pretending to glance around at Stack's décor.

Stack asked why she was not married. She replied that she had been, had divorced last year. What could be more casual?

A divorced woman with big boobs and several missing teeth should be easy, but when Stack tried to put his arm around her, she moved imperceptibly away, so he let his arm fall to the back of the sofa.

He wanted what he wanted, and he wanted it without any foolishness. Seduction was old-fashioned, childish, nonsensical, he decided. He was certainly not going to try to seduce her. She either capitulated or not, her choice.

She proved to be a militant talker.

Shortly Stack's heart ceased to beat hard. This wasn't going to work. And, if it wasn't, he would just as soon she went on home.

"I've forgotten your last name," Stack said. He had forgotten both names.

She told him, and he forgot it again.

Her dress had begun to split along the seam at her waist. He traced this line with his finger, a sexual advance she might respond to. If not, to hell with her.

She leaned away from his finger. "You really have a very nice apartment, you know that?"

Suddenly she began to talk about a transatlantic telephone call she was expecting. That's a hot one, Stack thought. In the middle of the night? He almost laughed in her face. When she got up, he accompanied her to the door—perhaps she expected to be accompanied all the way home—and gratefully closed it on her.

But later he lay in the dark feeling nervous and irritable. He wished the girl had turned out as he had expected—a quick, violent lay. It wasn't often Stack felt this much need for a woman. Power and sex were the same, he believed, whenever he thought about it, and if a man had the one then he didn't need the other very much.

But by morning he had forgotten sex and was preparing for his meeting with the chairman and Johnston, which would settle his immediate future with The Company. If he played his cards right, then he had seen the last of Bordeaux.

This meeting in the chairman's office began with praise from the chairman.

"The question now becomes whether or not we want to shake up a winning hand," said the chairman. "You follow me, Charlie, don't you?"

Stack followed him all right. He was about to be offered his old job back, or perhaps something better. Someone else would be sent to cope with the wine division. This was exactly what he had hoped for, was it not? Then why was he suddenly so confused?

To give himself time, Stack said: "No, I'm not sure I do." They were merely snatching the wine division away from him. That wasn't the way the game was played. They should offer him something else first. They should discuss alternatives first.

"Wine hasn't been exactly your bag, Charlie," said Johnston. "You're a great drug man. No one ever said you weren't. And you've handled this assignment like a wizard. We're all agreed on that. But, with the type of investment we're making in Bordeaux, it seems to both Warren and me that perhaps we ought to hire a wine man to run the division."

Stack perceived that his real defeat was about to happen now, and his instincts rose against it. "You make me feel like a man who's carried the ball to the one-yard line, and then the coach wants to take him out of the game," said Charlie Stack.

"You want to stay on in Bordeaux then, do you?" asked the chairman, smiling.

Trapped.

"Johnny, I told you that's the way he'd feel," said the chairman. "And really I think this young man has done so well that we have to let him make the choice."

"Of course," said Johnston.

Trapped. Stack took off his horn rims and rubbed his eyes.

The chairman moved behind his desk. It was a transparent glass table. The glass was about two inches thick, and was supported by chrome scaffolding. On this desk were a photo of the chairman's wife and two or three envelopes which had been slit open. Nothing else. The chairman liked a tidy desk. On the back of one of the envelopes the chairman had evidently made notes. "Charlie," said the chairman, "the next question becomes this. Should we hire some important wine guy to work under you. Would that be the best kind of insurance we could take out here? Just a suggestion. Of course I did cause an investigation to be done. We can get the guy who works for Rothschild to work under you. He's been there a long time. They don't pay him much. I've had all that checked into. We could double his salary and give him a long-term contract. He could run the château for you."

Stack thought: That's why Warren is chairman. First he traps you, then he shows you he's also working behind your back.

Stack said obstinately: "I'd rather take care of the operational end of it myself, decide myself exactly what sort of talent I need, and then hire it." Stack managed to chuckle lightly, adding: "And possibly if we stole their guy the Rothschilds would get mad at us. I suppose they're not really in our league in money, but they do have a lot of it, and I'm not sure that we want to antagonize them at this point."

The chairman said thoughtfully: "I hadn't thought of that angle."

The three men nodded at each other.

The chairman said: "Is there anything you do want, Charlie?"

The chairman wanted to give Charlie Stack something, and Charlie, though sick at heart, had to think of a suitable present fast. "I'll need that lawyer, Saar, from Paris," said Charlie Stack.

"You've got him, Charlie. Anything else?"

"I'll make a list."

"You just say the word, Charlie. Johnny and I are behind you one hundred percent, aren't we, Johnny?"

"Right you are, Warren."

A shaken Stack left the office. They had manipulated him like a child. A burst of laughter came through the closed door. Were they laughing at him? Had he seemed that foolish to them? Or were they laughing about some other subject entirely? They hadn't had to condemn him to Bordeaux at all. He had condemned himself. He was furious and filled with self-pity both.

When he got back to his office he ordered his secretary to enroll him in the most intensive French-language course she could find. At the same time she was to send over to Brentano's and buy every book on wine they had in stock or could get their hands on. She was to find out which universities had courses in oenology—the University of California at Berkeley was the best place to start. She was to find an oenology professor who could be hired to fly to New York to give Charlie Stack, class of one, a cram course in the subject.

That would do for a start.

Taking off his horn rims, he rubbed his eyes. He felt like crying.

BOOK TWO

1

The shipper Édouard Bozon at the wheel of his white Mercedes drove slowly past the place, looking it over. It looked perfect. It looked deserted too, though the old man must be somewhere about, for where else could he go? Bozon U-turned and drove past a second time, looking the place over from the other direction. It was the best he had seen. He did not expect to find better.

Presently he turned into the dirt driveway, got out of his car, and went looking for the old man. The front door of this "Château" Cracheau hung open. The château was a three-room farmhouse: kitchen, bedroom, and a utility room jammed with rusty old tools. There was no sign to indicate that the old man was inside the house—unless he was lying dead in there, which would happen one day no doubt. The police would find him after a week or more, after the stench had reached the road.

Bozon walked up the slope toward the top row of vines. His shoes got gummy with mud. The vines had lost their leaves as well as their grapes by now, and these vines, Bozon saw, were in as poor a state as the farmhouse itself. From the look of them they had not been pruned in several years. From each root branches and shoots went off in all directions, as tangled as a head of hair. At the top of the slope stood a row of fruit trees, and from there the slope dropped down the other side. This was the side of the property that faced south and that had always borne the best grapes. The soil was much poorer on this side, meaning of course better for grapes, more stones than dirt, and there-

113

fore both draining perfectly and holding in the daytime heat during most of each night.

Once Château Cracheau had been one of the best-known small holdings on this side of the river. Not a great château wine, but a full-bodied and charming minor vintage. Quite a lot of this wine was made in the good years too.

The fruit trees along the ridge were as badly tended as the vines. Bozon saw that the old man sat alone at the base of the most distant tree, his wooden leg pointing straight out in front of him. He must be nearly blind, as well as nearly deaf, for he had not noticed Bozon yet.

So Bozon stood a moment longer on the crest of the slope looking downhill in both directions, and then appraising once again the small, shabby farmhouse, with the old stone chai out back. There were no other houses Bozon could see from here—which meant more precisely that nobody's house overlooked this place either. One could not be accidentally spied on here, it would have to be deliberate, and to notice anything one would have to drive almost to the front door. Except for the road, the vineyards themselves were entirely surrounded by forests, and the road itself led from nowhere to nowhere.

Château Cracheau was exactly as isolated as Bozon remembered. Each time he had had to reassure himself of this. The place he was looking for had to be isolated, of course, but not so isolated that any traffic to and from it would attract attention. Bozon had considered other possibilities, but always returned here. The place had this added advantage: when Bozon took it over, if he took it over, a good deal of heavy equipment would have to be moved in, and this activity could be supported by the past reputation of the place. It would appear that the new ownership was planning to bring back a formerly good wine.

Bozon strolled over and reached down to shake hands with the old man. "Good to see you again, Monsieur Cracheau."

"Hah, haven't you been out here before?" demanded the old man suspiciously. "Don't I know you?"

"I'm Bozon. I'm the one you sell your wine to each year."

"Bozon. I know that name."

"I should hope so. I see that you've got all your wine in. Why don't we walk down to your chai and see how it tastes? After that we can talk about price."

Bozon reached down to help the old man to his feet, but Cracheau rejected Bozon's hand, levered himself into position with his one crutch, and lurched upright. They moved down the alley of mud to-

114

ward the farmhouse. Cracheau, despite his age, was a big man with enormous shoulders, and with each step his pegleg and his crutch sank into the mud. Each time he jerked them out they came free with a slurping noise.

"I'm warning you, young fellow, I sell dear," muttered the old man, moving faster than Bozon.

Bozon noted that the old man was surrounded by an odor as palpable as a cloud of gas. Probably no longer cleans himself properly when he goes to the toilet, thought Bozon disgustedly.

The old man pushed open the door to the farmhouse. They found themselves in the kitchen. A loaf of bread on the table, a knife standing in it; a calendar nailed to the back of the door. The bread looked stale and the calendar featured a naked blond with pneumatic breasts and dated from ten years ago. There were cobwebs up close to the ceiling and chickens searching for crumbs on the floor. Shooing the chickens out into the yard, the old man swung his crutch at the door and knocked it closed.

The old man hobbled around until he had found a pad and pen. "That's to do my calculating on," he explained. "Do all my own business. I've done all my own business all my life."

Bozon nodded. "I'm willing to buy your entire harvest, just like last year," Bozon said. "How much wine did you make?"

"Twenty tonneaux," said the old man.

That translated into eighty barrels, about three hundred bottles to the barrel, assuming they were all sound, about twenty-four thousand bottles. Last year, though the harvest was less copious than this year's, the old man had made more, and in past years he had sometimes made as much as four times more. But in those days he had had a wife and children living at home who did his bidding or else, and the kids had had pals they could bring onto the land to pick the grapes. Now the old man was alone. The forest was moving in on his vines, and his children had moved off the land. One had moved to Toulouse, Bozon believed, and the other to Paris. They came grudgingly back to the land in response to imperious telegrams from the old man each harvest time, each worked a single weekend, and then went home—and not simultaneous weekends either since the children didn't get along, not with their father and not with each other. There was also a nephew who came out from Bordeaux on consecutive weekends, no doubt thinking he might someday inherit the place. This year, Bozon knew, the old man's harvest had lasted until the last weekend in October, never more

115

than five people picking the grapes at once, and nobody on weekdays. The family then called it quits, leaving the rest of the grapes to rot. The old man had made his wine by himself.

The old man poured out a glass of wine for Bozon. Bozon sipped it, and they began to negotiate the price of this year's harvest. The old man was grinning happily, apparently loving the negotiations, feeling important.

They traded figures back and forth, and finally the old man settled for a price well under what Bozon had been ready to pay. The old man knew nothing about the wine boom, and very little about currency inflation. The price no doubt sounded like a fortune to him, for he spent nothing. He had his vegetable garden, his chickens, his cow, and his wine. He paid his children off for the harvest in wine. When he needed anything else he caught a bus into the village, wearing his old army knapsack. After filling the knapsack with provisions, he caught another bus back. He had lost his leg in the First World War. Probably he received a pension for that still. Looking down, Bozon thought: You'd think he would at least buy himself a new leg with his money. The pegleg was scarred and splintery. Probably it was the same leg the old man had come away from Verdun with in 1916.

The old man led the way next door into his chai. There were no lights inside the chai. Sunlight filtered through filthy windows and bounced off the filthy floor. It was enough to turn Bozon's stomach. The walls were humid and green with mold. Cobwebs hung from the rafters. The eighty barrels of wine ranged down the center of the room, held in place by chocks. In the chais of the great châteaux they used barrels only once, but old Cracheau had no doubt used these same barrels for twenty or thirty harvests. They were stained nearly black from the wine they had soaked up. In Bozon's warehouse there existed a contraption which sent jets of steam in through the bung hole, both cleaning and sterilizing the inside of each barrel. Not here. Bozon knew that the old man had no tools for cleaning barrels out each year. Probably he gave them a rinse with a garden hose, and that was all.

During the harvest the old man's relatives dumped the baskets of grapes in through that window there, into that bin, in which probably the old man stood with a pitchfork, pitching forkloads of grapes into the oldest, rustiest stemming machine Bozon had ever seen. As he waded in grapes the old man's one boot and his pegleg were probably clotted with cow manure, for Bozon had noted he was none too careful where he walked. If the Americans could see such a sight, Bozon thought, they

116

wouldn't buy the sauce I'll throw his wine into. Fortunately, the fermentation process sterilized the wine, and all solid impurities fell to the bottom in the dregs. Still, if the Americans could see this old guy standing in his grapes, they wouldn't buy.

Wine was both more delicate and more hearty than any outsider knew, Bozon reflected. On the surface it was inconceivable that a man like this could make drinkable wine, but the wine Bozon had tasted in the kitchen was not bad at all, and now the old man, using a pipette, filled a rather thick, filthy glass with new wine out of the nearest barrel.

"Fine," said Bozon, swirling it around in his mouth. He looked for a sand-filled basin to spit the wine into, but of course there was no such thing in this place, so he walked to the door and blew the wine out of his mouth into the dust.

"Hah!" said the old man. "Isn't that good wine?"

"Fine."

"Isn't that good wine? Now I ask you, isn't that good wine?"

The old man was chortling. Bozon thought: The Americans have the right idea about old people. Put them in a home. Get rid of them. Get them out of sight. The chai was swarming with fruit flies. Also, it was damp and cold. Bozon went outside into the sunlight. He stood looking up the slope at the vines.

The old man stood beside him. "How much deposit you gonna leave me? Show me the color of your money, boy."

"I'll give you a check," said Bozon. He led the way back into the kitchen. It was full of chickens again. Bozon saw that there was a trap in the door such as one might leave for a dog or cat. The chickens must butt their way in through the trap. The old man could nail it shut of course, but he must like having chickens in there for company.

Bozon sat down at the kitchen table. "I've got a proposition for you."

"I know, you want me to sell out," the old man said. Bozon thought: The old bastard is sharper than one would think.

"It isn't good for a man your age to be alone here," suggested Bozon. "If anything happened to you, no one would even know. You could lie here suffering for days, for weeks."

"At my age I'd be more likely just to drop dead, don't you think?"

Bozon guessed that the old man enjoyed talking about his own impending death. It made him feel important. He was about to embark on the big adventure. The subject was not going to scare him into selling his place.

117

"I'm sure your children worry about you. You owe it to them to move into town, perhaps move into the very neighborhood where your children and grandchildren live. Then they wouldn't worry so much about you."

"Worry about me? When have my children ever worried about me? One weekend a year is all they give me. The only reason they come down here is to stand around dividing up who gets what when I croak."

"You could get a good price for this place."

"A young fellow told me that a month or so ago."

"I think that was me," said Bozon, alarmed.

"Could be. All you young fellows look alike to me. The fellow left his card." The old man rummaged through some papers on the sideboard near the sink, and clomped forward holding Bozon's business card.

"That's my card," said Bozon, relieved. Bozon should not have worried. Surely nobody came by here anymore. Five or six years ago there were many potential buyers of this place, but the serious ones negotiated with the old man and gave up. The only sensible thing to do was wait till he died.

Now Bozon was in no mood to wait. This was the perfect place. This was the place he needed. His plan could not go forward without it—or at least something like it. And there wasn't anything else like it. Not that he had found so far, and he had been looking hard for months. There was just this place. This one perfect place. This one perfect, above-suspicion place.

For the next half hour Bozon drew figures on the note pad, pushed the pad across in front of the old man, received no reaction, dragged it back and made new figures. The figures proved that, if the old man settled for this much, then his income would be this much, assuming he left the principal intact. Or he could nibble away at the principal year by year. Bozon had started very low. Cautiously he raised his price. No reaction. He doubled his price. Still no reaction. Surely the sums he was now mentioning must astonish the old man.

There was so little reaction across the table that Bozon began to wonder if the old man was asleep with his eyes open. Or perhaps he had died and rigor mortis had already set in, Bozon thought angrily. Bozon began to mention some of the glorious possibilities so much money opened up. The old man could live in Paris next to his daughter, or in Toulouse next to his son.

"What do I want to live next to those idiots for?"

118

At least he was listening. Bozon began to talk of the trip around the world he might take. Or a small villa in an unfashionable seaside resort might be a possibility. No reaction.

Exasperated, Bozon said: "This place is falling in around your ears. What do you want to stay here for?"

"Don't talk stupid. This is my place."

"You can no longer take care of it properly."

"That's good money you pay me every year."

"But why?"

"Why? This is my place."

As a businessman Bozon had only one flaw. When he wanted something, he wanted it so urgently and negotiated so hard that his whole body became tense. After a period of time sweat would break out on his brow, the antithesis of the poker face, the dead giveaway. He could feel himself sweating now, even before the old geezer chuckled and then chortled: "What are you sweating for, boy? I'm too quick for you, huh?"

Bozon was furious, but gave no sign. The old man pushed the original glass of wine across the table under Bozon's nose. "Talking so hard makes a man powerful thirsty. Have some red."

Bozon rose to his feet. "Think it over," he said.

"Come back any time," the old man said with a grin, "and we'll negotiate some more."

Fruit flies were buzzing around. For the first time Bozon noticed a bowl of fruit on the sideboard, most of it rotten. There were apples and peaches on the bottom whose sides had caved in, and the fresher fruit on top had sunk down on top of them. Maybe he could get the health department to close up the farm as a menace to public health. Bozon was so angry he was almost trembling. He had to hold himself tight so nothing would show.

Outside in the mud the old man said: "Got to go tend my cow," and without saying goodbye he turned and started up the slope. Bozon watched him tread on a cow patty. In went the wooden leg, plunk. The old bastard seemed to have done it on purpose. Ahead was another. Plunk. Bozon turned and strode back to his Mercedes.

2

A negotiation was an emotional thing, Édouard Bozon knew. The negotiator strove to develop an emotional climate favorable to the bargain he wished to strike. In Paris Bozon arranged to lunch with a man named Claude Barrier, son-in-law of Cracheau. Barrier, who wore a shiny dark suit, was a postal clerk by trade. He was somewhat awed to be meeting with Édouard Bozon at all. Bozon wore silk clothing, even his underwear was probably silk, and with lunch he had ordered a Château Lafite two decades old, worth a week's salary to a postal clerk. Bozon would have a stupendous bill to pay when this meal was finished.

Bozon began by asking Barrier to state his opinion of his father-in-law. His opinion was as Bozon expected. Years ago the father-in-law had been autocratic, had made the postal clerk feel like dirt and unworthy of Cracheau's daughter, yet for a decade now the old man had played on family solidarity to get his wine in. Each year Barrier was obliged to drive south—he had his own car now, you understand, monsieur—with his entire family at great expense, donating at least a weekend of his time, sometimes more when the crop was heavy, and for this what thanks did he get? Later he would be obliged, once the wine was bottled, to make still another long, expensive trip south in order to fill his trunk with the wine that was his family's fee for making the harvest possible at all. "And the farmhouse, monsieur, you have been inside it? You have smelled it?"

Bozon nodded his head sympathetically. Yes, he had been inside it. Yes, he had smelled it. He had also smelled Barrier's father-in-law, an aroma which carried twenty meters even on a windless day.

The postal clerk was no stupider than most postal clerks, Bozon realized. Already the man's mind was proceeding ahead, bounding about like a kangaroo, trying to fix on the purpose of this meeting.

A shrewd negotiator never allowed his adversary time to guess too much. Surprise was paramount.

120

Bozon said: "I find myself needing to purchase your father-in-law's property."

"And the old fart won't sell, right?" said Claude Barrier.

"I'm not entirely sure that the old man is mentally competent," said Bozon solicitously. "If he were my father or father-in-law, I would be seriously worried about his mental state. I'd go to bed nights imagining that he might be lying in there dying, with no other human being within miles of him."

This was the opportunity for the postal clerk to turn pious, and he did not disappoint.

"My wife loves her father, of course. And I myself am filled with admiration for the old man. He asks nothing from anyone. He gets on entirely by himself—except for the goddamn vendange. He uproots our lives every harvest time. He thinks it's his right. He doesn't even say thank you. We have to go down there, because he's only got one leg, and he's over eighty years old, and if we don't he'll starve to death and we'll have to support him in an asylum somewhere."

"I'm glad you brought up that word 'asylum,'" said Bozon. Bozon gazed at the tabletop. The postal clerk leaned forward gazing at Bozon's eyelids.

"Have you considered having your father-in-law committed?" inquired Bozon. "Wait a minute, don't answer. I know how any devoted daughter feels, any loyal son-in-law feels. I myself went through all this with my own father only last year." This was a lie, Bozon's father having died of a heart attack in an alcoholic stupor at the age of forty-six.

Reaching out, Bozon put his hand on the postal clerk's shiny shoulder. "Say no more. Say nothing for the moment. Let me explain what's happened in my own business. You're a businessman yourself. You understand these things."

Across the table the postal clerk beamed.

"There are eighty human beings working for me. That means eighty families dependent upon my business. And my business is going very badly at this time. All wine merchants are obliged to pay scandalous prices to the château owners for the famous makes of wine. We are forced to pay so much for this wine that every bottle sold represents a substantial loss to our firms. You may ask, how do we make this up? The answer is that we make it up in volume. Each of us buys wine from growers such as your father-in-law. We blend these small wines and sell the blends in quantity at small markups all over the world. When you come right down to it, the prestige of all France depends upon the wine of men like your father-in-law. What's come to pass at this time is unfortunate for my firm, unfortunate for your father-in-law, unfortunate for you as the acknowledged leader of the family of Monsieur Cracheau. And unfortunate also for—La France."

As he spoke the name of the motherland, Bozon clapped his hand over his breast. Across the table from him the postal clerk solemnly nodded.

"I go out there to buy your father-in-law's wine as always. It is poor in quality. You saw how many of the grapes had rotted. You're an experienced man in wine. You have done many harvests. You have watched much wine vinified."

The postal clerk nodded again.

"More wine?" inquired Bozon. He poured Château Lafite into the postal clerk's glass. "Tastes quite like the 1929 Lafite, wouldn't you say?" asked Bozon.

"No, it tastes more like the 1930 to me," said the postal clerk, snatching a vintage out of the air, not knowing that no Château Lafite was bottled under the château label after that dismal harvest.

"Well," said Bozon, "the old man makes bad wine, and less and less of it each year. I am forced to buy the wine. I am forced to send it out all over the world, and it disgraces all of us, even you and your wife and your children, who helped pick it. I look over your father-in-law's property and I see that five or six times as much wine could be made there each year, and of a quality five or six times superior to what was made this year. So I go out there and I offer to buy the property from your father-in-law. I offer him far more money than the land is worth to him, so much that I wonder if I can even make a profit myself working that land. Perhaps in ten years' time there will be a small profit. Perhaps not. But this is the road I feel obliged to take. And I offer your father-in-law a fantastic price, and he laughs at me."

"You should try to talk to the old fart when you're only a son-in-law."

"I can well understand what your problem must be," said Bozon. "As you are well aware, fewer vines are producing there each year. The forest comes in closer on the vines each year. Already many rows are overgrown with underbrush. The former reputation of the place is entirely gone. Only a few relative old-timers such as myself realize what good wine once was made there. I have looked into the documents. Your father-in-law owns planting rights to land he has not planted.

122

Eleven years ago he ripped out a number of parcels. You know the law. If these parcels are not replanted within twelve years—that means next year—they cease to exist. It would become necessary to go to the government and buy them back, and you might find that permission was refused. In other words the productive size of the property is shrinking, and unless something is done within a year it will have shrunk irretrievably."

Across the table the postal clerk was getting more and more agitated. That was his inheritance Bozon was describing. Bozon was bringing him into the exact emotional state Bozon had been hoping for.

"If your father-in-law died today, half of the value of his property would come to your wife—and to you, of course. You would not become a wealthy man overnight, but you would be able to spend this money —probably you would choose to use it to educate your children. I can tell that you are a serious man."

The postal clerk nodded piously.

"I was with your father-in-law only last week. Physically he is as healthy as a horse. Mentally, as we both know, he has failed badly. Your half of the inheritance, when it finally comes your way in five years or ten, will, sadly, be much diminished. I fear there won't be enough left then even for a big new car."

The postal clerk cleared his throat. "What are you proposing, monsieur?"

"We both know that your father-in-law has become, sadly, mentally incompetent. If he were declared so legally, then disposition of his property would rest in the hands of your wife and her brother. I come to you, the leader of the family. If this sad state of affairs were to occur, and your father-in-law were to be declared incompetent, I would ask you to give me first refusal rights on the purchase of the property. As one businessman to another, I assure you you could make no better deal than to sell the place to Édouard Bozon."

"I think I can see what you're getting at," said the postal clerk, nodding sagely. "And we have talked about the incompetence of my father-in-law among ourselves. However, it is very complicated to get a man declared incompetent, and very costly. So we have done nothing."

"As loyal children, you have decided to let nature take its course as far as your father-in-law is concerned, am I right?"

"We talked about it, but we couldn't see any way out."

123

"I have made a certain investigation," confessed Bozon now. "I have talked to some lawyers and also to some psychiatrists. I have spoken to these people—hypothetically, of course—and they tell me that in the case of your father-in-law, once certain fees are paid, it's virtually an open-and-shut case. There would be a hearing, of course, at which all of you children would give your testimony. If you had a single strong outside witness, so I'm told, someone who does business with your father-in-law, and who knows first hand his mental state, someone like, say, myself, then it seems almost inevitable that the court would declare him incompetent, and commit him."

The two men stared at each other.

"Are you suggesting, monsieur—"

"Precisely."

The postal clerk drew in a deep breath.

"To preserve appearances, you would have to subpoena me to give testimony at the hearing," said Bozon. "But I think you can count on what my testimony would be. So far as I know I am the only merchant to have dealt with your father-in-law in the last three or four years. The lawyers say my testimony would carry great weight."

The postal clerk had become so excited he could scarcely talk, but he was trying to hide this.

"Inasmuch as it would be my testimony which would make all this possible," said Bozon, "I know that you would in no way betray me after the hearing and attempt to sell the property to someone else."

"Oh, no, monsieur. How could you think such a thing?"

"What I propose is that you speak first to your wife, and then to your brother-in-law and his wife. If you're all agreed, then we should meet in my office in Bordeaux and agree upon a price for the property. I can assure you I will be most generous."

The postal clerk was nodding and breathing hard simultaneously.

"One other thing," said Bozon. "Since you would be acting, in effect, as my agent during this transaction, I would expect to pay you an additional commission totaling twenty thousand francs. This would be paid to you in cash after all the papers were signed, and I see no reason why any other members of your family should be made aware of it."

Across the table the postal clerk was blinking his eyes rapidly.

"Did you say something?" inquired Bozon.

"We'd only be doing what's best for the old man."

124

"I heartily agree with you," said Bozon.

"The old fart will be much better off in an asylum."

Bozon raised his arm and wagged it vigorously. "Waiter, the check, please."

3

Bozon, before leaving Paris, telephoned Aline Conderie.

"I thought you might like to have dinner with me."

"What for?" she asked bluntly.

"I was up here negotiating a little business deal and—"

"How did the swindle work out?"

"I'm afraid you'll never understand business, my dear. Your father either, poor fellow."

"Don't call me that."

"But you are dear to me. You'll always be dear to me. What about dinner? The Tour d'Argent? Maxim's?"

"No."

Bozon chuckled softly. "There's no reason why we can't be friends. Good friends."

There was silence at both ends of the line. The amused Bozon thought: She'd like to slam the receiver down, but considers herself too well bred.

After a moment, amusement plain in his voice, Bozon said: "You don't object if I come into your shop this afternoon?"

"Anybody can walk in off the street. That's what it is. It's a shop."

"I'd like to buy a gift for a special friend."

"This is a very expensive shop. In addition, we would not have her size."

"Ah, my dear—"

"Don't call me that, I said."

"How I regret that I cannot look at you at this very moment. You are always most beautiful when you are, shall we say, aroused." Bozon began to laugh, then added: "Till later, then."

But she had hung up on him.

Bozon began chortling merrily. He felt in a rare good humor.

Aline's shop was on the Rue du Faubourg St.-Honoré, nestled among the art galleries and the haute couture houses. Bozon lunched late outdoors on the terrace of a café within sight of it, and from his table watched the shop.

It was a cold gray day. The glass was up around the café's terrace, the heaters were going in the corners, and condensation had misted over the glass in places. Bozon did not bother to give total attention to the shop. Nonetheless, he saw no clients enter during the nearly two hours that he made his luncheon last.

Backbreaking rent and no clients, Bozon thought.

He had started on cold Belon oysters, the opened shells nestling in their bed of seaweed and crushed ice. After testing the edge of each oyster, Bozon squeezed lemon juice down onto each, watching them retreat anew. Then he forked each oyster slowly into his mouth, chewing contemplatively, drinking the briny juice of each shell afterward, from time to time eating slices of buttered black bread. During this portion of the meal he drank a bottle of cold Riesling from the Alsace.

Next Bozon ordered fat hot sausages, which were served with this café's special potato salad. The small, firm potatoes had been cut into slices and marinated in oil and vinegar, and they were served cold. With this course Bozon ordered a stein of icy-cold dark German beer, and drained it, ordered another stein, and drained that too.

Now Bozon asked to be presented with the tray of cheeses. He selected a soft, runny goat cheese from the center of France, a wedge of Gorgonzola, which he considered to be the only Italian cheese worth talking about, and a quarter of a Camembert so creamy it was oozing out from under its crust before his eyes. France was a country of three hundred cheeses, and Bozon, a gourmet of cheese, knew most of them, and Camembert was his favorite of all. There was a basket of crusty French bread beside his place, but he ate little of it. Each bit of bread went into his mouth overwhelmed by a chunk of cheese; that was the way to eat cheese, Bozon believed; it wasn't a sandwich. The cheese was the taste Bozon was glorying in, not the bread. With the cheese course Bozon ordered a half bottle of 1947 Figeac, which, to his surprise, he had found on the wine list. A great cheese would make almost any wine delicious, but a great cheese and a great wine together were a rare treat

126

whatever the price. Bozon's bill when it came would be astronomical for this café, but it was his own palate he had regaled; he himself deserved only the very best. The price, whatever it would turn out to be, was justified.

After the cheese Bozon selected a mille-feuilles from the pastry tray. The thick layers of fresh whipped cream were interspersed with thin leaves of the finest, flakiest pastry. The top of the pastry was dusted with powdered sugar. Such a pastry was difficult for Bozon to eat. The whipped cream went squishing out the sides when he pressed with his fork, and before long his upper lip was decorated with the powdered sugar. Licking this off, he called for a tiny cup of strong black coffee, together with a marc, a dry grape brandy that was a specialty of this particular café.

During his meal Bozon watched, whenever he thought of it, Aline's shop. He saw her come back from her own lunch, reopening the locked shop shortly before 2 P.M.; he had just started on his oysters at that time. When he finally paid his bill nearly two hours later, he had still not seen any clients enter the place, though of course he could have missed someone.

Putting his cashmere topcoat on, he strolled over to her shop and peered in at two salesgirls studiously pretending they were not bored. He could not see Aline, but a curtain hung in a doorway leading to secret recesses in the back.

In the window against a scarlet velvet backdrop was pinned a single black dress. Perhaps the connoisseurs would call it an exquisitely simple dress. It had no ornamentation of whatever kind. Bozon couldn't see even what shape it might turn out to be. There was no price tag.

When Bozon entered, one of the saleswomen came forward promptly. She was beautifully dressed, groomed, and manicured, and she had a beautiful voice.

"And what may I show you, monsieur?"

Bozon glanced around. There were other expensive dresses in glass cases on both sides of the shop. Covering part of the parquet floor was a Persian carpet, no doubt worth a fortune. Bozon noted a number of Louis XV armchairs, and toward the rear a valuable antique desk which no doubt served as the shop's cash desk. Naturally there would be nothing as gross as a cash register in a shop like this.

"Madame la patronne is not in?" murmured Bozon.

"Yes, of course, monsieur." Moving to the rear of the store the saleswoman called: "Madame, someone wishes to see you."

127

The doorway drapes parted and Aline stepped out. She already wore her prepared smile, but when she saw Bozon, this smile ceased to exist.

Bozon grinned. "It may be that you can assist me."

Assuming Bozon to be madame's private client, the other two women stepped out of the way, though wondering, Bozon felt sure, why madame was not smiling. Why did she seem to be wringing her hands together?

Bozon almost wanted to laugh. "That dress in the window," he said.

Aline said nothing.

"I'd like to see it."

"Odette," called Aline, "please show monsieur the dress in the window."

"But of course, monsieur."

"No, no," murmured Bozon. "I'm sure madame would like to show it to me herself."

After a moment Aline strode toward the window and leaned in, one by one plucking out the pins that fastened the dress in place. When she had returned to where Bozon stood, she thrust the dress out, holding it in both hands. She held it by the shoulders so that it hung limp and unattractive between them.

"Very nice," said Bozon. "Very elegant indeed. And what is the price of this little number?"

"More than monsieur would like to spend on such a dress, I'm sure."

Aline was stony-faced, Bozon grinning. The two salesgirls seemed mesmerized. Appearance had always counted so much for Aline, Bozon thought. She was always so proper. Suddenly she finds herself part of a scene she must hate. What a treat for the two salesgirls. What explanations—or lies—Aline would be forced to come up with after Bozon had left the shop!

It was all Bozon could do to keep from laughing.

"No price is too high for a gift for that special someone," murmured Bozon piously.

"Monsieur must be an especially generous man," said Aline sweetly.

So she was recovering fast. Obscurely, this pleased Bozon.

"You must think very highly of it, or you would not have put it in the window," suggested Bozon.

"That's right," said Aline grimly.

128

When Bozon asked its size, Aline gave what was, to him, a meaning-less number. "I judge it would fit you perfectly," suggested Bozon. "Would you mind trying it on for me?"

Aline said: "That is out of the question."

The two saleswomen stared.

"It reminds me of the dress you wore in Biarritz that night."

"We would of course alter it for you," said Aline.

"What was the name of the young man you took a shine to that night? In Biarritz I mean?"

Bozon was grinning. Aline stared at the toes of her shoes.

"Yes," said Bozon, suddenly expansive. "I have made up my mind. I'll take it. Please wrap it for me. A gift wrapping, of course."

Aline carried the dress to the antique desk, where she instructed one of her saleswomen to wrap it. She waited. She looked as if she were trying to keep from shuddering. She looked as if she were suddenly standing in an ice-cold room.

"Here you are, monsieur." She pushed the package forward.

"How much did you say it was?" Bozon withdrew his checkbook.

"We do not accept checks."

"Surely, the prices you charge, you're obliged to accept checks. You can't expect a man to carry this much money around in cash."

Aline did not answer.

"Surely there are exceptions, madame," suggested Bozon.

Aline, gazing at the checkbook, said: "For long-time clients."

"Then I qualify," said Bozon firmly. He began writing out the check. "Otherwise I would find myself in the impossibility of making this purchase. All of us would be losers, your shop, myself, and the recipient of this little gift as well."

Aline would not meet his glance. A small smile playing about his lips, Bozon watched her face and saw, or thought he saw, that awful octopus, greed, snake its tentacles around her. This single sale might represent the profits for the entire day, if not the entire week.

"Very well, monsieur."

Bozon signed the check with a flourish and pushed it across. It lay there like a telegram representing news of some awful disaster. Aline stared at it. She seemed unable to pick it up.

"Well, then—" said Bozon. With his package under his arm he called out a cheery "Au revoir, madame."

The two salesgirls smiled for him as he passed them.

In the street, moving through crowds with his package under his

129

arm, Bozon began to giggle. Back inside the shop those salesgirls were going to demand explanations. What was Aline going to tell them? What fantastic tale would Aline invent?

Reaching his hotel, Bozon handed his package to the concierge, giving orders that it should be delivered to Aline's apartment; Bozon gave the address from memory.

That was another little scene he would give much to witness: Aline's face when she ripped the wrapping off and saw the dress coming back, compliments of Édouard Bozon. She would be so mad. Tears of rage would fill her eyes.

Then she would do—what?

In his suite, Bozon slipped off new shoes bought that morning—they pinched—and asked the telephone operator to put him through to his bank. It was his intention now to stop that check. Fun was fun, but one did not throw money away.

However, once the connection was made, Bozon abruptly hung up. There was no need to stop the check, he reasoned. A woman as proud as Aline would never cash it. She would take that dress back to her shop and hide it in a rack among other expensive models, its place in the window and in her affection lost forever. She would not be able to bear the sight of this dress now. The check would go into the drawer, where Aline would glance at it from time to time. But her anger and most of all her pride would never permit her to deposit it. She would not give Bozon the satisfaction. She would not take his money. Bozon respected most businessmen, simply for being businessmen. The businessman's role was hard. But Aline Conderie was not a businessman; she was a woman. She was also a fool.

On his bed Bozon sat massaging a pinched foot. By not stopping the check Bozon risked losing a great deal of money. But the risk seemed small. And that's what the excitement of business was all about, really. You made your decision, you backed your judgment, and then you waited to see if you had been right or wrong.

Bozon's only regret was that he would not be there tonight when Aline ripped open that package. Grinning, he went on rubbing his sore silken foot. It had been a good day. A very good day.

As the shop door closed behind Bozon, its little bell merrily tinkling, Aline felt as if she had just been punched in the solar plexus. She had difficulty catching her breath. She felt almost nauseated.

When the two saleswomen looked questioningly at her, she tried

130

to control her face. Knowing she could not control her voice, she gave her head an impatient shake, as if shaking her thoughts onto more important business, and disappeared into the back of the shop, where she stood in the tiny room, smoking, trying to think about nothing. About five minutes passed before one of the women called inside: "We were wondering what you wanted put in the window."

Aline went out into the shop. The three women went through the racks. She told the saleswomen nothing. Why should she?

Aline settled on a dark red suit with flaring jacket and patch pockets. The three women discussed the suit. Was its price appropriate? Was it chic enough? Would it attract buyers into the store?

Removing their shoes the two saleswomen stepped into the window and pinned up the dark red suit. Aline hid in the back room and stared at the walls. Her heart no longer thumped. The knot in her stomach was smaller than before. She began to congratulate herself. It was over.

Then why were her fists clenched, her nails biting into the palms of her hands? She loosened her fists.

She dismissed the saleswomen early, not wanting today's witnesses around, but stayed open until 7 P.M. as always, before making her way home through the dark and the crowds. Reaching her building she pushed the button, and one of the wrought-iron doors swung open. The concierge's loge was just inside this door, and the woman popped out now, holding a package.

"For you, madame."

"For me?"

Aline saw the wrapping, recognized it, and had to force herself to take it from the woman's hands. As she and her package rode the birdcage elevator up through the building, Aline's emotion was so intense that she expected at any moment to break out sobbing. I will not cry, she told herself. I will not cry.

Inside her own apartment she moved carefully, meticulously. The gift-wrapped box she placed on the dining-room table. She placed her handbag next to it. She had also been handed some letters by the concierge. These she placed on the table without opening them. She went through into the bathroom and began to run a hot bath. She got undressed. She stood beside the tub watching it fill. When it was at the proper level she tested it with her toe, then got in. She let the water cover her to her chin. She was concentrating as absolutely as she could on her body and on the pleasure of the hot water. She was attempting

131

to give herself over totally to the hot water, though her mind kept getting away from her.

She thought of her shop, which she knew now she would lose. She wished she would not lose it, but knew she would.

What does a divorced young woman need to distract her? A shop to run. So that is what her father gives her, and she loses money religiously for five years. She learns the business the hard way. She makes mistakes buying and also selling. Her competitors arrange for her deliveries to be late, for her tailor to make inaccurate alterations. She fails to build up any sort of faithful clientele. She keeps hoping business will improve and it does—slightly. She refuses to accept defeat—until tonight.

Aline's eyes filled with tears, though she fought them. Abruptly she stood up in the tub. The sudden movement seemed to stop the tears. As the water dripped from her body, she peered down at one of her breasts, perceiving no scar, though she twisted it this way and that under the light. Once at a party Bozon had burned through the bosom of her dress with a lighted cigarette because she had chanced to flirt with another man. She had never been to Biarritz again. Her eyes blurred and she lost sight of it but—look—it came swimming back, a perfect female nipple. Probably it still worked—it had never been tested after all—and the true scar was on her soul.

In her robe she padded down the hall, flicked on the dining-room light, and stared at the box on the table.

Today Bozon had merely shown her that she was a failure at running a shop.

She opened her handbag and went through today's meager receipts, almost all of it in checks. Withdrawing a package of cigarettes, she stuck one between her lips. She struck a match, lit Bozon's check by one corner, let it burn halfway down, and then lit her cigarette with it.

But this only made her eyes fill with tears again.

She fought them off, whirled, and marched back to her bedroom, where she began to get dressed. Tonight she had been invited to the première of the new play of one of the most celebrated of the new playwrights. A reception and dinner would follow. Many celebrities would be there. It was the place to turn up in Paris tonight, and she had been to a number of galas like it in the last several years. Her name had served as her introduction into such circles, and her youth and good looks had served to keep her there. She was of the proper social class and the proper age, and she was unattached, making her an especially rare bird and a godsend to hostesses planning parties. Also, she suspected, hostesses liked to watch unattached males knock each other down trying to reach the side of Aline Conderie. She had learned how to frighten men off, and possibly that was an entertaining spectacle too. Perhaps she was considered a freak. She did not know and had told herself for years she did not care, which was a lie—of course she cared. She was trying to fight her way through the world on her own terms, and it wasn't working. The world was too tough a place for a young woman alone. Men stuck together and humiliated women if they could, and it had always been that way and always would be, and the Women's Lib movement couldn't change that. Men would allow only a few token women to get through. These would be women who weren't smart enough, or hard enough, or good looking enough to constitute a threat to man's supremacy. She herself had no chance. It was hopeless.

In slip and slippers she went into the kitchen and fixed herself soft-boiled eggs. That used up three minutes. See, time could be made to pass in a whirlwind, if you kept busy. Activity could keep heartache out of a room indefinitely.

She ate an unflavored yogurt, and drank a glass of wine. At the reception later she would not eat at all. But what am I saving my figure for? she asked herself suddenly. The answer came back: for myself— myself alone. It was an insufficient answer, but the only one she could find for the moment.

She washed the egg cup, and rinsed out the wine glass.

She put on her sleekest dress. It hugged her figure to the floor. In the mirror she shimmered. She would cause a stir when she entered the room. Why did she crave the admiration of men's eyes, but not their hands? She penciled on eye liner, and with ten fingers fluffed up her hair. Putting on her fur coat, she went downstairs and out onto the street. Up at the taxi stand on the corner she climbed into a cab. Sitting back, she watched Paris pass outside the windows. The taxi entered the vortex of the Étoile and was flung off down the Champs Élysées. Aline Conderie moved slowly in traffic. The cinema marquees passed by and the lighted, crowded cafés with their glassed-in terraces.

For a moment Aline saw herself as others might: unescorted lady in an evening dress about to arrive alone in a taxi. Was this not an indignity, and might not the addition of a man, any man, have changed it to a triumph in the eyes of onlookers if not in her own? But she would not depend on any man, not ever again, for that was the worst indignity of all. She had once depended upon her father, who seemed so charming, so debonair, so strong. Oh, he was charming all right, and he loved her in his way, but had no strength at all. He had handed her off to her husband, the strongest man she could find, a man who destroyed, she soon learned, everything he touched, a powerful sexual force whom she came to equate with death. In those days, being younger and softer, she cried a lot. Now she was hard. The world was a wasteland, but she knew how to survive. She loved no one. She was self-sufficient. Nothing could make her weep.

4

That day Paul Conderie was in Paris too, having fled Bordeaux, scene of the latest defeat in his life, and the most ignominious too, he supposed, though who kept score except himself? And he could place the defeat in any category he chose, even into the category of victory. He had not phoned or contacted his daughter yet, though sooner or later he would have to explain how he had lost her inheritance, 150 years of family ownership stopping before it ever reached Aline, stopping with himself. Aline had never liked the place anyway, or so he told himself, but he could not have faced her now, could not have admitted how—how outflanked he felt. He imagined himself not overpowered but tricked. It all might somehow have been prevented, and Aline would see this, and would reproach him, either with words or with the expression in her eyes. She had eyes as expressive as her mother's were once. Conderie had never been equal to Aline's mother either in strength or devotion, though he always prided himself that his flair was superior to hers, superior to Aline's now, assuming flair was what counted this year, assuming that's what points were awarded for in life. Aline's mother had left him and then died, very convenient in the long run. The divorce would have been messy. This way the grief-stricken husband with the cute little girl, a man betrayed by the cruelty of life, remained a hero to all who knew him, number-one object of sympathy to the warm-blooded French.

Conderie sometimes felt lucky to have been born French, not American; for the Americans were absolutely pitiless; only victory counted there. In France in defeat you could be a bigger hero than if you had won. Conderie had experienced many defeats in the past, but had come away from most of them more a hero than ever, at least in the eyes of certain of his friends, those he kept, and also therefore in the eyes of himself. Like most men Paul Conderie avoided people who refused to see him in the light in which he saw himself. To Conderie flair was what counted, a man was what he appeared to be, and Conderie liked to surround himself with people who felt the same.

But he had fled Bordeaux, fled the corpse-strewn battlefield, and was holed up in Paris waiting for his wounds to scar over, waiting to be able to convince himself that he had not lost but won.

He could not face his daughter.

Let her read about it in the newspapers. He didn't suppose she would really care, except for the money. Everyone cared about money. There was still money left, perhaps not very much but surely he had equity in properties here and there; he would have to call his solicitor to find out how much, and he didn't want to do that just yet either, for fear the news would be bad. As long as he didn't know any exact figure he could convince himself that said figure must be enormous, and once he had convinced himself he could convince anybody. Even Aline.

Aline had a way of making him bleed with a single reproachful glance. Like her mother.

Conderie could not use his apartment—the Swedish diplomat was still in there and was resisting hints to leave. But Conderie had a number of rich friends, and he dealt his life out among them, one or two nights at a time. Obviously it was out of the question that a man of Conderie's stature stop overnight in a common hotel, even one of the palaces for which Paris was so famous. Mere money stayed at the Ritz or the George V. Personages of stature like Paul Conderie did not.

As always when in Paris Conderie passed one extraordinarily busy day after another. This morning had required several hours with his tailor, much of the time being poked and prodded, Conderie wincing nervously as pins were poked into the cloth. The session had ended in some distasteful haggling.

Conderie had come to submit to the final fitting for his winter

135

wardrobe, and preliminary fittings for his spring wardrobe. The latter came first. For an hour he fingered through spring samples.

"I'm trying to think how this would look on me."

"Monsieur could wear any suit elegantly and well." The tailor was sweating.

"Before I decide, I'd like to go back through those first samples again."

"Of course, monsieur."

The spring selection was finally settled.

"You will take all new measurements, of course?"

"That won't be necessary, monsieur. We have your measurements taken only a month ago."

"But I've been on a diet recently. I think you should take new measurements."

"Of course, monsieur."

At last the tailor brought out the three winter suits nearing completion. Conderie tried each on in turn, standing in front of the triple mirror studying himself. The tailor hovered behind him, a short bald man with a little mustache, tape measure draped over one shoulder.

"I'd prefer a more tapered line here. And no cuffs of course."

"But monsieur specifically ordered cuffs only a month ago."

"I think cuffs are passé now, don't you?"

"Not at all, monsieur. The mode this year—"

"I have small feet. I look better without cuffs. Please have them removed."

"Oui, monsieur."

The second suit pleased Conderie, except that he decided that the sleeves were a centimeter too long and would have to be redone.

"Of course, monsieur," said the bald tailor, chalking them.

Conderie suddenly declined to buy the third suit. "I've changed my mind. I don't think I'll be taking this one at all."

"I consider that the most elegant of the three," said the tailor nervously.

"It appealed to me too at first. But it's too—too unusual."

"Original, monsieur. I considered it the most original pattern we were offering this season. And, of course, once delivered to Mr. Conderie, then we automatically destroy the rest of the cloth. No one else will wear that pattern but you."

"However," said Conderie, surveying himself in the mirror, "I've decided against it."

136

Behind him, the little tailor bowed his head.

"Cheer up," said Conderie, slapping him on the shoulder, knocking the tape measure to the floor. "Your suits are so well made that you'll have no trouble selling this one to someone else."

"Very good, monsieur."

Most of Conderie's afternoon was spent in the "salon" of a barber known as Marcel, who called himself "Coiffeur to the Stars."

Marcel was an Alsatian or a German, it was difficult to tell, a homosexual of course, a tall, cadaverous individual of thirty-five or forty, Conderie decided; one could never guess the exact age of such people. He had been in business on the Champs Élysées for about two years now. There was no doubt that he was the "in" barber in Paris.

Conderie had stipulated from the first that no one but Marcel himself should cut Conderie's hair. Evidently all of the so-called stars stipulated the same, so that it had become Marcel's practice only to shape each haircut. Prologues and epilogues were left to his subordinates. Marcel did no preparatory shampoos, and no tidying up afterward. If Marcel barbered most of the rich and famous men in Paris this year, it was because, all his clients told each other, Marcel had a special way with a pair of scissors. In addition, as far as Conderie was concerned, Marcel had a secret product, a rinse which took the gray out of a man's hair without also draining its highlights.

Today Conderie's hair was shampooed by a short, sturdy girl with thick, hard fingers. Marcel then appeared, scissors sticking out of his pockets, to ask a few innocuous questions in his heavy German accent before snipping at Conderie's hair. Meanwhile, the shoeshine boy was busy on Conderie's thin Italian shoes, and a second girl was manicuring his nails. Conderie gave himself up totally to the sensuousness of the experience. Through the leather he could feel the shoeshine boy's fingers massaging his toes, while the girl worked meticulously on his nails and Marcel's scissors worked delicately within millimeters of his sensitive scalp.

After a second shampoo, Marcel returned to apply the rinse. This required the steep tilting of the chair until Conderie's skull lay submerged in a basin. The original shampoo girl kneaded the rinse into his scalp. Simultaneously the manicurist was working on his left hand and the shoeshine boy on his left shoe. A session wearing a hairnet under the dryer followed, and last but not least Conderie ordered himself shaved.

Distributing lavish tips, Conderie came out into the streets of Paris

137

with the afternoon almost gone, and the main business of the day still before him.

This business could have been done on almost any of the chic streets of the city, but he had worked the Champs Élysées carefully in the past, and so decided to seek a new site, opting for no particular reason for the Avenue de l'Opéra, to which he had himself delivered by taxi. Stepping down from the cab, he began to stroll along peering into shop windows in a way that might have appeared casual, unless the observer watched how carefully Conderie conducted himself, and how long the process took.

He ambled along very slowly, according the contents of each shop window only a moment or two before glancing through to study the sales personnel. If these were exclusively men, then Conderie ambled on. If they were women, then Conderie would spend some time before the window, alternately studying the goods displayed and the women inside until he had been able to appraise totally but unobtrusively every salesgirl in the shop, measuring each against a checklist in his head.

That one?

No, not that one. The one behind the cash desk then? No, she must be fifty.

And he would walk on to the next shop.

That one?

No. If she's more than sixteen, I'd be surprised.

He turned into the Rue de la Paix, walking almost all the way to the Place Vendôme, staring in at gloves, belts, lingerie, diamonds. He stared into two dress shops not unlike his daughter's.

A perfume shop held him. That one in the tight blouse?

He glanced at his watch. Why not?

He entered. An older woman invisible from the street came forward to block his path, but he dodged her and presented himself to the girl in the tight blouse.

"Monsieur?" she asked, wearing her professional smile.

"I need to buy some—" he glanced around, somewhat frantically reassuring himself that he was indeed in a perfume shop—"some perfume for a rather special girl." He gave her his most dazzling smile.

He knew she had noticed him outside the window. He had made sure of it, waiting until their eyes met, nodding at her with a half smile. He had done this at another shop a hundred yards up the street, but the girl there had turned coldly away, his nod unacknowledged. This one had turned away too, but with a half smile to match his own, and only

138

after having met his gaze for a few seconds. Conderie had judged his chances nil with the first girl, better than average with this one.

Which was why he was here now, asking her to show him perfume.

"Of course, monsieur. What type of woman is she? Is she old? Is she young?"

"Does it make a difference?"

"Of course, monsieur. Certain perfumes are rather heavy, musky. Definite come-ons."

"I see."

"You wouldn't give such a musky perfume to an old lady, or to a young girl either. So you should tell me who the perfume is for."

Conderie nodded, smiling warmly. "She's about your age, I would say."

"What type of skin does she have?

"Quite like yours. Rather creamy. Almost flawless. A skin so smooth a man wants to reach out and touch it."

They were both smiling. Both understood now what game was being played out. Neither knew where it would lead. Conderie looked very pleased, but the girl looked pleased too.

Conderie eyed the girl up and down. "She's about your size. She has long dark hair which she wears very much as you do. She has—" Conderie hesitated momentarily—"blue eyes. A rather deep, dark blue."

The girl seemed trying to keep from grinning. "Is she a person of much experience?"

"I would guess she has had some experience. Not too much, of course."

From a display case the girl took down several spray bottles of perfume. Holding Conderie's fingers, she sprayed a dab on the back of his hand and pushed it gently toward his nose.

"Very nice."

The girl sprayed a second sample onto Conderie's other hand.

"That's very nice too. What else do you have?" The girl got down more samples. Some she sprayed or dabbed on the backs of her own hands, and part way up her exposed forearm. Each area she then held to Conderie's nose. They were grinning at each other now, and once Conderie said: "Say, I like this."

"This particular perfume?"

"No, testing all these perfumes with you."

Across the shop the older saleswoman was staring stonily out the

139

front window. Outside it was beginning to get dark.

"How will you get all this perfume off?" asked Conderie.

"After you go, having made a substantial purchase, I hope, I'll go into the back room and scrub my arms with a brush."

They both laughed. "How interesting."

Conderie was almost sure, but wanted to be absolutely sure. "Surely a girl as lovely as you is married."

"No, monsieur."

"The perfume that you were wearing when I came in here, what was that?"

"Fleurs de Rocaille, monsieur."

"That's your own favorite perfume?"

"Oui, monsieur."

"Why don't I take a flacon of Fleurs de Rocaille. Will you gift wrap it for me? The biggest size, of course."

"It's very expensive, monsieur," said the girl doubtfully.

"Money is no object," said Conderie expansively.

As he watched the girl gift wrap the perfume, Conderie said: "Say, you've been so kind I was wondering if I could offer you an apéritif as a gesture of—appreciation."

"Monsieur, I don't know—"

"You'll be closing in a few minutes, and it would mean such a lot to me."

The girl smiled. "Very well, monsieur."

In the café a few minutes later, looking flushed and a little dazzled that this had come to pass, the girl ordered Cinzano over ice with a twist of lemon peel. Conderie sipped whisky. "Do you know what I thought when I first peered in the window at you?" asked Conderie.

"What?"

"That French girls dress so beautifully."

The girl looked pleased.

"I don't suppose they pay you a fortune in that shop, and yet you look so chic. So very chic. What's your name?"

The girl told him.

Conderie asked about perfume. The girl turned out to be a fountain of information. She knew the most expensive brand, Joy, and the least expensive—one Conderie had never heard of, naturally. She knew which had jasmine base, and which contained principally musk or ambergris. She had been obliged to attend courses at various of the great perfume houses when she had first gone to work in that shop. She had finished school at sixteen, and had been working in that shop ever since. She was twenty-four, and had almost married last year. Her life sounded to Conderie rather drab. But she had by now recovered her poise at least, and she was even better looking than Conderie had at first supposed. She smiled a lot and had good teeth. Conderie got her to talk more about perfume, and at the appropriate moment broke in to remark that perfume was really a good deal like wine, for the flowers that went into them had to be grown just so, picked at the exact proper moment, and then blended according to a rather rigid formula. There were even vintages in these flower harvests, Conderie understood, that were exactly comparable to wine vintages.

The girl confessed that, although she drank wine with meals as all French people did, she really knew very little about it.

"And what is your favorite wine?" Conderie inquired.

"What is yours, monsieur?"

Conderie said it was Château Conderie, of course, of which château he happened to be the owner. Her eyes went wide, and then her entire face seemed to turn shrewd. She studied him, her mind no doubt whirring, and Conderie observed with pleasure how impressed she was.

"And what is your name, monsieur?"

"Conderie, Paul Conderie. You must call me Paul, of course."

"Oui, monsieur."

"Paul."

"Monsieur Paul."

"No, just Paul."

The girl managed to get the word out: "Paul."

Conderie laughed. "Such a lovely name when your mouth forms the word." And he studied her mouth.

The girl watched him shrewdly.

"Say," suggested Conderie, "why don't we have dinner together tonight? If you are free, that is?"

"Well, I don't know, monsieur—"

"Paul."

"Paul," said the girl.

"I thought we could go to the Tour d'Argent." This was one of the most expensive restaurants in Paris, and Conderie saw by her eyes that the girl realized it.

"Well—"

"It's settled then," said Conderie. The perfume he had bought earlier stood on the table, and he pushed the package across to her. "By the way, I'd like you to have this. I'll buy another one for the other girl in the morning."

But Conderie noted for the first time that her eyes were not as young as the rest of her face. Suddenly he began to feel uncertain about the evening. It would no doubt be a long one.

Conderie said: "I must make a call first."

Stepping to the bar's cash desk he bought a token, then descended to the telephone cabin outside the rest room. He had previously made a date to attend the opera with a party organized by the Marquise de Polignac, but he would break that now, though promising to attend the reception beginning at midnight.

In the restaurant later Conderie and the shopgirl sat by the window looking down on the sinuous black Seine, and across onto the floodlit roof of Notre Dame.

When the waiters made a fuss over Conderie, the girl was impressed. Conderie worked hard at being charming. The girl laughed, or pretended to laugh, several times.

Conderie ordered half a bottle of the '53 Lafite, and half a bottle of his own wine of the same vintage. "Now I ask you, my dear, which do you prefer?"

"Compared to yours, the Lafite tastes like Coca-Cola." To Conderie's ears a somewhat sacrilegious joke.

But they smiled at each other, pretending to be old, warm friends.

Over coffee, Conderie explained about the reception he must attend. The reception would follow a benefit performance at the opera. He confessed he hated opera, and had been glad to dine with her rather than go, but he would have to attend this reception, and hoped she would accompany him.

This was the real purpose of the entire charade up to now.

She protested, predictably, that she was not dressed for such a soiree.

They could run by her place first.

She hesitated.

He would wait downstairs for her.

Still she hesitated.

"Should be quite a few important people there," Conderie suggested. "Belmondo is coming, I expect."

Conderie had no idea who would be there. "You're a stunning-looking girl, and I'm anxious to be seen with you," he said. This was true, though he was glad to see from her smile that she didn't quite believe him.

"All right, then."

Conderie was relieved. He had put too much into this to fail now. She lived in an old building near the Place des Ternes.

"I'm sorry I can't invite you up, but there's only the one room."

One room. He did not want to go up there. It sounded too—sordid.

"Think nothing of it, my dear. I have some business calls to make."

"At this time of night?"

"I can see you don't know much about business."

Conderie was paying off the taxi in the street.

"Take your time, my dear. I shall make my calls in that café on the corner."

There were no calls. In the café Conderie ordered a tisane to calm his nerves, and a copy of *Paris-Turf.* Sipping his tea, he studied the form charts for tomorrow at Longchamps in the Bois; he would be there wearing his derby hat and his tweed shooting jacket, carrying his big binoculars. He knew he would bet Cessez le Feu, an old favorite of his, in the feature, and now he began to mark horses in the other races.

When he next looked up, thirty minutes had passed. He was in no hurry. He was relieved to be alone. The girl was handsome to look at, but a strain.

When she appeared outside, knocking on the glass to attract his attention, she wore a long black dress and gold earrings. Her jacket was some kind of fur, probably rabbit.

"You look lovely, my dear." It was true. It was hard to remember her as the shopgirl he had picked up only a few hours ago. Now he was confident that the evening would be a success.

The party was crowded. Conderie handed the girl a long-stemmed glass of Dom Pérignon champagne off a waiter's tray. They touched glasses and sipped.

The hostess came forward. After she and Conderie had embraced and gushed over each other, Conderie turned to introduce the girl. Too late he remembered he had forgotten her name.

"And this is Michele—Michele Durand. That isn't her real name. We're keeping it secret. Won't help her reputation to be seen with an old reprobate like me."

"Paul is so charming, mademoiselle."

"My name is Geneviève Lemothe," said the girl. "This is very nice champagne."

"She's stunning, Paul. How do you do it?"

Conderie beamed with pleasure.

Conderie had Geneviève's arm; they cruised, so he could sop up compliments. Other men drew him aside.

"She's a knockout, Paul, where'd you find her?"

"Would we know her name, Paul?"

"Here's a hint. It's well known in the perfume trade." Conderie, beaming, selected another glass of champagne off a passing tray.

Leaning close to his ear, the girl whispered: "I don't see Belmondo."

"I'll find out," promised Conderie.

An old friend grabbed his arm: "How do you keep coming up with these stunning-looking girls?"

"The bachelor life has its compensations," answered Conderie, gazing proudly across at his girl.

The girl was surrounded by admirers. Luckily she was impressed enough by the furnishings, the servants, the crowd to keep silent. From her silence her admirers would read poise and breeding. The secret was safe until she opened her mouth.

Conderie was surrounded by admirers too.

"I read about the sale of your château, old boy."

"Yes. In a way I hated to part with it, but the offer was stupendous and, the tax laws being what they are, my lawyers assured me I had no choice. I'll still control it, of course. What would France be without a Château Conderie?"

Conderie reclaimed his prize. Geneviève hung on his arm.

Someone called out to him: "Paul, your daughter phoned asking for you," and he nodded.

"Is that marquise I met a real marquise?" asked Geneviève, on his arm.

"Indeed she is."

"How old is your daughter?"

"In her early teens, my dear, early teens."

It was time to leave. The evening had gone perfectly, and he did not want to risk spoiling it now, risk more questions about his lost château, or the daughter he was unwilling to face, or the shopgirl who had been treated like a princess.

144

"Come along, my dear," he said, guiding her away. "We must be going."

"What about Belmondo?" she whispered.

"He's ill. He's not coming."

"Too bad," said the girl wistfully.

"Evidently came down with something late this afternoon."

Outside in the cab, Conderie sat back and his eyes involuntarily closed. He was tired.

The cab driver peered over the seat awaiting directions.

"I really am very tired," said the girl firmly.

"Yes, it's late," agreed Conderie equably. He gave the girl's address, and settled back in his seat. The diplomat was in his apartment anyway. A hotel was always embarrassing. In any case, he wasn't really in the mood.

In front of the girl's house, Conderie and the girl shook hands.

"Thank you for a lovely evening," she said.

"My pleasure."

Conderie did not get out of the cab.

"Well, goodnight."

"Goodnight, my dear. We must see each other again soon."

The cab motored off. Tomorrow Conderie would have to contact his daughter. He couldn't avoid her forever. Why was he so sure she would reproach him? And he'd have to think up a way to ease the Swedish diplomat out of his apartment. In addition, he had the racing tomorrow afternoon, and a dinner party with old friends tomorrow night. All in all, another busy day.

5

Stack stalled a month in New York while in Bordeaux legal formalities dragged on. He was hoping for some dramatic reprieve, not that the deal would break down, but that some other crisis would develop on the thirty-seventh floor that would cause him to be called in as savior; and cause someone else to take over the wine division. This reprieve did not happen. He stayed long enough for the consummation of a drug acquisition which he had initiated some months before, as if hoping that, in his absence, men would throw credit his way during however many years the drug acquisition made money. Vain and hopeless hope. He wound up his affairs, cleaning out his desk but keeping his apartment.

Most of another month he spent in Paris, still stalling. He needed a visa, a residency permit, permission to work. He had to fill out French income-tax forms. The functionaries he dealt with were in no great hurry and neither was he, preferring Paris to Bordeaux any day.

At last the chairman flew over for the long-delayed ceremonial signing of the sale agreement, which was to take place in the Maison du Vin in the center of Bordeaux. Stack had assured him that the sale of such a famous château would be front-page news around the world, provided the chairman himself attended. The chairman's presence was essential if The Company was to capitalize publicity-wise on its new acquisition.

The chairman, sounding over the transatlantic wire pleased at the idea of himself appearing on international TV, had agreed, and The Company's executive jet, after stopping at Paris to pick up Stack, had touched down at Bordeaux airport an hour ago. The chairman was accompanied by Johnston, by The Company's corporate vice-president for public relations, and by two lesser executives.

The press conference, Stack had determined, was to be preceded by a reception at which Château Conderie wine would be served to throngs of journalists. More Château Conderie would be served to these throngs after the ceremonial signing.

The chairman's delegation, Stack included, strode importantly into the reception hall about ten minutes early.

The chairman glanced around. "Where is everybody?"

"It's not time yet," answered Stack, concealing his sudden doubts. Press arrangements had been made by Stack from Paris.

Now, peering about the nearly empty room, Stack wished he had saddled this responsibility onto someone else. There was no throng of journalists present.

Stack brought over Conderie, who appeared nervous.

Poor bastard, thought Stack, he seems to have realized for the first time that he's lost his château.

The chairman looked unimpressed by Conderie.

"Where's the mayor?" demanded the chairman imperiously of Stack. "I want to meet him. He's talked of as possibly the next president of France, you know."

"Mayor?" inquired Conderie. "I'm afraid he's in Paris today."

The chairman shot a hard look at Stack.

Scattered about the reception hall were a number of local dignitaries, and now Stack watched Conderie lead the chairman through the room. The chairman was outwardly charming and effusive, but it seemed to Stack that he kept glancing about as if counting reporters.

As waiters began pouring out 1962 Château Conderie, Conderie himself seemed to become visibly more cheerful.

"There's an old saying in the wine business," Stack heard Conderie tell the chairman as trays of cheeses also moved through the hall, "when you're selling wine serve—"

Stack sidled up to Saar. "Find out how long we should wait before starting. Are other crews coming, or what?"

But Saar came back leading the journalist Fernand Front. "He wants to do an interview with you."

The chairman, Stack noted, kept glancing across at him, no doubt blaming Stack for the scant turnout. Stack said to Saar:

"No, the chairman is the one he should talk to."

Saar and Front conferred in French. "He says he never heard of the chairman. It's you he wants to interview."

Stack got angry. "Tell the seedy little bastard that it has to be the chairman."

Conderie drew Stack to one side. "I say, old man, shouldn't we start?"

"There aren't too many reporters here yet."

"Nonsense," said Conderie, now sounding cheerful and confident. "This is a marvelous turnout for Bordeaux." He gazed approvingly about the room.

"By New York standards it stinks."

"I wouldn't know about that, of course. But I find myself in a bit of a rush. I must catch a plane to Rome in less than an hour—I have a business matter there."

A horse race, more likely, Stack thought.

At last Stack ordered the press conference started. He placed Conderie, the chairman, and the president of the Bordeaux wine-growers association at a long table, and the few radio and TV mikes were arranged before them.

147

Conderie began with a short speech, which was evidently charming, for the room was filled with smiles as he spoke, and when he finished there were laughter and applause.

It was the chairman's turn. He began reading a prepared text. The reporters seemed interested in this speech, Stack thought, for about thirty seconds, after which the single TV reporter signaled his cameraman to cut, and most of the radio tape recorders were snapped audibly into the off position. Stack saw the chairman observe this—for an instant the rhythm of Warren's speech altered. Then he went on reading into dead mikes.

At this point Stack watched a strange thing happen—Conderie suddenly took over the press conference as if it were his own.

The chairman had ended his speech by asking for questions, and when there were none, Conderie interjected a joke which brought the spotlight back onto himself. As Stack watched aghast, a great many questions now were addressed solely to Conderie—who answered them all, apparently with wit and charm.

Stack saw that beside him, totally ignored, the chairman burned.

This is awful, Stack thought. But he saw no way to stop it.

The corporate vice-president for public relations leaned over to Stack. "Pass the word to the reporters to ask some questions of Warren."

Stack turned rather desperately to the reporter behind him. "Do you speak English?"

"Non, monsieur."

A second reporter leaned forward. "Maybe I help you, sir?"

For a moment Stack felt enormously relieved. "Do you speak English?"

"A little."

"Is there someone here from the *New York Times?*"

"Is myself, sir."

Jesus, Stack thought, the *Times* didn't even send a staff man. The newspapers hate The Company so much that even when we do something nice, like buying a wine château, they won't cover us.

Now Conderie, seeming to realize the chairman's discomfort, asked the reporters if they wouldn't like to ask any questions of Monsieur Warren Endicott. Conderie offered to translate. Conderie's attitude toward the chairman was rather too gracious. In fact, Stack saw, it was condescending.

The result of Conderie's offer was even worse, for the first question had to do only with the spelling of Warren's name.

While Stack squirmed Conderie began to spell it out for them, but the chairman interrupted harshly: "Tell them it's on the goddamn brochure we gave them."

The second question had to do with Warren's function. What exactly was his title, and what did he actually do?

Stack watched the beaming Conderie turn to Warren and translate the question. The chairman managed to contain himself. "Tell them that that information too is in the brochure. In both French and English, I believe."

Conderie, translating, must have added a joke, for everybody laughed.

After the three men at the table had signed the phony document several times for photographers, the press conference ended, and Stack watched Conderie move through the hall making jokes, shaking hands. He shook hands with everybody. A politician could not have done it better.

"That was a pretty bad show," murmured the vice-president for public relations to Stack.

Stack said nothing.

Both men moved forward to encounter the chairman.

"I didn't see anybody here from the *New York Times*," said the chairman tightly.

"Oh, yes," said Stack. "I talked to the guy myself."

"Why didn't he talk to me?"

"I thought he had," Stack lied. "Anyway he has your speech. Overall we had an excellent turnout, I thought. You'll be all over the news broadcasts tonight."

The chairman seemed to perk up at this remark. Stack had once believed that a man as intelligent and powerful as the chairman would see through flattery instantly, but at this moment Stack hoped he wouldn't.

"Yes, he has your fine speech," said the corporate vice-president for public relations.

"You did your usual fine job, Warren," said Johnston.

The chairman said: "Where's that fellow Conderie?"

"Gone, I'm afraid," answered Stack.

"I wanted to talk to him. He works for me now, doesn't he? He should have waited."

"I'll tell him when I see him."

Later Stack and the New York delegation drove out to look over

149

the château and property. The chairman was impatient. He kept glancing at his watch. He had reports to read on the executive jet, and meetings that evening in Munich, he said. In the chai he refused a taste of last year's wine and so, therefore, did everybody.

As he was about to climb back into his limousine, the chairman said: "I was a little disappointed in the press turnout."

"Were you?" answered Stack, with pretended confidence. "Given the press's hostility toward The Company, I thought it was excellent. I also think that your idea to start a wine division is exactly what the doctor ordered as far as combatting that hostility is concerned." It was the best Stack could do for the moment.

The chairman patted Stack on the back, stepped into the limousine and was gone.

Dust from the limousine's passage hung above the vines.

Stack turned and went into the empty château. He began glancing into rooms, but soon tired of it.

When he came downstairs his suitcases still stood in the hall.

In his absence a tennis court had been built at the edge of the meadow behind the château. Stack walked out onto this empty court and stood looking around. He was stuck here for good now. Here in Bordeaux.

I didn't deserve this, he thought.

He swung an imaginary racket, driving an imaginary ball back at an imaginary partner. He felt terribly alone.

Upstairs, distributing his few things among many drawers, he ceased feeling sorry for himself and began to get mad. He'd show these bastards. Whatever profits they might be expecting, he'd give them twice that much.

But when he slammed the closet door shut on his empty suitcases, his courage left him again. He thought he had never felt so lonely in his life.

He had ordered a suite of offices built in one of the chais, and a bilingual secretary installed there. Stack looked in on her later, asked her name, and ordered her to buy a certain tennis-ball machine. He gave her the particulars. It would throw a hundred tennis balls across the net at him, hard, without needing to be refilled.

The secretary was part of his new staff. The lawyer Saar had been moved to Bordeaux with his family; Saar was part of his staff. There was also an accountant, French, who knew his way through the glut of paperwork that choked the wine business.

150

In ensuing days Stack prowled his domain, learning how wine was made, cared for, stored, sold. He learned the names of the fieldhands and their wives. In his absence, he noted, the vine leaves had turned to gold, then fallen, and the wind still blew them up and down the alleys between the rows. Most of the vines were already pruned. Each hectare contained six thousand roots, which wine men spoke of as "feet," and now that the leaves had fallen Stack saw that each root had spread its dozen canes up along the wire like the fingers of a Japanese fan. Before the pruning season ended each root would get ten of its dozen fingers amputated.

While the men pruned, their wives trailed behind them collecting the cut branches. Many of the days were gray and cold. The men and women bicycled out to the distant fields and leaned their bikes against the stakes that supported the wires. The women wore heavy cloth coats, and many wore scarves tied around their red faces, and they bundled up the branches with their red hands, tied them, and carried them to the ends of the rows. Later the branches were forked up onto trucks, and from the trucks they were forked into a barn back close to the château. When the barn was full, no more bundles were brought in, and the branches were tossed onto bonfires at the edge of the fields. There were columns of smoke from burning vine branches rising into the air all over Margaux.

Stack had never seen vineyards in winter before. Foot after foot, row after row, field after field was pruned until at last nothing was left but the bare brown truncated stumps, the two arms as short and malformed as a dwarf's, each ending in single canes that seemed to be giving the finger to the sky. Rusty old wires were replaced. Sometimes when the new wires caught the sun just right an entire field would glitter like some gigantic spider web.

Each vineyard in turn was plowed, the tractor straddling a row of vines, dragging two shares behind it, sharp noses aerating the stony soil and throwing it up over the base of each root, covering the permanent scar of each root's graft against the coldest weather still to come.

Conderie had not been there all autumn, Stack discovered. During those weeks no one was in charge, and the work got done anyway, and was still being done. Stack found it hard to understand what he himself was doing there. They didn't need him. The soil did all the work anyway; one merely collaborated with it. There were no politics to play; a man's back was no more vulnerable than any other part of him. Farming was altogether too tame. Stack hated it here.

151

His ball machine came. He put on his tennis whites and went out and adjusted it. For the next hour it lashed balls across the net at him, and he hammered them back, driving them into first one corner, then the other. He was hitting the balls with all his strength. He began driving them at the machine as if to smash it. He hated this place. He had his machine, he didn't need anyone else. He would leave when his time was up, and not before. He was like a man in prison exercising furiously to make time pass.

But the next day he gave himself a lecture. He was earning more money than ever before in his life. Making great wine would perhaps prove interesting, who knew? He must give it a chance. He had been exiled perhaps, but the months would pass, and then however many years, and he had best begin to enjoy whatever there was to enjoy. Enjoy the absence of pressure. Enjoy the absence of fear. Enjoy the money. Enjoy the luxury.

He would fly to Italy, and come back driving a cobalt-blue Ferrari —why not? He could afford it. He could also afford to fly to New York for the weekend from time to time if it got too mortally dull here, though it wouldn't do to let the chairman see him there too often.

He was obliged to submit detailed reports once a month. The Company believed in and relied upon reports. The idea of reports from Bordeaux made Stack uneasy. He didn't know enough about the business yet. Hell, he didn't yet know the names of everybody who worked for him. Reports were like saluting in the army. No one noticed that you had sent one in, but men would have noticed instantly if you hadn't. Reports were also like fingerprints at the scene of a crime. Once the crime was discovered, it could be traced via those reports directly back to its perpetrator—you.

But he sent his first report. He described the pruning of the vines. He described the ripping-out of some thirty-five thousand very old vines, five percent of the total, and attempted to explain to hard-nosed businessmen why five percent of their income-producing terrain should now be allowed to lie fallow for five years. They may all have heard of crop rotation in school, but it was sure to sound to them like owning a store and leaving five percent of the counter space vacant.

Stack described the weather—it was best they come to understand quickly that their investment hung by its fingernails on sun and rain. He described how the new wine, eight weeks old and clumsy as a kitten, had been run off into casks, each cask filled to the bunghole, that bunghole covered only by a sort of heavy glass globe, the theory being that

152

the wine was breathing now, growing accustomed to its new life. Every other day men had to top up each cask, compensating for what had evaporated, filling each cask always with wine from the same vat in which it had been made. Every other day for a year this would be done.

The report described how some of the workmen, now that the weather had turned cold, had moved indoors to take down and in some cases rebuild the tractors, the stemming machine, the pumps. The report described how now, just before Christmas, it was time to *fine* last year's wine. For this purpose some six thousand fresh eggs had just been delivered to the château. They were stacked in one of the chais almost to the ceiling. Each cask of the fourteen-month-old wine would be racked for the fourth time—pumped out of its cask into a clean cask, leaving behind sediment and at the same time refreshing itself on the air it supposedly gulped in great drafts. The dirty cask would be rolled off and flushed out with live steam, then returned to receive the contents of still another barrel. As soon as all the wine had been racked, the whites of six or eight eggs would be stirred into each cask, and this froth would then fall to the bottom of the cask like a veil, taking most of the remaining sediment with it. The six thousand egg yolks would be given away to the workers.

After the fining was completed, Stack's report concluded, it would be time to bottle, crate, and ship out the wine from three harvests ago, wine that was now two years and two months old and already owned by the big shipping houses in the city.

Stack's report said nothing at this time about the role of the brokers. The chairman and Johnston were not going to like the idea of paying these men two percent commission when it came time to sell off the new crop. These brokers had sworn to an oath of office in civil ceremonies, but otherwise they acted for private gain, and hardly a drop of wine in all Bordeaux was sold without them. Like all agents or brokers, they contributed their contacts and their geniality and their knowledge. They structured deals. They knew which merchant was looking for which type of wine, and which grower had such wine to sell. They moved back and forth between buyer and seller. Once they closed the deal then it was they who were legally responsible that the wine was what the grower claimed it to be, and that the purchaser would come up with the money he had agreed to pay. As in every part of the wine trade the brokers usually handed their businesses down from father to son, and many of them also bore English names and boasted distant English blood.

153

In the very old days the brokers had served as guides and body-guards to potential wine buyers, for the Médoc was a wild place then; there was a wall along the river to keep pirates out. The brokers guaranteed both sound wine and a safe passage. In a different sense they still did.

Even the great château wines usually were sold through brokers, but New York was not going to like the idea. New York, Stack felt sure, was going to want to cut the brokerage commission out, and Stack did not yet know enough about the business and its traditions to advise on this one way or the other.

In the first few weeks several brokers stopped by to meet the new owner, Stack. A few tourists still stopped by also. Conderie took charge of the tourists.

"There's an old saying in the wine business: when you're selling wine serve cheese—" The words began to ring round and round in Stack's head like a too-stale song.

This seemed the only line of chatter the former owner knew, and the only work he volunteered to do.

One day Stack said to Conderie: "I was thinking of inviting all the other owners to a reception here as a means of meeting them."

"Reception?"

"I was thinking of hiring a pavilion tent. We could put it up on the lawn over there, maybe hire a small combo or something. You know, a kind of big cocktail party."

"Cocktail party, old man? Here in the Médoc?"

"Yes. We could hire some barmen. The invitation could say something like: 'The new American ownership of Château Conderie invites you to a housewarming'—you know, the French equivalent, something like that."

Conderie stared at him so blandly that Stack was becoming uncomfortable. "You don't seem to like the idea too much."

"When were you thinking of staging this—this cocktail party?" Conderie inquired.

"How about the Sunday after next?"

"I'm afraid I won't be able to be here that particular Sunday, but you go ahead with it if you like."

"What are you trying to tell me?"

"I'm afraid they wouldn't come, old man."

"They wouldn't come?"

"You don't invite them, you see. They invite you."

154

Stack said, not meeting Conderie's eyes: "I'd really like to meet some of them. I'd particularly like to meet any of the ones who might play tennis."

Conderie said nothing.

"There must be some of them who play tennis."

Conderie only nodded.

"How do I get to meet these people then?"

"It's a problem."

"Would you do me a favor?" Stack said. "Would you get me invited into some of their homes?"

"Let me work on it," promised Conderie.

"Thank you."

"It may take a little time."

"How much time?"

"Let me work on it."

Nothing happened.

Inside the great empty château the two men, it seemed to Stack, rattled around like billiard balls. After the initial coldness had worn off, they had begun to take dinner together—they were alone in the château after all. Stack found Conderie a charming dinner companion. Conderie was also a man always on the move to fulfill social engagements in one international playground or another. Sometimes Conderie was gone a week. When he was not there Stack felt lonelier than usual.

Stack joined a tennis club in Bordeaux, and the pro set him up matches with other members, who did not, however, invite Stack home with them to meet the wife and kids—not that he had any desire to meet anybody's wife or kids, he told himself.

But the French social circle was harder to crack than he had thought.

He invited two couples out to the château for lunch one Sunday; one came and the other declined. The man's wife did not speak English, and the lunch was a terrible strain on all three. These people were not even in the wine business, and the contact, such as it was, was no use to Stack at all.

Several times he invited one of the pros out to play with him, but this was rather too expensive to make the tennis much fun. In addition the décor—meaning principally the château itself—seemed to make the pro uncomfortable.

Stack appeared at receptions at the Maison du Vin in Bordeaux, where he shook many people's hands and contributed small talk in both

English and bad French. He offered to serve on several committees. Brokers and merchants seemed friendly to him. Owners were polite and no more.

Notified that his Ferrari was ready, Stack flew to Italy and came back driving it. He was as pleased with it as a little boy. He wanted to show it to somebody. He swirled to a stop in front of the château and leaned on the horn. Several of the vineyard workers crowded around. Women came out of the château.

They were full of admiration, but it was Conderie's approval Stack was looking for, he could not have said why.

The former owner came out of the château.

"I got a new car," said Stack proudly.

"So you did."

Conderie walked around it, but did not say anything.

"What do you think?" asked Stack.

"It's a bit theatrical, wouldn't you say?"

"No, I wouldn't say."

"I've never been one for these Italian cars. They tend toward the garish, I find."

"I see."

"I'm sure it cost a good bit of money."

"Yes, it did."

"There was quite a vogue for cars like this about ten years ago. Then people seemed to switch to more sober cars. The Mercedes is a good car, I find."

Stack walked completely around his new car. "I like it," he said.

"Yes," said Conderie, and went back into the château.

Two days passed before Stack again found pleasure in his new car.

One day Édouard Bozon stopped by the château. He was the only merchant, so far as Stack knew, who bought directly from the château. He seemed to have some long-standing personal arrangement with Conderie. Stack might decide to change this later, but needed time to look into it first. He stepped forward to shake hands with Bozon, whom he found a big hulking man with an aggressive voice and an aggressive manner.

"Good to see you again," Stack said.

"Oh, have we met before?"

"I came by your place late one night with Paul. I think he was trying to borrow money from you."

Bozon showed all his teeth. "Oh, yes," he said.

Bozon, Stack decided, had a mirthless smile. Stack watched him draw Conderie aside, and they talked quietly in French for a long time. The merchant then left hurriedly, and without tasting the new wine, which Stack thought strange.

"Who is this guy Bozon anyway?" Stack demanded.

"He's a shipper from Bordeaux," explained Conderie.

"I know that. But what is he to.you?"

"That goes back a ways and is too difficult to explain," said Conderie stiffly. "I shall have to go up to Paris tomorrow for a week or so."

Stack resolved to look into this Bozon matter, whatever it was. "Suit yourself," he told Conderie.

Stack went out onto the tennis court, plugged in the machine, and started hammering balls across the net. After about twenty balls, the machine turned into the chairman before his eyes, and he began slashing backhand volleys at it—the kind that tied the chairman in knots. He found himself shouting, "Your backhand stinks, Warren!" "How'd you like that one, Warren?"

When he realized what he was doing, Stack thought: I'm going to go crazy before I get out of this place.

Though the machine was still throwing balls past him, he had stopped swinging. Leaving the court, he walked up to the château. Behind him the machine was still popping balls. Like anger, or even love, it would shut itself off when it was empty.

6

Each time any among Bordeaux's three thousand châteaux changed hands, whether big château or small, papers on the sale reached the desk of Alexandre Dupont at Fraud Brigade headquarters at 37 Rue Labottière. Each of the fifteen agents assigned to the Bordeaux region had his own techniques, and this was one of Dupont's: he liked to go out and chat with new owners.

Often the new owners these days were not wine people, and did not know the Fraud Brigade existed. The appearance of Agent Dupont could well shock them into taking the wine laws seriously. Dupont's sudden appearance—he hoped so anyway—might stop dishonest behavior before it started.

Some of the châteaux, the problem ones, changed hands many times. Dupont, stepping out of his car, knew the problems better than the new owners did, and he would chat with them, apparently endlessly, appraising their knowledge, energy, and chances, hardly considering possible criminal aspects at all.

Other times the new owners were celebrated men, persons Dupont could never have hoped to meet otherwise.

Dupont preferred these chats to serious investigations. He did not like responsibility. He regretted even the heavy fines he sometimes brought down on owners. Compared with his own salary, such fines seemed enormous, even though he knew most owners could afford them. Most fines weren't even equal to profits that the owner had made through quick dealing.

Major investigations were an ordeal for Dupont. The Fraud Brigade had no manpower. Major investigations were rare, and performed by others under his direction. He was unhappy when commanding gendarmes and detectives he did not know and who perhaps would find him dull or ineffectual.

He much preferred winter visits such as today's. He had a list of six châteaux. Probably he would not see them all today. Such visits took time.

His first stop was in the Premières Côtes de Bordeaux, an unfashionable region of low-priced wine across the river. A Japanese syndicate had just bought a property there, paying millions for it, an outlandish sum, a sum so vast that it had no meaning to Alexandre Dupont, who did not even own a car—the small Renault he was driving today belonged to the service.

As he stepped out into the court in front of the aging sheds, the dust rising up to cover his shoes, two middle-aged Japanese men came forward, all grinning teeth, and shook hands with him.

"Agent Alexandre Dupont de la Brigade de la Répression des Fraudes, at your service," declaimed Dupont. He hoped to intimidate people, not with himself, but with the weight of the law.

But Dupont realized from the unchanging grins that the Japanese gentlemen understood no French. They jabbered at each other in their own language. This was the first time Dupont had ever heard Japanese

158

spoken. It sounded odd to him, like the high-pitched chattering of birds, and he marveled at it, even though it was no more incomprehensible to him than, say, English.

One of the men held up a forefinger—Dupont should wait—and ran off toward the chai. He came back leading a Frenchman.

"Alexandre Dupont de la Brigade de la Répression des Fraudes," announced Dupont, shaking hands with the Frenchman.

"Enchanté, monsieur." The Frenchman, after giving his name, explained that he was the new régisseur of the property. The two Japanese were its managing directors.

"How do you communicate with them?" inquired Dupont. "Do you speak Japanese?"

"No. They are supposed to bring another Jap in here in a day or two who speaks French."

"It's said they paid a fortune for this place," suggested Dupont conversationally.

The Frenchman pulled out a half-crushed package of Gauloises, and lit himself a cigarette. "I think they plan to ship all their wine back to Japan. Genuine French wine. Apparently they can sell it at a good price there."

When he got back to his car Dupont would make a note of this idea. Also of any other details he might pick up. He never took notes while "chatting" with people lest the visit seem too official.

Now Dupont was given a tour of the sheds like any tourist. He tasted last year's wine. He did not consider himself an expert on wines. Still, it tasted quite ordinary. No Frenchman would pay a high price for this wine, but Japanese people might. Dupont knew nothing about Japanese people.

At the time of the sale the income-tax men had gone over the books thoroughly and had inventoried the stock. These things were not Dupont's concern. He had come out here to get a feel for the new owners, and to nose around. To see if anything struck him as odd or false.

In a reception room at the end of one of the sheds one of the Japanese indicated that Dupont should sign their guest book. They opened it for him, and he saw the names of only three visitors so far. This was not the type of place to attract many visitors. Did the Japanese gentlemen imagine they had bought Château Haut Brion, Dupont wondered? He was not a tourist and would not sign. He closed the book, nodded his head, smiling, and said "Merci beaucoup" several times.

159

Just then he noticed empty bottles high up on ornamental shelves close to the ceiling. They were back-lighted by concealed spotlights. Their labels extended for three-quarters the length of each bottle. The top half was printed in French, the bottom half in Japanese.

Exactly what information a wine label must contain and what additional information it might contain were stipulated by law. The law was strict. It stipulated the exact sizes of the lettering that each key word must bear in relation to other key words.

The French part of the label looked okay to Dupont.

He had no idea whether the label's Japanese characters conformed or not. This would have to be checked into.

He asked for a copy of the label, and the Frenchman went to fetch him one. The Frenchman all along had been neither more nor less polite than he had to be. He had been correct. Dupont would note as much in his notebook later. He put the label in his pocket.

The two Japanese gentlemen escorted Dupont back to his car, where Dupont said formally: "Thank you for your hospitality."

As Dupont motored away, they stood in the gateway, grinning, waving after him.

The next name on Dupont's list was Château Cracheau. He had to turn off the main road and onto a secondary road which started out asphalt but became dirt. He lost his way once, and had to go back and start again. He remembered having been out here once some years before. A one-legged World War I veteran had the place. He had been old even then. Now the château had changed hands; Dupont supposed the old man must have died.

At last he could see the farmhouse—you couldn't call it a château —part way up the slope. He drove up there, parked, and got out of his car.

Two men came out of the shed. They looked tough. "Who are you?" one demanded.

"Agent Alexandre Dupont de la Brigade de la Répression des Fraudes."

Did sudden fear flash across one man's face? Dupont assured himself he was imagining things.

"Have we done something wrong?" the man asked in a milder voice.

"Not at all. Just routine. I always like to drop by when a château changes hands."

160

Dupont shook hands with the second man too: "Alexandre Dupont."

"Giuseppe Ferraro."

Dupont realized that the second man was an Italian. He felt a vague annoyance. All these new owners were foreigners.

"The Italian is just a handyman," the first man explained.

Dupont took out a pack of cigarettes. "Smoke?" he offered.

"No." The Frenchman waited. He looked wary.

"Did the old man die?" inquired Dupont conversationally.

"Old man? What old man?"

"The old man with the wooden leg who used to have this place."

The Frenchman hesitated, then said, "I didn't know about any old man."

"You're not the owner?"

"The owner's in Paris."

"Well," said Dupont, "I'm sorry to miss him. I like to talk to new owners. Then, if anything happens, we know each other."

"What could happen?"

Dupont gave a mild smile. "Probably nothing, I'm sure."

"That's right, nothing."

Dupont leaned back against the fender of his Renault, puffing nervously on his cigarette. He felt physically intimidated by the two men. They were bigger and a good deal younger than he was. He was not armed. He did not like trouble. This place was nothing to him. He had no suspicions to check out. It was really just a social call, and these men did not want to be sociable.

"What are your plans for the place?" he asked conversationally.

"Plans?"

"Are you the régisseur? Are you going to run the place or what?"

"Ask the boss."

"You say he's in Paris?"

"That's right."

Dupont pushed his rump away from the car. He resolved he was not going to be pushed around. "Do you mind if I look the place over?"

The man said nothing. Dupont strolled toward the shed. The door was ajar. He stuck his head inside, eyes squinting after the bright sunlight. There was very little light in there. Nonetheless, he made out two gleaming new stainless-steel vats. This surprised him. Such vats cost real money.

161

"The old man had concrete vats," Dupont said conversationally.

The man behind him said nothing.

"I guess you took the concrete vats out."

The Frenchman's eyes were hard. "What does it look like?"

Dupont nodded, as if impressed with the wisdom of this remark. He walked all the way into the chai. To his right, pushed into the corner, was a bottling machine. This surprised him too. The old man had always sold his wine in bulk, Dupont believed.

"I guess you're going to bottle your own wine from now on, eh?"

He expected another hard answer from the Frenchman, but instead the fellow said grudgingly, "Put the words 'Chateau Bottling' on the label, and you can sell the bottle for a few francs more."

"Good idea," said Dupont. When he came out of the chai the sun felt hot. He almost hurried back to his car. The man followed him all the way. Dupont opened his car door.

"Here," Dupont said, handing the man his card. "If you have any need of me, this is my phone number."

The man put the card in his pocket. He said nothing.

"And you're the manager?" said Dupont.

"That's right."

"I don't think you gave me your name."

"Claude Maurice."

Dupont drove out of there. But half a mile down the road, out of sight of the château, he pulled over and got his notebook out. He wrote down the date, the time of day, the name and location of the château. He wrote the word "Régisseur," but then couldn't remember if the régisseur's name was Maurice Claude or Claude Maurice. He put a question mark after the name and drew a circle around the question mark.

The visit had been thoroughly unpleasant. In itself this meant nothing. A good many people were thoroughly unpleasant to Dupont, even when he gave them no cause to be. A good many people hated anyone who represented the law. They didn't need an excuse. The hatred was just there.

On the next line Dupont wrote: "Two new stainless-steel vats." He guessed at the approximate capacity and put it down: "Perhaps 4,000 liters each." On the next line he wrote the words "Bottling machine."

He paused to wonder about such expensive vats. A place like this didn't need such vats. Of course it was possible the new owner had bought or leased one or more of the neighboring properties as well,

162

intending to make all the wine here. Dupont might check into it. The idea of château bottling the wine was a good one, if you could afford it.

Dupont was annoyed at himself for having felt intimidated up there, and he was annoyed at himself now for imagining that he had noted anything suspicious. What was suspicious? Nothing, that's what. There had been a lot of loose dirt around. Piles of loose dirt. Someone had been digging. What was wrong with that? Obviously they were redoing the place.

And no sign of any woman. It was hard to imagine two men living way out here with no women.

Dupont pulled his notebook out of his side pocket once again and wrote on the page devoted to Château Cracheau: "Much loose dirt lying about." He thought a minute then added: "No sign of women." Then he shrugged and rammed the notebook back in his pocket. The notebook dated back almost sixteen months and contained entries relating to dozens of châteaux that Dupont had visited, made notes about, and then forgotten.

He drove north toward Blaye, where the ferry was, for his next château was on the Médoc side of the river, but when he reached the dock the ferry was just pulling out into the water. So he settled down in a restaurant that overlooked the river and ordered a nice lunch.

By the time he had finished his coffee the ferry had come back. Dupont paid his bill, went outside, belched, and drove his car onto the ferry.

About that time, the shipper Bozon strode aggressively into a café opposite the Bordeaux railroad station. The café was crowded. Bozon glanced around, found his man, and strode through to the back of the café.

"I'm a busy man," Bozon snapped. "Make it fast."

"We had a visitor," said Claude Maurice, handing Bozon a business card.

"An elderly man," Bozon announced, looking up from Dupont's business card. "A quiet, meek little guy. I know him. So what?"

"He didn't seem meek to me. Look where he's from."

Though furious, Bozon decided to calm Maurice. Bozon's face broke into a mirthless smile and he clapped Maurice hard on the shoulder. "A routine visit from a meek little functionary," Bozon asserted, "and you panic. I thought you were a man with balls, but you're not."

"How do you know it was routine?"

"What did he do? Did he even go inside the chai?"

163

"He looked in the door."

"If you've lost your nerve I'll get someone else."

"What made him go out there at all? That's what I want to know."

"Routine. They drive by a place, those fellows, and they stop and ask a few questions. Makes them feel important. Nothing to worry about."

"Nothing for you to worry about, maybe. But I'm the registered owner of that place."

"Nobody's the registered owner," snapped Bozon. "The registered owner is a man that doesn't exist."

"I signed the papers."

"If you followed instructions," Bozon said sharply, "you presented a false identity card, you were wearing a beard at the time, and you made a false signature that you had practiced over and over again for two days. At least that's the way I instructed you to do it, and the way you assured me you did do it."

"You don't have to get mad."

"Nothing can go wrong, I assure you," Bozon said more calmly. "I've thought of everything."

"The Italian is worried, too," said Maurice. "It turns out he's been in jail before for this kind of thing. I didn't know that."

"How do you think I found him?" said Bozon impatiently.

"How did you find him?"

Bozon ignored the question. "He's completely trustworthy, I assure you. He's got more to lose than anyone. You can trust him."

"What about my false identity card."

"I destroyed it," lied Bozon. "Nothing connects you to the sale except a false signature, and the solicitor's memory of a man with a beard."

The waiter came over. "Bring me a Pernod," ordered Bozon. "And bring my friend some cognac for—" Bozon gave his hard, mirthless laugh—"for his nerves."

The waiter went away. The other man said: "I'm glad you think it's so funny."

"I don't think it's funny. I just think you're exaggerating. I assure you, you have nothing to worry about."

"What about the three Spaniards who did all the digging?"

"All right, I'll arrange for the police to receive a call about those Spaniards. They'll be picked up and deported. They'll be gone by to-morrow."

164

The waiter set the drinks down on the table. When he was gone, Maurice said, "The less that's left to chance, the better I like it."

"Relax. You haven't even done anything yet."

"I know it. That's why I got so upset. It looked like they were on to us before we even started."

"A routine visit, that's all it was."

"And the stuff is coming in Thursday night?"

"That's right. Thursday night you go into business."

Bozon drained his Pernod, put money down on the table, and stood up.

"You won't forget about the Spaniards?"

"I won't forget," snapped Bozon.

Leaving the bar, Bozon programmed his scheme through his mind. There were no loopholes. The visit of Dupont could only have been an accident. At the merest suspicion of a second such "accident" Bozon would sacrifice Maurice, the Italian, and the scheme itself. Until then it would go forward.

On the way back to his office Bozon stepped into another bar, where he bought a token and telephoned the immigration police. He denounced the three Spanish families by name, giving the address of the building in which they lived. He said he knew them to be illegal immigrants, and that because of them and their brats the hallways were full of filth. He said he was a tenant in the same building, refused to give his name, and hung up. The police would know what to do. The menial laborers of France were mostly Spaniards these days, and those who had entered the country illegally had no rights.

Only one of the three Spanish families had a phone. Bozon waited several hours, then dialed this number. The voice of a Frenchman came on the line: "This is the police, monsieur. Who is calling?"

Bozon hung up.

The three laborers, their wives, and their multiple children would spend tonight at the commissariat, Bozon believed, and tomorrow would be shipped back across the border under guard. They would be allowed to take only what they could carry. All the rest—beds and furniture, cooking gear, food, TV set, toys (they had been here a number of years)—would be sold at public auction, and the chances of any proceeds reaching them back in Spain were slim.

They would not know who had denounced them, of course.

They didn't know anything anyway. They had dug a hole without knowing what for. Maurice and the Italian had done the rest. At the commissariat the wives and kids would cry most of the night. This was no concern of Bozon's. Business was business, and the Spaniards should not have entered France illegally in the first place.

Later that same afternoon Alexandre Dupont drove into the court formed by the aging sheds at Château Conderie. There was no one about. Dupont glanced into one of the sheds, found a workman there, and sent him in search of the patron.

Dupont peered down at his dusty shoes. Glancing around, he quickly rubbed first one, then the other against his pants legs.

Two men came under the arch into the courtyard. Dupont recognized Paul Conderie and shook hands with him.

"Charlie Stack," said the second man. He looked a big, aggressive man, and he had a hard, heavy grip.

"You must be the new owner," suggested Dupont to Stack.

Conderie translated.

When Stack grinned, all his teeth showed. He said to Conderie in English: "Just translate the hard lines. I can handle the easy ones myself."

"What did he say?" asked Dupont in French.

"He welcomed you to Château Conderie," said Conderie.

"Very good," said Stack to Conderie, still grinning.

"Very good," repeated Dupont in English, adding in French: "I know that phrase: Very good."

"This is too comical for words," said Charlie Stack in English.

"What did he say?" asked Dupont.

"He asked in what way we can help you," replied Conderie in French.

Nodding his head, Dupont offered his business card to Charles Stack, saying: "Alexandre Dupont de la Brigade de la Répression des Fraudes, at your service."

Stack studied the card a minute, then asked Conderie in English: "How important is this guy?"

"It depends how much evidence he has against you."

"I see."

"He's been out here before. We give him a look around and a bottle of wine and send him on his way."

Dupont kept looking from one face to the other. It annoyed him when people spoke foreign languages in his presence. Furthermore, his stomach suddenly felt distinctly uncomfortable. That rabbit stew had not gone down well at all.

166

"Right this way, inspector," said Conderie, ushering him toward the chai.

"Not inspector, monsieur, at least not yet," protested Dupont.

"If you're not an inspector, you ought to be, a man with dedication like yours," commented Conderie blandly, and they entered the first-year aging shed. The new owner, tagging along, wore a grin as broad as the two Japanese gentlemen had worn this morning, no different, and to Dupont this owner's language was just as incomprehensible. Dupont was irritated.

Conderie plunged his pipette into the nearest cask of wine, extracted it, and raised his thumb. Wine ran out of the pipette into the glass he held in the other hand.

"Have a piece of cheese, inspector," suggested Conderie, handing over the glass. "You know the old saying in the wine business—"

"You don't need me," said the bored Stack in English. "I'll wait outside."

"When you're selling wine, serve cheese," finished Dupont politely.

When Dupont and Conderie came out of the sheds Stack was standing in the sunlight in the dust.

"Does he speak French at all?" asked Dupont.

"A little, inspector, a little," Conderie said.

In English, Stack said to Conderie: "I had them stick a case in the trunk of his car. Is that all right?"

"How old?"

"Nineteen sixty-two vintage."

"Bit of a waste, that. These government fellows never appreciate good wine."

Stack smiled. "I wanted to give him something to remember me by."

Dupont knew they were talking about him. Mocking him, no doubt. A government functionary could not really hope for better from rich owners. Still, it was extremely irritating.

Two kilometers down the road Dupont pulled off and got his notebook out. He wrote down the name of the château and the place and time of his visit. He noted the names of Conderie and Stack and added one phrase: "Nothing of significance noted."

On an impulse, he got out, walked around his car and opened the trunk. The wooden case of Château Conderie wine stared up at him. A single bottle he might accept with good grace, but a case in these days

167

of high prices was excessive. It was almost bribery. He ought to bring that American up on charges.

Unfortunately the American would be defended by high-priced lawyers, the case would fall through, and Alexandre Dupont would get reprimanded.

Dupont ran his fingertips over the rough wood of the case. Agents of the Fraud Brigade were not allowed to accept gifts, but Dupont didn't see what he could do with this gift now except accept it. It was worth plenty, and he wished he could sell it, but he couldn't take the chance. He and his wife would have to drink it. He doubted they would enjoy it. It was too valuable. They would be too conscious of how much each mouthful was worth. It would be like swallowing money.

When he got to work the next morning his chief asked how the day had gone, and all his irritation came back.

"All the new owners are foreigners," Dupont grumbled in his mild way. "I don't understand it. Americans, Italians, Japs. The foreigners are taking us over. Before long, France, I fear, won't be France."

The chief laughed and patted him on the shoulder. Alexandre Dupont sat at his desk and began to brood. Then he got his notebook out and stared at yesterday's notes. That man Stack had exuded power. The two Japanese gentlemen in their way had exuded power also. Dupont did not understand who these people were, or exactly what their power might be, but he was mildly afraid of them. People got annoyed at you, people made trouble for you. Dupont had learned this the hard way over the last thirty years.

But that fellow out at Château Cracheau, that pseudo tough guy, he exuded no power at all. He was worried about something. Dupont had no idea what. And Dupont had no idea who he was.

Dupont also had nothing planned for this morning. He felt at loose ends. So he put a call through to the solicitor who had handled the sale of Château Cracheau.

"Just a routine call, you understand, maître. But I was wondering about old man Cracheau selling his château. You know the old man I mean. The old man with the wooden leg."

"The sale was handled by the son-in-law. The son-in-law came in here with power of attorney."

"Where is the old man? Is he dead?"

"According to the papers, he was adjudged incompetent and committed and that's why the son-in-law was selling the place."

"Committed where?"

168

The solicitor gave Dupont a name. "It's an old man's home, as I understand it. It's supposed to be a nice place, as those places go."

"The new owner, this man Aubervilliers," Dupont asked, reading the name off the official papers, "what kind of man was he?"

"A man of about thirty-five, as I remember. Wore a beard. Lived in Paris, according to his papers."

Aubervilliers's Paris address was on Dupont's copy of the document.

"Aubervilliers was an odd kind of man," the solicitor added. "Kind of a tough guy. He didn't seem to me the kind of man that should be buying a wine property. But you never know, these days, do you?"

After hanging up, Dupont sat drumming his ballpoint pen on the desk. An hour later he sent a communication through to the Paris office, asking them to make a discreet background inquiry on this Jean Marc Aubervilliers, who was to be found at the following address.

7

Françoise, home during the Christmas holidays, stepped out of the cold, bright sunlight into the gloom of the chai of the first-year wine. For a moment she could not see.

"You must be old Jean's daughter," said a voice beside her in awkward French.

Françoise peered up at him: the new owner. The man her father was so in awe of.

"Charlie Stack," the man said.

Françoise was trying to see him. All she could see was white teeth. "Enchantée," she said, and offered her hand. He loomed up next to her in the gloom. A big man with a big hand. She had done what any well-schooled French girl would have done. Her hand had shot out. But he held on to it rather a long time.

"Vous êtes Françoise, n'est-ce pas?" he said. "I have noticed you here and there," he added, still in French.

Good manners obliged Françoise to answer in the language in which she was addressed. "Je suis Françoise, monsieur," she agreed.

"Vous êtes très jolie," said Stack. "I have noticed you here and there."

If she switched to English, he might be insulted. Perhaps he was even proud of his French, though in it he was making such a fool of himself.

Françoise said: "Perhaps you would prefer to speak English."

Stack's face immediately brightened, and he gave a laugh. "Am I that bad in French?"

Françoise had not expected Stack to be charming. Stack's charm had not come through her father's reports. Her father seemed in awe of Stack, principally because Stack had come all the way from America. Her father found it hard to believe that places so far away really existed.

To her father Stack was a "grand monsieur."

"No," lied Françoise with a smile, "your French is not bad at all."

"How is it that you speak English?" he wanted to know next.

"I went to school in England for a little while."

"How long?"

"Two years."

"Where did you go?"

Was he really interested in knowing about her? "It's a school you probably never heard of."

"Tell me."

Françoise gave the name, adding: "Aline went there too."

Stack was nodding at her. "That's a very good school."

"You've heard of it?"

"Of course."

Françoise suspected that he was lying. Nonetheless, his interest was flattering.

"And what did you learn there?"

"English, sort of."

"You speak English with a charming accent."

The smile faded from Françoise's face. "When I first came back to France I spoke English like a proper English girl," she said. "Now—"

If she had been able to keep her English pure, this might have made a difference somewhere someday. But with lack of practice her French accent had come back. A lot of things had gone wrong in her life already and she was only nineteen.

They stood there in the gloomy chai.

Françoise thought: That takes care of language as a topic of conversation. Did they have any others?

"Do you come from the wine country of California?" asked Françoise.

"Of course not."

"Oh."

"I'm from New York."

"You made wine in New York?"

"No. I'm a businessman.

"Oh."

"A good businessman," asserted Charlie Stack, "can handle any business anywhere in the world."

Françoise was regaining control of her emotions. "I came in here looking for my father," she said.

This chai was more than two hundred feet long. Rows of casks of last autumn's wine stretched away from them toward geometric infinity.

Nearby two men were racking this wine. As each barrel was emptied, its wine pumped into a clean barrel, one of the two men would roll it out of the shed into a room where it would be rinsed out with live steam. Then the pumping process would be repeated with the next cask in the row.

"I find winemaking so fascinating," said Charlie Stack.

"They're racking the wine," Françoise said.

"Fascinating."

"They do it to each cask four times a year for two years," Françoise explained. She didn't know how much he knew about winemaking.

"Your father explained it to me."

"And you find that fascinating?"

Stack laughed. His laughter was so engaging that Françoise laughed too.

"It's all in the point of view, I guess," Stack said. "But it seems so —normal. It's so unthreatening. People here seem to move at the same pace nature moves. No one is trying to knife anyone in the back."

Françoise was unable to determine the meaning of these remarks.

"Look out," Stack said, grabbing her arm and pulling her backward. He also had pulled her against his body.

One of the workmen was rolling a barrel past them, not very close. Stack had both Françoise's arms. He was holding her against his body, safe from nonexistent danger.

171

Françoise was surprised. She was trying to figure everything out on too few clues.

"I have to go find my father," she said.

Stack eyed her up and down. She was wearing shoes, blue jeans, a windbreaker. Her clothes certainly did not display her figure, so what was he staring at? He could see her face framed by her dark hair, and her hands, and her white ankles, for she was wearing no socks, and that's all.

Françoise was confused. Before Stack could notice she said: "It really stinks in here, doesn't it?"

Both of them sniffed the odor of scores of years of spilled wine.

It seemed to Françoise that she could still feel his fingers through the cloth of her jacket, though he stood now two yards away. "Well, I've got to go," she said hurriedly.

Outside in the courtyard the sunlight made her blink her eyes. The air was cold and clear. Across was another chai. As she stepped into its humid gloom, her nostrils were once again assailed by the rank odor of spilled wine.

She found her father beating the whites of six eggs in a wooden bowl. He was using a brush made of twigs. The twig brush stirred the whites to a froth. Now a workman emptied half a pipette of wine into her father's bowl. He whisked the twigs around until the froth turned blue, then dumped the contents of the bowl into the bunghole of the nearest cask. Her father's helper inserted the prongs of the stirring machine, and Françoise listened to the hum of the motor. The froth was being dispersed throughout the wine.

The door behind Françoise opened. As sudden sunlight stabbed in, Françoise turned. It was Charlie Stack. Françoise assumed that he had followed her. Now she was no longer confused.

"Do you find this process of fining the wine fascinating too?" Françoise asked him.

He was grinning at her. She was conscious of his big teeth.

"Oh, yes."

Her father was cracking and opening eggs with one hand, leaking the whites into his wooden bowl. He was really quite deft, Françoise thought.

Turning, Gorr dumped the leftover yolks into a tub already half full of viscous yellow eyes, then tossed the empty shell into the crate the eggs had originally come in. There were rows and rows of unopened

172

egg crates stacked against the wall.

"Some of the châteaux use chemicals for this," Gorr explained to Stack. "But here at Château Conderie we do it the traditional way with egg whites."

"Ah, oui," Stack said.

"It costs us about six thousand eggs a year."

"You understand what he says?" Françoise asked Stack.

"Ah, oui."

Françoise thought that he didn't, but wasn't sure.

"When the egg whites will have fallen through the wine," Françoise explained in English, "the sediment at the bottom of each cask will be four to five inches thick."

"I ought to hire you as interpreter," Stack said, smiling. "I ought to put you on the payroll."

This only reminded Françoise of how little money she had. She wished she could find some way to earn a little money.

Gorr's twig brush whisked more egg whites to a froth. Françoise realized her father was showing off for Stack, and was annoyed at him.

"Isn't it wonderful the way monsieur takes an interest?" said Gorr to his daughter.

Françoise flinched. Whether or not Stack understood the words, he would recognize obsequiousness when he saw it.

The froth had been thoroughly stirred inside the first cask, and the machine withdrawn. Her father's helper now drove a wooden bung into the hole by hammer, rolled the cask tight against the others, bunghole to the side, and chocked it there.

"That bung is leaking slightly," noted Stack in English.

"It will swell very quickly," said Françoise. "It will be airtight before you know it."

Stack was standing too close to her, and she was afraid her father would notice. She was conscious of the weight of Stack's body. She felt like an animal being stalked, and she did not like it.

Her father, she saw, had noticed nothing.

Though she stepped away from Stack, he quickly moved close again.

In French her father said obsequiously: "Monsieur learns very fast. We'll make a winemaker out of monsieur in no time. Right, monsieur?"

"Ah oui, ah oui," said Charlie Stack.

Her father, deftly, rapidly, was whisking up a new batch of egg whites.

"Are there famous recipes with leftover egg yolks here?" Stack asked Françoise.

"There aren't any at all. Some people make rich sauces. Most just live on omelets. The French peasant is not imaginative enough to think up any gastronomic dishes. The Médoc, you may have noted, is not one of the gastronomic centers of France."

"You're right," said Charlie Stack, and she looked up into what she saw as a predatory grin.

Françoise said to her father in French: "Papa, I have some errands in the village. I need the keys to the truck."

Balancing the wooden bowl on a cask, her father fished out keys.

"If you need to borrow a car," Stack offered, "take mine." He held out the keys to the Ferrari.

She stared at Stack's keys.

"Take my Ferrari."

All the kids would see her at the wheel of a Ferrari. Those who didn't see her would hear about it. People would come out of their houses. They'd collect from all over.

Françoise's mouth got hard. "No thank you, monsieur."

"Sure. Go ahead."

The keys dangled before her eyes.

Her face had become sulky. "Thank you, but I prefer the truck."

"I'll drive you down if you like."

She stared at him, saying nothing. At last he put his keys away.

"How dense of me," Stack said. "You're probably meeting a boy friend down there."

Françoise said nothing.

"A girl like you probably has lots of boy friends."

Françoise said nothing.

Her father, understanding no English, swirled his twig brush around the wooden bowl. "Did you ever think how many eggs the Médoc imports each year at this time?" he asked cheerfully. "If you multiplied the number of châteaux by six eggs per cask—it probably goes into the millions. Of course monsieur is better at figures than I am."

"Ah, oui," said Charlie Stack.

Françoise turned and left the chai.

Her truck bounded down the dirt lane toward the road. In Margaux she made purchases of groceries for the house, and in the pharmacy for

174

herself. After that she felt at loose ends. She went to the post office and put in a telephone call to her boy friend, who had gone home to Nice for the holidays. But when, after a short wait, the operator told her there was a forty-five-minute delay for Nice, Françoise canceled the call.

A former school friend named Carmen Rivière worked behind the cash desk at the butcher shop. Françoise looked in there but a crowd of women waited between her and Carmen. So Françoise went to sit in Pierre Jacot's father's café, where she sipped an apéritif. Pierre Jacot came down from upstairs and sat with her. He had nothing to say, and Françoise was not in the mood to talk to him anyway. She tried to pay for the apéritif, but Pierre Jacot told the barman not to take her money.

Later Françoise prepared lunch for her father. When would Christmas come? How these vacation days dragged. In summer you could usually get a gang of kids and drive down to the river, or drive all the way across the Médoc to the beach. But it was not summer now.

After dinner Françoise decided to take a bath. She hated the tub, which was half sized, for her father had decided to economize when the bathroom was installed. The floor of the tub was in two levels. One didn't stretch out, one sat up in it. The water did not come up to her breasts. Since the hot-water heater operated only as the water ran through it, you had to fill the tub slowly in order for the incoming water to be hot enough. Meaning that by the time the water reached optimum level it was already cooling.

Françoise put on a tight dress with a short skirt. It was the only dress of this kind she had. In a real city she might have worn such a dress to a fancy restaurant or a night club. In Margaux one wore such a dress only to a wedding or a funeral. She stood in front of her mirror darkening her eyebrows, penciling in eye shadow. Her lips were rather red naturally, she thought. She put on a lipstick with hardly any color, but it made her lips glisten.

She had no real jewelry, but some of her costume jewelry was rather nice. She put on earrings and pinned a matching brooch below her left shoulder.

She had no idea why she was getting all dressed up. Her thoughts had gone no further than the pleasure of doing it. Once finished, probably she would undress and go to bed.

She gazed at herself in the mirror. She was used to wearing woolen shirts and big sweaters. She looked peculiar to herself. What she really thought she looked was old-fashioned.

She had a satin evening bag. She emptied the contents of her leather bag into the satin bag. The satin bag had a rhinestone clasp, which she snapped shut.

In the other room she could hear her father padding about in his stocking feet. She decided to display herself to her father. But, because she wasn't used to wearing high heels either, she tripped over the door sill, dropped her handbag, and nearly went sprawling. Her father caught her.

"Don't you look nice?" he remarked. He beamed with pleasure.

Françoise gazed at him.

"Who are you going out with tonight?"

"No one. I just felt like dressing up."

Neither had yet glanced down at the contents of the handbag sprayed across the floor, but Françoise feared the worst.

She dived for her belongings, trying to sweep them unseen back into the handbag. Some of what she was hiding disappeared in time, but not her cigarettes.

"I won't have you smoking."

Françoise felt relief. He had glimpsed nothing except her cigarettes.

"Give them to me."

"No."

"While you're living under my roof, you will do what I say."

Françoise gazed at him without expression.

He lunged for the handbag. Françoise, fearing the entire contents might spill again, allowed her father to snatch away the cigarettes.

"No daughter of mine is going to smoke."

Françoise gazed at him.

"A real lady wouldn't smoke. Aline Conderie doesn't smoke."

"She does so."

"Not Aline. She's a lady."

Her father was breathing hard. They glared at each other. Then Gorr's face softened. "You certainly do look lovely. You're the most beautiful girl in Margaux."

"That's not saying much, is it?"

"What have you got against Margaux?"

Françoise made no answer.

"I knew you shouldn't have gone away to that university. It's given you all the wrong ideas."

Françoise edged toward the door.

176

"Where are you going?"

She had no idea where she was going. She just wanted to get out of this stifling little house. "Up to the château to see mother."

Her father said: "Give your daddy a kiss before you go."

Françoise thought: Why not?

Her father had papers spread out on the table. Probably he would do paperwork for the next two hours. Paperwork, Françoise knew, was agony for him.

She went up to him and kissed him on both cheeks. Unexpectedly he embraced her.

"Your father loves you very much, do you know that? Your father loves you more than anything in the world. Your father wants you to do the right thing and be happy." Gorr removed his glasses and rubbed his eyes. "I have no ambitions for me, only for you, little one. That's why I'm rough on you sometimes. It's just because I love you very much."

He held her tight. Françoise released herself.

Outside, the night was dark and cold. She shivered—she should have brought a coat or wrap—but she was not going back in there to get something. She plodded up to the château in her high heels, often stumbling, and entered through the kitchen door.

Her mother was supervising the final cleanup of the kitchen. The two Spanish girls worked at the sink. Copper pots and pans hung gleaming on the walls. Her mother instructed one of the Spanish girls to go into the main room and collect used glasses.

Françoise said: "I'll get them."

She hadn't noticed any cars parked in front of the château. She assumed that the main room was either empty or else that Stack was there alone. She did not much care one way or the other. She was not afraid of him.

She went through the swinging door and crossed the dining room. When she came into the big main room, there was a fire blazing, and Charlie Stack was staring into the flames, a cognac glass in his fingers.

"Oh, hello," he said.

Françoise watched him.

"You look terrific. Are you just going out, or just coming in?"

After a moment, Françoise lied: "Just coming in."

"Have a brandy with me then."

Françoise made no answer.

Stack marched to the sideboard and poured cognac into a snifter. "Here."

Stack was eying her up and down. Françoise regretted that she wore a dress. She understood why men liked girls to wear a dress. To a man, a girl was a cross between a piece of meat and a piece of jewelry. A man wanted to see exactly what he was buying. Her father was no different from the rest.

"Where did you go?" Stack asked.

After a moment, Françoise lied: "To a party."

"Have fun?"

"Oh, yes," Françoise said.

Stack glanced at his watch. "It's over rather early, isn't it?"

Françoise decided not to answer. Instead she began to tour the room, studying the paintings on the walls. She found that Stack was at her elbow, that he moved from wall to wall as she did. Françoise began to regret coming up to the château. If Conderie had been in residence, she wouldn't have come, for she didn't like him. She saw Stack, who was breathing on her, as big, rich, and confident, and told herself she didn't like him either. Why then had she come?

She told herself she had only wanted to be inside the château once again, to look through rooms she had admired as a child. Now that she was here, she was not going to let herself be frightened away. She was not afraid of anybody.

She sat down in a chair facing the fire. Ignoring Stack, who settled into the opposite chair, she sipped her cognac.

A long silence ensued. Suddenly Françoise felt like talking. "You must miss New York."

"Not at all," asserted Stack. "I've rather been enjoying the peace and quiet. I haven't had much of that in my career. As a matter of fact, I find Margaux a charming little town."

"That's hard to believe."

Stack laughed. "I sense you hate Margaux. Why is that?"

"I don't know how you can stand this place after New York."

"Have you ever been to New York?"

"I may go with some kids next summer, if I can get the money." But she knew there was very little chance of such a trip. Where was the money to come from? No one she knew at the university, none of the grand messieurs she had met at this château, knew what it was like to be Françoise Gorr, to start out in life with no money whatsoever. She hated the fact that Conderie, not her father, was paying for her education. She hated going out on dates and letting boys pay for everything, for this established her role as subservient to the boy's role. It made her a sex object. She was supposed to pay them back in the only currency she had.

Françoise heard the swinging door pushed open, and her mother, carrying an empty tray, came into the room and began gathering up soiled glasses. "I wondered where you had got to," she said to her daughter. But it was clear from her mother's nervous manner and red cheeks—burning with shame—that she had come in here to spy on her daughter.

Françoise, studying her, said nothing.

Stack's grin showed all his teeth. "Françoise has been informing me about that which is her life at the university," said Stack in French.

Mrs. Gorr nodded. There were no more soiled glasses, nothing to keep her there. She met nobody's eyes. She concentrated on the floor. "It's late," she said to Françoise. "It's time you were getting home to bed."

Françoise made no answer.

Though Madame Gorr still stood in the doorway, Françoise turned back to the fire and sipped her cognac, staring into the flames. She was conscious of her mother standing there. After a moment she heard her mother's footsteps clomping away across the dining-room floor. Then the swinging door into the kitchen swung, and her mother was gone.

Stack gave Françoise a rather too bright smile. What does that smile mean? Françoise asked herself.

He squirmed in his chair as if trying to get comfortable there.

Françoise's thoughts were fixed on the center of her universe— herself. She stared into the flames.

Stack began to question her about drugs. Yes, there were drugs at the university, she answered reluctantly. Yes, she knew people who took drugs. Yes, she knew people who sold drugs. Yes, she had smoked marijuana, hadn't everyone?

But she was pleased that he was interested in her.

"And you," she asked. "Have you ever smoked marijuana?"

"As a matter of fact, no."

Françoise was incredulous. "Never?"

"Well, I've been rather busy, and in the circles where I move, the subject doesn't often come up."

"I thought everyone below my father's age had tried marijuana. I mean, how can someone not experience something as important as that?"

"What about sex?" asked Stack. He stirred in his chair.

179

Françoise gazed at him. "What about it?" she asked truculently.

"How old will you be when you marry?"

Françoise said: "I don't know, twenty-five, maybe twenty-six."

"And how many men will you have gone to bed with by then?"

An interesting question. "Maybe five, maybe six."

"Maybe more?"

"Maybe."

"And who will these men be?"

"Three or four will be love affairs. The rest will be men that just happened to be there in a situation I couldn't get out of."

Stack's eyes seemed overly bright to Françoise, but she was still focused on his last question. What would become of her?

Behind them, the swinging door again swung, and her father came into the room. He had papers in his hand. "I have some papers for you to sign," he said to Stack. But he could not meet Stack's eyes, nor even his daughter's. "Françoise, get to bed."

"Papers?" asked Stack in French.

"Got them right here. Françoise, I said something to you."

Stack thumbed through the papers. "These will wait till morning."

Her father's face was white. "Françoise, come along."

Stack handed the papers back to his cellar master. "I'll see her home a little later," Stack said coolly.

For a moment the two men stared at each other. Then Stack suddenly grinned, showing all his teeth, a death mask to Gorr. Her father's face was ashen.

"Françoise—" her father said.

"Before you go, Jean," Stack said coolly, "throw another log on the fire, will you?"

Françoise looked from one to the other. Her father stared at Stack.

"On the fire, Jean."

"Oui, monsieur."

Her father moved to the fire, where he dropped a log into place. The flames blazed up.

Gorr gave a strained laugh. Stack said: "That will be all, Jean."

Gorr turned and stumbled from the room. When he was gone, Stack asked Françoise: "What was that all about?"

"I think he's worried about his daughter's virtue," joked Françoise.

"And is there anything to worry about?"

Françoise said into the fire. "Who can tell?"

From the corner of her eye she saw Stack staring at her, weighing

180

his chances. Then he was standing beside her chair. He reached a hand down for her. "Come on upstairs with me. I want to show you how I'm going to redo my part of the château."

Françoise kept her face blank, letting him wonder what her answer would be. Abruptly she drained her glass and rose to her feet. She allowed Stack to take her hand.

She allowed him to lead her up the marble staircase. She had her purse in one hand, his hand in the other. His eyes were overbright. Her own were overbright too; she could feel it. Hand in hand, king and consort, they mounted to the upper reaches of the castle, where Stack threw open a door and described how he would put an office into what was now Aline's room. Poor Aline, Françoise thought. Aline would be shoved off into the other wing of the château; Conderie already had been. The new office would have a leather sofa and matching leather armchair, Françoise heard Stack say. The desk would be glass with chrome legs. He had it all figured out. There would be a coffee table in front of the sofa, and on the walls blowups of sports scenes.

Françoise peered around Aline's room, saying goodbye to it.

Stack led Françoise by the hand into the master bedroom. She had never been in this room before, Conderie's room in the past. As Stack explained it, there would be a Persian rug on the floor extending even under the queen-size bed, which seemed to Françoise a waste of a good rug. There was an ordinary double bed there now and no rug at all, only mats. At the other end of the room would be another sofa, two arm-chairs, and a coffee table. Françoise tried to concentrate on these de-tails. The walls would be decorated in framed prints from the Napo-leonic Wars, if he could find any. There would be portraits of Nelson, Wellington, Napoleon, and a number of battle scenes. There would be a bar in one corner, a rolling tray containing bottles and glasses. There would be book shelves along one wall, the shelves mostly empty: a few books, a few records, a stereo turntable.

"Nice," said Françoise, envisioning it.

Stack loomed suddenly over her. She thought: He really uses very expensive aftershave lotion. It smells expensive anyway.

He was a decisive man. She felt his hands on her shoulders, his hands turning her around. He kissed her, raping her with his tongue. After a moment she let him.

Françoise was confused. Climbing the staircase she had had the illusion that he was leading her to her bridal chamber. All she had to do was follow. After that she would live happily ever after. This illusion

181

was now dispelled. She could feel his hand on her back fumbling for her zipper. Reality meant taking her clothes off. He found the tab and pulled it down several inches, but she stopped him by grasping his arm. She might have slipped away or even laughed, but didn't or couldn't. She was trying to decide but couldn't manage that either.

Her mother's face and thick red fingers filled her mind. Her mother would never have been confronted with the choice confronting Françoise now. Her mother would have been constrained to answer no, or else been labeled whore. Françoise, neither saint nor whore, could answer any way she pleased and remain unchanged. Either way Françoise could remain—Françoise. She and her mother belonged to different worlds. Her mother was, and always had been, condemned to Margaux for life, whereas Françoise might yet escape.

In her mother's day a girl was—different. Today a girl was a person just like everyone. A girl obeyed the same rules as a man. There was no difference between male and female. Françoise believed this, or believed she believed it. The consequences for a girl would be the same as for a man, neither more nor less.

She was nineteen years old and believed she saw the world clearly, and her own role in it clearly. She refused to be a sex object to anyone. She would take part in this as an equal or not at all. She would initiate this act now herself, so as to make her own role in it clear to him. She was trembling, and did not know why.

Face flushed, eyes fixed on his, she reached across under his belt and pulled at the tab of his zipper. Her modesty shrank from the job —he might think ill of her—but she felt constrained to perform it, her own idea of herself being more important than his. But the zipper was stuck; it would not budge.

She kept tugging. Her thoughts were muddled. Nothing was as clear as she had thought.

The zipper came free. His fly bulged open, which seemed funny to her, but she didn't laugh. They faced each other, separated by two feet of air.

Reaching behind her back, Françoise tugged down her own zipper.

Stack threw his jacket on the bed and began rapidly unbuttoning his shirt. He was faster than she and moved to help her with her clothes. She would do it herself, she told him; she did not need him. But he insisted, and she suddenly felt so weak she let him.

He was more muscular than she had supposed, and seemed vain

182

about his physique. She laid her head against the matted curls on his chest while he worked with the last of her clothing.

She tried to tell herself that nothing significant was taking place. She was not unique, nor was he. What they were doing was not unique. Nothing was unique. Pinch a person here, she thought, and cause her pain. Rub a person there and give her—oh—pleasure. She was concentrating hard. He was taking her where she wanted to go. He was taking her out of Margaux.

She heard a stair creak, or thought she did, and stiffened under him, imagining it was her father. That spoiled it for her, though obviously not for him. He lay moving in and out of her, enjoying himself apparently, while she listened for more creaking stairs.

No, there was nothing. Nothing to fear. Her father would not dare enter this room. Her father would not want to catch her at this. Her father would not dare challenge Stack, acknowledged lord and master.

She pushed at Stack's chest, and he rolled off her. Her clothes were in heaps on the floor. She gathered them up. Stack sat on the bed grinning, watching her. She had lost an earring. Tugging on her ear, she glanced about, searching for it. With her clothes still draped over one arm, she got on her knees. She searched under the bed.

From above her, Stack said: "You've got a very provocative bottom."

Françoise, kneeling upright, gazed at him.

She could not afford to search longer. She tugged the other one off and slipped it into her handbag on the sideboard. As far from him as she could get without leaving the room, she began to dress.

"Come back here," Stack called.

"I have to go."

"Come back here," Stack ordered.

Françoise gazed at him without expression. She wondered who Stack was comparing her to, and what he thought of her. She continued getting dressed. Reaching behind herself, she managed to get her zipper pulled all the way up. She stepped into her shoes.

"Come back here," Stack called.

She picked up her handbag off the sideboard, moving past the bed to the door.

"You can't leave me like this," said Stack. He was swelling before her eyes, grinning hugely, obviously pleased with himself.

"I have to go."

"How would you like to go on the payroll?" Stack inquired.

The thought of money stopped her. She stood with her hand on the door.

"I could use you as an interpreter. I could use you to show visitors through the chais."

"I have to go to school."

"Well, when you're home from school."

At the door Françoise hesitated.

"I could pay you, say, five dollars an hour."

Françoise translated this into francs. A fortune.

"Why don't you stay, and we can discuss it?"

His conversation was of money, but she looked down at him, and clearly his thoughts were not. Françoise turned the door handle.

"You can't leave me like this."

"I have to go."

The hall, once the door had slammed behind her, was as dark as a night at sea. She groped for a light switch. Behind her she expected to hear him laughing through the door, though no sound came. She found the switch, and in the stairwell the crystal chandelier suddenly blazed. She ran down the marble staircase and out into the night.

Françoise stumbled as she hurried down the path in her high-heeled shoes. When she saw that lights still burned in the cottage, she became tense. They were waiting up for her. Outside the cottage she paused to compose herself. She waited till she was breathing normally. Her cheeks felt hot, and she waited for that to stop, but it didn't. Well . . .

She stepped inside.

Her father looked at her with stricken eyes. Françoise passed her tongue over her lips, tasting the almost-colorless lipstick.

"Where have you been?"

"What do you mean, where have I been? I was up at the château."

"Your guilt shows in your face," her mother hissed.

Françoise decided to try to bluff it out. "What did I do?"

"You went upstairs with him," her father said.

"Of course I didn't," Françoise said. "What do you think I am?" But she was having trouble controlling her voice.

"You let him take advantage of you."

Françoise made no answer.

"Did you? Tell me. Did you?"

184

Françoise's face was impassive. Turning her back on them, she stepped toward her own room.

Her father spun her around. "I'm your father. I have a right to know."

"What I do with my life is my own affair," Françoise said.

Her father slapped her. The slap rang in her ears.

"There are ways to find out how far it went," her mother hissed.

"I'm sick of your village morality," Françoise shouted. "You're old-fashioned. You're out of date."

Her father slapped her again. When she was a child he had sometimes given her terrible spankings, but he had not raised his hand to her since she had reached puberty, no doubt believing in his old-fashioned way that he might somehow damage her ability to bear children. To men like her father, females were fragile.

She was breathing hard, and to her surprise she was on the verge of tears. "Nothing happened. Nothing at all," she said, and began crying.

She could see he wanted to believe her.

"How can you mistrust me like this?" she wept. "How can you believe such things about me?"

Her mother looked unconvinced, but her father moved forward and embraced her. His shoulders were shaking.

In her room she put her pajamas on, not removing her underpants. It would never occur to her father to search out such evidence, but her mother might. Her mother was perfectly capable of it. Françoise would wear the evidence until morning, when she would wash them out.

Awakening at dawn, believing himself filled with well-being, Stack decided to fly to New York for the holidays, why not? At this château and most others work started at 7 A.M., meaning that when Stack phoned down to the chai Gorr was already there. Stack asked his cellar master to drive him to the airport.

The cellar master was waiting out on the gravel, beret in hand, when Stack came out carrying a small valise. But Gorr rushed to relieve him of it. They crossed to the garages.

"Monsieur looks well this morning," said Gorr ingratiatingly.

Stack was pleased with his cellar master, who always showed the proper amount of servility. In New York Stack's underlings called him Charlie. America was overdemocratized. No one showed deference.

Immediately Stack was ashamed of himself for enjoying servility.

Gorr threw back the garage doors, exposing the château's several cars.

"We'll take the Ferrari, Jean," decided Stack. Probably the cellar master, less proud than his daughter, had always wanted to drive the Ferrari. Today he would drive it home from the airport. Today his lord would grant him this boon, one of two.

"Why don't we put the top down?" suggested Stack. It was a cool morning, but in New York a few hours from now it might be snowing.

While Gorr folded back the Ferrari's canvas top, Stack stood on the gravel and brooded about Françoise. He was ashamed of himself for that too.

Stack intended to catch the 9 A.M. flight to London, and connect to New York. As they drove along in the cool early morning, Stack suddenly announced that Gorr would remain on as cellar master.

Stack had been on the point of replacing the man. Gorr was a winemaker, not a decision maker, and Stack had heard of two men who might be available who were both. God knows I need more help than he can give me, Stack thought. But he couldn't do it now. Not after last night.

Stack told himself that he owed Françoise nothing. A casual roll in the hay was nothing. One owed no girl anything for that. Why then rush off to New York? Why not wait all day for a glimpse of Françoise's sunny face?

But he didn't want to face Françoise's face. By the time he got back she'd be gone. Her face, unencountered on a staircase or in the yard, would not reproach him.

She was asking for it, he thought.

Not from me, he thought.

And why not fire the old man as planned?

He just couldn't do it now, that's all.

Stack held his Ferrari in the long sweeping curve passing Château d'Issan, and felt the wind on his face and arms.

"I'm sure you'll do a fine job for me, Jean."

The gesture would not even earn Gorr's especial loyalty. The cellar master's loyalty was for the vines.

Gorr rode with a kind of bemused smile on his face. The idiot appeared perplexed, Stack thought, as if unsure he understood his pa-

186

tron's French. Evidently it had not occurred to Gorr that his job, which his father and grandfather had held before him, was ever in jeopardy, but it had been.

Gorr knew nothing about the workings of New York conglomerates.

Stack was nodding at him: "I thought you'd be pleased, Jean?"

"Oui, monsieur."

Stack had questioned other owners about his cellar master; they said Gorr knew how to make wine.

Stack could make the decisions himself, could he not? The fact that Gorr spoke no English was perhaps an advantage. Stack chose to concentrate on this advantage, if it was an advantage. Such a man could not be secretly subverted by the chairman. Such a man could not turn out to be the chairman's spy at the château.

If the lawyer, Saar, was not the chairman's spy already.

Stack brooded again about Françoise. "You've got a lovely daughter, Jean."

"Oui, monsieur."

Stack told himself he was running to New York out of high spirits, not remorse. He wanted a few days with his own kind.

"Yes, she's a beautiful girl."

"You flatter me, monsieur."

At the airport the cellar master grabbed Stack's bag. Stack went to buy a newspaper, taking his time, while Gorr waited with ticket and valise to check in for him.

"I'll be back in a few days," Stack said at the boarding gate, thinking: If he knew, he would kill me, or himself. He seems old-fashioned enough.

"Oui, monsieur."

"Take care of things in my absence."

"Have a pleasant trip, monsieur."

Gorr, beret crushed in his thick fingers, waited at the gate, Stack noted, until the passengers were led out of the waiting room and across to the plane.

Françoise, awakened by the sound of her mother moving about in the kitchen, came forth. Her mother did not acknowledge her presence. Françoise prepared herself a café au lait. Breaking off part of the bread, she sliced it down the middle and smeared butter on both sides.

Her mother would not speak to her. Françoise ate the bread and drank the coffee.

After locking the bathroom door, Françoise stepped out of her pajama bottoms and underpants. Her breasts shook inside the loose pajama top as she washed out the underpants.

She thought she would walk up to the château as soon as she was dressed. Standing at the sink, she stripped and washed her body all over with a washcloth. She spent a long time in front of the mirror primping, but in the end decided to dress in blue jeans and her plaid lumberjacket.

Stack would be up by now, she thought.

But up at the château one of the Spanish girls informed Françoise that monsieur had just gone to New York.

"New York?" said Françoise.

Imagine flying to New York on a moment's notice, commented the Spanish girl in broken French. What a romantic figure monsieur was.

Françoise went through into the living room, but it was empty. The ashes still lay in the fireplace. Françoise went upstairs to Stack's bedroom, but that was empty too. The bed was still unmade. She could see in the pillow the imprint left by his head. She began to search for her earring. She did not want her mother, who cleaned this room, to find it.

It lay on the floor under the tangled counterpane. She found it easily. If she hadn't run out of here so fast last night she would have found it then. If she hadn't run out, monsieur might not have flown to New York today.

Françoise threw the counterpane back on the bed. The earring she slipped into the pocket of her jeans.

Sudden tears crowded her eyes, and she told herself she did not know why. She rubbed them away. When they were gone, she bit on her lip, surveyed the room one last time, and went down the stairs and out of the château. She decided she would walk into the village. Maybe she would gossip awhile with Carmen at the butcher shop, or with Pierre Jacot at the café.

8

The reply from Paris did not come back for eleven days, by which time Dupont had virtually forgotten his original request. Someone came in and handed him the telex. Sitting at his shabby desk in the brigade's shabby offices, he read:

NO ONE NAMED AUBERVILLIERS AT ADDRESS LISTED.

Dupont read the message a second time. The words did not change.

Dupont, puzzled, sat tapping his ballpoint pen against the edge of his desk. Perhaps Aubervilliers lived or worked at the address given, but in an apartment or office listed under the name of an associate or relative. Perhaps the agent assigned to check out Aubervilliers was inexperienced or careless or lazy. Dupont's request had suggested no urgency. Perhaps the agent assigned had not even gone around in person. Paris was shorthanded too. The agent might have attempted to look up Aubervilliers in the telephone book; it was conceivable that Aubervilliers had an unlisted phone.

It was conceivable that the concierge at Aubervilliers's building was new, and that Aubervilliers was not often in residence there. It was conceivable that the concierge had not recognized the name, and that the agent sent to check had let it go at that, and had repaired to a café to make the assignment last all the rest of the afternoon. A good many agents, especially the younger ones, were not as conscientious as they should be.

It was conceivable that the notary who had transcribed the sale—or the notary's clerk—had made a mistake of one digit in the number of the address, putting the building in question across the street or blocks away. It would take a conscientious agent to find the true address.

Many things were conceivable.

Dupont had no knowledge of who the agent was or how conscientious he had been, only that the Paris office had treated Dupont's request lightly, had taken eleven days to check out a simple address. He kept drumming his ballpoint pen against the edge of his desk.

Dupont's in-basket was piled with reports to be studied and verified. A second pile of reports was stacked neatly in the middle of the desk. Dupont was a neat, meticulous little man. Those two piles of reports would take him the rest of the day. Probably he would have to work late. His wife would be annoyed at him when he came home late for dinner. She would reproach him in her mild way. He decided he had best get back to work on those reports.

Before filing the telex from Paris, Dupont read it one last time. It was a simple statement of fact. There was no indication there or any-where else of illegal conduct by anyone. Abruptly Dupont folded the telex in four, so that it was the size of a playing card, for he had decided not to file it. From his middle desk drawer he took out his notebook and a single straight pin. Opening the notebook to his visit to Château Cracheau he pinned the folded telex message to the page, working the straight pin carefully through the thicknesses of paper, being careful not to prick his finger. Then he closed the notebook, and returned it to his drawer, closed the drawer, and took up the pile of reports once again.

But when he got to work the next day Dupont got out the phone book and began to phone up plumbers.

"This is Château Cracheau," Dupont said into the phone. "I'm calling about those stainless-steel tanks you installed for me not long ago—"

"Excuse me, monsieur, but I think you have the wrong plumber."

Dupont went down the list, first calling plumbers in villages close to Château Cracheau, then gradually widening the circle.

One plumber asked him to wait while he checked invoices. "I'm sorry, monsieur, but I have no record of doing that job."

Dupont worked doggedly all morning. When he came back from lunch, he went back on the phone. Soon he was calling plumbers more than twenty-five kilometers away from Château Cracheau. He began to worry about the phone bill he was running up—the Fraud Brigade was poor and he would hear about it—but by now, intuitively, he knew he was on to something. Those two great new tanks, that shiny new bot-tling machine, these things constituted capital investment too great for a château of that size, and now he couldn't find the plumber who had installed them.

By eleven o'clock the next morning he was dialing plumbers in

190

Libourne. He judged Libourne to be nearly fifty kilometers from Château Cracheau.

But the third plumber apparently remembered the job perfectly.

"That's right," said Dupont. "You installed two big stainless-steel vats for me."

"No, no," the plumber said. "You're calling from Château Cracheau, right? The little farmhouse halfway up the hill."

"That's right."

"But the vats I installed for you were cement. I hooked them up, and I hooked up the septic tank too. Has something gone wrong?"

"Not at all," lied Dupont. "I'm the accountant for the château. I'm just trying to figure out what all these bills mean, and where to enter them on the books. Now that I've got it straight, I think I'll be okay. Sorry to have troubled you."

Dupont sat tapping his ballpoint pen on his desk. He was worried that he might have made the plumber suspicious; the plumber might decide to phone up the château. Maybe the plumber would do it, but Dupont, who knew plumbers, did not think so. No plumber went looking to complicate his life.

But one phone call by that plumber was all it would take. The evidence would disappear. The illegal operation, whatever it was, would close down.

Which might be for the best. The wine trade did not need a scandal. Dupont did not really want to get anyone in trouble, thereby risking getting in trouble himself.

Though he spent the rest of the afternoon calling more plumbers, widening his circle to ever greater distances, he found no one who remembered the stainless-steel tanks, and so came to the conclusion that the tanks had been bought far away, had been trucked in there by night, and had been hooked up without the intercession of a professional plumber. As for the cement vats, Dupont had not noticed them. He had seen only stainless-steel tanks. Where were the concrete vats? Was it possible that they were under the floor?

It was quitting time. Dupont's chief came out of his office with his hat and coat on.

"Still here?" he asked Dupont.

Dupont got up and, in the corner by the door, picked his coat off the coat tree and put it on. The two men went down the stairs. On the sidewalk his chief said: "Do you have anything heavy that you're working on?"

191

"I'm not sure."

"Want to tell me about it?"

"Perhaps not yet, inspector."

"Well, goodnight, Dupont."

"Goodnight, inspector."

9

Aline's father came on the line. "How's my little cabbage?"

Aline, phoning from Paris, said: "I've decided to sell the shop."

Her father, not knowing what to say, said nothing.

"I've already done it. I've closed up and turned it over to a real-estate agent."

It was cruel to confront her father with something like this. He wouldn't be able to cope with it.

"Oh," her father said. "Oh. Well. What do you know?"

Her father moved scared down the corridors of life. The sudden opening of any door—any door at all—usually sent him into a panic.

"Could I come down there for a few days?" Aline asked humbly. She hated the sound of humility in her own voice, but felt so defeated she couldn't help it. She could not bear to stay in Paris. The streets seemed to mock her and the idea of her former shop, waiting empty for a buyer, was more than she could endure. She refused to admit it to herself but, like a little girl, she wanted to go home.

"Of course, my dear. Shall I meet you at the airport?"

The unexpected kindness in her father's voice nearly undid her. They had had a terrible fight when she learned that her father had sold the château.

"Is—that man there?"

"No. He's been here, but he's not here now. He hasn't really taken over yet."

"Then it would be all right if I came down."

"I'll meet your plane. It will be lovely to have you."

192

In her bedroom Aline began packing. Tears came to her eyes, though she hurriedly forced them back. She would go home to the Médoc because she had no place else to go. She would go home to the Médoc and try to come back to life.

She was trying to ignore the fact that it wasn't home anymore.

Her father took her to lunch near the airport. It was a mild day and they dined at a restaurant in the forest, first sipping an apéritif outdoors on a terrace overlooking a duck pond. Presently they went indoors and ordered. Her father demanded a bottle of champagne—"to celebrate your coming home," he told his daughter cheerfully.

He was cheerful all through a quite good lunch, and charming, and made her laugh. But as each sipped a tiny cup of strong black coffee, Aline began to ask the hard, important questions. "Will you stay on at the château, Papa?"

"Oh, yes. That is, I can if I want to. It's in my contract."

Aline wet her lips, then asked: "And me. Would it be all right for me to stay on for a little while? All right with—him?"

Her father grinned at her. "Of course. That's in the contract too."

"Contract?" Aline asked, puzzled.

"That's in your contract with me, my dear. That's in the contract I signed the day you were born."

At the château, except that her father had been banished to the other wing, nothing seemed changed. Aline went into her old room and it was as she had left it.

When she came back downstairs her father stood in the drawing room.

"He's not such a bad fellow," Conderie said. "That fellow Stack, I mean."

Aline nodded.

"He looks up to me, you know, I don't know why."

Both realized that they were standing not in their own home but in someone else's. They were ill at ease, not with each other, but with this familiar room.

"He was here most of last month. I expect him back any time now."

Home was where one was safe from all outsiders. For them both Château Conderie was no longer such a place. They felt insecure there.

"Will he live here permanently?"

"So I understand. As permanently as that type does anything."

From birth until her marriage Aline had lived secure in her homes, her schools, her name; and although she had known almost no security since, her girlhood was not so far away that the mood felt irrecoverable. She was still young. Security—somehow—might come back. But her father's security, she had come to realize, had been getting whittled down for decades.

She felt suddenly so sorry for him that she reached out and stroked his face. He caught her hand. He had an ebullient personality and seldom stayed depressed for long, a quality she much admired. Already he was smiling cheerfully.

"My name and family heritage," said Conderie, "that's what the fellow looks up to. These Americans scarcely know who their grandfathers were. No background. Nothing to help them through the tight spots in life. Fellow may own the château, but our name is still on the label, isn't it? No one's going to change the name to Château Stack, are they?"

Aline forced a smile. Though she felt dispirited to think that someone else owned these rooms now, she said cheerfully: "We're safe until he comes, anyway."

Aline went back to her room and, fully dressed except for shoes, lay down on her bed. The strain of closing her shop, the strain of coming home today had drained her. She fell asleep.

Someone was rapping on her door. Her father or one of the maids, she thought. Groggy, tousled-haired, clothes rumpled, she opened the door on Charlie Stack.

"Sorry if I've disturbed you," he said, and perhaps he was.

She had the normal female reaction: I don't look my best for him. It made her angry. "You didn't disturb me," she said sarcastically. "I was only taking a nap."

He had the grace to stare at his shoes. "Well, anyway, could we have a little talk?"

"Wait for me downstairs," she said, and closed the door on him.

Changing into fresh clothes and shoes, she dragged a comb through her hair.

He was waiting in front of the cold fireplace, one hand on the mantel.

"You wanted to see me?" Aline asked.

He got straight to the point. His words were direct and forceful and left no room for argument. He was not embarrassed. He showed no tug of sentiment. He spoke with absolute authority. He would need her room. He would need that entire wing of the château, as a matter of fact.

194

"Excuse me, I don't understand," Aline said, shocked. "Are you kicking me—out of the château altogether?"

"Not at all. Your father is entitled to live here by contract, and so are you as far as I am concerned. I suggest you establish yourself elsewhere in the château. I'm merely saying that henceforth that wing is mine."

Aline nodded numbly but felt like weeping. Lost was not her own bedroom, but in some measure her childhood. Her childhood was being moved like a piece of broken furniture to one of the unheated rooms in the rear.

But she was trying to recover, to face him as an equal.

"It will be better all around," said Charlie Stack, favoring her with what she saw as a false smile. "You don't want a room close to me anyway. You might be disturbed by the dancing girls."

Aline snapped: "Is that supposed to be charming?"

Stack frowned, so that Aline immediately thought: I mustn't speak to him this way. I'll get kicked out, and then where will I go?

"I'm sorry," said Charlie Stack.

He turned and walked from the room, but at the door stopped to say to her: "Why don't you get a couple of men in from the chai to help you move?"

"Right away?"

"If it wouldn't be too much trouble."

They nodded at each other, and he was gone.

Aline lit a cigarette, puffed three times, and flicked it into the ashes in the fireplace. She went up to the rooms in the other wing of the château. It was years since she had been in those rooms. They smelled musty. She turned the radiators on, and one began to clank almost at once. Sometimes during harvest these rooms had been used to house extra guests, though not in a long time. She peered out a dirty window. The view was the same—stakes, wires, and unending vines. Gnarled, arthritic fingers groping up out of the mud, clawing at the sky. She moved from room to room, deciding which she should take. She and her father would have to share a bathroom. She looked it over. This particular bathroom had been installed before the Second World War. The tub stood away from the wall on claw legs. It had rust stains in it.

Dinner Aline found unendurable. He was host now, not she. The three of them sat spread out around the vast table, while Madame Gorr ladled out soup. A plate of cold meats was passed around, a bowl of potato salad, a green salad with oil and vinegar. The cheese and bread came, then the coffee. Stack talked somewhat loudly about American politics. Her father made a glum audience at first, but later cheered up and began to take part. She herself said almost nothing. It was like certain lengthy ship voyages of long ago; a stranger whom they found incompatible had been assigned to their table, and would be with them throughout the voyage.

Aline excused herself and went up to her shabby new rooms.

The next day, as Aline was reading a book in the salon, Stack entered accompanied by two effeminate decorators, with whom he was attempting to communicate in French. Aline, ignoring him and them, went back to her book.

Suddenly Aline heard Stack say: "I'm sorry, I'll never learn this damn language. Aline, won't you help me?"

She looked up. "I thought you were a man who didn't need help from anyone."

Stack smiled. "It's a front I put on so people won't realize what a babe in the woods I really am."

Aline felt herself momentarily won over by this remark.

"Won't you help me?" he begged.

After a moment Aline said: "What is it you're trying to tell them?"

Stack explained. The wallpaper in this room was not wallpaper at all but canvas which had been affixed in place hundreds of years ago, and on top of which some unknown artist had painted a single, vast hunting scene. Horses carrying men in frock coats and tricornered hats leaped hedges and streams in pursuit of a stag. A pack of dogs was involved. The entire countryside was laid out in front of the hunt, which covered three walls out of four. But the artist, whoever he was, had been either unskilled, Stack felt, or a practitioner of some primitive style, for many of the parts of the whole were out of scale, or badly drawn.

Stack wanted this hunting scene torn down. "Tell them," he said, "that I'd like the walls hung with some sort of red velvet material. Tell them I'll pick that out in the next couple of days—"

Aline stared at him incredulously. "What?"

"I'm getting rid of this wallpaper or whatever it is. I don't like it."

"What?"

Stack grinned. "Go on saying 'what' like that, and you'll have me believing I can't speak English either."

"You can't do that," Aline gasped.

196

"Why not?"

"Because—because these old paintings are charming. They represent the charm of the château." She felt almost speechless. She could not think of anything else to say.

"Well, I don't like them."

He had decided. The matter was closed.

"The château is famous for those scenes," Aline cried. "Ask anyone. Any château in the Médoc would love to have them. The museums would love to have them."

"I don't like them."

"They're worth money. They're worth lots of money." It was the only argument she could think of that might move him.

Stack said: "I know very well they're worth money. Do you think I haven't checked into that? As a matter of fact I thought you might help me get the best price."

Aline was filled with contempt. Money was all this man understood. "No thank you," she said, and turned coldly away.

"Aline, the start-up costs of an operation like mine are really tremendous," Stack explained. "Selling these hunting scenes, which I don't think are particularly attractive anyway, would offset some of that."

Aline said nothing.

"So who's the best antique dealer. I'm really depending on you, Aline."

When she did not answer, he added: "We should air-condition the entire château, of course, and I need to know who to go to for that, too."

Aline said icily: "If it gets too hot for you, why not try just opening the windows?"

After a moment, Stack said to her back: "Do I have your permission to get some functional furniture in here?"

Furiously Aline spun around. "The furniture is worth a bundle too. You better have that appraised while you're at it. Each of these pieces is several hundred years old. Each is unique. Do you always make decisions before you know what you're doing?"

She saw she had impugned his faith in himself as a businessman, and was glad.

"As far as I'm concerned," Stack shot back, "the Salvation Army can back its truck up to the door and take it all away."

Turning her back on him, Aline stared out the window with her arms folded across her breast. Behind her Stack attempted to talk French to the decorators. All three men left the room, and she heard them go upstairs.

That night, unable to bear the sight of Stack, Aline dined on soft-boiled eggs and cottage cheese in the kitchen. Through the swinging door she could hear her father and Stack in the dining room. Finished, she slipped up the back stairs to her room.

From then on she avoided him as much as she could. He was often gone from the château anyway, twice to Paris, other times to Bordeaux. She had no idea what he did in Paris and did not care to know; in Bordeaux, so she understood, he served on a committee, though what he contributed she could not imagine, as he knew little about wine and spoke poor French.

Some days Aline went for long walks through the woods. By avoiding Stack, she could make believe nothing had changed. The weather was warming fast now, and it seemed to her she could feel herself getting stronger, as if recovering from a long illness. The peace and quiet were good for her. Sometimes she drove down to the river and walked along the banks. She had hoped to come back to life in the Médoc, and despite the new owner, it seemed to be working.

She saw a good deal of her friend Odette Brown, Nathaniel Brown's wife, with whom she had once attended an exclusive Catholic girls' school in Bordeaux. Odette had a horse too, and their château gave onto the other side of the forest. The two young women would meet in the forest where there were long straight gallops under the trees, and on warm days they would sit together in the sun while their horses grazed nearby.

Odette probed for details behind the sale of Château Conderie, but Aline gave none.

"I gather the American is a rather gauche person," Odette suggested.

Aline felt uncomfortable. If she answered with the truth, then she would be obliged to defend both the sale of the château and her own presence there still.

"You met him at our house one night last harvest time," Aline temporized.

"Yes. I remember he didn't speak French."

"He can be quite charming," suggested Aline.

"And he's quite good looking. Between the two of you is there any—"

198

"Of course not," said Aline.

"Maybe we should invite him to dinner one night."

"I wouldn't go that far."

"You said he was charming."

"As you noted, he doesn't speak French."

When Stack had gone to Paris or New York or wherever he went, Aline would convene some of the Conderies' friends for dinner, and in Stack's absence the château seemed almost as much her own as in the past.

Since they lived in the same house it was impossible to avoid Stack altogether. One day they met as she was going up the marble staircase and he was coming down. Her eyes dropped to her shoes and she attempted to step by him, but he blocked her.

"I asked around. I checked up on what you told me about those hunting scenes, not because I doubted you but because I wanted to impress upon myself how wrong I had been. I had no idea that the château was so well known for them."

Apparently he awaited some reply, but Aline gave none.

"I mean, how was I supposed to know? That's a new field for me. I appreciate your setting me straight."

Stack stepped past her and descended the stairs. From the bottom he called back: "By the way, I'm having your bathroom torn out. You'll have to use the one downstairs."

Aline, furious, opened her mouth to cry out, but Stack was smiling up at her. "In the matter of bathrooms, I am an expert, and I'm putting in a new one for you. I hope you're not going to tell me that the one you have is a valuable antique and can't be touched."

At the front door, his hand on the handle, he added: "The plumbing guy is up there right now with his books of samples. Pick out what you want." With a negligent wave, Stack stepped out into the sunshine. Behind him on the staircase, Aline stood dumbfounded.

That night at dinner Stack and her father chatted cheerfully, but Aline found it hard to bring words out: "I've given instructions for the bathroom, Mr. Stack, and, well, thank you."

"Charlie," said Stack.

"What?"

"Call me Charlie."

It seemed to Aline almost like an order and she bristled. "I don't know that I want to."

"You called me that when I came here in October for the harvest."

199

"Did I? You didn't own my home in October."

That silenced him, she noted grimly. He looked almost hurt, though it seemed inconceivable that mere words could hurt such a man.

One afternoon Aline came upon Stack trying to communicate with Madame Gorr in the kitchen. He turned toward Aline: "There's no dishwashing machine in here."

"Is that such a surprise?"

"It is to me. Tell her I'm buying her a dishwashing machine. Tell her I'll have the guy out here tomorrow."

Surprised, Aline translated. Madame Gorr became so happy and flustered she was virtually in tears. She kept thanking Stack.

"Yes, well," said Stack edging toward the door.

"That was nice," Aline told him when they were outside. "You made that poor woman very happy."

Stack seemed embarrassed by her praise. "You have to bring these people into modern times," he said. Suddenly he grinned rather impishly: "Besides, she'll break fewer dishes that way."

Aline said: "You made her feel that she's important. She'll brag about her dishwasher to all the other women in Margaux."

"Maybe so. I just thought she ought to have a dishwasher."

He really did seem embarrassed. Aline was surprised and confused. She almost liked him.

Stack said: "I've decided to leave the main rooms of the château just the way they are. I'm having my own office and bedroom done over according to my own taste, and I assume that's all right with you." He hesitated, glancing at her, then said: "It is all right with you, isn't it?"

Was there a twinkle in his eye?

Aline answered seriously: "Yes, of course."

"I'll need things to hang on the wall. I was wondering, if you had the time, if you would mind going with me into Bordeaux to the shops to buy some things."

Aline was flattered. Also, she told herself, whatever he bought would be in better taste if she were at his side. Did she not owe it to the château to go with him?

The next morning they went through the big department stores, paused for lunch, and in the afternoon visited antique shops. Aline found a series of framed engravings of the Napoleonic wars which Stack was enthusiastic about, and they bought them. They bought an ornate Louis Quinze desk for his study, which surprised Aline. Stack had been thinking in terms of chrome and glass, and now this. They bought lovely

200

old brass andirons and a matching stand of fireplace tools. This was to ornament the fireplace in Stack's bedroom—many of the bedrooms in the château had fireplaces.

They were out on the narrow, crowded sidewalk when Stack suddenly said with a grin: "Now all I need to put in front of that fire on a cold winter night is a bear rug and a naked girl."

Ordinarily Aline would have been repelled by such a remark, but this time she smiled. Stack took her arm and propelled her around people. "Now I'm going to buy you a cup of tea," Stack announced.

Over tea, curious at last, Aline began to question him. Why had he never married?

"A man can only marry one thing at a time. I married The Company. I set out to be president of The Company." Suddenly he added: "I chose a life that doesn't leave a man much of himself, didn't I?"

Was this a new insight or a thought he had been pondering for some time?

"If you feel that way—" began Aline.

"I don't know what I feel. My feelings are beginning to change."

"Please don't misunderstand my interest," Aline said hastily. "I'm just making conversation."

"I assume you know nothing whatever about American business," said Stack. "The company I work for is ruthless, it's absolutely rapacious. To move upward in such a company demands absolute concentration. It's such an enormous challenge that for a long time the challenge itself is fascinating. You look neither to right nor left. The only place you look is up. You put in fifty-five or sixty hours a week. About ten or fifteen of those hours are constructive. The rest are spent protecting your flank, studying ways to acquire more leverage or to use what leverage you have to influence people one or more rungs above you inside The Company. Every executive in that company goes about armed to the teeth—figuratively, of course. You keep your knife in your hand at all times. You attend stupid meetings, which are called only to display someone's power to call such a meeting. You introduce products to the market place for which there is no real need, and you force the public to buy them through skillful packaging, merchandising, and advertising."

Stack sipped his tea. "Hot," he said.

Aline looked at him with new respect. "But if you see all this so clearly, how can you give yourself to it?"

"You hear a lot of talk these days about men not understanding women. That always hands me a laugh. Women don't remotely understand men. I could talk to you for an hour, and I don't believe you could understand a word of what I might tell you."

There was a moment's silence, which Aline found far more intimate than she was ready for. She took a gulp of tea, which burned the inside of her mouth. She put the cup down.

After a moment Aline said: "I'd like to hear you try to tell me."

"A man's basic psychological need is to be respected—and in some cases feared—by other men, even men he might despise. That's where his sense of manhood comes from. The artist who tells you that he doesn't mind that no one buys his stuff is lying. Success is what men crave. High pay checks, high rank. I don't know if it was like that in caveman times; I only know it's like that today. You get into a company like mine, and you find that you will do anything, anything at all, to achieve the higher pay, higher rank. If everyone else is ruthless, you must be more ruthless. I was doing well in that company, but I did make one or more mistakes. I was guilty of a momentary lack of attention, and I got sent here to do penance. The publicity release called it a promotion, and it was accompanied by an apparent raise in rank, and a raise in pay, but inside The Company it was a stab in the back, and everybody knows it, and nearly everyone was glad to see it happen. At corporate headquarters in New York for the moment I'm something of a joke."

"I'm not sure I understand," said Aline.

"I didn't expect you to understand. A man doesn't do what he does in order to show off to a woman, but to show off to other men. And defeats hurt not because they diminish a man in front of a woman, but because they diminish him in front of other men. The struggle is at corporate headquarters in New York, not in Bordeaux. I'm like a player who has been put out of the game. I can't score any more points until I can find a way to get back into the game. I'm not sure that I can do that here in Bordeaux. Maybe I can."

"Are you sure you want to get back in the game?"

"Of course I'm sure," said Stack almost irritably.

"You don't care about the château or about wine at all, do you?"

Stack studied her. He sipped from his teacup, and put it down carefully. "I cared nothing about this place at first. I do care about it now, I don't know why. I don't know how much I care about it. I'm not a farm boy. I don't understand anything about the land. But I think I have discovered that the land exerts a pull over everyone on it, whether such a pull is welcome or not. These last few weeks have slowed me down, made me take stock, affecting me more deeply than I would have

202

supposed. On the land you have to wait for things to grow. You can't force anything. And nobody's coming at you with knives."

Aline had begun to resent these apparent confidences which this strange man across the table was showering upon her.

"Well," she said briskly, "that was a nice cup of tea. What shall we do now? Shall we go on with the shopping?"

Stack signaled the waiter. They were seated behind glass on the terrace of the Hotel Splendide. When the waiter, standing beside the table, had totaled up the tickets, Stack withdrew money and pushed it toward him.

Holding Aline's coat for her, Stack said carefully, "I'd like to know if you plan to stay around here for any length of time."

Aline bristled, and he saw this and said quickly: "Please don't be so touchy. I don't mean to hurt you."

After a moment Aline said: "I haven't decided how long I want to stay. Do I have to ask your permission?"

"No. It's just that I understood that you had a shop in Paris."

"I've sold the shop."

"I didn't know that."

"The shop was doing very well, but I found myself getting a bit tired of it, and then I got a nice offer." Offer? The shop was still empty so far as she knew, a staring obscenity on a chic street.

"So I sold out." There, she had managed the same lie any man would have managed. The lie was done.

But why did she feel such an overpowering need to lay her head on some man's shoulder? Why did she want to be comforted? A man wouldn't want to be comforted, she told herself.

She judged that Stack had perceived more of the truth than she might have hoped, for he was nodding solicitously. "The reason I asked," he said, "is that if you're going to be around here, and if the idea interests you, I'd like to have you work for me."

"Work? What do you mean, work?"

"I can't run this place properly by myself. I probably can't even run it at all. I need help. Your father's no help, I regret to say. I have a lawyer, Saar, who's come down from Paris, and he's some help in legal matters, not much. I can call upon the staff of the Paris Profit Center, but they're too far away, and besides they report back to corporate headquarters. For all I know Saar does too. I don't need to be spied on. I need help. I need someone who knows the wine business, and who speaks the language."

He led her through the tables. "Just don't say no before you think about it," he said, and they went out onto the street.

There was a park opposite with rows of bare plane trees, all of which had been repeatedly, almost brutally, pruned in the French manner, so that the trees resembled gigantic vines, same gnarled arms and fingers groping for the sky.

Stack had taken her arm, but Aline turned to face him. "What do you imagine my duties would be?"

"You've run a shop. You know business."

Aline stared at her shoes. "Thanks for the compliment."

"We could call you executive assistant. Where I go you would go. You could introduce me to places where I need introductions. You could get me invited into these people's houses, for one thing. You could talk for me, and God knows I need that." As they walked along the sidewalk, Aline was conscious of his fingers through several thicknesses of cloth. It was not unpleasant.

"One other thing I would like," Stack said, "for at least an hour every day I would like you to teach me French."

She stopped walking and stared at him.

"That's not an essential," Stack said quickly. "I could hire somebody else to do that, I suppose. But you're there, we're living in the same house. It would be simpler. But you can forget about that aspect if you prefer."

After dinner, when her father had gone up to bed, they stood in front of the fire sipping cognac, and Stack named a salary, explaining that he had checked with the Paris Profit Center, which had come up with the figure. It was equivalent to what other French women in such jobs were earning.

It seemed an enormous sum to Aline. How inexperienced in business matters I am, she thought.

"All right, I accept," said Aline abruptly, "but with one condition."

"Which is?"

Aline felt her jaw go hard. "This is strictly and solely an employer-employee relationship. Is that understood?"

Stack stared into the flames as if his feelings were hurt. She watched the play of firelight on the planes of his face.

"Of course," he said.

And so, for the first time since her divorce, Aline Conderie found herself in a position subordinate to a man.

204

10

Decorators, masons, and other artisans swarmed over the château, and for most of the day it was an unpleasant place to be. Stack asked Aline if she wanted her wing of the château redone. After hesitating half a day, she told him yes.

"Speak to the decorator then. Tell him what you want."

It was Stack's château, of course. Improvements only enhanced its value to him. Nonetheless Aline guessed that the redecoration of her wing exceeded Stack's mandate. He did it just to be nice. Kindness from Stack only confused her.

At Stack's request she also ordered surveyors out onto the land. The property, Stack had found, had not been surveyed in a hundred years. He wanted to know the exact limitations of his land, especially those plots which fell within government limits and were thus entitled not only to be planted in grapes, but to produce wine entitled to the appellation Margaux. It was Stack's notion, he explained to Aline, that the survey would show that certain plots, perhaps many plots, had shrunk by a row of vines over the years, perhaps even several rows of vines. Either underbrush had been allowed to creep in upon the vines, or else footpaths had taken over where grapes formerly grew, or turn-around areas for the machinery. He wanted such rows replanted if possible. He wanted to know also which parts of the various meadows he could legally plant in grapes. He wanted to know if he could cut down part of the forest and plant that in grapes.

One afternoon he went out with her to look at the meadow where the two horses and two cows grazed.

"Find out for me if we can legally grow grapes in this meadow," Stack said, "and what appellation they would be entitled to."

Aline protested. The meadow was more than was needed to feed the horses and cows, and of course the horses could go and the cows could go. They could buy their milk and cream in the shops like everybody else. But the meadow gave the property character. Too many vines made for monotony. The view down over the meadow toward the forest was beautiful, was it not? To plant grapes there would change everything.

Because they were on friendly terms now, her appeal was somewhat impassioned. Stack shook his head, cutting her off.

"This is a business. Our primary object is to make money for the stockholders. If we can plant this meadow we can increase production by, I should judge, ten percent or more. At the price wine brings in these days that's too much money to throw away on two horses, two cows, and a view."

Aline, angry, turned away from him. For the rest of the day she would not speak to him except to answer yes and no. That night at dinner Stack pleaded: "Maybe you're right. I'll think about it. Now will you please talk to me again?"

He had a boyish quality about him sometimes which quite undid her. Her father, puzzled, looked from one face to the other but said nothing.

She saw that Stack worked hard and was full of ideas. One day he had her dictate a request for an audience with the mayor of Bordeaux. This particular mayor was evidently running for president of France, and was rarely in Bordeaux.

"Don't think I'm interested in meeting the mayor of a jerk town like Bordeaux," Stack told Aline. "But I'm in business here, and he could be important. I've got to get to him."

An answer came back signed by a secretary. The mayor was too busy to accord an audience at this time. Stack said to Aline: "Write him another letter. Send a case of our wine along with it. Allude to his interest in the presidency, and suggest that my company might be able to help him. Tell him we want the interview within a week."

This letter went out, and the following day, to Aline's surprise, came a telephone call from the secretary. The mayor would receive Monsieur Stack Friday morning at 10 A.M. Aline accompanied him to the interview. The mayor's executive secretary spoke English, and the mayor himself spoke about as much English as Stack did French. Aline watched Stack's deportment with amazement. Stack was confident, boisterous; he kept attempting to make jokes in French. Although the jokes did not turn out well, everyone laughed anyway. At the end of half an hour, they left. Stack and the mayor patted each other on the back at the door.

206

Once in the hallway, Stack said to Aline: "In a month he comes to dinner. A month after that I'll invite him to play tennis with me. It's an important contact, and contacts you work at." Almost as an afterthought Stack commented: "Send him the invitation tomorrow. Add a line to the effect that the right kind of political leadership is important to all businessmen. Tell him that my company might be willing to make a modest campaign contribution when the time comes."

Aline was shocked. "I hate this kind of thing," she said. "You're corrupting a politician."

"No, I'm not," snapped Stack. "Politics corrupt the politician, not me. I'm just trying to stay afloat in a corrupt system. It works that way in America and every place else I know of, so don't be surprised."

The surveys were duly completed, showing places where vines could be planted. Very little wine made from these extra rows of vines was entitled to the Margaux appellation. But grapes would grow on the rest, out of which Stack had conceived the notion of making a sweetish rosé wine.

Aline was horrified.

"The Portuguese have been selling sweetish rosé wine to Americans for several years now. They're making a fortune at it. There's no reason why we can't cash in on that. We'll call it Conderie Rosé, or maybe on the label we'll put our name very small. I haven't decided yet. There's money in sweetish rosé, and we can produce extra grapes to make it with, and the land isn't being used for anything else."

Aline refused to talk to him the rest of that day too, but this time he was amused. "You're going to have to talk to me when you give me my French lesson this evening," he said.

When the weather was fine the French lessons took place outdoors on the terrace at the back of the château. The meadow with its two cows and two horses drooped down toward the trees. Madame Gorr served them each an apéritif. Aline favored red Cinzano with ice and a twist of lemon. Stack changed his order from day to day. Occasionally he asked for a dry martini. Most often he drank beer. There was always a bowl of olives, and sometimes of potato chips.

There was something ferocious about Stack's attempt to learn French. During the hour that each lesson lasted he never once reverted to English. For the first twenty minutes he liked to point out objects and name them. Of course they were the same objects every day but there were many of them, and he was committing them to the deepest part of his memory so that they would pop out in the future without thought,

207

like a great tennis shot. Day by day his accent improved, and he attempted ever more complicated conversations. Often he talked about himself, and about American business and his own philosophy as a businessman. Today he spoke of his curious realization that, as president of the wine division in France, he didn't need to court success, he really didn't have to do a thing. The wine boom would take him along with it. By the curious rules of American business the wine boom would be credited to his account as if he had caused it, no questions asked. In his clumsy French, Stack added: "It will be seen in the United States that it is I who has increased profits by twenty percent, next by thirty percent, who knows? But, even though I will be a big success here, I'm not sure if it will help me. Those who are my enemies need only keep me here to win over me. Every day that I spend here is a losing day. And yet it comforts me to think that in the meantime I can be a human being again here, and not all the time knock people down. Here I can enjoy. Here I can enjoy a sunset, such as tonight. Look, Aline."

The sun was dropping behind the trees. There was no sound that they could hear. "Hear that the night is without sound," said Stack in French. "In New York there is never a moment without sound. Here I can enjoy the sunsets, and the peace."

Did he mean it, or was he just practicing his French? In French he could speak as irresponsibly as a drunk. Because he was not in control of his words, he could not be held to account. She was irritated to see that this gave him an advantage over her.

"Drink," Stack suggested in French. "The hour in which I must speak French is coming to an end, and I am glad, for I am very tired of it."

He studied his watch. "Voilà, the hour in which I must speak French is terminated."

Although there was a chill to the air he wore only a short-sleeved sweater open at the neck. His arms were muscular and his forearms were covered with dark hair. He was smiling at her. Aline said coolly: "You're doing very well. All you need now is practice and a little more confidence."

Stack said: "They finished my office and my bedroom, and this morning I hung the prints we bought. Want to see how it looks?"

Aline almost declined. In his bedroom he might choose to misread her interest and her mood. However, she did not want to offend him, and it was she, after all, who had shopped with him.

"Lead the way," she said.

The Louis Quinze desk had been installed in his office. Behind it rolled a leather armchair which reclined when one sat back.

"Very comfortable," Aline conceded from the chair. On the walls, she noted, he had hung his American university diplomas, and also a framed montage of newspaper clippings about himself over the years: Charlie Stack, boy wonder. There were bookshelves containing many books on wine. Atop them stood a photo of, she supposed, his mother and father.

How hard to believe that such a man had a mother and father, had once been a baby.

"Come next door," Stack said, leading the way.

On the long wall of his bedroom Stack had arranged eight of his Napoleonic prints, and on the short wall four. They were quite handsome and formed almost a narrative history of the war.

"Very nice," Aline said. "We'll have to go looking for something to put over the fireplace next."

"Fine," agreed Stack. "When? Shall we go tomorrow?"

"Okay."

He had stood exceedingly close to her all along. She had been conscious of this. He was too close, there was going to be trouble, but now as she turned from the prints she found herself unexpectedly in his arms. He was attempting to kiss her. She moved her face this way and that, but his mouth clamped down on hers anyway.

She made no response. After a time the kiss ended.

She said: "I'd rather you wouldn't do that again."

"Why not?"

"I work for you; you don't own me."

"Who said own?"

She said nothing.

"Wasn't it fun?" he asked.

"No."

He shrugged and walked away from her. She followed him out of the room and down the stairs. Male vanity, she told herself. The trouble with men is that they can't take no. Women take it all the time. They ought to try being a woman for a while.

But Stack several times flew to New York, once staying there a week, and during each absence Aline found that she missed him. Not him personally, she convinced herself, but his excitement. Things happened when he was there. The Médoc no longer seemed so drowsy. It must be marvelous to be a man, and as important as Charles Stack, who had just flown four thousand miles to a directors' meeting. To rule on the fate of men and investments, to move millions of dollars about the world seemed to her something to be envied. In any case, she missed not having him there.

11

But for Stack the board meetings were not that marvelous.

In New York he stood beside charts on an easel. Around an oblong table sat the seven members of the planning committee. But Stack's attention was concentrated on only two of the seven: the chairman and Johnston. In the months Stack had been in Bordeaux, Johnston's power had increased dramatically. Such was the corridor gossip, and such Stack now in this room felt most strongly.

"This chart shows the land we own," Stack began. He adjusted the unfamiliar horn rims on his nose. "Note how the château is placed more or less in the center of our acreage. The shaded areas are those currently under vines."

Johnston said: "I see a lot of unshaded areas, Charlie." He was wearing a purple shirt, and his face looked florid.

"Strange as it may seem," Stack said, "one can't simply plant vines any which way in France."

"It's our land, Charlie boy," said Johnston. "We can do what we want."

"Unfortunately we can't," said Stack, who was being heckled, and knew it. He replaced the first chart with another showing the entire Médoc region. "Our plan was and remains to increase our acreage under vines as much as possible. However, there are legal restrictions. Our primary product is our château wine. Our château is in the village of Margaux and is allowed by law to carry on its label the appellation contrôlée Margaux. This is the highest designation it can carry, which is important. That's the designation people pay money for. You might think that any land lying within the village of Margaux is entitled to this appellation. Not true. A number of years ago a government commission came out and tested all the soil. In effect they wrote zoning laws. Wine made from the most apt land in the village of Margaux is entitled to be called Margaux wine. All of our acreage currently under vines is entitled to this appellation. Then there were other lots where the soil was not quite so apt. The commission ruled that such lots were not entitled to the appellation Margaux. However, such wine could call itself Haut Médoc wine. Still other lots were rated less good than that, and can be called only Bordeaux Supérieur. The fourth category would be wine from still less apt soil, and such wine could only be called simple Bordeaux."

The chart showing the Château Conderie acreage went back on the easel. Stack was using the pointer. "A certain amount of our acreage, here and here, not currently under vines would be entitled to the appellation Margaux. All such lots will be planted this spring. Eventually this will increase our yield by ten or twelve percent. You must understand that by law no wine can be made from the newly planted grapes until after the fourth harvest."

Stack's pointer tapped the chart: "Note this area here. This is the meadow behind the château. Part of it would be entitled to the appellation Bordeaux Supérieur. Under the circumstances, I've decided to leave the meadow unplanted. The price we could get for wine made on it would not justify destroying the meadow and the setting of the château itself."

"There must be some way around these regulations, Charlie," suggested Johnston. "There always is, isn't there? I mean, if a man is sharp enough to find it."

Stack looked from Johnston to the chairman. Stack didn't know what had been going on politically at the top of this company. Perhaps the chairman was contemplating early retirement. Perhaps he felt himself threatened in some way. Perhaps he had decided to push Johnston forward as the abrasive force in The Company. Perhaps he had turned against Stack because of that fiasco of a press conference in Bordeaux. The chairman, watching Stack closely, kept silent. His face gave no clues.

"Any law can be got around, I suppose," said Stack. "But I'm not sure it's a good idea in this case. If we got caught there'd be a stink. I thought we bought this property in the first place so as to upgrade our image. Or am I wrong on that?"

This time the chairman smiled. Johnston's eyes dropped to the table, and he began leafing through Stack's last report.

A map of the commune of Margaux now stood on the easel. "I've been negotiating to lease land here, here, and here," said Stack using the pointer. "The first area would come to about fifteen acres of grapes entitled to the appellation Margaux. Legally we will be able to throw such grapes into our Château Conderie wine—even though the acreage is several miles away from our château—and I intend to do so. The other two parcels would be entitled only to the appellation Haut Médoc, but once we plant vines there we could launch a second lesser brand using the name Château Conderie in some way, as most of the other great châteaux do."

The chairman spoke: "Lease, Charlie? I don't like the word 'lease.'"

"I don't like it either, Warren, but for the moment we don't have much choice. The people who have this land are peasants. They don't want to part with their land. They don't believe in money—although they're demanding a high enough price for it."

"How long a lease are we talking about?" asked the chairman.

"Thirty years is the best I can do so far."

"Thirty years?" demanded Johnston. "That's a derisory amount of time, wouldn't you say? I would say that was derisory."

"Mandatory retirement age here is sixty," commented Stack dryly. "None of us will be here when this lease runs out."

They'd all be dead by then, except possibly himself.

"The Company will still be here," said the chairman in a quiet voice.

Hypocritical bastards, thought Stack. Nonetheless, he had made a mistake which he now sought to repair, declaring apologetically: "I would hope my loyalty to The Company is as unquestioned as your own. I don't like such short-term leases any better than you do, and I would hope we could upgrade them as time goes by. This is the best I can do now."

"Maybe you need some help over there," said Johnston.

Stack and Johnston eyed each other. He's sure enough of himself even to wear purple shirts, Stack thought. Stack's hand pushed the horn rims home, a nervous tic. There were rumors that in Washington Johnston's brother was about to be given a cabinet post. Was this the explanation?

"Let's say we lease this land," said the chairman quietly. "What will it yield next fall?"

"Nothing. It's not planted."

"Just lying there?"

"Yes."

"If the farmer isn't using it, I don't see why he won't sell it outright."

"This brings me to another problem," said Stack, "the planting of vines. Even when we have leased the land and we're entitled to the appellation that we're looking for, we still can't go out and plant vines. We have to buy planting rights, and then we have to get permission from the government to plant."

Johnston said: "I don't get it, Charlie boy."

Stack glanced at Johnston. Once Stack had been Johnston's protégé. Johnston had brought him up fast within The Company. Johnston had put Stack in jobs where he could shine. I even thought he liked me, Stack thought.

Obviously Johnston now saw Stack not as a protégé but as a threat. Johnston, Stack had heard, had a new protégé now, a twenty-seven-year-old graduate of Harvard Business School on whom he had begun to bestow lavish projects.

"I've been searching around to buy up planting rights," Stack explained, peering over his horn rims. "You find a farmer here, a farmer there who has the right to plant vines on his land and isn't doing it. He sells you the document for about a thousand dollars an acre. The price keeps going up and such farmers get harder and harder to find."

"But you're finding them, Charlie?"

"I've found some. I'll find more."

"Do I read you right, Charlie?" asked the chairman. "You want us to lease land for only thirty years when we don't even own the legal right to plant vines on such land?" The chairman was tapping his fingers on reports sent from Bordeaux to New York at the rate of one a month by Charlie Stack.

Stack decided to flash a confident grin. "You have my reports. I've got everything under control."

"What about the hotel?" demanded Johnston.

Stack had been too busy to launch the hotel scheme, which he had decided could be left to ferment slowly in its own juices, so to speak.

213

He had looked over one or two dilapidated old châteaux down by the river. And that's all he had done.

"Work is progressing on that project, too," Stack said.

"But not fast, eh, Charlie?" said Johnston.

So far, none of the other five members of the planning committee had said one word during Stack's presentation. They had nodded from time to time. They had looked interested.

This company is ruled by fear, thought Stack.

The function of the chairman was to distribute generous doses of fear, though at the moment the chairman was acting with a certain aloofness while the fear was distributed by Johnston. What am I trying to get to the top of this Company for, Stack asked himself for the first time. It's an artificial goal. It's like trying to be first into a swamp.

"I thought it prudent to proceed slowly," said Stack. "We are not in the hotel business."

"Yet, Charlie, yet."

Stack was exasperated. "Look, I'm trying to learn the wine business. I found and purchased this château quicker, cheaper than anyone else could have done. I had to renovate the buildings, build up a staff, learn the laws and regulations, make the contacts with politicians, and now I'm trying to lease land and buy planting rights. So lay off me on the hotel for the moment."

It was an unfortunate speech, and Stack knew it. Johnston had been throwing darts at him for an hour. Now, reacting with irritation, Stack had revealed the accuracy of Johnston's aim.

Every dart had stung. Stack had shown weakness.

"If you need help, Charlie boy, we can get you help," said Johnston.

How could he ask for help on that basis?

Johnston, obviously with the approval of the chairman, was trying to push him to the edge. If Stack fell off, he could be replaced by someone better. Or at least by someone newer, more energetic, more enthusiastic. Or perhaps, instead of falling off, Stack would be goaded into a super performance. Either result was good for The Company. The Company, all pretended, came first.

Stack decided to say only: "That's all I have for now."

The seven members of the planning committee began to gather up their papers.

"How's the Conderie woman working out?" asked Johnston conversationally.

Stack looked at him. After a moment Stack said, "Fine."

214

"You've been seen with her rather a lot."

Jesus Christ, Stack thought, I've got a spy working for me. Saar, probably, who sends back even malicious gossip.

"That's only natural," said Stack. "She's my executive assistant, and also I've been relying on her as an interpreter at times."

"I would have thought you'd be fluent in French by now, Charlie."

Stack was furious. He wondered if Johnston had ever tried to learn a foreign language or knew how hard it was.

"Getting there, getting there," said Stack with a big grin. "Another month or two and I'll have it cold."

"Is she a hot number, Charlie?"

You whore, thought Stack. But he was still managing to grin. "To tell you the truth, I've been too busy to find out."

The chairman said: "Let me have all that lease business in writing, Charlie. I'll make my decisions based on that. But you know how I am. A guy with a really good success pattern I'll go along with."

This remark stood for praise.

"In next month's meeting I want to hear more about the hotel possibilities."

The seven men filed out, leaving Stack with his charts.

What are you upset about, Stack asked himself. Today is a perfect example of the way the game is played. And you love the game, don't you? Don't you?

That night Stack flew back to Bordeaux.

Aline, driving Stack's Ferrari, met him at the Bordeaux airport.

"You didn't have to meet me yourself," he said, surprised. "You could have sent someone."

"Your baggage should be along in a minute," said Aline, flustered. He was right. Why had she come here anyway?

Stack held up his small valise. "This is all I have."

"Oh," said Aline. But she felt ill at ease. He might get all the wrong ideas. She had met his plane only because she had thought it would be fun on this lovely spring morning to drive the open Ferrari through the quiet, empty country of the Médoc. She had meant nothing personal.

Outside the chrome-and-glass airport Stack got into the Ferrari on the driver's side. Aline got in on her side and handed him the keys.

"Well, what's happened in the last week?"

On firmer ground, Aline told of two farmers who had been located on the other side of the river. They had pulled out their own vines several years ago and replanted their land—one in cabbages, the other

215

in potatoes. Between them they still held planting rights to ten hectares of vines which they would sell for a bit over $30,000.

Stack whistled. "Christ, the price keeps going up."

Still, he was pleased. The two farmers no doubt imagined they were stealing money from the rich American château. Any wine they could make themselves was worth less as a cash crop than cabbages, but transfer their planting rights to Stack in Margaux, buy and plant the equivalent number of vines, and you could pay off the cost with the first usable crop four years from now.

"Congratulations," Stack told Aline.

To her shame, she blushed.

"You look nice when you blush. What the hell are you blushing about?"

Aline looked sideways at the passing country, so he could not see her face.

"What else?" demanded Stack.

Aline told of conferences with the lawyers who were drawing up the leases in Margaux that Stack had already contracted for.

Again Stack nodded.

She risked a glance at the line of his jaw. He was a good-looking man, but he had sat up on an airplane all night, then spent an hour or more in Paris between planes, then come on here. He was unshaven and looked tired.

"How do you feel?" asked Aline. "I mean physically?" The minute she used the word she could have bitten her tongue off.

Stack leered at her. "I feel fine—physically. How do you feel—I mean physically?"

He was only teasing her, she told herself.

But she did not like being teased.

"I wouldn't mind a café au lait," said Stack. "How about you?"

"The trouble is there's no place to stop," said Aline. It was true. In a nation famous for its cafés, there wasn't a single pleasant café in the entire Médoc.

They had come out of the forests into a country of copses and pastures. The fields showed clover and cow parsley, nettles and vetch. Briars and brambles in hedgerows separated the farms. Despite the shallow pitch of pink tiled roofs and the occasional isolated palm tree (imported long ago) this was Atlantic country, not Mediterranean. The trees were oak, ash, chestnut and elm. Overhead billowy clouds drifted across the vast sky.

216

Just short of Cantenac, two bars and a gas station faced onto a crossroads. One bar had two iron tables out front in the sun. Stack stopped the Ferrari and they got out. The two iron tables had been heavily painted many times, and both were wobbly, for Aline tested them with her hand.

Stack stuck his head through the beaded curtain into the bar and called out: "Anyone here?"

Behind him Aline said: "Very good accent. You're coming along."

"Thank you."

A man came out wiping his hands on an apron. Stack asked him for two big cups of coffee. Turning to Aline, Stack asked: "Cognac?"

"At ten o'clock in the morning?"

Stack turned back to the barman. "One cognac."

They sat in the warm sun. Presently the barman came out bearing a full tray.

Aline started to pour milk into Stack's coffee.

"No thanks," said Stack, upending the cognac into his coffee. When Aline grimaced, Stack laughed. "Just a nasty little habit I've picked up in France. But it will help keep me awake another few hours.

After a moment Aline asked: "And how did things go in New York?"

"Couldn't have gone better," Stack lied. Why should he tell her anything? He put his hand on the paint-encrusted table top and wobbled the table. "Isn't it odd that in the Médoc, a bit of land worshiped by every gourmet in the world, this café is as good a café—and as good a restaurant too, I suppose—as any gourmet could find if he came here?"

Thirty minutes later Stack stopped the Ferrari at the edge of the river and got out. The doors slammed. He stood looking at the river. The water was brown. The far bank was two miles or more away but they could not see it. There were two islands—sand banks really—in the way. The deep-water channel was between the far island and the far bank. The water ran brown and cold in all three channels.

Aline watched Stack. Inland sheep grazed on what had once been the front lawn of a château. The château was a dilapidated eighteenth-century building. It faced out over the river. It had round towers on either side, and a steep slate roof in between. No vines grew near it.

There was a saying in the Médoc that none of the great wines were made within sight of the river, and Aline knew this was true. The old château was surrounded by overly rich black earth, for the river overflowed its banks often enough, carrying silt. Such earth was no good for grapes.

Half a mile inland the land started to slope upward, and that's where the grapes began to grow.

Aline had no idea to whom the dilapidated château had once belonged. People had lived in it when she was a child. Wine wasn't selling then, and the Médoc was going through one of its periodic times of misery. A lot of the châteaux changed hands for very little money; the owners of others died. Roofs fell in, and no one cared. Many of the great châteaux of the Médoc came to look as if they had been shelled, though of course no war had ever come near the place.

Abruptly Stack turned to Aline: "What would you think of buying that château over there and turning it into a small luxury hotel?"

Was he serious, or just making conversation? But the idea delighted Aline. "It would be fun to decorate it," she said.

Stack smiled. "That's a very unbusinesslike way to look at things."

Stack began to walk upstream along the bank, approaching the château, but had to give up. The ground was too marshy.

"How many rooms do you suppose you could rent out in such a place?"

Aline had no idea. "It looks pretty big."

"It's got chais out back. They could be transformed into rooms too, like a motel."

He was studying the château, calculating its size.

Aline said: "Are you going into the hotel business?"

"God knows the Médoc cries out for a hotel."

"This ground is marshy."

"There must be trees or bushes that could be planted that would soak up much or most of that moisture. We could give the château a fancy name, maybe even the same name it used to have, and we could plant vines."

"Land along the river is called the Palus," said Aline. "It has the right to no appellation contrôlee at all."

"I know that. But no one's going to know it in Idaho or Japan. We could make wine here, give it a big advertising budget, and possibly get a pretty good price for it. No one ever heard of the words 'appellation contrôlée' in Idaho, or in Japan either."

Stack studied the château. "It would be kind of small," he muttered suddenly. "I don't know if they'd go for it. What they're thinking of

218

probably is a ten-story Holiday Inn."

Filled by whom? Tourist buses sometimes went down the main road, stopped to taste the new wine at one or two châteaux where previous arrangements had been made, then continued out to the end of the Médoc peninsula, where they crossed back to the mainland by ferry. The river was seven or eight miles wide up there, and the ferry trip took nearly forty minutes.

"If you put up a ten-story hotel here," Aline said, "you'd change the character of the land forever."

"I know that."

Aline wondered if he had come to like the character of the land the way it was, and if he resented whatever pressure was making him consider changing it. The world here moved more slowly than he was used to, and perhaps he had begun to move at its pace.

"A small, quite-elegant hotel in this spot," Stack said, "with an excellent restaurant, would fit in here, don't you think? A man could be proud of having built that." After a moment he added: "The château owners might be glad to have it here, a place to go for dinner once in a while apart from each other's houses." Stack suddenly grinned. "They could foist off all their unwanted guests on this place. And we could make the prices high enough so that such guests wouldn't be eager to come back." Stack and Aline started to laugh. The morning sun shone on the front face of the dilapidated old château, and on the cold brown river, surging soundlessly past it.

"I want you to get up some figures for me," Stack ordered. "Find out how many people have gone across on that ferry in the last year. Find out how many tourists approximately have come out here in the last year. At the same time I want you to find out who owns this château, and how much land goes with it. Find out if it's for sale. Once you have that information I want you to get some contractors out here that I can talk to. I'll talk to them myself. For the time being we won't think any more about the ten-story Holiday Inn–type hotel."

They climbed back into the Ferrari. The doors slammed and the engine roared. The sun was warm on Aline. She could feel it on her bosom through her sweater. They surged uphill, parting the vines. In a few days now the vines would begin to push out new shoots and leaves. The soil would begin to assert its strength, pushing grapes up from under the earth. By fall the grapes would be hanging there in their tight, heavy clusters.

12

The cellar master opened the main door of the Château Lafite with a great key. To one side Stack and Aline caught a glimpse of an elegant living room. Then the cellar master had opened a second door directly ahead, and was ushering them down into a small vaulted cellar. This was the château's private wine cellar. No tourists entered here, Aline had told Stack, and precious few outsiders of any kind.

A bare bulb hung down, making enough dim light to show that the vaulted ceiling and the stone walls were covered with dark mold. And it was enough to show the treasures lying on their sides in sand-filled bins along the walls. The bins were like stone sepulchers. They were filled with sand to within inches of the top. The rare old bottles lay on the sand, each vintage partitioned off from the next by a board standing on edge.

"Old wines are terribly sensitive to vibration, and also to light," Aline explained. "That's why the light is so dim here, and why the old bottles lie in sand."

Stack looked impressed. The first bin was marked 1797—a single bottle. The bottle was covered with dust, of course, and Aline watched Stack extend a hesitant forefinger, touching for the briefest possible moment the bottom of the bottle.

"That's the oldest bottle of wine in the world," Aline whispered. "It's still alive. That's the way I suppose you have to talk of old wine. It's still alive, and changing every day in the bottle, though less now, I suppose, than when it was young."

Why was she whispering? She felt almost reverent down here, like a child in church.

The cellar master, who had stepped back, watched them as carefully as a bank guard. A single bottle lay in the bin marked 1798, and also in the one marked 1799. From there the bins extended forward in time, growing more crowded. Some contained two bottles, some up to

220

six, but there were gaps in the years, for some years the wine was stillborn, and in others it had died young. The bins continued up through the 1800s.

Aline and Stack looked down on wine contemporary with events they had studied in school, battles perpetrated by Napoleon or one of his successors, massacres under the Commune. This wine here might have been drunk by the Impressionists when it was young and vigorous. Of course it would taste far different now. The wine marked 1864 was harvested during the American Civil War, Aline recalled.

Most of these old bottles would never be drunk, for to drink a bottle would be to kill it. One day the wine inside would expire. If you loved wine, you really wouldn't want to drink any of these. There was more pleasure just imagining that such wine still lived on in this soundless cellar, still enriched the world with its existence.

The last bin was marked 1914. That was the year the world ended for Europe. The world began again a few years later, but it was different. Aline supposed that Stack would not understand such a notion as that, and she feared he would not understand these few old wines either. In a moment they would go upstairs and outside into the sunlight, where he would probably make some joke. She herself felt as awed as if in the presence of a Beethoven symphony that the rest of the world had never heard, or a Rembrandt lost for centuries and found only now.

"It's cold," murmured Stack, who was wearing only a short-sleeved shirt.

"About fifty-five degrees," said Aline. "Something like that."

"Aren't you cold?"

"I suppose so. I don't mind it." She was in the presence of something she didn't clearly understand. Looking down at the sand-filled sepulchers and the dusty old bottles, she felt deeply moved, though she could not comprehend why. At the same time she realized there was no understanding this type of thing ever. One either felt it or did not.

"How much is all this worth?" Stack murmured.

"It's priceless."

"Priceless means that a man who cared about this would give ninety percent of all he owned to have it."

Aline was pleased with this remark. You couldn't talk about these old bottles in terms of money, but nonetheless one wanted to find a way to talk about their value. They were without price.

Rothschild's cellar master cleared his throat. By the door he stood

221

fidgeting. Obviously their time was up. Aline sighed.

"I suppose many of the châteaux have something similar," Stack mused when they came outside into the sunlight again.

Aline, somewhat offended, assured him that the cellar they had just seen was unique. A few of the great châteaux owned a few old bottles, none older than the last decades of the nineteenth century. That was all.

Stack's shoes scuffed the gravel. Aline felt a relief from tension. Why should the contemplation of rare old objects produce tension?

"Thanks for bringing me here," Stack said. "I'm very impressed."

A few miles away he steered up to the château of the second Baron Rothschild, and sprang out of the car. Stack's secretary had made advance arrangements here too, and the inevitable peasant in blue work clothes came forward to serve as guide.

"I thought the baron himself was going to show us around," Stack said.

"That would not be possible, monsieur," the guide answered, leading them into the wine museum. "The baron is a grand monsieur."

Glass cabinets set into the walls contained the loot of centuries: golden goblets and chalices, many encrusted with precious stones; shelves of woodcuts and engravings on the wine motif; busts of Bacchus sculpted out of marble, or cast in bronze, or molded in faïence with a necklace of grapes painted ruby red, or carved in bas relief on barrel ends, a popular art in Austria in the 1700s.

"But we had an appointment with the baron," insisted Stack stubbornly.

The guide pretended graciously not to understand. Stack ungraciously got angry. "—I didn't come here as a tourist, but to talk to the baron. He agreed to the meeting, we were told."

"I'm sorry, monsieur. But the baron is resting."

"Wake him up."

"Impossible, monsieur, begging your pardon."

"Rank has its privileges," noted Aline.

"At least tell him I'm here," insisted Stack.

"He has been informed."

"But he's resting," said Stack. "I think we'd better go, Aline."

Aline refused. "Let's look at the museum first."

She stood before another Bacchus, this one in polychrome-and-white glazed faïence, wearing only a few vine leaves for clothes, purple

222

grapes in his hair, sitting astride a wine barrel, his cheeks rouged, obviously drunk.

"I'll be in the car."

Stack stomped out.

But she had wanted him to see all this. She had wanted to stroll with him backward and forward in time. Here there was a collection of Greek amphorae. She wanted to say to him: "The Romans and Greeks knew no other way to keep their wine than to put it in an amphora, put a stopper on it, and pour wax on top. When the Romans came to Bordeaux, they learned the art of making barrels from the Bordelais."

All this would be a surprise to him. She wanted to show him that the history of wine went back thousands of years, that artists for centuries had celebrated the wine and grape, the harvest and the festival, in many different mediums.

"Wine has always been awfully close to the heart of man," Aline wanted to tell him. "Artists used it as a symbol of joy, and as a symbol of extravagance. Look at all this gold and silver and jewelry."

She wanted to hear him say: "It's beautiful."

It was no fun seeing it by herself. She went outside to the car. Though angry at him, she forced herself to say: "The baron and his wife collected all this personally."

"The baron has a lot of money."

"And a lot of taste."

"And he doesn't keep his appointments. Get in. Let's go."

He stopped at a café on the river front at Pauillac. Aline was still annoyed at him. He could be so crass at times.

"This café is as seedy as the one we had coffee in the other morning," Stack asserted.

He ordered two portions of fresh salted shrimp and a bottle of cold white wine.

"I wanted to ask the baron why the Rothschilds haven't put up a hotel out here somewhere. They're already in the hotel business for God sake."

Aline broke open a tiny shrimp, pulled the flesh out, and popped it into her mouth with manicured fingernails.

Across the narrow street was the river. They ate their salted shrimps, drank the cold wine and stared across to the far bank some five miles away.

"That's good wine country over there too," Aline said.

"But not as good as this side."

Stack tore the head off a shrimp and worked the flesh loose. Then he took a gulp of the cold white wine.

I don't like him, Aline told herself, and he doesn't like me.

Stack said: "This river reminds me of the Mississippi. It's even wider than the Mississippi. But it's too muddy for swimming and too swift for sailing. You'd think a river this grand would be important to the lives of the people who live on it, but it's not."

"In its way it was very important," said Aline. "What do you think formed the wine country on both sides of the river? Tens of thousands of years ago, maybe millions of years ago, as the Ice Age receded, or whatever it did, the river must have extended outward along both banks, covering what is now the wine country for ten miles on both sides. Then the river got narrower and began to cut the bed it runs in now. But on the higher ground it left behind all that sand and gravel. And that's what produces the great wine. It's really unique soil. The great wine grows in what used to be river beds."

When the barman, wearing a dirty apron, came out onto the sidewalk, Stack began interrogating him about the café's wine list. Stack wanted to know what kinds of wines he stocked, and what kinds his customers asked for, but the barman gave unsatisfactory answers. Stack turned to Aline and said in English: "This guy doesn't seem to know anything about wine."

"Why should he?"

"Because he's a barman in the most important wine area in the world. Eight or ten of the greatest wines in the world are produced within five miles of his bar."

"You forget that great wines cost money. Great wines are drunk by the educated, the sophisticated, and the well-off, not by this barman. You wouldn't expect this barman to know about Mozart or Rembrandt, would you?"

"Those guys weren't French."

Stack gave the surprised barman a five-dollar tip, then said to Aline: "Come on, let's go."

That evening Stack took Aline to dinner in the Savoie in Margaux, where he again studied the wine list.

"Amazing," he said in English after a moment.

Aline watched him. With the wine list lying open on his lap, he began to interrogate the owner-waiter about wine.

224

The owner seemed to know little more about wine than the barman at Pauillac that afternoon.

They ate a sturdy, unpretentious dinner: a homemade vegetable soup, steak with a wine sauce, fried potatoes, salad.

"So today I've learned two things," said Stack. "First, that the history of wine goes back thousands of years, and that there are collections both of art objects and of rare old bottles that are worth a fortune. And the second thing I learned is that the ordinary barman in Pauillac and Margaux doesn't know a goddamn thing about the subject."

Aline began to laugh.

"I'm not so sure it's funny though," said Stack. He led her out into the barroom, where they ordered coffee.

Moodily Stack stirred in sugar.

Just then the door opened, and a number of teenagers came in. Among them was Françoise Gorr.

"Françoise," Aline called out.

Though Françoise shook hands with Aline, she seemed unwilling to shake hands with Stack, Aline thought. She seemed to force herself to do it.

Françoise answered Aline's questions monosyllabically. Yes, she had just got home. No, she could stay only a few days. It seemed to Aline that Françoise resolutely refused to look at Stack. Although Aline addressed Françoise in English, Françoise's brief responses came in French.

Plainly Françoise wanted to get back to her friends, and Aline let her go.

Stack would not look up from his coffee.

"She doesn't seem to like you very much," commented Aline. "What did you do to her?"

"What do you mean, what did I do to her?" said Stack defensively. "I hardly know her."

"She's like a sister to me," explained Aline. "We even went to the same school in England. Not at the same time, of course. I worry about her and wonder what will happen to her."

From the bar, Aline noted, Françoise was staring at the back of Stack's head.

Stack drained his coffee. "Come on, let's go," he ordered.

13

After brooding about it a week, Alexandre Dupont decided to go see old Cracheau in the sanitarium. The place, it turned out, wasn't a sanitarium at all, but a three-story stone building with its back up against the railroad cut. Below it ran the Bordeaux-Arcachon line. In front ran one of the main streets of this crowded suburban town. Buildings pressed close to either side. It had a minuscule garden surrounded by a spiked fence. In the garden, as Dupont approached the gate, several old men stood aimlessly. Though it was a warm spring day, they wore overcoats and mufflers.

Inside, Dupont asked to see Cracheau.

"Do you have the doctor's permission, monsieur?" inquired the nurse at the desk. Perhaps she was merely a receptionist. She wore a white uniform and had a hard face.

"Oh, no," said Dupont mildly. "Is that necessary?"

"Then I'm afraid you won't be able to see the patient," the woman said. She gave him a false smile. "We have strict rules about that."

Dupont had been dismissed. She was already busy with some papers. Dupont drew out his credentials and announced: "Alexandre Dupont de la Brigade de la Répression des Fraudes."

The woman appeared flustered. "Oh, police," she said. "Well, I'm sorry, monsieur. Well. I didn't know."

It occurred to Dupont that he should correct her. He was not the police. He did not like to think of himself as the police. He was merely a government functionary. However, he had come out here to see Cracheau, and had to get by this woman first.

"If monsieur will come this way—"

He followed her into a reception room, where she left him. A few minutes later Dupont was conscious of a thump-thump in the hallway. The door opened, and an old man in a faded blue bathrobe hobbled into the room. Tangled white curls showed at his throat. But the hair on his

226

head had been shaved off. He was leaning on one crutch. His false leg was of the latest modern design: two bands of chrome steel descended from the hem of his bathrobe and were joined in a kind of rubber heel at the floor.

"Who are you?" the old man demanded. "Do I know you? What do you want?"

Dupont came forward, hand outstretched, but said automatically: "Alexandre Dupont de la Brigade de la Répression des Fraudes."

The old man began to cackle. "Fraud Brigade, that's a laugh. Did you catch me doing something? Did I fail to fill out your fool papers? Maybe I forgot to declare my stock on the thirtieth of the month. Guilty Put me in jail."

The old man began cackling wildly.

Dupont had not known what to expect, and still didn't. Was the old man insane? Senile? What had Dupont come out here for anyway? Probably the old man knew nothing. Even if he had information to give, the testimony of a man committed to an institution would not be worth much in court.

"Go ahead, put me in jail," cried the old man. "Anything would be better than this dump."

"I'm sure you're very comfortable here," murmured Dupont.

The old man waved the crutch at him. "Comfortable? Who's crazy here, you or me? Comfortable? Have you had a look at this place? Have you talked to that battle-ax at the front desk?"

Dupont judged that the old man was close to tears. Tears of frustration? Tears of rage? But he did not sound crazy.

The old man began cackling again. "Whatever I did, you can't get me now. I've been certified. I'm not responsible."

The cackle ended, and the old man rubbed his eyes. "So I guess I'm stuck here. I can't even get myself put in jail. I never thought I'd want to go to jail."

His unshaven cheeks were caved in on his nearly toothless mouth.

Dupont watched him attentively.

"I don't suppose you could get me my old leg back, could you, young feller? No, I guess that's asking too much. Look at this leg." The old man hiked his bathrobe up. His own leg ended at mid-thigh, and the truss for the two chrome steel struts started there. "This is no fit leg for a man. Besides, it hurts my stump. I wish I could get my old leg back. They won't tell me what they've done with my old leg. Probably chopped it up for firewood by now. They said it was dirty. They said it stank. So what. It wasn't their leg, it was my leg."

The old man gave a sob. "I miss my leg, boy. I miss my land."

Dupont, much moved, said nothing.

"I guess you think I'm crazy."

"No," said Dupont. "I don't think you're crazy at all. I wonder if you'd tell me how you happened to come here."

"A judge certified me senile, that's how I happened to come here."

"I imagine there was more to it than that," suggested Dupont.

"My children signed the papers, of course. They wanted my money. They wanted to sell my place and get my money. They couldn't wait a couple of years till I died. Can't live forever at my age. They couldn't wait."

The things people did to each other, thought Dupont. It was sad. It was sad for the whole human race. After a moment Dupont said: "What's the procedure of a thing like that, anyway?"

"It isn't a trial in a proper courtroom, if that's what you mean. It's not a criminal procedure. You don't confront your accusers. They just come and get you. The fellows in the white coats, they come and get you. They stick a needle in your arm, and you wake up here. I was rude to that psychiatrist fellow. That's where I made my mistake. How was I supposed to know he was a psychiatrist? I thought he was just someone who wanted to buy my land. I was always rude to people who wanted to buy my land."

Dupont waited.

"Fellow comes out on my land. He starts asking foolish questions. So I give him foolish answers. Then I ran him off. That was the court-appointed psychiatrist. He testified against me, so my lawyer says. My children testified against me, and that other fellow who wanted to buy my land, he testified against me too. I don't have a lawyer any more. I don't have any money left to hire a lawyer with. They took all my money. They signed over my army pension to pay for this place. I don't have a sou for a lawyer. You're not a lawyer, boy, are you?"

"What other fellow testified against you?" asked Dupont carefully.

"That other fellow. Testified to the irrationality of my acts. Said I liked to stomp in cow shit. So I like to stomp in cow shit, so what? What else is a wooden leg good for? It wasn't like putting your shoe in it. It was just a wooden leg. What's irrational about that?"

"Do you remember the name of that fellow?" asked Dupont carefully.

"Oh, yes. My lawyer showed me all the papers. That fellow Bozon.

228

He used to buy all my wine. Lately all he wanted to do was buy my place. I led him on. I teased him a bit. I let him make a fool out of himself. I guess he didn't like it. He testified to the irrationality of my acts. He said I liked to stomp around in cow shit."

That name Bozon again, thought Dupont.

"He wanted my place real bad. I guess he's got it now."

"Not at all," said Dupont. "Your château was sold to a man from Paris. A fellow by the name of Aubervilliers."

The old man snorted. "A man from Paris? I don't believe it. Look into that fellow Bozon. He's behind this. He used to buy my wine. He kept after me to buy my place, so I raised the price of my wine on him. That's why he did this."

The old man looked close to tears again. But Dupont's mind was buzzing with other thoughts.

"Say there, young fellow, you wouldn't want to help an old man, would you? You wouldn't want to help me get out of this place would you? I've been certified as a madman. I'm not crazy. Do I sound crazy to you, young fellow? I'm not crazy, am I? You can help me, can't you, young fellow? Can't you help me? I'd so like to get out of this place."

Dupont shook the old man's hand and headed for the door. "I'll do what I can," he said, knowing he could do nothing. "You'll hear from me again."

"No, I guess I won't hear from you again."

"Yes, you will. I promise."

"It's asking too much, I guess. But maybe you could help me get my old leg back. If you asked them, maybe they'd give me my old leg back. This one hurts my stump."

Dupont went out of there.

Back in his office Dupont angrily took the Bozon dossier out of the filing case and read it. Then he went to the truck yard to interview Armand Picot. The trucker was not there. They said he was due in an hour, and stared solemnly into the inscrutable face of the man from the Fraud Brigade. Dupont nodded, and went out through the gates and sat in a café for an hour. His anger passed. He sipped his wine and tried not to think of the old man. When he re-entered the yard, the truck was in and Armand was standing there. Dupont interrogated him. Dupont's questions were formless, and almost meaningless. He wondered why he was there at all. He had nothing specific to ask this man. He could only hope the trucker would let some fact drop.

The trucker sensed Dupont's confusion and became arrogant. His answers became monsyllabic, surly. He had been nowhere near Bozon's warehouse for the last six weeks at least, and a visit to the trucking office, where the brother-in-law got out the truck's papers, confirmed this.

"What's this all about?" the brother-in-law demanded.

"Just routine," said Dupont.

The brother-in-law glanced from Dupont to Armand. "What the hell have you been up to?" the brother-in-law demanded of Armand.

"Someone has denounced Monsieur Armand Picot," Dupont lied. He did not know why he lied, or why he was speaking at all. "It's not a denunciation we take seriously, but I must check it out."

When he left there, the brother-in-law was worried, Armand was shaken, and Dupont was annoyed at himself for having wasted the entire afternoon.

Back in his office he ordered down the two young gendarmes who had stopped Armand's truck so many months before. They arrived on their motorcycles about two hours later. They came in through the door and stood in front of his desk, guns flapping, helmets under their arms, gauntlets off and clenched in their fists.

"Do you remember this report?" Dupont asked, pushing it across.

The young man who had written the report acknowledged his signature. He said he remembered stopping the truck, since it was the first night he had ever been asked to check wine trucks.

"Your report says that it was red wine."

"Oui, monsieur."

"How did you know in the dark it was red wine?"

"I licked some off my finger, monsieur."

"Then you could have been mistaken."

The young gendarme said: "Monsieur, I was not mistaken. I am a Frenchman."

Dupont dismissed them. Why had he even ordered them in?

Dupont was stalling. He had been rather idly investigating the sale of Château Cracheau, but had stumbled upon Bozon again. He was convinced Bozon was up to something. Dupont did not know what. He had no idea where this new trail would lead, should he decide to follow it all the way, but he was afraid of where it would lead, and he did not want to go up against a man as rich and powerful as Bozon. He could not imagine a man like that soiling his hands in a petty swindle. If Bozon was involved at all, then he was involved big, and it was possible that the honor of French wine depended upon him, Alexandre Dupont, a minor government functionary. And this notion troubled him. It troubled him very much.

Dupont decided to request authorization for a trip to Paris as part of a confidential investigation. After a week the requisition came back stamped approved. The next day Dupont rode up to Paris in a second-class carriage. This was the only type of transportation authorized for members of the service except under extraordinary circumstances. Dupont's wife had packed him a lunch, and he munched this contentedly while staring out at the countryside flashing by. The train averaged nearly a hundred miles an hour—how remarkable French trains are, Dupont thought, as the houses whizzed by. He was in Paris by early afternoon. He did not know the city, and did not want to spend money on a taxicab, so he took the Métro, overshot his destination by two stops, and walked back.

The address given for Aubervilliers, purchaser of Château Cracheau, was 72 Boulevard de Lannes. When he came to this address, Dupont pushed the buzzer, and the great wrought-iron door of the apartment house swung inward. He then rapped on the door of the concierge's loge.

The door opened four inches and he looked in at the face of an officious little woman. But, when he had presented his credentials, she looked frightened. She stepped out into the hallway, and Dupont opened his briefcase. She knew no one named Aubervilliers, she said, never had. Dupont began to show her eight-by-ten blowups, asking if she recognized any of these men, under Aubervilliers or any other name. She kept shaking her head. When the photos ended, Dupont closed his briefcase, thanked her, and went out into the street again. Paris seemed much colder than Bordeaux to him, and it was getting dark fast. Dupont turned up the collar of his raincoat. He could perhaps parade up and down both sides of the street showing his photos and someone would recognize one of the faces. This is what he would do all day tomorrow, most likely, but now on a hunch he walked up to a policeman and asked if, in addition to the Boulevard de Lannes, there was not also a Rue de Lannes, or Avenue de Lannes. Often, when giving false addresses, people merely changed their real ones slightly. Dupont had no idea what this proved—perhaps only that the perpetrator of the fraud sought to give a false address he could easily remember. Perhaps he found security in an address so like his real one. Perhaps it showed merely the stupidity of the criminal mind.

The policeman directed Dupont to the Allée de Lannes, a narrow alley with only one building entrance.

Dupont rapped on the concierge's door.

"Do you recognize this man? No? What about this one?"

The first photos were of colleagues in the Fraud Brigade. Then came one of Claude Maurice, a replica of the photo on Maurice's official identity card.

"That looks like Mr. Maurice," the concierge said. "Of course he wore a beard when he lived here."

Dupont's face remained impassive. He shuffled through the remaining control photos. "Do you recognize this man?"

Dupont was afraid his hands would start trembling, but they did not. He thanked the concierge, and went out into the night. He was elated. He breathed in the air. He felt like singing. Then he thought: Yes, but what have I proved. That Claude Maurice had lived on the Allée de Lannes and worn a beard, and that no one named Aubervilliers lives at No. 72 Boulevard de Lannes. That's not much, is it? Dupont thought. It's not even a crime. But what else is going on, and when, and how? Though Dupont was suddenly full of questions, he could ask no more here, fearing that Maurice, if he checked back from time to time, would hear about it.

Dupont decided to find a cheap hotel, and tomorrow he would catch the day train back to Bordeaux again. He would work out a plan.

But as he thought it all out he began to see the enormous problems ahead, and to lose confidence. He had no evidence, only suspicions. That night as he ate his soup in a small restaurant, he decided to tell his chief all his suspicions when he got back to Bordeaux. Dunking his bread in the soup, Dupont mulled over this idea, but by the time he had eaten the soupy bread, then reached for his wine glass, he had changed his mind. His chief would not be impressed. His chief would tell him to go out and dig up hard information.

Dupont's boeuf bourguignon was placed in front of him. His fork stirred it around.

What information? Where?

He could go to Château Cracheau. He could hammer a hole in the floor and see if false vats were down there. But, unless he found fraudulent wine in those vats, then he still had no case. And the bureau would have to pay damages, both physical damage to the premises and damages to the reputation of the Château Cracheau and its wine.

232

If anything serious was being planned there, such a raid would merely scare the perpetrators underground.

No, all he had so far was a hint, a wisp of perfume floating by. His nose sniffed something, but when he reached out, he caught only air.

Dupont lifted his glass to his lips. Wine: it was as normal as bread. It was as normal as blood. It was as necessary as either or both. It was vital to the economy of France. It was vital to each Frenchman and Frenchwoman at each meal, and to millions of other human beings around the world. It was the job of himself and a few others to safeguard it, and tonight he felt plainly inadequate. What he had found out so far was insignificant, and the true problem was that he had no idea what to do next.

Each year the Fraud Brigade discovered two hundred or more infractions, mostly because disgruntled employees or competitors informed. Usually violators were fined. The laws involving wine were so complicated that many additional paper violations were discovered each year, but were not cited. Only major frauds were prosecuted, such as the adding of sugar and water to the vats to stretch ten thousand liters out into twelve thousand one-liter bottles, for instance.

Another popular fraud was overproduction, for each property was limited by law to a specified maximum amount of wine. Some growers tried to plant extra vines in unapproved terrains, or to prune their vines in such a way as to increase productivity beyond what quality would support; and some growers from time to time would try to falsify labels, slapping an expensive label onto a cheap wine and shipping it, usually, out of the country fast.

Perhaps the new proprietors of Château Cracheau were trying one of these tricks. Perhaps the new concrete vats under the floor were meant only to hold the overflow. Such owners deserved a good fine, if they could be caught solid.

Perhaps Bozon was not involved.

Dupont, forcing a chunk of bread and a wedge of cheese into his mouth, wanted to believe he had stumbled onto nothing serious. It was impossible that he could have stumbled onto anything really bad. He had no right to alarm anybody yet. He would go on nosing around a little longer. Time was not of the essence. He would tell nobody yet.

But exactly how would he push his investigation further? All he could think to do was to call in gendarmes, surround the place, and raid it. And that simply wouldn't work. He had no evidence.

The little agent went back to his cheap hotel, where he paced the threadbare carpeting, smoking. He didn't have enough to go on. He could only wait. Perhaps nothing would happen. Perhaps he was imagining things.

BOOK THREE

1

In the Médoc sky clouds built up every few hours. Except for the hottest part of summer, Stack had been told, rain would fall frequently all year, and so far had. Certainly winter had been an almost constant drizzle, and although spring had come early—there were burgeons on the rose bushes by February 1—it had produced a solemn procession of overcast days that seemed to last forever.

During such days the two remaining canes on each vine root had been trained outward along the wires in graceful crucifixion. Stack had watched men tie each cane with raffia, rounding them into gentle flat curves so that (according to Gorr) the rising sap could not race straight to the ends, dripping future wine nectar into the dirt.

By May some twenty-five thousand new vines, looking like double-length pencils, had been thrust into the soil at one-meter intervals on ten other acres, which now came back into service. Stack had planted one row himself. In some obscure way this made them his personal vines, and he watched them carefully for days, waiting for them to burgeon and show life.

The first of the four yearly plowings had taken place, the high straddling plows moving along above one row of vines, aerating the soil on either side. One plot Stack plowed personally. Keeping the machine straight was harder than it looked, but Stack learned it and worked for an hour, delighted with himself, while its driver stood in his rubber boots at the edge of the field looking conspicuous and uncomfortable.

Soon the vines were throwing up shoots in all directions, and men

237

moved down the rows each day, leaving some shoots, pruning the surplus. Stack helped with the pruning of the field he had plowed and, when the time came, personally sprayed it blue with chemicals, making it safe—for a while—from mildew and pests. Afterward he stood looking over his handiwork, glowing with pleasure.

On May 25 Gorr strode about the place rubbing his hands confidently. The risk of frost was over, he said.

Stack had never realized there was any such risk this late in the year.

"Oh, yes," said Gorr. "Until May 25."

"On May 25 exactly, the danger automatically ends?" asked Stack.

"That's the tradition."

Stack was amused. "I see. Frost operates according to tradition."

"Tradition is important in wine," said the cellar master.

The vines flowered. The flowers were tiny, almost invisible to the naked eye, but decided the quantity of grapes that would be harvested next fall. Hail—or even heavy rain—could wash off the flowers, decimating next fall's crop here and now, but during the two weeks that the flowering lasted, no precipitation fell. This was rare.

"We should have a huge crop this year," Gorr gloated to Stack.

Stack put it in his monthly report to New York. Huge. The word sounded like a rash promise. Charles Stack's report, not the soil, not the vines, not nature itself, became responsible for pushing forth next fall's huge crop, as far as New York was concerned. The Company would blame Stack if said huge crop failed to materialize.

According to Gorr, you could count 120 days from now to the vendange: "The grapes will swell, their skins will thin and turn purple."

Gorr was happy at the prospect, as was Stack. You could count on it. Gorr was talking about a sure thing, almost the only sure thing left in life in these modern times. The soil would push forth its fruit on a schedule of its own, and no chairman or company could decree otherwise. One could not count on men or human events. One could count only on the land.

For once Stack's life seemed based on something solid.

He felt himself coming alive in ways that were new to him, and there were days when he thought of the New York business world as akin to riding out on the wing of an airplane at thirty thousand feet. It was too cold and rare out there and you had to hang on so hard there was no fun in it at all. You couldn't see, hear, and enjoy. All you could do was hang on.

238

Immediately he reacted against such notions, thinking: Let's not get seduced by the easy life. You knew when you came here that it would not demand much of you. That was always the special danger of the place.

Today, for instance, he had nothing much to do, though it was Thursday, supposedly a business day. At the moment he lounged in the archway, sucking on a blade of grass, gazing across at the château. The main job of the day was a phone call to the chairman, but he could not, because of the time difference, make it for several hours yet. Warren was invariably at his desk by 7:30 A.M., so the call would be placed at lunchtime, Bordeaux time. Stack meant—once again—to invite the chairman to spend a relaxed week, or even just a weekend, at the château. He should bring his wife. He and Stack could play tennis, and Aline could show his wife around the other châteaux. They'd both enjoy it.

Stack had made the same invitation previously, but the chairman had ignored it.

Stack had been brooding about the unfortunate press conference. It was possible that Bordeaux had become fixed in the chairman's mind as a place where he had been made a fool of. Stack did not want to let the chairman's mind harden any further, because if it hardened against Bordeaux then probably it would harden against Charlie Stack too.

Stack had acquired a few new leases he could report on. That would be the ostensible reason for the transatlantic call. Though he dreaded the call in advance, Stack knew he would come on cheerful once the connection was made.

He doubted the chairman would accept the invitation. Although they had attended meetings and conferences together, Stack had not once managed to see the chairman alone since the day of the press conference, meaning months ago, and this had begun to seem ominous.

Just then Aline came out of the château and crossed to her car. He stalked her with his eyes. Was she so unaware of her effect on him? When she waved to him, he waved back.

An hour later Aline and her childhood friend Odette Brown sat under dryers at a hairdresser's in Bordeaux. The weekly trips to get her hair done were a ritual with Aline; usually she was back at the château for lunch, but today she and Odette would make a day of it. After leaving the hairdresser's they lunched with another former schoolmate, whose husband, a lawyer, had come home for lunch to join them.

Aline and Odette went from there to Aline's dressmaker, where

Aline had herself fitted for two new dinner gowns.

"What did you do when you had your shop?" inquired Odette.

"Wore the best ones once each, then put them back in the window. But I had to be so careful not to soil them that it was hardly any fun."

Afterward the two young women strolled in the streets, peering into shop windows, eliciting glances from men and giggling about it once the men were out of earshot. Late in the afternoon it became time to pick up Odette's two small children at their private school.

On the way home Odette said: "Would you and your father like to come to dinner tomorrow night?"

"My father's away, but—" Aline hesitated, then said: "I wonder if you'd mind if I brought Monsieur Stack."

Odette gave a grin: "Is there something between you two?"

"Of course not. I just thought it was time you and Nathaniel got to know him, that's all. After all, you are neighbors."

Odette was smirking, which made Aline acutely uncomfortable. "He really can be quite charming at times, and he speaks creditable French now."

"We'll be delighted to have him," said Odette.

When Aline had parked in front of the château and got out of her car, Stack came toward her across the gravel.

"Where have you been all day?" he demanded.

"I took the day off," answered Aline defensively. "Why, do I have to ask your permission first?"

"You do work here, you know."

"What's gone wrong?"

After a moment Stack answered: "The chairman's not coming."

"How did he sound?"

"Abrupt."

"Don't blame me just because you've had a bad day. I myself had a lovely day."

"And where the hell is your father?"

"Right at this moment I believe he's floating around the Mediterranean on the yacht of a friend."

Almost despite himself, Stack looked impressed by this news. "He never tells me where he's going or when he's coming back," Stack grumbled.

"Is that so surprising? He does have his pride, you know."

"He's got a lot of gall, too. I just found out he took a case of 1934 vintage with him. Presumably that's what he pays his room and board with when he goes on these yachts. I've just learned he takes a case every time he goes anywhere. Do you know how much those old cases are worth? And it's not his wine to give away, it's my wine."

"It's the company's wine, surely," amended Aline mildly.

"When he comes back I want you to tell him he's forbidden to take any more of that old wine."

"I can't tell him that."

"I'll tell him myself."

"If you feel you must."

"I'll put a padlock on it."

"I'm sorry the chairman's not coming. That must have been hard for you."

"I want you to tell your father he doesn't own this château any more."

Aline said: "I've got some good news for you. You're invited to Nathaniel Brown's château for dinner tomorrow night."

"It took you long enough. Did I finally pass inspection? Whose inspection did I pass, yours or theirs?"

"I thought you'd be pleased."

"I'm sorry. I am pleased."

"There'll be other couples there too."

Stack managed a smile. "You mean I'm about to make a social breakthrough, eh? If I don't start barking like a dog at the dinner table, I'm in."

"I'm glad you're feeling better now."

"That wine your father takes is worth a lot of money, Aline. I wish you'd tell him. I don't want to have to hurt his feelings."

"All right."

"And thank you for getting me the invitation."

Sunday came. The weather had warmed. Stack became restless. He felt penned in here. It was too quiet. He wanted to go somewhere, now, today. On this triangular peninsula few directions beckoned. Half a mile east ran the river. Twenty miles south was Bordeaux.

A Sunday drive, why not? Stack invited Aline, who hesitated, but agreed. "I'll get my things."

They drove out toward the ocean in the thundering Ferrari. In each village people stared. Stack was pleased to be on the road, pleased by the sun on his arms, pleased by the girl beside him. The man who had made good wore ornaments. The Ferrari was an ornament; the girl

241

was an ornament. He was rich enough to decorate his life, and had decorated it.

The young prince thundered through villages in a cobalt-blue chariot, making heads turn.

Aline's seat was half reclined, her head on the headrest, her eyes closed, her blouse open down to the cleavage. Something inside him stirred to look at her.

He moved toward the ocean, wearing his Ferrari like some splendid decoration on his chest, the Congressional Medal of Honor of the business world. He was thirty-five years old, president of a division of one of the mightiest conglomerates in the world. He was proud of himself.

And Aline?

She was efficient. As a business associate she did quickly and accurately what she was asked to do. He relied on her and bounced his ideas off her. Who else did he have? He told Saar almost nothing. Saar handled the leases; Saar kept the château inside the wine laws. Old man Gorr cared for the wines aging in the sheds, and directed the workers in the vineyards.

For as long as he did not attempt to approach Aline physically, she was as warm and friendly as one could hope for. Many times he had been moved to touch her shoulder or her hand—and who knew where the thing might go from there? But each time, at his touch, he had felt her stiffen.

What the hell was the matter with the woman? he wondered.

From the top of the Pilat sand dune they looked down on the shimmering ocean. This was the tallest dune in Europe. A hundred or more summer homes, many owned by rich wine merchants from Bordeaux, clung to its summit and slopes. These were substantial Mediterranean villas with orange tile roofs, but they faced out over the Atlantic, a colder sea. Trees shaded the steep, twisting streets—mostly maritime pines, and long slippery pine needles carpeted the gardens.

One slope of the dune was a vast place of pure blowing sand. On it a German blockhouse faced out over the ocean, waiting out eternity. A modern castle: no ramparts, no towers, no battlements. A mighty concrete cocoon with a small steel door in the back, and a gaping aperture in the front from which the stout nostril of a twelve- or fourteen-inch gun must once have extended. The walls and ceiling were three feet thick at least. Stack and Aline stood looking across at it.

"How many tons does the thing weigh?" Stack asked Aline.

For a moment he imagined the invasion here which never took place. The cannon, mightiest phallic symbol of its day, bombarding the ships, the ships bombarding the blockhouse.

The mighty blockhouse no longer looked formidable. Part of the dune had collapsed underneath it. It was almost teetering. Presumably the winds and rain of a very few more years would finish it off. The sand underneath would dwindle further; one day the blockhouse would pitch forward on its face. It would tumble down the dune into the sea.

Stack could hardly believe the Germans had built such a heavy blockhouse on top of a sand dune. A few shells landing ten or more yards underneath might have toppled the whole thing into the sea in 1944. A few near misses might have destroyed the blockhouse more quickly than direct hits.

Turning, Stack looked back on the town of Arcachon at the edge of its vast inland sea. The sea was almost perfectly round, and in the sunlight shone like glass. Except for its channel to the ocean, it would be a lake. North of here, Aline had told Stack, there were two other vast lakes much like it—coastal lagoons with no channel to the sea.

The Ice Age, or whatever it was, had done strange things to this bit of land: towering dunes, funny coastal seas, and, a few miles inland, isolated patches of stony, sandy soil that produced the great wines, patches so unlike any others in the world that it was as if they had fallen like gigantic rugs from the sky.

"The bay of Arcachon is full of oyster beds," Aline said. "Would you like some oysters for lunch?"

From their restaurant terrace one flight up they looked out on moored fishing trawlers, and at sailboats gliding across the bay. They had oysters with black bread and white wine, followed by a tray of cheeses with a bottle of red wine, followed by pastry and coffee. In France, Stack was beginning to realize, one did not have to eat expensively to eat beautifully. The crusty bread, the incredibly flaky pastry were the same everywhere. The oysters would be equally cold and salty in a seedy pub, the cheeses would be as fresh, and there were hundreds upon hundreds of wines to taste, very few as splendid as the great wines of the Médoc but all fun to drink and talk about.

Stack put his hand on top of Aline's on the table top. "I'm really beginning to love to eat," he said.

Aline, almost casually, removed her hand from under his.

"In America one doesn't dine, one refuels," Stack commented.

243

"One feeds." He felt the need to explain something to her, or perhaps to himself. If France was winning him over, food was a large part of it. "In this country, no matter what you choose to eat, the eating of it tends to delight you. I'm not used to that."

They decided to go swimming.

The road north ran straight and flat through a vast pine forest. All this area, Aline explained, was once an immense beach. The prevailing wind was always from the sea here, and the sea had kept pushing sand onto the continent. The sand had gained ground at the rate of seventy-five feet a year. Rivers trying to find their way to the sea got blocked —they gathered inside the line of the dunes in shallow stagnant lakes. Elsewhere the sand drifted over the soil until it did not drain, so that each rainfall created vast swamps. No one lived in this whole region but a few shepherds who herded sheep on stilts. From the Middle Ages on there had been talk about somehow stabilizing the invading dunes, which made the rivers mill about inland. One river, the Adour, trying to find a channel to the sea, changed directions every hundred years or so. Each terrible storm would block its present channel and it would have to start another. Eventually it was threatening the city of Bayonne. In 1578 a channel direct to the sea was opened for the Adour. Men and beasts dredged this channel through two kilometers of shifting sand dunes, the most massive engineering project of the age.

Elsewhere the sand had still gained on the land. Two hundred more years passed before an engineer named Bremontier planted a two-hundred-kilometer-long wall of pilings in the beach about seventy meters from the highest tides. Dunes began to accumulate against this palisade. The engineer kept planting new palisades on top of the new dunes. He created in effect a solid sand dune fifty feet high from the Spanish frontier to the tip of the Médoc peninsula, and seeded it with a bush that was actually a kind of vine—it sent down an enormous number of roots and spread quickly.

Now the engineer applied himself to the problem of the drifting interior dunes. Various kinds of bushes were seeded. Mixed with these seeds were the seeds of a maritime pine. The bushes grew fast enough to stabilize the sand until the pines were high enough and strong enough to take over the job. As the pines grew, the bushes underneath rotted, furnishing fertilizer for the mostly sandy soil.

The work took a hundred years but it saved the entire peninsula, which today was principally pine forests. The pines went right up to the edge of the wine country, which was really just a strip of land sixty miles

244

long and twelve miles wide along the bank of the river. The rest of the peninsula was timber.

"I guess it's the richest timber land in Europe," said Aline.

They had reached the beach village of Lacanau, whose one street ended at the edge of the high dune. They looked down at the ocean far below. The beach extended as far as the eye could see in both directions. Wooden stairs descended to the beach. There were many swimmers.

When Stack came out of the changing cabin he had all his clothes rolled up in the tennis satchel. Walking to the water, he stood looking out to sea, the satchel in his hand. The salt wind was in his face, as was the sun. Hot sand pushed up between his toes.

Because of the wind and breaking waves, Stack did not hear Aline's cabin door open and close. Nor did he hear her footfalls on the sand. Abruptly, she was standing beside him. They were separated only by his tennis satchel, her straw bag, and the few bits of cloth that constituted modern bathing suits. He looked at her.

He had never seen her legs before, he suddenly realized. He had never seen her in a dress or short skirt, just long trousers or dinner gown. Now she stood before him more naked in many ways than if she were completely naked. Complete nakedness was usually a prelude to sex and one tended to look right past it, but he was not looking past it now. A man and a woman had suddenly revealed almost all of their bodies to each other, under the pretense that this was not important. It was bad form to stare at another's body, Stack reflected, or to comment upon it, even though to stand together like this signaled a rather violent change in their relationship. A great many very important secrets were being handed over. One's visual knowledge of another person suddenly increased by about ninety percent. One's understanding of another person too, perhaps. It was like tearing down a fence. One could now see across.

She wore a wide-brimmed, floppy straw hat and dark sun glasses, and was staring out to sea as if afraid to look at him. He looked down along the line of her throat, out the slope of her chest, encountering the cloth there. His eyes moved down over her flat stomach, past the other bit of cloth, down her thighs, down her shins and out across her feet to her painted toenails. It was as if his eyes were scissors cutting out her silhouette. He thought: Did she paint those toenails for me?

His gaze started up from the knobs of her heels up over her calves, up the back of her thighs where the cloth—very briefly—interrupted

245

again. The cloth was smooth and silky, elastic nylon probably, and it was white. It was so brief it barely reached the top of her behind, and so tight that he had an urge to stroke it. His gaze moved up her back, skipped over the string bow, encountered her hair. Their eyes met. Because of the dark glasses, Stack could not read her face.

"Very nice," said Stack with a grin.

She frowned.

The modern sexual revelation had been accomplished. Their bodies stood revealed. Was she eyeing his figure too?

He dropped his bag on the sand. "Is this a good enough spot?"

Stack walked into the waves. The wind off the sea was warm and blew spray in his face. He waded on out, let a wave smash over him, and began to swim. He swam out a good way. When he looked back, Aline stood letting the waves wash up over her feet. Stack saw German blockhouses at the base of the dune. They were about a mile apart.

Swimming back toward shore, he let a wave catch him and it dumped him in a storm of sand and pebbles at Aline's feet.

Aline watched him.

"Are you coming in or not?" Stack asked.

He waded on out again. When he looked back, she was entering the water, high stepping. She swam out. He came close and put his hands on her soft narrow waist.

Aline frowned. "I wish you'd keep your distance."

"I don't get it."

"We're not teenagers, you know."

"I still don't get it."

"As I recall, teenagers always like to handle a girl underwater. They imagine they can get away with something underwater that they wouldn't dare try on dry land."

Jesus, thought Stack.

He swam in and toweled himself off. When he looked back, she was walking slowly out of the water. He went up to the cabin and changed back into street clothes. Climbing the staircase, he stood on the boardwalk on top of the dune until Aline, also dressed, appeared at the bottom of the stairs. Stack stared out at the sea. Her head appeared at the level of the boardwalk, but Stack ignored her. Presently she stood beside him. Aline's hair was wet and black. The wet hair hung down the back of her neck, exposing her ears and the sides of her neck. She looked very much younger and more vulnerable than before.

246

When they got back into the open Ferrari, the seats were so baking hot that Aline squealed girlishly, but Stack still ignored her. As he put the key into the ignition, Aline said: "There's something I should tell you."

"There's nothing you have to tell me."

"I feel I owe you an explanation."

"You don't owe me anything."

She stared at her hands in her lap. "It's hard for me to explain."

"Then don't."

She said in a low voice: "You have a right to be mad at me."

Stack, exasperated, said: "I'm not mad at you. As a matter of fact I've sort of given up trying to figure you out."

"When I got divorced I was twenty-two. That was five years ago. In those five years I haven't—that is—there hasn't been—"

He waited.

"You probably think I've had lots of lovers since then."

"That would be normal."

"Well, I haven't."

"You haven't had lots of lovers. Fine."

"No, I haven't."

She was wringing her hands in her lap. "I haven't had any lovers at all." This was a lie. She had, though not in a long time.

"Not one?"

She said nothing.

"I don't believe you."

"Don't then," she mumbled.

Stack's hands were on the wheel. He stared out through the windshield at the Atlantic Ocean.

She was trying to tell him something, but what? "If I've hurt you at times, I didn't mean to, it's just—"

"If you prefer girls to men," said Stack harshly, "just tell me and I'll stop pursuing you."

Aline seemed to stiffen in her seat. "I'm not a lesbian. I used to like making love, and then I didn't like it, and in any case, this is all academic as far as you're concerned. I don't need you sniffing around me. I don't need any man. I can get along quite nicely all by myself, thank you. You seem to forget women are not mere sexual objects any more. They are people now."

Stack, feeling the heat of the leather through his trousers, said:

"This is so melodramatic it's almost funny," but he didn't laugh. After a heavy silence, he said: "That must have been some marriage you were in."

"Someday perhaps I can tell you about that," said Aline in a low voice.

"Were you in love?"

"You don't believe in love, do you?"

"I believe in a number of things. I'm not sure that I believe in love."

"I do," murmured Aline.

"Next you'll tell me you're saving yourself for Prince Charming who will sweep you off your feet because you're pure. It's a bit too late for that, isn't it?"

"It would be nice to fall in love again as I did when I was a young girl. But that kind of love is impossible except out of innocence. It requires a headlong quality on both sides, doesn't it?"

She was looking at him, waiting for an answer. Stack thought that this conversation was almost as idiotic as the kind teenagers had with each other.

Stack said: "I see what you mean," although he didn't.

In her eyes Stack thought he saw a vulnerability and a need that he had never noticed before. Stack said: "You're going about it wrong. You ought to jump into bed with guys. Maybe the love would come afterward. In this day and age it damn sure isn't going to come before."

"I don't believe you."

"No? Your five years' experience proved the contrary, I suppose?"

He gave the ignition key a vicious turn, and the Ferrari began to thunder. He backed the car around. When he glanced at her, she was looking away from him, her jaw hard.

2

Alexandre Dupont was called in by his chief, who wanted to know what he had accomplished in Paris. Dupont gave a vague answer: he had met with confidential informants. In police work the world over, the words "confidential informant" enclosed privileged terrain. No cop asked the identity of another cop's confidential informant. Usually, once those words appeared, no cop asked further questions at all. The phrase could be used to cover any progress in a case, or to cover up any lack of same.

Now his chief nodded, but said: "You'll have to give me a report. A trip like that has to be justified."

Though his chief waited for an explanation of some kind, Dupont, unsure of himself, preferred to keep his suspicions to himself. No point alarming anyone yet.

"I'll do up a report," he said vaguely. After thirty years in the service, Dupont knew how to write reports that would justify unusual expenses. His chief, lighting a pipe, nodded. The interview was over.

But Dupont felt pressure. Signing out a car, he drove across the bridge and out into the wine country on the other side of the river.

It was midmorning when he entered the minor road that led past Château Cracheau, and he drove along it from north to south, passing the château. At a café five kilometers distant, he ordered café au lait, which he sipped until it went cold. Glancing at his watch, he forced himself to wait over the half-filled cup of cold coffee until an hour had passed. Then he drove back the way he had come, passing in front of Château Cracheau a second time. At the other end he had lunch in a restaurant, then made the same drive a third time. After that he drove back over the bridge and so to his office.

He had had three glimpses of Château Cracheau, totaling perhaps thirty seconds, and using up almost the entire day. The glimpses would suffice to reinforce his original impressions of the place. Château Cracheau could not be put under surveillance without the inhabitants knowing about it. Dupont had considered sending a man or men along this road with a telephone repair crew. Perhaps some job could be concocted so as to keep the place under surveillance for several hours, but now Dupont had seen that the telephone lines were so meager that work by such a crew would fool no one. Two strands passed in front of the château. The telephone poles did not even carry crosstrees. How long could you keep a crew of men busy on two strands of uninsulated wire?

So surveillance was out.

However, a panel truck had been parked in front of the château during Dupont's first two runs; it was gone the third time. Dupont, straining his eyes, had managed by the end of the second run to copy down the numbers off the plate.

As for activity, two men had been pruning vines in the field close to the road during all three runs. Dupont recognized them as Claude Maurice and the Italian. If Château Cracheau was a front, then it was a good one. The vines next spring would be in better shape than ever in recent years, judging from what work had been done previously, and the additional work which Dupont had seen done today.

When he got back to his office, Dupont began tracking down the license plate of the truck. The truck had to lead somewhere. One had to show identity papers to buy or rent a truck. In two hours he had traced it. This particular truck proved to have been rented in Dax, a small city a hundred forty-two kilometers to the southeast. Why Dax? Was Dax a false trail? Another dead end?

Dupont noted that all trails so far had led him immediately out of the Bordeaux wine region. Someone, presumably deliberately, was breaking up each trail, making it hard, perhaps impossible, to follow. The plumber, the vats, the owner, now the truck, all led in different directions. They were different-colored threads, and all they did to Dupont was confuse him. He still felt no certitude that all of them together would ever lead anywhere.

The name of the truck renter was given as Emilio Buonocorso, who was perhaps the Italian who worked at Château Cracheau.

The weekend was coming up. Dupont decided he would think about all this over the weekend.

Monday morning, after hanging his suit coat on the coat tree in the corner, he sat behind his desk, unlocked it, returned his keys carefully to his back pocket as always, so that he was sitting on them and could feel them there all day, and looked through the papers in the dossier he had begun on this case. As always, the dossier told him little, and he soon replaced it in the drawer. He then went through his in-basket, marking several routine reports for rerouting. It was midmorning before, abruptly, he sent one telex to customs and a second to Interpol in Paris. The first asked customs to check when and where one Emilio Buonocorso had entered France, if this was possible. The Interpol telex asked for a background check on Buonocorso, and hopefully, a photograph of him. With these two messages out of the way, Dupont returned contentedly to routine tasks, the case for the moment being out of his hands. For the moment any mistakes were being made by others, and Alexandre Dupont could not be held to account.

Now the days began to pass, and to his surprise Dupont found that he could not get his mind off Château Cracheau. Several times he got the file out and went through it. It still gave back no answers, and it seemed in no way connected to the other file, the one on Bozon. Why should such a man as Bozon be involved, if he was involved? Dupont wondered time and again. Bozon's involvement continued to seem implausible to Dupont. Such a rich man could not possibly be a criminal. It didn't make sense. Dupont himself, if that rich, would not even consider committing a criminal act. Of course Dupont, poor, wouldn't consider it either. But surely he, Alexandre Dupont, had calculated wrong somewhere.

His telex messages had gone out, but did not come back. So far, not a word.

And so that month ended, and the next began. Dupont, troubled, went around to see Le Grand Jo on the street behind the Quai des Chartrons. Within three hundred yards of Jo's bar were five major wine shippers. There were other bars, and by day it was such a busy street that unusual activity of whatever kind would be difficult, perhaps impossible, to notice. But at night it became just another dark, empty street, and Jo's bar was the only one open.

Dupont asked Le Grand Jo to phone him at home at any hour of the night whenever there was activity inside any of the nearby shipping houses. Jo looked mystified.

"It's a routine matter I've been asked to look into," lied Dupont. Nodding confidently he sauntered out of the bar.

That was at 7 A.M.—Jo went off at 8, and to see Jo, one of Dupont's best informants, he was obliged to go by very early or very late.

Dupont had drunk a glass of wine with Jo. Leaving the informant, Dupont waited in another café for his office to open. His rank was not high enough for him to hold custody of a key to the place.

Later Dupont checked out a car and drove some forty-five kilometers northeast of Bordeaux to interview the plumber who had installed the concrete vats at Châteaux Cracheau. One had to be most careful in a matter of this kind. Dupont wanted to hear the plumber tell the same story twice, and he wanted to know exactly where the vats were. He wanted to see a receipted bill if possible. He wanted the plumber to sign a statement attesting to the facts he had given. Only then could Dupont be confident that the plumber's evidence would stand up in court. Only then could Dupont feel confident that such evidence existed at all.

"Alexandre Dupont de la Brigade de la Répression des Fraudes," the little agent said, showing his credentials.

This shook the plumber. Presently Dupont followed him back to his house. There the plumber showed Dupont the entry in his log book. Dupont copied down the date and the amount of money received.

"Is that all the job was worth?"

Dupont knew that the plumber had entered a smaller sum in his books so as to cheat the government in income tax.

"It wasn't such a big job," said the plumber, flustered.

Dupont gave him a hard look. Dupont wanted him intimidated and thus cooperative. "Do you always work for so little?"

"It only took me half a day," insisted the plumber nervously. "It wasn't a big job."

The fellow began to protest that business was bad, and a plumber had to accept any fee he could get.

"Were you paid by check?"

"Oh, no, monsieur. Cash. This guy peeled the bills off a roll."

Sitting at the man's kitchen table, Dupont began to write out in longhand a description of the job, giving the date, the approximate capacity of the concrete vats, their location, the amount of pipe work involved.

"You say the vats were below the level of the floor?"

"That's right, sir."

"I'd like to ask you to sign this."

The plumber, worried, asked why he was being investigated, and what would happen to him. He began to protest that everybody cheated on their income tax a little.

Income-tax violations were not Dupont's affair, but he did not say so.

It was true, the plumber admitted, he had been paid slightly more

252

than he had declared, but very little more, and he had meant to enter the correct sum, but had forgotten.

A few minutes later Dupont left with the signature of the shaken plumber. Behind him, he imagined, the poor man was pouring himself a stiff shot of cognac and had begun to worry about going to jail.

That night Dupont's phone rang. The telephone was in the front hall. Stepping groggily out of a warm bed, Dupont hurried barefoot along the hall. The floor was freezing on the soles of his feet.

It was Le Grand Jo. "There are lights on Chez Bozon across the street, and somebody is unloading a truck."

"A tanker truck?"

"No, it's a panel job."

Dupont had arranged to keep one of the brigade's cars overnight. He had asked to keep the car a week, but had been granted only three days, and tonight was the last of them. He drove quickly through empty streets. Turning off the Quai des Chartrons he reduced speed, and he drove past the back of Bozon's warehouse as slowly as he dared.

Parked outside was the Château Cracheau truck. No one was in the truck or in the street. Dupont continued along for a distance of about three hundred yards, then pulled over under a street light. In his notebook he noted down the exact time, the exact location of his now parked car, and the sequence of the night's events: the call from his confidential informant, the plate number of the truck parked outside Bozon's warehouse with its back doors opened. He then signed his name in the notebook. In court, notes taken contemporaneous to an event carried great weight. Dupont then thrust his notebook back into his pocket, and cruised past the warehouse a second time.

Two men had begun unloading the truck. They appeared to be unloading cases of bottled wine. Their faces had been turned away as he passed, and he could not identify them. Further down the street, he stopped under a street lamp again, wrote these additional details into his notebook, together with the exact time, and again signed his name. That was all he could do tonight.

When he got home, though he was exhausted, he lay awake until dawn. Now he knew that Bozon and Château Cracheau were connected. What else did he know? Nothing.

On his desk next morning he found a telex from the Customs Service. No record of anybody named Buonocorso, Emilio, entering France had been found. Customs pointed out that tens of thousands of people entered France legally by car, and no record was kept.

Dupont sat staring at the message for several minutes, nodding his head over and over again. It was like a game, he thought. Nothing serious. It was like a masked ball. The object was to guess at the identity behind the mask.

If he broke into Bozon's warehouse right this minute, he might find a few cases of mislabeled wine, or he might not. It was extremely difficult to prove mislabeled wine under the best of circumstances, and virtually impossible if the documents had been skillfully altered. Dupont shook his head in disappointment. He still didn't have enough hard evidence to warrant calling the integrity of the entire French wine industry into question. For what? On mere suspicion? He didn't know where hard evidence was to come from either.

Unless Interpol came up with something.

But Interpol seemed to have forgotten that any request for information from one Alexandre Dupont had ever existed. This wasn't too surprising when you thought about it. He was only a minor government functionary. No reason why anyone should listen to him.

3

Sundays in summer in that open, vine-covered country felt hotter than other days, Stack thought. And emptier. You did not see the workers or their families. You felt them all around you but didn't see them. Stack was bored and restless. The sun was implacable. No air moved. In the afternoon, because all his potential tennis partners were at the beach, he had hammered a hundred balls back at his machine, then quit. It was too hot. The soles of his feet burned through his sneakers. After a shower he felt cool for a time, then began to sweat through his shirt again.

Madame Gorr was off Sundays, and Conderie had gone somewhere —he was seldom there this summer—so it was Aline who prepared an early supper. They ate on the terrace and drank a bottle of cold rosé. Aline seemed trying to be nice to him these days. But this only increased the sexual tension between them.

Stack pushed back his chair and stood up. He had conceived the idea of a drive, perhaps to the beach. It would be cool in the car, and perhaps if he did go to the beach he would find a breeze off the sea. He needed to go somewhere: he felt cooped up. In his restlessness he had begun to worry about New York again—what was happening there? Surely in his absence lesser men were jumping ahead of him in the queue.

He moved toward his car. To his surprise Aline followed.

"It's hot," she offered.

"You'd think the grapes would shrivel up in this heat," he said, glancing off across the vines. But in fact they thrived on heat, and it was against the law to irrigate them.

"Where are you going?" asked Aline.

"To the beach." Stack hesitated. "Want to come?" What the hell, he thought; he had no choice.

"You don't have to invite me," she said humbly.

"I wanted to. Get in the car."

He drove straight into the setting sun. He had the sun visor down and wore dark glasses, but behind them he was squinting. Presently the Ferrari entered the forest, plunging into sudden cool. The pine trees were dark and cool. It seemed to Stack that he could smell the odor of resin and pine cones.

Soon it seemed he could smell the sea too.

"Turn left here," Aline suggested.

The great ridge of dunes was not far ahead, and there had begun to be houses beside the road. The new road ran between the houses, and then the houses ended and there was only the dune between them and the sea. The road had become a narrow strip of solid concrete that ran along parallel to the dune. It was not much wider than the width of the Ferrari. It was solid. It was like a strip of runway made to handle heavy jets. Stack imagined that the road was three feet thick. It had been laid in sections twenty or so feet long, and some of them had tilted slightly from the movement of the sand.

The forest was on their left, and on their right was the dune. The dune rose far higher than the trees, and on the other side of the dune would be the sea.

"How far does this thing run?" asked Stack. He wondered why any-one had laid this minor beach road in thick concrete segments. Here and there chunks were missing, creating dangerous potholes. Evidently the road menders didn't even take care of this thing. Stack was confused.

"Do you know what this road is?" asked Aline.

"It's a very odd road."

"The Germans built it. It runs twenty or thirty miles down the coast behind the beach. It was made to carry tanks, I suppose. They used it to supply their blockhouses along the beach. Then the war ended and they went away, leaving their bloody blockhouses on the beach forever. Leaving this road here forever too. Pretty soon you'll find it just runs out. It just stops."

It was beginning to get dark. There were clouds above their heads, and the setting sun was beginning to paint them in violent colors.

"Turn in here," suggested Aline.

Stack turned off the concrete road and bounced along a kind of dirt trail in the direction of the dune. He parked the car and they got out. Ahead was the solid bulk of the two-hundred-kilometer-long dune.

Aline had come to this spot often as a young girl, she told him. She felt comfortable here.

"Do you feel like climbing to the top of the dune to watch the sunset?"

He looked at her attentively.

Because the way his eyes clamped on hers confused and unsettled her, this time as always, she suddenly began to climb the dune alone. Halfway up she took her shoes off. The dune was steep. She kept sliding backward. The cuffs of her trousers became full of sand.

When she came up onto the summit, she could see the sweep of beach and ocean. Chunks of red cloud floated overhead.

She sat down on the sand and hugged her knees. Stack came up and stood a few feet away. There were great streaks of color all across the sky. She glanced over at Stack.

"Nice," he said, and sat down.

She looked back at the sunset. The clouds turned scarlet. Presently the scarlet became violet and then mauve, and then she was sitting in a plum-blue dusk.

Aline stood up and began slogging down the dune toward the sea. Her heels dug in. She strode down the dune, skidding.

When she had skidded to the bottom she called up to Stack: "You ought to try that. It's fun."

In his turn Stack strode down the wall of the dune, heels digging, carrying her shoes in one hand and his own in the other.

"Let's walk down the beach," suggested Aline. "Leave the shoes there. We'll find them when we get back."

Stack looked dubious. She saw that he was worried about getting lost. "It's a big beach. Supposing we can't find our car again?"

"We won't get lost," said Aline confidently.

"It will get dark awfully fast now."

She saw Stack checking over the terrain. There was a kind of saddle in the dune where they had come over, and their heels had scarred the wall. They should be able to find that saddle again, even in the dark.

They began to stroll south along the beach, walking in the wet part of the sand, leaving footprints. They walked about a kilometer.

It had begun getting dark fast. "We'd better walk back," said Stack. It was the first time she had ever seen him unsure of himself.

The stars came out as they retraced their steps. When they got to the shoes again Stack picked them up and started toward the dune. Aline stood facing the hot, dark sea.

She took her shirt off and her bra, dropping them behind her. The hot wind blew at her, hot as hands. Stepping out of her trousers and underpants, she walked forward into the darkness. The warm waves smashed over her white body.

Stack had dropped the shoes and taken several steps forward. She saw his hand go to his belt, but for a while he did not move. She stood up to her bosom in the sea, peering back at him. The water rose and fell around her.

She felt power over him and all men. He'd like to come after me, she thought, but he's probably got an erection. She saw an erection as a sign of vulnerability, a sign of weakness: he would never let me see that. An erection testified to the truth. The truth was not written in a man's face, but halfway up his abdomen in language any woman in the world would understand. Aline thought: There is no language barrier; women who speak only Hindi would understand. The infallible lie detector. The truth stares up at you, and the man is ashamed.

And the woman is afraid.

Except in the bedroom, of course, where a different set of rules applied.

This was not a bedroom. Stack seemed paralyzed, and Aline almost laughed. She was glad she was not a man coping with this repeated problem.

She watched him begin to get undressed. His movements looked feverish. He walked toward her, lifting his knees high. He was moving straight toward her, so she swam away from him. The water felt cold

257

all over her body. She was swimming. Her nipples were hard and her legs felt smooth.

It had got very dark. The white of the beach and the crests of the breaking waves made a kind of luminous light, but in the sky there was now no moon, no stars, no light of any kind.

Stack was standing on the bottom, the water up to his curly chest, watching her. It was as if they were in different rooms. She swam in her room, and he swam in his.

"It's raining," Stack called across to her.

She raised her face. Now she could feel a few drops. She began to wade hurriedly toward the shore. A wave smashed against her back and she stumbled forward. The next wave hit her in the buttocks. She heard Stack moving out of the water too. Lightning split open the sky. For a moment it was bright as day, revealing them to each other. Drums rolled. Then it was dark again.

She bent to gather up her clothes. Stack was doing the same. There was a streak of lightning, and another peal of thunder—followed by more lightning. The beach became very bright. She looked across at Stack. She had her shoes in one hand and her things in another, and was trying to cover herself. She had counted on night, not sunshine.

It was raining as she tried to sort out her underwear.

Stack called: "Bundle it up and run for the car. If you get dressed here you'll be soaked by the time you get over the dune."

They ran up the dune, scrambling. Aline slipped and fell. Sand stuck to her knees, to her abdomen, and to both breasts. At the summit as lightning flashed again, Stack stared, raking her with his eyes. He made her feel clinically naked. The lightning that had exposed her to him seemed to last an hour.

In darkness they started down the other side. Lightning streaked again, but this time Stack searched for and discovered only the car. Rain was pelting down hard. Aline was trying to move fast down the dune. She was digging her heels in but the sand gave way, and she skidded down on her bottom, the cursed lightning exposing her to Stack's eyes and sudden strident laughter.

Stack, running, reached the car first, threw up the lid of the trunk and tossed his clothes in. "Give me your things," he called.

She handed over all she owned without knowing exactly why. Naked she stood stupidly beside the car in the pouring rain.

Stack, a patch of lighter darkness, moved fast, undoing catches. He knelt in the driver's seat and pulled the top up over his head and down

258

onto the windshield. She heard the catches snap shut. After rolling up the passenger window, then the driver's window, he stepped out into the pouring rain, slamming the door behind him. He had come out her side of the car, and stood now far too close.

"Might as well let the rain wash the sand off," he suggested.

The cursed lightning repeatedly invaded her privacy.

"You've got sand stuck to your breasts," he said. "How'd you do that?"

She stood naked in the warm rain because she had no choice. The sand on her body was being washed off now. Stack went around to the trunk, lifted the lid and reached out a towel.

"Want me to brush you off?"

"No, thank you."

Lightning crackled regularly. Stack was as naked as she, Aline noted, but it wasn't the same. She was conscious of his size. He was eight inches taller and seventy-five pounds heavier than she. She would have no chance against him.

If he raped me, I would deserve it, Aline thought.

Rape. At the moment, a semi-delicious thought.

Aline stood with her eyes closed and her face lifted, being struck by points of warm rain. She forgot Stack's presence, or thought she did. She told herself she was standing safe in a bathtub facing up into the shower. The water ran down her body, carrying the sand away.

Stack's voice startled her: "You're not cold, are you?"

"No, I'm not cold."

He handed her the towel. She stood with the towel over her shoulders. "Can I have my clothes now?" she asked facing him, disdaining to cover herself.

In a flash of lightning she found herself looking into what she saw as his leering grin. "Suppose I say no?"

"Don't be funny."

He reached into the trunk and lifted out her bundled clothes.

"Do you want the shoes too?"

"No, leave the shoes."

Taking the bundle, she extricated her underpants. Holding the bundle under her left arm, she stepped into them.

A gentleman might have glanced away, but Stack watched her every move.

She separated out the trousers, and hurriedly, clumsily stepped into them, streaking the inside of the legs with sand and mud. Wearing

259

only trousers, she opened the car door. The light flicked on, dazzling her, and she slid into the seat under a spotlight. Slamming the door she put her bra on in darkness, then her shirt. She made a turban out of her towel and tied up her hair.

In a moment Stack got in on the other side, barefoot, wearing pants. Behind the wheel he was using his towel to dry off his face and hair. Rain drummed on the canvas top. The windows were fogged up.

After wiping them Stack threw his towel into the back. He worked his shirt over his head and down over his torso.

There was tension in the car.

"Well, that was unusual," Stack said after a moment.

Aline said nothing.

Stack started the engine, put the car into reverse, and backed around. The windshield wipers swept back and forth. The headlight beams dragged them back onto the concrete road. Aline felt the car bounce up onto it. Stack increased speed. They moved along a concrete road built for German tanks several wars ago.

"What barbarism a country lives through," said Stack. But Aline saw herself still standing naked on the dark beach. In the pale light of the dashboard she stared at the backs of her hands.

Why did I do that? she asked herself. Was I trying to attract him or torture him?

At last Stack pulled up onto the wet gravel in front of the château, and they went inside.

"Would you like a nightcap, before you go up?" asked Stack.

Aline shook her head and went upstairs.

She lay in bed in the dark. Reflected moonlight slanted through the shutters. She lived in a vast, high-ceilinged room, with two sets of tall French windows, both fully open. But the room was hot and it seemed to her she could not breathe. She got up and threw back all the shutters.

Back in bed she lay under a sheet but was still too hot. She threw the sheet off. She wore a thin transparent nightgown that no one had ever gazed through but herself.

After a while she sat up and took the nightgown off, but the heat still oppressed her. Lying on her bed, as naked now as on the dune, she found herself lusting after past sexual gratification—to feel a man's hand on her body again, caressing her here—and here. But her door was locked, there was no man in her room, and the hand caressing her was her own.

Would it ever happen again?

She fell asleep.

260

4

Françoise, wearing jeans and a man's shirt knotted at the waist, approached the tennis court, where Stack at the base line was driving serves into the opposite corner. She noted that Stack's tennis whites were soaked through, his face was sweaty, and his hair bothered him. It kept getting in his eyes as he threw the ball up. He was smashing the ball so hard she could barely see it.

Aline, who leaned against the gap in the fence watching Stack, called hello. Françoise waved back, but did not go over to Aline's side of the court. After a moment Aline walked around to Françoise's side. She hadn't seen Françoise in days, she said, where had Françoise been?

Days? Françoise had been in Toulouse all summer. Françoise thought: If she cared about me, she'd know where I've been.

Françoise explained she had been taking summer courses at the university. Françoise, as usual, was not wearing a bra under her shirt; and she noted that Aline, looking her over, disapproved. Her father disapproved also. What was the matter with these people, Françoise asked herself. What century were they living in?

Stack came over. He had his racket under his arm and was wiping his face with a towel.

"Can't either of you girls play this game?"

Aline, with a smile, shook her head.

Which made Françoise say: "I'll play with you."

"Fine. Come on then."

"I'll get some sneakers."

When Françoise came back, Aline was gone, which was as Françoise had expected, and Stack was driving balls into the corner again.

Françoise thought: She thinks I'm not good enough for him. She couldn't bear to see me with him, not her.

Above her jeans, Françoise now wore the top of a bikini. In sneakers she stood at one end of the court while Stack hit the ball to her gently. Often she returned it. She had played tennis before, but not much.

After a while Stack called her to the net, and began to give her instructions.

Taking her to the base line he showed her how to hold the racket, how to stroke a forehand, how to stroke a backhand. He leaned over her, his shirt and chest pressing against her bare back, manipulating her arms and wrists. He was practically embracing her and her knees went weak. She was hardly conscious of the racket in her hand, only of his body draped over hers.

Once when she glanced up, her father was standing out in the middle of the vegetable garden, watching her, a stricken expression on his face.

She and Stack separated. She came out of her trance and they hit balls to each other. Stack stroked the ball regularly to the same spot, and she hit most of them back. She felt healthy and alive. She began to sweat. Her eyes were salty, and sweat was running down her back.

"How about letting me hit a few serves now? I'll hit them into the corner. You just collect them and throw them back."

From the base line he began blasting serves at her. She stood against the fence, dodging them. He had only about twelve balls. Some rolled toward her. Some she had to go after. She bent over to gather them up. Her bosom hung in the bikini top. The jeans were stretched tight across her behind.

But she began to get irritated. She told herself: He's not playing tennis with me. He's just using me.

So she stopped picking the balls up. Leaning against the fence, she watched him blast the last of the balls into the corner. He waited for her to throw them back, but she didn't.

"Throw them back."

She walked toward the gap in the fence, where she said: "I don't want to play any more."

He came toward her all smiles. "Let's go in the kitchen and have a beer."

This pleased her. Immediately she brightened. She gave him one of her rare, shy smiles.

The kitchen was empty. They sat at the table that her mother cut up vegetables on. Stack had brought two pewter steins out of the

262

freezer. They were glazed with frost. He opened two bottles of Alsatian Kronenbourg.

"This is the best beer in France," Stack asserted. "It's one of the best beers in the world."

Matted curls showed at the base of his throat.

"I don't know much about beer."

"Don't the kids drink beer at the university?"

"Not so much."

"When I was in college, that's all we did. Drink beer."

"Today the kids pop pills."

Stack was immediately interested. He leaned forward, giving his big grin. "Tell me about that."

"I never did," Françoise lied.

His face was tanned and still damp. Her own body was damp too. She was conscious of a drop of sweat running down her breastbone, and that Stack kept staring at her bosom.

Françoise told herself: He likes me.

He had sweatbands on his wrists, with which he wiped sweat out of his eyes. He gave her an intimate kind of look that made her feel weak.

He likes me a lot, she told herself. He likes me better than her.

"Let's take these inside," Stack said. "The shutters are closed and it's cool in there."

Did he mean inside or upstairs?

She did not want to go upstairs with him. What did she want? She didn't know. But he was moving across the dining room toward the hall and the marble staircase. She had to follow or lose him. They heard a door slam upstairs in the hall, but it hardly penetrated her consciousness. He had hard muscular legs.

Aline appeared on the landing. Aline descended the staircase, glaring, it seemed to Françoise, down at her.

Françoise felt her face go red. Guilty as charged. She tried to tell herself: I haven't even done anything yet. But the guilt remained. She refused to meet Aline's eyes.

If Stack was embarrassed, it did not show. "Hello, there," he said cheerfully.

He walked past Aline. Françoise followed him. They went down the hall into the cool salon. Françoise could feel Aline's eyes on her all the way.

Stack put his beer mug down on the desk. "Aline thinks a lot of you, you know."

"No, she doesn't."

"What makes you say that?"

Françoise said nothing. She was waiting for something to happen. She thought of the bedroom upstairs, redecorated now, she had been told.

"She told me she considered you like a sister to her."

Stack now seemed cool, distant. Nothing's going to happen, Françoise told herself.

"What's the matter with her anyway?" demanded Stack. "She's really an uptight kind of woman, isn't she?"

"She used to be more fun before her divorce, I guess." Françoise wasn't interested in the subject of Aline. She judged that Stack had not been able to get close to Aline. What was so surprising about that? No one else had either. It was common gossip among the workers. Throughout the village of Margaux too, probably.

Stack had his towel. She watched him wiping his face with one end of the towel, and it felt as if he were wiping hers. She felt her cheeks go red again.

"Hot, isn't it?" he asked amiably.

"Yes."

Now he might kiss her. Although she told herself she did not want to be kissed, she could feel in advance the way her bikini top would flatten against his wet T-shirt.

But he only said: "Is everything all right at school?"

She nodded.

"Good," he said approvingly.

He drank some of his beer.

Her own mug felt icy in her hand.

"I've had most of the upstairs redecorated," he said. "Have you seen it yet?"

After swallowing some beer, she began to feel in control of her emotions again. "No, I haven't."

"You must take a look at it sometime. It came out rather well, I think."

Françoise said nothing.

"Even Aline seemed pleased with it, and you know how hard it is to please her."

After a moment, Françoise said solemnly: "My mother says the bathrooms are fabulous."

Stack's quick grin glowed, it seemed to Françoise, with pleasure. She guessed he was proud of what he had done to the château.

The phone rang.

"I can't hear you," Stack said into the receiver.

The connection was apparently terrible.

"I can't hear you," Stack shouted.

He hung up.

"That was New York," he explained. "They're going to call back."

They nodded at each other, then waited in silence. For five minutes Stack stared pensively at the phone.

When it rang again it made Françoise jump.

"That's better," Stack said into the receiver. To Françoise, he said: "This will take a minute. Look around if you'd care to. You're part of the family, you know."

Part of the family. How many times had she heard those meaningless words?

"Hello, Warren? Good to hear your voice."

She was not part of the family. She was the cellar master's daughter and meant nothing to any of these people. Stack's attention now was given entirely to the telephone.

Apparently he was being summoned to a conference in Paris. He was jotting down notes.

Carrying her beer mug, Françoise wandered out of the salon. When she reached the staircase she hesitated a moment, then started up. She felt an intruder. She kept expecting to meet someone—though whom?—who would order her out of the château.

She began looking into rooms, though there was only one she wanted to see again.

At last she came to it. The bed had been changed. It was bigger. That was the first thing she noted. She stood in the doorway expecting that some significant thought, observation or emotion would come to her. But nothing happened. The room was as meaningless to her as any other that belonged to someone else. The momentous event she remembered had been momentous only to her, and could not be found again in this room or anywhere. It was irrecoverable, gone, no more real now than if she had read it somewhere.

She felt an acute sense of loss, and for a moment was on the edge of tears.

The bathroom was indeed fabulous. She stepped into it. The bathtub was huge compared to the two-level, sit-up tub in her father's cottage. There was even a stall shower. There was even, she noted with amazement, a telephone fixed to the tile wall, and below it one of the buttons glowed, indicating, she supposed, that downstairs Stack still talked to New York.

Behind the door was a full-length mirror, and she closed the door all the way, the better to peer at herself. Her face was streaked with dust and sweat. So was her chest.

Françoise set her beer mug down on the sink and took off her bikini top. In the mirror she appraised herself.

Her attention kept flickering between the full-length mirror and the glowing telephone button.

She was still hot and sweaty and considered washing her face, but the stall shower caught her eye again—what luxury. A man who could afford that could afford anything. She had not taken ten showers in her life, and longed to take one now, wash away the sweat and dust, in some measure make herself ready for the future.

Suppose Stack caught her there? But the button showed Stack still spoke to New York. She would know soon enough when the call ended. Even if he did catch her there, so what? He might not even mind.

She got undressed and opened the stall shower. It took her a moment to adjust the temperature of the water. The nozzle was a foot in diameter and the water came down hard, encompassing every part of her. It felt glorious. She found shampoo on a ledge and decided to wash her hair. Water coursed down over her head and face.

She imagined Stack standing in this shower. Then she imagined the two of them in it together, imagined him embracing her, cupping her bottom in both hands. He began to soap her, which felt nice. The water pouring down united them inside a circle. They stood together inside the water, inside the stall, inside the room, inside the château, inside the world.

"You have a nice ass," she heard Stack say.

This was not what she wanted to hear. It only made her feel like a cellar master's daughter. He went on about her bottom, stroking it, but she wanted to hear him talk about her as a person. She wanted to find somebody who saw the world as she did, and who would care about her more than anyone else, and she felt like crying to realize there was no such person in this château.

266

Stepping out of the shower stall she toweled herself off and put her sweaty clothes back on. She felt a touch of panic to realize that the mirror was all steamed up. She wiped it with the towel, but it quickly steamed over once more.

Her eyes flicked to the telephone button, which still glowed.

On the staircase she met Stack coming up. Both gripped beer mugs.

"I hope it's all right," she said. "I took a shower." She had left behind a wet towel and a steamed-up mirror, and she was afraid he might shout at her, but he only grinned.

"How was it?"

"Nice."

He went on up the stairs. "Thanks for playing tennis with me," he called over his shoulder. "We must do it again sometime."

Leaving her mug on the kitchen table, she went out of the château. The kitchen door slammed behind her, and she moped down the lane toward her cottage.

Her father was waiting for her just inside the door. He slapped her. He hit her so hard she nearly fell down.

"Whore."

He must have looked into the kitchen and found her gone into the main part of the château with the patron. Perhaps he had stood under Stack's window and thought he could hear her voice.

Her hair was as wet as if she had been swimming, but her clothes were dry, and it was not a rainy day. Perhaps he imagined she had taken a shower with Stack.

"Whore," he cried, and smacked her with great force with the other hand.

Françoise, who supposed she now had finger marks on both cheeks, moved woodenly into her own room and began packing a small bag. She heard her father sobbing into the fireplace. When her bag was full and she came back out, her father stood watching her with tragic eyes.

"Where are you going?"

"Away from here."

"I forbid you to leave this house."

Françoise gazed stolidly at her father.

"I'm your father."

Françoise moved toward the door.

"If you go out that door, you're never coming back."

The door slammed behind her. As she cut through the vines to the main road she worried that Stack might see her from his window. She need not have worried; he lay naked on his bed, asleep. Reaching the road, Françoise put her thumb out to cars that did not stop. As Françoise saw it, the Médoc was smothering her. Ritual and tradition ruled everything. The Médoc never changed. She had to get out or die.

She counted her money. Only about twelve francs, and when night fell she would get hungry.

A fertilizer truck bound for Bordeaux picked her up. Through the back window she watched the last of the vines that surrounded home.

It was over. She was leaving the Médoc forever. She told herself: You can't be a woman there.

Stack was awakened some time later by the noise of an explosion. He threw on a bathrobe and rushed downstairs. Smoke was coming out of the kitchen above and below the dining-room door. He pushed through and bumped into Aline.

"What—"

The sun was slanting low through the windows into a room full of smoke. In the far corner one of the Spanish girls, minus her eyebrows and the front part of her hair, sat weeping.

"Don't worry your pretty head," Aline told Stack icily. "Carmen was just trying to light the oven."

"Looks like she nearly blew up the château. Where the hell is Madame Gorr?"

"Madame Gorr sent word that she's ill. You can take modest credit for that, I should think. Françoise is gone and I imagine they're having quite a fight down there."

Aline told the Spanish girl to go home for the day.

Stack was peering about the kitchen as the smoke gradually dissipated.

"Carmen was preparing your dinner," said Aline, "but that idea just blew up. Why don't you go down to the Savoie instead."

"Why don't you? This is my château."

They glared at each other.

After a moment Aline crossed to the stove, scratched a match and lit the oven. She pushed a Pyrex casserole into the oven. "I will have monsieur's dinner prepared shortly. I suggest that monsieur go put some clothes on. Certain people around here may prefer monsieur in the altogether, but the cook does not."

Despite himself, Stack started to laugh.

"You don't have any shame, do you?"

"Shame for what?"

268

"For what you did to that child."

"She's not a child, or hadn't you noticed? In any case I didn't do anything to her, not today, not ever." Now each had lied to the other about past sexual events. Both suspected as much, but neither was sure. "I was just trying to be nice to her," Stack said. "I wanted to make her feel at home here. If you want to know the truth, I've begun to feel a kind of fatherly responsibility for all these people." After a moment he added: "I hope she'll be all right."

Aline glared at him.

He came toward her. "You're the one I want to make love to, not Françoise."

He put his hands on her shoulders and drew her to him until her face was against his bathrobe. She was stiff in his arms but at least she did not withdraw.

"The Americans, the English, the Japanese—everybody's fighting to get a toehold in the wine world, and a kid like Françoise can't wait to get away," said Stack.

5

No reply from Interpol. Looking up the date of his telex, Dupont was surprised to find that nearly a month had passed. It did no good to nag bureaucracies, he knew. Whatever the popular notion, Interpol was not a police force, it was an information depot. They had no information of their own, they had to send out for it, and their clients learned to wait. Nonetheless, Dupont decided to send a second request. Possibly a reply had been prepared but was lying on a desk somewhere. Such things happened in the Fraud Brigade, Dupont knew, and in most other bureaucracies, he supposed. He would send a second request.

Within an hour the reply came back. When Dupont read it his breath started to come very fast.

The telex read: "Alonso del Greco, also known as Cosimo Carlucci, and Emilio Buonocorso. Male, Italian, 34. Born Milano. Profession pharmacist. Arrested by police of Nuclei Anti Sofisticatori. Charged 18 counts concocting false wine for public distribution. Convicted on all 18 counts. Thrity-four others also convicted. Four bottling plants closed. Expert witnesses testified to presence in false wine of noxious chemicals, including ferrocyanide of potassium, astringent alum of rock, chlorocarbonate of etile, ox blood. Small amounts of strychnine also found. Principal ingredients water, sugar, and dregs. Del Greco sentenced to eight years prison. Released on technicality after six months. Failed to appear for resentencing. Warrant issued. Current whereabouts unknown. Believed to have fled Italy. Photo and details follow."

Dupont began drumming his ballpoint pen on his desk. He drummed harder and harder, louder and louder, until one of his colleagues across the room called with irritation: "Cut that out, Dupont."

"Sorry," said Dupont contritely.

But still Dupont hesitated to move on his information. He would await arrival of the photo of this Buonocorso before alarming his chief —and a good many other important men of France. Dupont was a cautious man. There could well be more than one Emilio Buonocorso. At this stage, a delay of one more day meant nothing. Better to be absolutely sure before he, a minor government functionary, rang the national fire alarm.

The package arrived special delivery airmail the next morning. Dupont's fingers tore at the seal, bent back the clasp. He pushed all of the papers out of the way to get at the photo.

The face staring up at him wore numbers around its neck. It was the face of the Italian at Château Cracheau.

Dupont, his face ashen, scooped all this material up, and went in to see his chief, Inspector Dompierre.

"I'm rather busy. Can it wait?" Dompierre said.

Dupont screwed his courage up. "No, sir, it can't. Inspector, I think I may have uncovered something terrible. Please read this. I have reason to believe that this man is in France. I have reason to believe he's mixing up noxious chemicals and selling it as wine. Here in France. I have reason to believe that one of our biggest shippers is involved."

"All right, Dupont, put the file there. I'll get to it right away."

An hour later the inspector called Dupont in. "I'll take over from here, Dupont. In a case of this magnitude the leadership of a superior officer is called for, as you know. It will be necessary to insist on personal interviews with the prefect. He will want me to present my case to Paris. The Ministers of Agriculture and Interior will no doubt become involved."

270

Dupont was vastly relieved. It was someone else's responsibility now. The case was out of his hands.

That night Dupont offered to take his wife out to dinner, a rare treat for them both. She said: "What's got into you?"

Dupont replied only: "I got rid of a very troublesome case today, and I feel quite good about it."

But soon Dupont began to fret. Emotionally this was still his case and nothing seemed to be happening. Though time passed, he heard nothing from his chief, who often seemed troubled and preoccupied. Dupont forbore asking about it. One did not question the techniques of inspectors. The case was in Dompierre's hands now. It was not Dupont's case any more.

In the meantime people were drinking ox blood and rat poison and thinking it wine.

The inspector was gone most of each day, and Dupont imagined him closeted with government ministers elsewhere in the city. But one night, as Dupont was leaving the office, he chanced to bump into Dompierre on the sidewalk.

"Anything new?" asked Dupont hesitantly.

"Coming along, coming along," said the inspector vaguely.

"That's good."

The inspector turned a fierce expression on Dupont. "I'll smash this ring. I'll give them a drubbing they won't recover from for a long time." Nodding his head vigorously, the inspector went into the building.

Dupont went home and had dinner with his wife.

The next afternoon Dupont was called into Inspector Dompierre's office, and interrogated fiercely.

"It all hinges on your identification of this fellow Buonocorso–del Greco."

"Yes sir."

"But you're not sure of your identification. How can you be? You've stuck me out on a limb, Dupont."

Dupont, worried, said nothing.

"You insist that this fellow del Greco and the Italian at Château Cracheau are the same man?"

"I think so, inspector."

"You only saw him once," Dompierre accused. The inspector was glancing through Dupont's report.

"Yes, sir."

"For less than five minutes apparently. Probably weren't even looking at that chap most of the time.

"Yes, sir."

"Then how can you say you're sure?"

"I don't know, sir."

Dompierre, studying Dupont, was breathing hard. "This fellow Bozon is big. Very big."

"Yes, sir."

After a moment, Dupont suggested hesitantly: "How about some wiretaps, inspector?"

"I put them in. I'm monitoring them twenty-four hours a day. I've heard nothing yet."

"If someone is concocting false wine," Dupont suggested hesitantly, "he would need an enormous quantity of sugar and also an enormous quantity of dregs. Can we check up on abnormal sugar shipments? Can we check the candy and jam factories? Can we check back through records on the dregs?"

"I'm checking into all that," the inspector said. "That stuff must be coming in from abroad, Spain probably. Probably coming right up the river in the dead of night. How am I supposed to find where they unload the stuff?"

"It's a big river," conceded Dupont.

"Exactly, Dupont. That will be all, Dupont."

"Yes, sir."

"I can't move until I can take them all."

"Yes, sir."

"That will be all, Dupont."

6

Aline was with Stack constantly. The sexual tension was always there between them. He was wearing her down.

More than ever she was his guide, interpreter, and adviser. Together they negotiated with peasants for the sale of planting rights, or for the lease of land. There were staff meetings: Stack and Aline, the lawyer Saar, a Frenchman named Bertrand, who was the château's accountant, and a bilingual young Englishman named Robertson, on whom Stack had hung the title assistant to the president. Other conferences of a technical nature involved Stack, Aline, and Gorr. There were meetings in Bordeaux with shippers or brokers or politicians. Always Stack wanted Aline at his side, and he seemed to rely on her judgment.

In addition, increasingly, Stack entertained at the château: lavish dinner parties that featured fine old wines. At first only Aline's friends came, but once he had passed inspection other owners followed. Most seemed surprised to find that he didn't eat with his hands, then impressed that he was such a relaxed host. At the head of the table sat Stack, pouring wine; at the foot making conversation, moving the servants about, and in other ways behaving exactly like his wife, sat Aline.

Doubtless some guests, perhaps most, believed them lovers.

At night she went alone to her room. She had begun to sleep badly. What did he think of her? What did he imagine she was going through? She would lie in the dark and think of him in his own room in the other wing. She had only to put her slippers on and take a few steps. His door was probably not locked. Even if locked, she need only knock. She did not imagine he would send her away. Once in the middle of the night, unable to sleep, she had paced the floor, considering it, but had done nothing.

He was wearing her down.

Stack found himself standing in the dark under the oldest part of the Count de Grenelle's château. This was the owner's personal cellar. It must have been a dungeon centuries ago. The floor was dirt. The walls were stone. The vaulted ceiling was caked with damp mold.

The path between the wine racks was not much wider than a man's shoulders. The Count de Grenelle's candle led the way. The man behind Stack, a shipper from Bordeaux, also held a candle.

Surrounded by rare old bottles, Stack murmured: "What's the oldest bottle down here?"

The count turned. The candle flame shone on his white hair. "I don't know," he said.

The racks were protected by padlocked grilles that were rusty and opened stiffly, and that were laced with spider webs. Some vintages were labeled. But the oldest were not. Labels would not last long down here, and most vintages were identified by dates chalked on boards and wired to each rack.

The count kept thrusting his candle close to boards, trying to read dates. In places the chalk had almost disappeared.

"Voilà," he said, "1906."

To have come upon one that old seemed to astonish him, though it was his château and his cellar. Stack realized that very few owners' cellars had ever been inventoried. In most cases, owners had no clear idea what was down there.

For Stack the important question came next: "And what's the oldest," he whispered, "you'd be willing to serve us tonight?"

The count laughed. "I never thought about it. I don't know; 1922 perhaps."

He had been peering past his candle into the racks. The rack marked 1922 contained twenty or more bottles. Older vintages would be represented by only one or two bottles each.

At dinner parties it was always the count's pleasure to lead his guests down into his cellar and let them pick the wines for that particular evening. It was an idea Stack intended to adopt.

Stack watched the count open the creaky rack marked 1922. "I don't know what condition it's in."

The count withdrew a bottle, holding its neck over the flame of the candle.

The candle flame showed the bottle to be only about two-thirds full, meaning that the cork had dried out. Part of the contents had evaporated. The rest would be undrinkable.

Stack felt almost a physical pain to think of such a great old bottle gone, having given pleasure to no one. The Count de Grenelle shook his head. He looked close to tears himself.

The candle flame showed a second and a third bottle to be full. The count passed one to Stack, who held it in a horizontal position, careful not to stir up the sediment inside.

Turning to the Bordeaux shipper, the count asked: "And what would be your pleasure?"

The shipper selected a 1953 Château Talbot.

"And I," said the count, "shall select a Burgundy. Let me see. How about a 1953 Bonnes Mares so that we can compare the same vintage in Bordeaux and Burgundy."

With wines this old, it was best to decant them before moving

274

them. The count had brought three crystal decanters down into the cellar. They stood on a table near the foot of the stairs.

Each of the bottles was laid into a straw pouring basket. The count's candle went down on the table. He pared off the tops of the three capsules, being careful not to disturb the bottles in the baskets, then pulled each cork, drawing each out slowly, disturbing the wine inside as little as possible.

Each time a cork came free, he unscrewed it, and held it to his nose. The candle flame showed him sniffing the cork, then nodding his head with pleasure. After that he passed each cork to Stack, who sniffed it before passing it on to the Bordeaux shipper. The odor of the corks would show whether the wine in the bottle was sound or not.

The count decanted the oldest wine first. With the neck of the bottle held directly over the candle flame he poured its contents very slowly into the decanter. As soon as tiny particles of sediment began to show in the wine flowing through the neck of the bottle, the count stopped pouring. Left in the bottle in each case was up to an inch of wine.

The count moved each bottle over the candle flame so that the three men could study the amount of muddy deposit left by the years. The count now handed Stack the decanter containing the 1922 wine, and also the empty bottle in its basket. The Bordeaux shipper was handed the wine he had selected in the same way. The count, carrying the decanted Burgundy, and the bottle it had come in, blew out the candle, and all three men trooped up the stone staircase, coming out into the château's kitchen. In the dining room, they set the carafes down on the table set for dinner. The empty bottles in their baskets went on the sideboard so that all of the guests could look them over. Part of the pleasure was merely to look at the very old bottles, encrusted as they were with dirt and spider webs, two of them bearing half-deteriorated labels, and the oldest not labeled at all.

Later, the youngest wines would be served first, and the oldest last, and as each was poured a certain tension would occur. It was like opening the door into a strange room. One never knew at what stage in life one might surprise the inhabitant.

Once poured, each guest would slosh the wine around, then raise it to the nose to inhale the bouquet. Stack no longer scoffed at this. It was fun to sniff wines, and especially to taste them. It was fun to talk about wine, and to speculate upon why one had lasted better than another, or whether a certain wine, which perhaps was already twenty years old, had or had not reached its peak. Such conversation seemed to focus all of a man's awareness on the wine he was drinking, and Stack had come to see that the pleasure factor thereby increased, and pleasure was what wine was all about.

Nor was it essential to know the wine jargon by heart. People who really cared about wine often referred to it in terms of music or sports. A wine could be a sprinter or a long-distance runner. It could be a tenor or a baritone. It could be a chorus of voices, or it could be a clear, hard sound such as the high note of a soprano.

Stack now could tell the origin of a great many wines after a single mouthful and was proud of this new skill. He had always scoffed at such claims in the past, and had been inclined to rate the claimers as pretentious frauds. No doubt some were frauds, but others he now knew were not at all.

Nor were all men frauds who revered only certain labels, though they could be mistaken if they carried their narrow prejudice too far. Some of those châteaux officially classified in 1855 no longer existed. Their vineyards had been absorbed by other châteaux, or by one of the expanding villages. Some parcels had gone back to bush or to forest. Every surviving château had expanded or contracted since 1855. Not a single one fit within its old boundaries. And so within the classification relative values had become blurred. The count's wine had been judged only a fifth growth. But some years the count made wine as good as anybody's, and some years one or another higher-ranked château had a poor crop.

It was a bit like horse racing, Stack reflected. Breeding often tells; not always.

The count considered himself in no way diminished because he owned only a fifth growth. His wine had been classified. It was of noble rank. The wines outside the classification were commoners.

Aline, Stack noted, had had a lot to drink that night. He watched her bid the count goodnight. He watched her climb into his car.

He judged she was pretending to be drunker than she was, a condition he was used to recognizing in women who craved sudden affection but were afraid to ask for it in any other way. So, instead of driving home, Stack drove down to the edge of the river and parked.

"Weren't those old wines marvelous?"

"Yes, they were," he agreed.

Her seat reclined slightly, and her head rested on the headrest. He watched her, calculating his chances.

276

"Which one did you like the best?" she wanted to know.

But this wasn't what he had parked there for. He said: "One tends to forget that wines are alcoholic, doesn't one?"

She began to giggle.

He watched her. He had watched her for weeks.

Aline looked up at the stars. "There sure are a lot of stars tonight," she said.

He was now certain that she was not as drunk as she pretended.

Past her face loomed the bulk of the deserted château he had considered as a hotel, and for a moment this distracted him. The studies had come in weeks ago. He had done nothing, and he was worried about what New York would say. But the project felt wrong. If a hotel was such a great idea, why hadn't the Rothschilds built long ago?

"You don't really want to open a hotel here, do you?" Aline asked, for she saw him studying the site, not her.

"No. A hotel would change this place, and I guess I don't want it changed."

"That's right," said Aline, slurring her speech a little. "Let's keep it the way it is for us."

So Stack leaned over and kissed her. He kissed her because he imagined this the best moment he would ever get finally to bed her, all that female coolness finally dissolved. It was absurd that he hadn't bedded her long ago; the challenge would be resolved tonight at last. And he kissed her because he was worried about New York's reaction to the non-hotel, but did not want to worry any more tonight. He kissed her calculatingly and efficiently, and felt her trembling, though he himself was in control.

In her half-reclined chair he was virtually on top of her. He let his weight down on her body. He was kissing her long and deeply, and when at last she began to kiss him back his principal emotion was elation. Got you, you bitch, he thought.

He began to paw her body, all the while planning her total seduction as scientifically as possible, given the obstructions. He felt slightly disoriented. In the days when he had used cars as bedrooms the seats did not recline, there was no control column separating the seats into two compartments, and the girls were not wearing trousers.

He was trying to work intimately but for this needed to slip a hand inside her belt, though the trousers fit her too snugly. In this age of presumed promiscuity, a mode of dress had been decided upon by women which militated against that very promiscuity: trousers. And under that perhaps panty hose. The world was crazy.

Stack, worried, supposed his only chance was to carry the walls at a single assault before Aline could marshal a defense. Probably she felt safe here. In an open car on a river bank what could happen beyond a hand job? Stack had other ideas—you're in for a surprise, lady—but was held up at her first sentry post—those trousers.

To his relief, Aline began to giggle. "How do teenagers do it these days?" she said. But she didn't move to help him.

Though sex was supposed to be simple today, physically it was harder than ever. Fathers of teenage girls were more worried than they needed to be. Stack was straddling Aline, kissing her, and his left hand worked the crank beside the chair. The chair was approaching a horizontal position, where all things presumably became easier, and there was still no protest from Aline.

He had been searching for a zipper at her hip, but found it where a man's would be, and yanked. He had to work several seconds at the waist clip before decoding its mystery. Room at last for a grope. His hand slipped under the band of her underpants, and he worked it down the part in her curls. He felt her body stiffen and expected protest now at last, but her arms only tightened around him.

She was sopping.

To his surprise, this made Stack angry. You bitch, he thought, you must have wanted it for months. What she had put him through no man ought to be put through, and she would pay for it now. He removed his lips from hers. "Say it," he growled.

Her voice was throaty. "What—do you want me to say?"

"Say you want to make love to me."

She offered him moans and hard breathing instead.

"Say it," he ordered.

"Someone will come by."

"No one will come by."

He was rubbing her. She was squirming and moaning.

"You want to make love to me. Say it."

"Let's go back to the château," she begged.

So that she could change her mind when they got there? He would defeat her here and now.

"Say it," he ordered.

"I—want to make love to you." He did not believe her. She wanted what she was getting, no more. Virginity was a state of mind into which her mind fit.

278

He began trying to work her trousers down her legs.

But Ferraris were not designed for such work. Nor trousers.

He half lifted her off the seat. "Turn over and get on your knees," he ordered.

Presumably wanting to be mauled, failing to see her danger, she complied. "What are you doing?"

In a moment she would know.

He had half lifted her onto her knees. The side of her face lay on the headrest. Kneeling between her ankles on the seat, he peeled her trousers down, her underpants after them.

Her behind shone milky white under the night sky. He peeled the different clothes down to the backs of her knees until they lay bunched up in the crooks. He could see the side of her face, and hear her moan, and with the side of one hand he massaged her cleavage.

With his other hand he undid the front of his trousers.

"Take me back to the château," she begged. "I—I want to make love to you."

He was sure she didn't. She considered herself still safe, relatively speaking. Necking in a car was safe, romantic too, like old times. A teenage girl might be in danger in a car, but not a woman who could turn the danger off any time just by offering something better, a double bed instead of a front seat. And then at the bedroom door offering a handshake.

Stack came forward, prodding her in unresisting places.

It was a moment before she comprehended what was happening to her. She attempted to jump sideways in the seat, but Stack's hard muscular arm encircled her hips. He held her exactly where he wanted her. She was in a vise and could only squirm, not escape. He almost wanted to laugh.

At first he thought her more excited than ever. Her lascivious squirmings pleased him. Bitch, he thought; this is one you'll remember. Then he realized she really was trying to escape him.

"No," she cried out. "Not on my knees."

"Yes, on your knees."

"At least let me lie down."

"I like you like this."

He felt her realize that he meant it.

The lovemaking turned into a grim struggle between them. There was something noble about her fight, conducted almost exclusively with her squirming behind. He could observe this and approve, but at the same time it increased his determination to defeat her.

"We'll go back to the château. I'll stay with you all night."

"I'll take it here. Now."

For a time there was silence, except for grunts. Stack had one arm around her waist, with her bare abdomen pressed against the hairs of his forearms. His other arm, braced to the seat, held her in place. Her bottom was squirming frantically. She was trying to wrestle herself off her knees or out from under him, and could not. Though he kept prodding her lips, she was moving too much, and he could not find what he sought.

"You're hurting me."

"Not as much as you hurt me."

Tension demanded release, though he still knocked outside the door. So he stopped, waving in the air a minute or more, holding her struggling body, waiting for the return of inner calm. The moonlight still showed his fierce grip and her useless efforts. She was still under him. She was very strong, but not as strong as he, and in a position of disadvantage.

"Oh, you bastard. Pig. Bastard."

"You whore."

He thrust forward against her again, attempting to spear her, but her knees were not spread very wide, and they were bound together by her trousers and panties. He needed a hand free with which to guide himself, but could not spare one.

He kept poking her. Once when he did begin to slip inside, she jerked away, and he stabbed at buttocks again.

"You filthy swine. Oh, you filthy swine."

"You don't understand. It's either fuck you or kill you."

"I'll scream."

"Go ahead and scream."

That he was seeking to humiliate her, not make love to her, both knew, and he could feel rage build up in her, and then abruptly she stopped moving at all.

The stars shone down on her placid white behind. Was this too good to be true? He relaxed his grip, ready to grab her again if necessary. But she did not move.

Two free hands spread her just enough and he glided all the way home. A little squirming now, if you please.

He felt her stiffen slightly as it happened. After that she did not move. On all fours on the seat under him, her head pointed straight ahead, she lay asleep or dead. She made no effort now to escape. She made no response of whatever kind.

Sliding in and out, he waited for the sweet, pulsing ache he was used to, but the sweetness had gone away and it neither pulsed nor ached. He was simply in there. Like a match it would spit flames when rubbed enough, but without giving pleasure to anyone.

At last he came. She made no response when this happened either. After a moment he climbed off her, zipped his pants, and hiked himself over the control column and behind the wheel again.

Aline opened the car door and got out. Standing on the dirt, she pulled her panties up, and after that her trousers. She buckled them, then zipped them up. She climbed back into the car and the door slammed. Her right hand worked the crank, and the backrest began to take an upright position again.

Stack did not speak.

"Take me home, please."

He started the car and did so. Something had gone wrong with his plans. Was it possible he had just made a terrible mistake? As he drew up on the gravel in front of the château, he decided to take her hands, talk to her, but Aline opened the door before the car stopped rolling, stepped out, and went in through the door.

Stack stayed to pull the top up, then wind up both windows—it might rain before morning—and when he got inside the château there was no sign of her. He went up the marble staircase two at a time and along the hallway to her room in the other wing. A light came out from under her door. He could hear her moving around in there. She was banging things. He considered knocking. He wanted to see her. Most of all he wanted to hold her in his arms and, if that was what she wanted, apologize.

But she was angry. Now was probably not the best moment. The conservative businessman—and he prided himself on being a conservative businessman—would wait patiently until signs were better.

The rarest of all virtues: patience.

Though his knuckles yearned to knock, he backed from the door down the dark hall.

Alone in his room, pacing, he found that he wanted her more than ever. Why had he behaved that way anyway?

Sex is the battlefield, he thought. And on it he had lost.

She'll come around, he told himself confidently. But would she?

In the morning he was out of the château earlier than usual. He got clippers from the tool room and went out into the nearly ripe vines. The roses were blooming at the head of each row. He clipped off about twenty of the best ones, came back to his office in the chai, and found and filled a crystal vase. Hearing movement in Aline's office next door he went in carrying the vase, wearing a big smile.

But it was only her father nosing about in there.

"Oh, are those for me?" asked Conderie cheerfully.

"I didn't know you were back," Stack said.

Stack set the flowers down on the desk. He was in no mood for jokes.

"I'm on my way into the city," Conderie said. "Anything you need?"

"No."

In his office Stack paced the floor. The mail came in, but he scarcely glanced at it. The accountant entered with checks to be signed. Stack signed them. A call came through from the Paris Profit Center. Midway through the conversation Stack thought he heard Aline next door. He cut the conversation short.

He stuck his head into her office, all boyish grin and cheerfulness, but to his surprise his hands were trembling. "I brung you some flowers, I did," he announced.

Aline stood with her back to him, staring out the window. She neither moved nor spoke. She was wearing a blouse and a nylon skirt. Her legs were bare.

"It's nice to see you in a skirt for a change. You have nice legs."

Still no response.

"Did you sleep well?" he asked her.

Nothing.

"Aline, about last night—"

She spun from the window. "I wanted to make love to you, not just fornicate. But you wouldn't know the difference between the two, would you?" Tears sprang to her eyes.

"Aline—" He tried to take her hand.

"Don't you ever touch me again," she cried. Brushing past him, she rushed outside. He heard her car start up, and from the window watched her drive away. At least she was upset, a better sign than pure coldness.

When he went across to the château for lunch her car was back, but there was no sign of her.

Late in the afternoon her father appeared again in Stack's doorway.

282

"I've brought somebody to see you," Conderie said. "He may have an interesting proposition for you."

Conderie looked pleased with himself. Behind him stood Édouard Bozon.

Stack rose, moving out to shake hands. Bozon's hand was as big and his grip as hard as Stack's.

Conderie stepped back as if, now that he had brought the two men together, his vital role was discharged. He looked pleased with himself.

Stack's glance swept back to Bozon. "What can I do for you?"

"That's what I like about you Americans," said Bozon. "You get right to business. You don't waste people's time. No tour of the chais—anywhere else and we'd be tasting wine for the next hour. My mouth would get so puckered I could hardly talk." He gave a big booming laugh.

Stack smiled too. "If you'd really like to taste the new wines—"

Bozon held up one hand. "Desist, desist, I beg of you."

Conderie watched, pleased that the two men were getting on so well.

Bozon now began to outline a plan whereby he would buy all of the château's output, bypassing the customary role of the brokers. In exchange for this exclusivity, and in addition to extra profit, he could offer Stack certain distribution advantages.

"Eddie is the third-biggest shipper in Bordeaux," Conderie put in. "Eddie's reputation is impeccable. With Eddie you wouldn't even need a contract. A handshake would be enough."

Stack considered most of Conderie's recommendations of no value to him whatsoever. He pushed down the button on his intercom. "See if Aline is in the château," he ordered his secretary. "Ask her to come over here please."

While they waited for her, Bozon passed around cigars.

"Eddie and I were about to complete just such an arrangement," Conderie said, "—when you took over here."

Aline appeared in the doorway.

"How are you, my dear?" cried Bozon, rising to his feet.

He took both her hands, but she disengaged them quickly. "You sent for me?" she said to Stack.

Now Bozon began to outline his proposition. His distribution network was weak in Germany, he admitted, but strong in the United States, Stack's main target, strong elsewhere too. By eliminating the broker's commission and by shipping to America in great bulk . . .

From her chair against the wall where she sat making notes on a legal pad Aline said: "The brokers will scream their heads off."

"Let them, my dear," said Bozon.

"Why should we care whether the brokers scream or not?" Stack asked Aline.

Aline said nothing.

Bozon talked on. He was suave. He was charming. He had answers to all Stack's questions.

Aline asked nothing. In his corner, Conderie merely beamed with pleasure.

Much later Bozon sprang to his feet. "Why don't we set another meeting in a week's time to work out the final details? No doubt you'll have to run this through New York."

"No, it's my decision to make," said Stack automatically. This was true—as long as he kept making what New York considered the correct decision every time.

"I'll drive you back," announced Conderie to Bozon.

Stack stepped forward for the ritual handshake with Bozon. In France one shook hands every time one saw somebody, and also each time the person left the room. It was ridiculous.

Bozon's hand went out to Aline too, but she ignored it, remaining in her corner. Her head nodded slightly, that was all.

"Interesting proposition, don't you think?" Stack mused, when the two men had driven away.

"No, I don't."

"I gathered you didn't. Why?"

"If you get involved with that man, you'll lose."

"Oh, I don't know," said Stack smugly.

"You think you're a pretty ruthless businessman, don't you?"

Stack smiled confidently.

"Next to him, you're a choir boy."

"What would you know about him?" inquired Stack.

"Who do you think I was married to?"

"I know very well who you were married to. Do you think I didn't check? What do you know about him as a businessman, that's what I'm asking."

Aline got up and left the room.

Stack called after her: "And I'd also like to know in what way he's mixed up with your father."

She reappeared in the doorway.

284

There was a long and heavy silence.

Aline's eyes were blazing. Her sudden fierceness made her appear to him absolutely gorgeous. For that moment she was the most beautiful woman he had ever seen.

"Forget about your father, for the moment," Stack said. "Forget about Bozon. What about you?"

She was to some extent twisted inside, he believed, and he had just seen her in the presence of the man who, presumably, had done the job. He had observed them carefully together a few moments ago, but had noted no clues.

He would like to know more, but did not dare question her in her present mood.

"I suppose you think that man damaged you in some way permanently," Stack said. He moved about the office, arranging his thoughts. "I would like to suggest to you that everybody is a bit twisted inside. You're not as unusual as you may think in this respect." The delicate nature of the subject was making him sound wordier and clumsier than he intended. He frowned.

"To survive in life a man—or a woman—has to learn to live with tomorrow, not yesterday. The past is over and can give neither pain nor pleasure, whereas tomorrow can give both."

Her flat, cold eyes met his. "Anything else?"

"Aline, please sit down."

They stared at each other. After a moment she rested her rump against his desk.

Stack attempted to pick his way through the minefield. "Let me explain what I mean as applied to wine. There is the pleasure of anticipation as the wine is poured and sniffed. And there is the lovely pleasure of drinking it—" Here he gave a smile to which she did not respond. "And then it is gone and the only pleasure is to contemplate another bottle tomorrow."

Aline stood up. "I have things to do."

To hold her there, Stack said: "We have business to discuss before you go."

"Such as?"

"This proposition of Bozon's—he's offering much wider distribution than we have now, cooperative advertising and—"

"He's a crook."

"In what way is he a crook?"

"I don't know."

Stack was annoyed. "Female intuition?"

"I lived with him."

"And you believe he brutalized you."

"In ways you can't even imagine."

"Such as?"

"That's not your affair, is it?"

"It might help you to talk it out."

"Not to you."

"I suppose you think I brutalized you too."

"I thought we were talking business, but if the business aspects of this talk are over—"

Again she moved toward the door.

"I would of course investigate Bozon's proposition very carefully."

"You won't find anything. He's too clever."

"Your father's mixed up with him in some way, isn't he?"

Her eyes blazed. "My father's an honest man."

"I didn't say he wasn't."

"My father gets from Bozon a feeling of strength and power such as he himself has always lacked. Bozon has an acute sense of commerce such as my father has always lacked too, and he admires that."

"And it was that strength and power that once attracted you to Bozon also."

"Perhaps."

"And of course he's good looking."

"He's good looking," Aline conceded. "Will that be all?"

Stack said hastily: "Then you recommend against the deal?"

"You know what I recommend."

"You don't mind if I investigate it?"

"Do what you want."

"Aline, about last night—"

"—I don't want to talk about last night," she said, nearing the door.

Stack stood in front of the door, blocking it.

"You must try to understand. You're a beautiful woman, an exciting woman. I've not only been living out here celibate for months, I've been living in the same house with you and—"

"Would you please let me out?"

"Not till I've finished speaking."

The phone on Stack's desk buzzed.

Both stared at the phone. Stack feared that if he went to his desk, Aline would escape. The phone buzzed again.

"Would you mind getting that?" Stack said.

After hesitating, Aline went to the phone. "Yes?" Stack heard her say. "All right, put her on." To Stack, Aline said: "It's the grocer's daughter from Margaux—"

"Tell her you'll call back."

But Aline began speaking animatedly into the phone. The conversation—something about a christening—seemed endless. Stack's own conversation with Aline had been broken into. The mood, such as it was, was gone. Once Aline had hung up he would have to begin again.

He waited.

At last the phone went back into the cradle.

"Aline—"

"She wants me to be godmother to her son."

"About last night—"

"It's a week from Sunday in the Margaux village church."

"For months it seemed to me that you were deliberately torturing me sexually. I mean we're both sophisticated people. There seemed no reason—"

"These village people always try to get prominent godparents for their kids. It's a way of insuring the future of the child as much as possible."

"I didn't rape you exactly—"

Her eyes were fiery. "Oh, no?"

"You led me on and on and finally—

"People such as the grocer know they won't be able to help their son very much in life, but maybe one of the godparents will."

"—And finally what anyone in his or her right mind might have expected to happen—"

"And every Christmas the godparents are expected to send lavish presents."

"—Happened," said Stack lamely.

"Still, it's flattering to be asked, don't you think?"

Stack said sarcastically: "Who's the lucky goddamn godfather?"

"It never occurred to me to ask. Will that be all?"

"Listen," Stack said hurriedly. "I want to ask you something. I want to ask you to have dinner with me tonight. We could go into Bordeaux and—" He stopped.

"I work for you from nine to six, Monday through Friday. I am at your disposal—in the business sense—during those hours."

Stack nodded.

"Was there anything else?"

Stack stared at his shoetops.

She went out of the office, leaving him astonished at her new ability to hurt him.

7

Bozon and Conderie dined copiously in a restaurant on the other side of the river. After studying the menu Bozon demanded the tray of sausages as a starter. The tray when it came contained nine different types: hard spicy salamis, blood sausages that were soft, almost runny, sausages from Germany, sausages from Spain. Some were as thin as a finger, some thicker than a man's arm.

They cut themselves generous slices.

Twice while they were eating sausages Bozon asked for the bread basket to be refilled, and they drank an entire bottle of an unlabeled red wine.

The second course was a terrine of pâté with bread, the third was broiled fresh trout, and the fourth was rabbit stew. It came with another basket of bread and a third bottle of wine.

Bozon saw that Conderie was nervous. Bozon thought: He wants to know about his money.

But neither man would have considered talking business during dinner.

Bozon found the stew delicious. The chunks of rabbit came away easily from the bone. The sauce was thick, almost black, and tasted of more spices than Bozon could identify. The potatoes were small and firm. The carrots, though swimming in the sauce, retained their own true taste, granted them by the ground they had been grown in.

Such conversation as the two men engaged in concerned the meal itself.

"Quite a nice little wine," Bozon said once.

288

"Yes, it is, and we could use more of it."

Bozon banged the bottle on the table. Presently the waiter rushed up with a fresh bottle.

"And I'll have another portion of stew, also," ordered Bozon.

"I love to watch you eat," said Conderie. "You're a marvel."

"I'm a big man. I have big appetites."

Still chewing, Bozon poured out more wine.

"The owner grows his own wine," explained Bozon. "Since he's selling it to his own clients, he takes proper care of his vines, and even buys new barrels once in a while. This fellow here could get quite a lot of money for his wine. But then he'd have to hassle with brokers and shippers. He'd have to label it. He'd rather sell it to people who come into his restaurant."

"Like us," said Conderie, pleased. "Pour me some more, will you?" Conderie had long since had enough to eat, but was still drinking.

After the rabbit stew Bozon demanded the tray of cheeses, helping himself to a thick slice of Gorgonzola and a wedge of goat cheese, and he also speared a big chunk of Cheddar.

Conderie refused cheese.

He watched Bozon eat. "I don't know how you do it," he said.

Bozon ordered still another bottle of wine. "It's so cheap we could drink it all day," he said.

"All night, you mean," said Conderie. Bozon noted Conderie was beginning to feel the wine. He himself felt fine.

The waiter came back with the cheese tray. Bozon helped himself liberally to seconds.

For dessert Bozon ordered a homemade strawberry tart topped with fresh cream.

"I'm stuffed," said Conderie.

"Nonsense," said Bozon. "Waiter, two tarts. If you can't eat yours," Bozon told Conderie, "I'll eat it for you."

Afterwards each drank a small cup of strong black coffee. The owner came forward with a bottle of plum brandy. They could see the plum in the bottle.

"He must have grown it in there," said Conderie. The owner poured out the brandy.

Bozon drained his glass. "What do you say we go take a look at your latest business investment," Bozon suggested.

The meal was over. "I was going to ask you about that," Conderie said nervously. "I want to get out."

"Come now," said Bozon soothingly. "You haven't even seen your latest investment yet."

"I don't want to see it. I don't want to know anything. Couldn't I just have my money?"

"No, you can't," snapped Bozon with irritation. "It's tied up right now—as you'll soon see." Bozon was sick of being importuned by Conderie for money Bozon had no intention of repaying any time soon. Tonight's visit would neutralize Conderie. It would scare him into silence.

In Conderie's Mercedes they drove up in front of Château Cracheau, got out of the car and approached the chai. No light showed. The night was very dark, and so was the chai.

"There's nobody here," said Conderie nervously.

"Be patient."

Bozon gave a series of knocks on the door. After a short wait the door was opened and the two men stepped inside into total darkness.

Someone flipped a switch, and Bozon stood blinking in the bright light.

"You ought to leave a few lights on outside," he said mildly. "It looks suspicious if the place is dark every night."

He shook hands with the man who had let them in. Conderie did likewise, though only first names were exchanged.

"I don't get it," the man said, jerking his thumb toward Conderie.

Bozon started to laugh. "This is one of the owners of this little enterprise."

The man, who was Claude Maurice, looked both angry and suspicious.

"Have no fear, have no fear," soothed Bozon. He laughed again. "Relax, both of you."

Conderie stood peering about, then said in English: "Is it something dishonest?" To Bozon Conderie looked as if he sounded stupid even to himself.

"Oh no," said Bozon. He began to roll with laughter. "Oh no."

Suddenly he stopped laughing. He realized he was quite nervous himself. Tonight was the night. There had been innumerable delays. The correct chemicals proved not easy to buy in quantity. The first forged documents had not satisfied Bozon. The sugar wholesaler in Spain had died and a new one had to be found.

Now at last all was ready. Everything had been set up flawlessly,

290

but if tonight the wine turned out to be undrinkable, the whole scheme fell to pieces.

"How is the brew?" asked Bozon.

"The Italian says it's fine. We were waiting for you." Claude Maurice gave Conderie a hard look. "We thought you'd come alone."

Conderie was glancing nervously over the chai. A row of burlap sacks along one wall attracted him. He peered into them. They were filled with a kind of red dust, which he held to his nose.

"Fertilizer?" he asked.

Bozon, under tension, felt the mirth bubbling up inside him. "That's a little ox blood we bought with your money. You know, dried ox blood. You may not know it, but you're now in the ox-blood business."

Bozon's laughter turned strident. "It's fertilizer all right. Only this time instead of fertilizing the soil, we're going to fertilize the wine directly."

Conderie, baffled, stared at the laughing Bozon. Bozon found this amusing too.

The man who had opened the door now released a catch of some kind, and began shouldering one of the stainless-steel vats aside.

Steps down into a secret cellar came into view. Conderie, mystified, stood at the edge peering down into full vats and a lighted cellar. Staring up at him was the face of a man he didn't know.

Bozon called down: "Hello there, Emilio." To Conderie, Bozon said: "That's Emilio. He's a master vintner."

Up the concrete stairs came Emilio, carrying a glass pitcher of wine. He handed this pitcher to Bozon, who held it to the light.

Bozon realized that a broad grin was fixed to his face. He was still on the edge of laughter. That's how much tension he was under. Conderie kept glancing about, as if trying to figure out what was happening.

The wine's color was dark red. "Excellent robe," said Bozon. "Bring glasses," he instructed Emilio.

Four wine goblets were plunked down on a barrel, and Bozon poured two inches of wine into each glass.

When Bozon raised his glass in a toast, the other three men did likewise. "To the success of our enterprise," Bozon said solemnly. "To the new wine." Giving a nervous laugh, he watched each of the three men swirl the wine around in their glasses. Each took a mouthful, each gargled the mouthful. The Italian and the man who had opened the door both spit their wine out onto the floor. Conderie swallowed his.

291

"Not bad," Conderie said.

Bozon gave another laugh, but abruptly his laughter stopped. Raising his glass, he tasted the wine himself.

What had he expected? He didn't know. He only knew that he had been very worried. It was one thing to concoct a "wine" which had never seen a grape. To sell it was another. If people would buy such a beverage, you could make a nice profit. But no one would buy unless the taste was good.

Bozon swirled the "wine" around in his mouth, then spit it out onto the floor. His face broke into a broad grin, which became punctuated by grateful sighs.

"Not bad," he kept saying. "Not bad at all."

The Italian was beaming. The Italian went around shaking hands with everybody. "Isn't that good wine?" said the Italian.

"To me," said Bozon, "it tastes like champagne. Pure champagne." Bozon was chortling. He banged the Italian on the back. "I can't taste any ox blood, can you, Emilio? I don't notice the chlorocarbonate of etile. The taste of the rat poison seems well disguised."

Bozon was grinning. Emilio was beaming with pride.

"Get it into the bottles," said Bozon. "Load it onto the trucks and bring it around to my place."

"I don't understand," said Conderie, looking mystified. "It's just another ordinary wine."

"That wine you just drank is not wine," explained Bozon.

"What?"

"Emilio here concocted it out of various things, none of them grapes."

It all dawned on Conderie now. He blanched. "What did I just drink?"

Bozon began to laugh merrily. "Nothing that will hurt you, old boy. The worst anybody risks who drinks that wine is heartburn. Maybe a little stomach ache, but probably only heartburn."

But Conderie looked as if he were about to vomit. Bozon hurried him out into the night air. Behind them the door to the chai was locked and barred. Bozon glanced at Conderie's Mercedes waiting in the moonlight. He was glad the car was Conderie's, not his own. No car had driven up tonight which could be traced to Édouard Bozon.

"You are now a master criminal," Bozon told Conderie. Bozon began laughing again. "This is the wine swindle of the century."

292

Master criminal.

The master criminal was himself, Bozon realized with pride, and he felt as he imagined certain racing-car drivers must feel—he was leading the race at great speed and might get killed at any moment but the exhilaration was intoxicating. He felt glorious.

He realized also that he had had to come here tonight. He had had to take that slight extra risk. Without risk there would have been no point to the scheme; he was not in this for money, but because he loved the excitement of trying to pull it off.

The risk was small. His forger, who would supply birth certificates for all the false wine, lived down by the Spanish frontier and did not know whom he was manufacturing the papers for. The plumbers who had installed the new vats and the various pumps and pipes had come from Libourne, or over in the Armagnac country, where no one could find them. The Spaniards who had dug the secret cellar had all been deported. Bozon was safe unless he actually visited the place—and was caught there by the police. He would not come again, but he had had to come tonight.

In the car, driving back to the city, Conderie asked in a shaken voice: "Whom do you plan to sell that stuff to?"

"Not to Frenchmen, old boy. You don't need to worry about that. Most of it I think I shall ship to South America. They don't know anything about wine there."

Conderie nodded glumly.

"And the profits. The profits will be really stupendous. You mustn't expect to realize anything on your share right away. But in about six months, I should say, you'll be in for a pleasant surprise. A very pleasant surprise. And I have set a limit of exactly one year. At the end of one year, we shall liquidate the enterprise." Bozon began to laugh. "Liquidate. That's a joke. Isn't that funny, Paul?"

It had become Bozon's idea to double his immense wealth in one year—just to see if it could be done—and then quit.

Conderie steered glumly back toward the lights of the city. As they were driving across the bridge, Bordeaux glowed against the skyline to the south, and Bozon said: "This calls for a celebration. I know where we'll go."

They stopped in a bar for Bozon to make a phone call, and each also drank a cognac. Bozon came back from the phone all smiles. He said to Conderie: "I called a woman whose place I have never patronized before. Nonetheless, the quality of her, ahem, acquaintances is said to be truly amazing." Bozon began to laugh. "Very young, very feminine —practically virgins."

Conderie gave him a distracted look.

"Finish up, they're waiting for us."

Following Bozon's directions, Conderie parked his Mercedes on the Cours Clemenceau opposite the public gardens, and they entered an elegant old house. The floor and staircase were marble. Bozon stopped the elevator, which could carry only three persons, on the third floor. There was only one apartment on each floor. Bozon rang the bell.

The maid who let them in was a young black woman in a uniform, apparently a Senegalese from Dakar, for she spoke little French.

She showed them into the salon, where a woman of about fifty, all smiles, came forward to greet them. She wore a gown down to the floor, and rings on both hands. She was carefully made up and groomed. Her hair was piled on top of her head and seemed held in place by lacquer.

She led the two men into the room. Seated on a velvet sofa were two young women. They were as carefully groomed as the older woman. They looked demure. When introduced to the two men they showed exquisite manners. Their voices were well modulated and showed no particular place accent. One was named Brigitte. She was tall and thin, though she had enough flesh in the right places. She seemed to be about twenty. The other was named Maude and was somewhat older. She was quite small. She wore a white dress with a low-cut bodice trimmed in lace. The ends of her sleeves and the hem of her skirt were also trimmed in lace. She had a pert upturned nose and nice teeth, Bozon noted.

The older woman, whose name was Madame Lasablière, had gushed out the introductions. For the second time that night, only first names were given.

"And to whom do we owe your presence here tonight?" asked Madame Lasablière cheerfully. "Surely someone recommended us."

Bozon gave a name.

Madame Lasablière nodded, a pleased expression on her face. "Oh yes, he's one of my nicest clients."

The maid came in bearing a tray of glasses and ice, and drinks were served. Polite conversation took place. Madame Lasablière and Bozon did most of the talking. The girls listened attentively and demurely, making self-effacing comments from time to time, laughing at the proper moments, showing their nice teeth.

294

"Well, my dears, I'm sure you don't need me around any longer," said Madame Lasablière after a proper interval. She had been watching the play of eyes for the last few minutes. She saw that Bozon had selected Maude, the girl in the lacy white dress. Being skilled at her job, she did not ask which man had selected which girl. This would have sounded crass, the selection of meat on the hoof. Instead, following her intuition and experience, she said only: "Maude, why don't you show Mr. Édouard the gold room. At the same time, perhaps Brigitte can be showing Mr. Paul the green room."

Conderie found himself in the green room with the girl named Brigitte. The door closed and Brigette locked it. She placed her handbag, open, on what looked to Conderie like an authentic Louis XV table. Conderie walked over and stuffed money into the handbag.

"How kind you are, Monsieur Paul," the girl said in her soft, well-modulated voice. "I wasn't really expecting such a nice present."

Like hell you weren't, Conderie thought.

Everything in the room was done in some shade of green. There was a green couch. The dressing table wore a green satin skirt. The wallpaper was green, of course, as was the coverlet on the double bed. A number of easy chairs were covered in this same green. There were always many mirrors in such rooms as this, Conderie realized, and much of the wall behind the dressing table was hung with mirrors, arranged only to highlight the dressing table—ostensibly anyway. Standing on the dressing table was a three-way mirror. The panels could be arranged in any direction inhabitants of the room might desire.

Conderie kept thinking of Château Cracheau. He wished Bozon hadn't shown it to him. Needing money, he had asked Bozon to make investments for him. That's all he had asked. The first scheme had lasted a year and ended weeks ago. Conderie had been nervous throughout that scheme, but not nearly as nervous as right this minute.

His return on the first scheme had been much smaller than he had hoped. So he had invested again. Bozon had talked him into it. He had invested without knowing the nature of the new scheme, but he knew it now. If they got caught they would surely go to jail.

The whore—Conderie had already forgotten her name—came up and stood before him. She was nearly as tall as he, and stood so close she was virtually breathing on his face. Her fingers, reaching out, loosened his collar and his tie. He took hold of the girl's wrists and smiled at her.

"You're a lovely girl," he said.

But he was distracted. He kept thinking of the police raiding Château Cracheau. After that they would come out to his own château to arrest the arch criminal, himself.

Smiling, Conderie said to the girl: "You have not been in this business very long, I can see that."

The girl, a skilled professional, accepted the role in which the client had apparently cast her. "You're right," she said demurely.

Perhaps the police would find only Bozon. In that case, would Bozon denounce him?

"How long?" asked Conderie, smiling.

The girl demurely studied her shoes. "Only a month, monsieur," she said in a low voice.

Conderie let go of her wrists. He could see liquor and glasses on the sideboard. His tongue licked his lips.

"Perhaps monsieur would like a drink?" the girl said quickly.

Conderie said he would prefer Scotch whisky, and the girl prepared it for him. She brought it over.

"You're not having anything?" Conderie asked.

"Perhaps just a sip from monsieur's glass."

The girl, smiling lovingly at Conderie, undid his shirt buttons halfway down.

"Oh, you want to play that game, do you?" said Conderie, and quickly unbuttoned her dress to the hem. He really wasn't interested tonight, but it was better than thinking about Bozon and the police.

He helped the girl step out of her dress. When she was naked, Conderie stood back and admired her.

"You have a very nice body," Conderie told her.

The girl's face showed pleasure.

That's probably genuine pleasure, Conderie thought. She does have a nice body and I guess she likes it when someone tells her so.

"I bet monsieur does too," the girl said. Moving close to him, breathing on his face, she took the glass out of his hand and set it down.

But Conderie abruptly crossed the room to a chair. Sitting, he said: "Do you know what would give me great pleasure?"

"What's that, monsieur?"

"Just to watch you walk up and down for a minute or two. Would you mind doing that? Just up and down."

"Oh no, monsieur."

The naked girl began to walk about the room.

"Why don't you just pretend that it's your own bedroom?" Conderie suggested. "Just pretend I'm not here. Do anything you might do. Comb your hair. Anything."

For a moment the girl seemed at a loss. She just stood there naked. Ill at ease, she brushed a lock of hair out of her eyes. A ring glittered in the light, and her right breast jiggled.

"That's the way," encouraged Conderie.

The girl began to pace the room, thinking it over. She had an indolent stride. She looked like a prostitute patrolling a sidewalk.

After a time, thoroughly bored, she sat at the dressing table and began combing her hair. Her breasts moved up and down. Conderie was seated in the opposite corner. He watched the muscles of her back move. Her breasts moved in the mirror.

The girl stood up and tried to decide what to do next. Apparently she couldn't think of anything. She began walking up and down again. Once she stopped directly in front of him. After a moment she thrust her bush against his nose.

Conderie took her hips and turned her around. Reluctantly, she resumed patrolling.

"Do you play golf?" asked Conderie.

"A little," the whore lied.

"Why don't you show me how you swing?"

The girl stood five paces away and began taking vicious swipes at the air. It was grotesque. Conderie almost laughed out loud.

Conderie called her over to the bed, where he pulled down the coverlet and the blanket. He read her thoughts: Now it would start and after a predictable time, end. She looked relieved.

"Why don't you lie down there now?" Conderie suggested.

The girl lay down with her legs spread. Red lips pouted twice. From the expression on her face, Conderie judged that she suddenly felt much more comfortable. In bed she was sure of herself.

Conderie, still fully dressed, pulled a chair up to the edge of the bed. Reverting to her former role, the girl asked demurely, "Will monsieur come to bed now?"

"As a matter of fact I don't feel quite myself today," Conderie answered. "I'm not as young as I used to be, you know."

"I don't believe you," the girl said. "You can't be more than forty."

"Forty-two," Conderie lied.

"You don't look nearly that old," the girl said. "I can't believe it."

"And how old are you?"

"Nineteen," the girl lied. "A month ago I was still in the lycée."

Conderie looked down at her. She was really quite a beautiful girl, and she had a lovely body. If he weren't so worried about Bozon and the police—

He took her hand and placed it between her legs. "Do that," he suggested.

The girl immediately remembered a role she had played before. "Oh, no, monsieur, I couldn't."

"Why not?"

"Please, monsieur, it wouldn't be right. Nice girls don't do that."

"Do it for me."

The girl allowed herself to be persuaded. "Well, perhaps for you it would be all right."

The girl began massaging herself. Once Conderie put a hand on top of hers, and the two hands moved in unison. Conderie pushed her hand down further. "Put one finger in."

They went through the same charade again. "Please, monsieur, don't make me do such an awful thing."

"Please. For me."

She had long red fingernails. Conderie watched first one, then several disappear inside her. He found himself getting mildly aroused. "Make yourself come."

"Please, monsieur, it wouldn't be nice."

Conderie took a hundred-franc note out of his billfold. "This is yours if you can bring yourself off."

The girl eyed the money.

"Don't fake it. I can tell the difference."

The pointed red fingernails disappeared, reappeared, disappeared again. It looked as though she were spearing herself. Her finger tips glistened red as blood. She had begun to moan and writhe on the sheet. The role was congenial to her. This she understood.

Conderie was fascinated by her performance. He had forgotten Bozon, forgotten the police. Her nipples were hard and her fingers wetter than ever. He watched avidly. He began to be confident he would lose his hundred-franc note.

In the gold room across the hall the whore called Maude was trying to cope with Édouard Bozon. Maude was twenty-four but had already been a prostitute nine years. At fifteen she had looked old for her age. She had started her career in Lyon, on the street, pounding the pavement with older whores who didn't know any better. Maude considered herself an aggressive, grasping woman—and smart. She had worked her way up to where she was now, a call girl in Bordeaux, and she was on her way to Paris. She did not consider herself a whore, but a call girl. The words had come over unchanged from the English. They sounded chic and expensive, which is what she was. Her real name was not Maude but Clotilde Berthier. She had changed her name and her town of business four times and her protector more often than that. She owned identity cards in four different names. That cost money but was worth it. Each time she had moved on she had also moved up. With a new name no one could trace her.

She had just reached Bordeaux. Here no man shared her earnings. She paid a percentage to Madame Lasablière, who arranged her "dates."

At first Madame Lasablière had monitored her performances through peepholes in the wall. It became a matter of pride with Maude that this should stop. Maude did not object for reasons of privacy, not her own and certainly not the johns'. But once the surveillance stopped —and it only lasted a week or so—Maude's future seemed to her assured. She had successfully acceded to new and higher rank. She had reached higher social strata. It was like being admitted to a new posh club. She was now assured more money for less work and her clientele was almost exclusively uppercrust.

She considered herself a pro. She knew everything about her line of work. All men fit into one category or another. Five minutes after entering a bedroom with a john she knew what category to fit him into. There were those who wanted to play games first and those who wanted to get right to business. There were those who liked to give oral gratification and those who liked to receive it. There were those who told her their troubles and who, afterwards, wanted either sympathy or contempt. At first it had shocked her to know that some men wanted to be spiritually flayed by her for their imagined deficiencies. She would have thought all men craved only sympathy, but it wasn't so, and she had learned to discern which man was which and act accordingly. The ones who wanted contempt from Maude got it, and usually afterwards such men liked to lie on their backs while she mounted them.

She knew how to simulate excitement and even orgasms. No man, watching her, could guess she was not in a state of transport.

She cared about only two things: that she not be physically abused, and that she get paid. She took pride in her work but only in the foreplay and the afterplay—in the social intercourse that preceded and followed the other kind. Any woman could lie on her back and get plugged, Maude felt.

She was a performer, and often thought of herself as a kind of actress. She liked to roll the words "call girl" round and round in her mouth. She liked the way the words sounded and also what they meant.

She had never seen Édouard Bozon before tonight, nor he her, but without knowing who he was, she had sized him up quickly. He was rich, he was important, he was used to being obeyed. As she locked the door to the gold room and turned back toward the bed she noted that Bozon was prowling about looking for peepholes or two-way mirrors. She watched him lift up and peer under paintings on the wall. She was amused.

"You can rest easy," she told him. "There's nothing in this room. The green room is the one with the peepholes. Madame Lasablière is probably checking up right now on Brigitte and your friend."

"I like to be certain," noted Bozon.

"You're a very forceful man," Maude said. "Anyone can see that."

"Come here, my dear. Let me remove that lacy white dress. Shall I tell you what you're wearing under it? Lacy white underwear. There, just as I thought."

Maude laughed as if with pleasure. This client was neither harder nor easier to read than any other. "What else can you tell me about myself?"

"That you like your job. That you love your job."

"Not always. But with a man like you I can tell it's going to be fun."

He was a big bruiser and, as his weight came down hard on top of her, she worried that, either deliberately or inadvertently, he might hurt her.

"I can't breathe," she gasped, exaggerating a bit.

He got on his elbows and began sawing. He sawed on and on. She pretended passion from the start, but presently began to worry. He showed no sign of approaching a climax. A sexual athlete. She had had sexual athletes before. On and on Bozon worked, until she began to doubt it would ever end. If he kept up much longer she'd get sore.

"Let's try it another way," she begged throatily, passionately. "I'm dying to feel what you feel like another way."

They came apart and then together again. She answered every thrust. She was working very hard now. She was glistening with sweat. So was he. He looked as if he had just come out of the shower. She began

300

to get really worried. He was big, both inside and out. He could hurt her permanently.

He had not spoken a word.

Now she lay on her back again. Astride her hips he sat facing her. His prick seemed to rise up out of her own pubic hair. Looking down, she saw herself as a man with an erection. He was pinching her nipples. She closed her eyes and began manipulating him with both hands until at last through experienced fingertips she could feel his climax nearing.

Thank God, she told herself.

Her eyes were still closed. His whole body seemed to go into spasms. She felt the hot viscous substance coursing down over her hands, which was normal, but also down onto her thighs, which was not. There was a moment of incomprehension.

—What's going on here, she asked herself.

Then the stench rose up, assaulting her nose.

"Jesus Christ," she cried out. She tried to squirm out from underneath him, but he was sitting astride her hips. She was pinned between his calves. She could not move the lower half of her body. She could feel the viscous substance spreading out over her thighs.

She tried to sit up, but his hands on her breasts pressed her down again. Tears came to her eyes. "You bastard," she cried, "oh you dirty bastard." She called him every name she could think of. He sat astride her, fouling her, laughing his head off.

8

In New York Stack gave a party, inviting all high executives of The Company and their wives, and also a good many high executives and wives from drug companies with whom he had once done business. Stack's bar was tended by two moonlighting cops. The waiter, who was a black man supplied by the caterer, wore a white coat and moved through the crowd offering canapés on a tray. Stack in scarlet sports coat with red-and-green-checked pants stood near the door, greeting guests, glass in hand. His pale rose shirt, open at the throat, was stuffed with a foulard, and his shoes gleamed. Even their dangling tassels gleamed.

The apartment was cool. The air conditioning hummed. The grin was fixed to Stack's face, and he was working hard, a human handshaking machine. Only a few hours previously he had stepped off a transatlantic jet, and his body was operating on a different time clock. His body thought it was nearly midnight and he still hadn't had dinner. His body thought that the day's work was long since over, and in fact it hadn't yet started.

Stack wished he were back in Bordeaux. Back in Bordeaux people would consider such a party uncivilized. In Bordeaux one drank for enjoyment, not to stupefy oneself. In Bordeaux one dined sitting down, and not on canapés.

In Bordeaux one did business in offices, not at parties.

The party unreeled, seeming unreal. Already Stack had told twenty middle-aged women how lovely they were. He had greeted their husbands as if overjoyed at the chance to shake their marvelous hands.

But the party was already a flop, for the chairman wouldn't be coming. Earlier his regrets had been expressed via a phone call from his secretary. The chairman hadn't even bothered to call in person.

What did this mean?

Stack's New York secretary had arranged the party a week or more ago. Though she had other duties too, now that Stack was in Bordeaux, she was still his; they were taking her away from him gradually. When she was gone completely it would mean something, though it was not yet clear to him exactly what.

Wearing the dark business suit he had traveled in, Stack had spent an hour in the office that afternoon, trying to gauge the climate—meaning his own stature. The chairman's regrets had been phoned in five minutes after Stack came in the door. Five minutes later Johnston had stuck his head into the office Stack was using.

"Charlie, great to see you again. You're looking great, Charlie."

"I'm always happiest right here in this office," Stack had said, grinning effusively. He was wearing his horn-rimmed glasses by then and through them peered owlishly at Johnston.

"Say, Charlie, about your party tonight—"

Stack, a shaken man, had thought: He's going to cancel too.

The point of the party was to meet socially with The Company's top

302

executives, especially the chairman and Johnston, to impress them with their lavish host, himself.

"Well, er, Charlie, my wife can't make it tonight. But, ah, if you don't mind, I might drop around without her."

"Swell," said Stack, relieved.

"You don't mind if I bring a friend, do you, Charlie boy?"

"Of course not."

What did "friend" mean?

Now the door to his party swung open, disclosing Johnston, all smiles.

"Charlie," Johnston cried out. "This is Charlie, honey. Charlie, you're looking great."

The girl was young and very small. She had enormous breasts for her size. She was wearing one of the shortest skirts Stack had ever seen. She had the slightly glazed look of invincible stupidity. A secretary, Stack thought automatically. Stack wondered if she worked for The Company—or for some other company. Surely Johnston would not appear in public with one of his own secretaries.

And what did it mean that Johnston dared bring such a girl at all? The chairman would not approve such conduct by Johnston or any other top executive. The chairman was quite a prissy guy, and Johnston knew it. Had Johnston risen to such sudden power within The Company that he could do what he liked?

Johnston's face was red and he was gushing. "Vera, this is the guy I've been telling you about. This is Charlie Stack. We all think a lot of Charlie." He socked Stack in the arm. "This is Vera," Johnston explained.

Stack gave Vera a handshake and his best smile. Her hand was tiny, and during the moment he held it her eyes searched the room uncertainly.

As Stack's door opened again, disclosing still another couple waiting to be greeted, Stack said to Johnston: "I hope we get a chance later on to talk for a few minutes."

"Sure thing, Charlie. Sure thing."

Stack, already shaking hands with somebody else, watched Johnston and Vera insinuating themselves deeper into the crowded room.

Secretary. One of ours? Or someone else's? Did it matter?

It did matter. In the morning Stack would appear before the committee monitoring plan fulfillment. He had to collect as much gossip as possible before then. What was going on inside The Company?

He had been away too long. He had come to enjoy Bordeaux, a more pleasant place to pass one's life than here. To watch the soil produce seemed more fitting for a man than these cheap palace intrigues.

But his career would be fulfilled or broken off here, not there.

After a while Stack was able to move away from the front door. He circulated, laughed, made jokes, groped for gossip. The rumor was that Johnston would be named chief operating officer. It was not known if the chairman planned early retirement. Perhaps there was a stock deal cooking of some kind.

Stack stifled yawns.

He tried to get close to the oblivious Johnston, the only person here he truly wanted to talk to, but Johnston's attention was fixed exclusively on Vera. Vera stood literally in the corner. Johnston was leaning in on her, one arm against the wall. Vera's head was using the two walls as a headrest. She was looking up at Johnston almost fearfully. From time to time Johnston would call out for a drink and one of the moonlighting cops would rush one over. Those cops know how to read power, Stack thought.

Stack kept waiting for Johnston and Vera to drift into the middle of the room, where Johnston could be separated from her and talked to casually, but at the same time pointedly, about Stack's role in The Company. But this never happened.

As people began to leave, Stack stood at the door again, effusively sending people he didn't care about on their way. The noise diminished somewhat. Stack wondered what Aline would have thought of his party, and guessed she would have found it grotesque.

Johnston and Vera remained glued to their corner. Stack, talking loudly, always grinning, was exhausted as he shuffled between goodbyes and the bar. He had had three drinks, perhaps four. He had eaten half a tray of canapés and was still hungry. He wished everybody would go. To hell with talking to Johnston. Stack just wanted to go to bed.

When next he looked around, Johnston and Vera were both gone. They couldn't have got past him at the door. Were they in the dining room? The hallway then? Stack hovered at the bathroom door. Not both in the bathroom together?

The bathroom door opened and a woman Stack didn't know came out. "All yours, pal," she said, marching past him.

Stack's bedroom was closed as he had left it, but when he tried the handle the door was locked from the inside.

Oh, Christ, he thought.

In the hallway stood Stack, watching his bedroom door, chattering inanely with a new group vice president and the man's dull wife. At last the lock to Stack's bedroom turned. The door opened, and Vera issued forth looking disheveled. A moment later came Johnston, straightening his tie, looking pleased with himself.

Johnston clapped Stack on the back. "Well, Charlie my boy, it's late, and I guess we ought to be shoving off. Wonderful party. Thanks for the invitation. You and I will have our chat in the morning, okay?"

"Right you are, Johnny," Stack said, accompanying both to the door, where he bid them an effusive goodnight.

Now came the night's worst chore: waiting out the last of his guests. Stack's body imagined itself still in Bordeaux. Though it was only midnight in New York his body thought the hour 5 A.M. Stack drifted on the edge of sleep.

At last everyone was gone.

When the door closed behind the two cops, Stack stumbled into his bedroom. He had a big bed with an expensive satin counterpane, now mussed. Staring down at it, Stack imagined he could see the outline of Vera's body and of Johnston's knees. On the counterpane between Johnston's knee prints there was a large wet stain.

Oh no, he said to himself. Not that too. A present from Mr. Johnston, Stack thought, disgusted.

Then he thought: Why should I be disgusted? Johnston is a powerful man, and he's only feeling his power.

Outside the village church of Margaux the line of cars, including a few small trucks belonging to local tradesmen, gleamed in the sun. They were all parked on a slant, wheels halfway down the rain gutter. Aline, godmother to be, parked as close as she could get, then walked down the dirt road and into the churchyard through the wrought-iron gates.

In the open space between the tombs of the graveyard and the weathered wooden doors of the church a great many people had congregated, all looking happy, all wearing their Sunday best, for baptisms were festive occasions in French villages, ranking third in importance, exceeded only by weddings and funerals.

The grocer and his wife came forward to greet Aline. The grocer's wife carried the baby, her grandson. Aline praised the baby and was

305

given it to hold, while the grocer went to find his son-in-law. The son-in-law, Aline knew, had started his working life as a clerk in the grocery, but now presumably could hope for better things.

The son-in-law came up beaming.

"Congratulations," Aline told him.

Both gazed rapturously down at the infant. It had been a long time since Aline had held a baby—any baby—in her arms, and it felt comfortable there, and she realized she felt quite happy.

Other people crowded around Aline and the miniature star of today's show including the butcher and his wife, the pharmacist, the old couple who ran one of the village gas stations. They treated Aline like a celebrity. They all thanked her for coming.

Paulette, the grocer's daughter, was not present, this being the custom, but would attend the luncheon reception at the Savoie later, and would accept congratulations—and presents—then. The grocer, Aline knew, could be depended upon to lay on a champagne feast for fifty people which would cost him the profits of half a year, but he would think the feast worth every sou. Even now he was gazing adoringly down at the baby in Aline's arms.

"Who's the godfather?" Aline inquired.

The grocer shot an anxious glance at his wife. After a moment the woman said hesitantly: "Paulette asked Monsieur Bozon to be godfather."

"Oh," said Aline. She frowned.

"I hope you don't mind."

"Why should I mind?" said Aline, thinking: And Bozon accepted just to humiliate me.

"I'm so glad," said the grocer's wife, relieved. "I told you it would be all right," she said to her husband.

"We're all adults here, aren't we?" said Aline. "I mean, we're all civilized, aren't we?"

The grocer's wife would not meet Aline's eyes. Your daughter is a ninny, Aline thought; or maybe it's you.

Oh, the crass, grasping mentality of the French peasant, Aline thought, here hoping to reunite the landed local gentry (herself) and one of Bordeaux's great commercial houses (Bozon) for the benefit of this cooing infant in her arms.

Calm down, she told herself, they're only trying to do what they think is right for the baby.

306

She peered at the tiny male human being in her arms, a responsibility she had willingly accepted, knowing at the time she was being used, though not how much. I mustn't take it out on you, she silently told the baby.

Just then Bozon, piously blessing himself with holy water, came out of the church. Sunlight glistened on the wet dab on his forehead.

"The curé is ready," he called.

Spying Aline, he came forward, all broad grin and outstretched hand. "And how are you, my dear?" he demanded.

Aline used the excuse of the baby in her arms to ignore Bozon's proffered hand.

"Let's go into the church, shall we?" suggested Aline to the grocer and his wife.

As Aline, Bozon, and the baby led the parade inside, Bozon took her arm. There was nothing she could do about it. It seemed to her she could feel all the village folk observing her, appraising her conduct toward her ex-husband.

The threesome stood in the gloom beside the baptismal font, which was marble and which had been worn to various smoothnesses over the centuries.

To Aline the holy water smelled as if it hadn't been changed in centuries either.

The curé, an elderly man in a worn and dusty cassock, stood opposite, intoning prayers out of a book, holding it sideways to catch a shaft of light coming down from a window high up. The rest of the multitude had crowded around.

Bozon still had her arm. She kept telling herself that this had no significance; she did not mind it. She didn't want to make a fuss in here, in front of all these people, and perhaps spoil the christening for them.

She began to listen to the prayers. Once she had been very religious. Even now she sometimes imagined that when she got old she would come back to the church.

She stood in the gloom beside her ex-husband, holding a stranger's baby.

The Margaux church was so old it seemed to her that she was inhaling the odor of centuries.

That, and the stagnant holy water. And the odor of Bozon's lotions.

In her ear Bozon whispered piously: "This is the first time you and I have been in church together since our wedding."

307

She glanced up sharply, remembering only at the last moment to transform anger into a wooden smile.

Their wedding had taken place not here but in the thirteenth-century cathedral in Bordeaux, and had been one of the major social events of that season.

It became her turn to make baptismal responses. Directed by the curé, she denounced Satan on behalf of the baby. She vowed to oversee the baby's religious education if this should become necessary. Bozon, sounding pious, did the same.

Bozon, Aline noted, had been an atheist as long as she had known him. The only thing he believed in was himself.

It was her own promises that rang in her ears. Today's were no more empty than most of the ones a woman makes in a lifetime, she decided. She was peering down at the baby who, wearing lace and bonnet, was asleep, but who, a moment later, would wake up yowling as she held him over the font, and the water was poured over his bare pulsing scalp.

Bozon gave her arm a squeeze. Aline, unable to take any more, yanked it out of his grasp.

More prayers were intoned. Aline was thinking of her father, and of Stack, both, for all she knew, under the spell of this brutal man beside her, and she resolved to try to talk to him outside when the ceremony ended. She was not afraid of him. No.

Ten minutes later Aline and her former husband stood amid the tombs. Nearby, the baby was back in the arms of its grandmother, the pair surrounded by laughing well-wishers.

"What are you up to with my father?"

Bozon lit a cigarette. "We have a little business venture going. Your father is about to make a good deal of money."

"Let him go. Leave him alone—"

Bozon laughed, teeth glowing below his mustache.

"Shouldn't you talk to him about it, not me?"

"And this proposition you've offered Charlie Stack—"

Bozon's grinning mouth mocked her: "Why, I do believe I detect affection for the fellow in your words."

Aline, suddenly on the defensive, said: "It's a good job. It means a lot to me. I don't want to lose it."

"Why should you care what happens to that fellow, my dear? He's just another pirate—like most businessmen."

308

"I've advised him against your proposition."

"It's a good affair for him."

"But a better one for you."

"Perhaps. In any case, I believe you're too late. As I understand it, he has gone to New York to seek final approval."

In her frustration, Aline glanced about. The baby was being passed from arms to arms, but she herself stood ankle deep in marble-covered tombs. The slabs lay like blankets as if to keep the cold away from people dead ten years, fifty years, two hundred years—or perhaps to keep them by sheer weight from suddenly sitting up. Scrolled and flowered wrought-iron crosses sprouted upward as if out of dead people's eyeballs. There were enameled photographs inset into some of the newer tombs; plastic flowered wreaths, guaranteed to bloom through eternity, lay atop others.

It was true. Her father was already hooked, and Stack had indeed gone to New York to seek approval. Aline was too late, as always. Bozon was again the winner.

He sucked on his cigarette to make the coal glow, then pushed it inexorably toward her bosom. Automatically she cringed.

How often had she cringed in the past? She had walked out, though not right way.

Now she stood straight, and thrust her bosom forward. "Touch me with that thing," she said, "and he'll kill you."

"The American?"

Aline, grim-faced, said nothing.

"So that's the way it is," commented Bozon.

"Let you be the first to know."

Bozon laughed and flicked his cigarette over a row of tombs.

"He's a lucky man," commented Bozon. "You are a very hot number, when handled properly."

The church and its graveyard were surrounded on three sides by vines belonging to Château Margaux, and on the fourth by a woods. Aline looked past Bozon's head down a row of vines. Each vine was the same height and width as every other vine. The rows were as constantly and as carefully cropped as a row of hedges, and as perfectly ordered as life itself was not.

Once Aline had come home to find Bozon having sex with some woman on their bed, with the bedroom door open. Mesmerized, or perhaps paralyzed, Aline had stood in the doorway watching and, once the woman was gone, had taken her place on the bed.

How could someone, meaning a woman as proud as herself, ever get over behaving like that?

"Do you know what I remember as the hottest I've ever seen you," began Bozon.

But Aline hurried away from him.

She was surrounded by death, meaning Bozon and the tombs, but also by life, meaning the baby and the vines, and she could not reconcile the two, so she handed over her present to the grocer's wife—a gold religious medal on a golden chain that had cost plenty—made her excuses, and fled both the churchyard and the champagne banquet that was to come.

By 6 A.M. on the morning following his party, Stack was fully awake. His body thought the hour coming up was noon, and could not be persuaded otherwise, and so Stack arose and began cleaning his apartment.

But at 10 A.M. he stood brightly before the committee monitoring plan fulfillment. Gone was the scarlet blazer, gone the checked pants and rose shirt. Stack wore the somberest of his business suits, and a somber tie to go with it. Peering through his horn rims, he spoke confidently, pointing out that the crop this year should be huge: "The oenological station at Bordeaux, after tests of sample cuttings, reports that the average grape in the region is twenty percent fatter than in an ordinary year."

"Spell it out in dollars and cents, Charlie," suggested the chairman.

But Stack refused. "No can do, Warren. We're not running a store. To a large extent we're at the mercy of whatever the weather will be during the harvest. On this side of the ocean wine is a business—and a booming business at that. On the other side of the ocean wine is agriculture."

Around the board table, Stack watched men squirm. They were not farmers, but businessmen. They wanted firm answers.

Stack stood beside the easel with his placards and outlined the percentages: so many good years per decade, so many poor ones. Wretched years were few, he told them.

"You're not waffling on us, are you, Charlie boy?" demanded Johnston.

No, but he wanted them to realize the risk inherent in all agriculture.

310

"We don't want to hear your doubts, Charlie," Johnston said. "We want the results you promised us."

Standing beside his easel, Stack wafted a pleasant smile across toward Johnston, while thinking: You left wet semen on my bedspread. He held up one hand. "All I ask is patience. Give me your patience, and I'll give you your profit."

Compounding felony with felony. If the weather should destroy the harvest, then the fault would be his—he had just said so, had he not? —and these people would replace him instantly with someone more "reliable."

He tried to tell himself that he exulted in such pressure. He liked being under fire. He liked the spotlight. He loved responsibility. But all he could think was that he wanted to be back in Bordeaux, where his only master was the soil.

Nature is not malevolent, he thought, only impersonal. Executives such as these men are malevolent and impersonal both.

Most of all such men were intolerant: intolerant of eccentrics, intolerant of rebels, intolerant of failure.

"Let's talk about this hotel," suggested Johnston almost amiably.

Stack, who kept seeing the semen stain on his bedspread, said calmly: "I'll have to ask you to hold off on that until after the harvest. "I'll have some reports ready by then. I have had my team in there and we're readying a complete report now."

A report had already been prepared, but it was negative and this was no time to submit a no to men who wanted to hear yes. The arguments for rejecting the hotel had convinced Stack, but would not necessarily convince these men. To Stack the project simply felt wrong. A half-dozen small factors indicated it was wrong, at least for this year. The price of land was too high this year, for instance, and it was going to be difficult, perhaps impossible, to buy enough of it from greedy peasants. Existing structures, for one reason or another, were unsatisfactory. The best way to build such a hotel would be with French government support, and gaining such support should fall to the Paris Profit Center, not to Charlie Stack in Bordeaux. Maybe government support was possible, maybe not. No one had yet checked.

The instant the harvest is in, Stack thought, I better get this hotel business settled.

It was time now to lay Bozon's proposed distribution arrangement on the table, and this could be done so that it seemed a triumph for The Company's man on the scene in Bordeaux, Charlie Stack in person.

Stack had had folders prepared complete with graphs and statistics. There were maps of various countries dotted with Bozon's claimed outlets. Stack's investigation had disclosed no unsound practices by Bozon. Stack's auditors had gone over Bozon's books, Stack's solicitors had checked over Bozon's documents. All was as it should be.

The folders lay in a neat pile beside Stack's briefcase.

Distribute them then, he told himself.

The committee members waited expectantly.

But Stack realized that this project rang false to him too, and he could not make his hand touch the folders. For a frantic second he asked himself what he was basing such a judgment on.

He could not say. He had been brooding about the deal ever since his reports had come in. Somebody had overlooked something somewhere.

Or was he being unduly influenced by Aline's view of her former husband? He didn't know. He hoped he was not. Perhaps he was in love with her, and this was warping his keen business sense.

At the head of the table he shook his head doggedly. His lips moved, though he did not know it.

"Well, Charlie?" inquired the chairman.

Push the goddamn folders forward, Stack ordered himself. Score points for yourself. You certainly need them. These people will flip for the deal. The folders are all the proof they will need. They'll practically give you a medal.

Stack forced a bright, confident grin. "That's all I have for today, gentlemen," he said.

The folders went into his briefcase and he zipped it shut.

Back in his own office, Stack stared out the window, considering Bozon's deal still again. The Company would gain increased profitability and wider distribution than heretofore. Bozon, who owned distribution rights to none of the top five wines, would acquire Château Conderie, the No. 6 wine. Château Conderie would become his flagship wine, the seal of approval on all the other wine he was marketing.

Fair exchange. It was the type of mutually advantageous deal businessmen agreed to every day. Stack could find no reasonable reason not to propose the deal to his superiors. His nagging doubts he should, as a businessman, ignore.

He resolved to call a special meeting tomorrow and present the deal then. He would let other men decide, knowing in advance they

312

would think the deal great, and would grab it. This was the decision that the success of his own career seemed to demand, and so he would make it.

Late the next day Stack taxied from the office to the airport, where he caught the night plane to Paris, a sleepless night spent staring out at the dark stars while the stewardess plied him with champagne. Once he tried to sleep but couldn't, and so sipped more champagne, which only gave him a headache. At Paris he hurried through the airport to catch the flight to Bordeaux, slept all the way, and stumbled up the ramp groggy.

A pleasant surprise: Aline stood there waiting for him.

Stack found himself grinning, his first genuine grin in many hours. "You did miss me, didn't you?" he asked her. "You couldn't wait to see me."

But Aline, on the defensive, began to talk of a reception he had been invited to that afternoon: "I thought you should know about it right away."

The reception was unimportant and, he thought, not why she had come to meet him. She could have sent anyone or no one, but was there herself. Taking her arm, Stack walked her happily out of the terminal. "And after the reception, we'll go to dinner together."

She disengaged her arm. "Dinner won't be possible."

"Why not?"

"I go off work at six."

"Zingo," said Stack.

But, as they stepped silently across to the parking lot, Aline said: "I'm sorry, I didn't mean to be as rude as that sounded."

"You just meant to be slightly rude."

"Yes," said Aline in a low voice.

"Then have dinner with me."

"No, thank you."

Sun glared off parked cars. After a moment, contritely he supposed, Aline took his arm.

When they had climbed into the Ferrari, Aline asked: "What happened about the Bozon proposal?"

"Nothing," said Stack. "It's still there in my briefcase. I didn't present it."

"Did I have something to do with that?"

"I don't think so, no."

When he glanced over at her, an irritating half smile played at the corners of her mouth.

Driving up the dirt lane to the château he stopped the car and walked out a few yards into the vines. He was so pleased to be standing amid his vines again that he thought he must be drunk with fatigue. Peeling back some of the leaves, he weighed in his hand a long tight cluster of grapes. It was almost like weighing a woman's breast. There was the same type of sensual pleasure to it.

Each cluster looked as if it would fill a bottle on its own. He picked off a grape and ate it, finding it too sweet, though to him at the moment delicious.

Aline was watching him from the car. He looked across at her and thought of Johnston and the chairman in New York.

Struggling with the soil is life, Stack reflected. Struggling with each other is madness.

A week later Bozon telephoned. "I thought I would have heard from you by now."

Stack said: "I don't have any word for you yet."

Bozon affected to be surprised. "You mean it's not decided yet?"

"No."

"I understood that New York would merely ratify your decision."

"That isn't the way it has turned out."

Bozon was silent.

Stack said: "I'll call as soon as I hear anything."

"I certainly wish they'd decide quickly," interposed Bozon. "The sooner we get started, the more profit for all of us."

"Right you are. I'll see if I can't hurry them along. I'll get back to you."

When Stack had hung up he said to Aline, who was seated beside his desk: "He's awfully anxious."

"Why didn't you just tell him you had decided against it?"

"This way is better."

"Sooner or later you're going to have to tell him."

"I don't need to make an enemy out of the man, Aline. He won't phone again for two weeks, and when he does I'll tell him that it looks bad. A week after that I'll tell him I did my best for him, but New York overruled me."

314

Aline said disgustedly: "Must big business be so dishonest."

"Yes, it must, just like politics. The first rule of business and politics both is this: never gratuitously make anybody mad at you. I may need Bozon sometime. Let him resent New York, not me."

"I wish I had taken the call. I would have delighted in making him gratuitously mad at me. I would have told him straight out."

"My way is better, believe me." Stack grinned at her. "Besides, circumstances could change. I might change my decision."

Aline did not grin back.

"It could happen," Stack pointed out gently.

In fact he had miscalculated. A week later Bozon drove into the courtyard formed by the chais and stepped out into the cloud of dust his car had raised.

Stack came forward and they shook hands.

"No word?" said Bozon.

"I'm worried," answered Stack. "It doesn't look too good, I'm afraid."

"What could have gone wrong?"

"I can't imagine."

Stack stared blandly across into Bozon's intent frown. Stack thought: He's not bashful, is he? If the answer is to be no, he wants it right in the face. And he wants to be sure exactly where it's coming from, too.

"Why don't we go across to your office?" suggested Bozon. "I want to go over the details with you again. Maybe we can figure out where we went wrong. That is, assuming you did recommend the plan—"

Stack, who had been on his way to Bordeaux to play in a members' tournament at the Primrose Tennis Club, demurred, saying that New York had all the information it needed.

Bozon interrupted, "I have some new projections."

The Ferrari, with Stack's tennis gear in the trunk, was parked ten yards away. Escape was that close.

Stack argued politely. He remembered all the details perfectly. New York had them and would decide.

"You assured me your decision would not be overruled," declared Bozon harshly.

"I guess I was mistaken."

Stack eyed his car. He could feel the racket in his grip in advance. He could see his forehand drives clearing the net.

"It's a brilliant deal for your company."

"Maybe they don't see it that way," Stack suggested.

"Maybe your presentation was weak."

"Maybe."

"Maybe deliberately so."

"Look, I've got an appointment in Bordeaux and—"

Bozon said bluntly. "My ex-wife told me she had advised you against the deal."

Stack was surprised to hear this. When had they seen each other? "Yes, she did."

"She hates me."

"Well," said Stack, "that's neither here nor there as far as the deal is concerned."

"I don't believe you."

Stack was annoyed. "I don't care what you believe."

"I open my books to your auditors. Your lawyers come in and look over my papers. All perfect."

"Yes, they were," Stack conceded, eying his getaway car.

"So, if you reject the deal, it's a personal thing."

"Look, I'm late, I've really got to take off now."

"Why don't you admit it? It wasn't New York that vetoed the deal. You did it yourself."

Stack said nothing.

"You let that bitch turn you against me. That vindictive cow."

Stack said coolly: "I'd really prefer it if you wouldn't talk that way about her."

"That's right, she told me you'd been screwing her."

Stack, trying to control his rage, said: "I don't think she said that."

"I thought you were a businessman out for the best deal for your company. But you enjoy my ex-wife's pussy so much you let her talk you out of it."

"I suggest you get into your car and drive out of here."

They glared at each other.

"Right now," shouted Stack.

"I'll hurt you for this. You can count on it."

Bozon's car, wheels spinning, roared out under the arch. Stack, who stood in the miasma of dust looking after it, was trembling from tension and rage.

Once the trembling had stopped, and Stack had crossed to his car, his principal emotion became amazement. He was amazed at the be-

316

havior of the man—the sudden, inexplicable violence. He would not mention the incident to Aline. It would only upset her. Starting his car, Stack drove thoughtfully toward his tennis club.

He had turned the man into an enemy despite himself, and had been threatened, but was not unduly worried. There was no way he could see that Bozon could do him harm.

9

Françoise in Toulouse wandered amid the counters of the Prisunic. Françoise liked Toulouse, which to her seemed a big city. Bigger than Bordeaux, anyway. And the people weren't all farmers married to a few stupid vines. Toulouse had factories. They even built jet airliners in Toulouse.

Françoise had no money. Not a sou. There was nothing in the pockets of her jeans but a few loose pills. All around her were things she needed, and also things she only coveted. The Prisunic was the cheapest of the French chain stores, the French equivalent of Woolworth's. Prices though low seemed high to Françoise. She needed new underpants, for example, and fingered some before dropping them back in the bin. And it would have been lovely to buy a bar of this scented soap. The next aisle brought her to the store's huge and crowded food department. She was not hungry. She really didn't eat much any more. And she certainly wasn't interested in those racks of wine.

She came to the lingerie counter again, where her hands stirred through the panties. She found some in pink that pleased her. There was lace around the legs and they would be stretched almost transparent when she wore them.

No one was watching her, though she glanced guiltily around to make sure. In her pocket the underpants made no more of a bulge than a handkerchief.

She strolled on until she came to the perfume counter. She would have really loved a bath, she realized. She was tired of washing herself all over standing in front of a cold-water sink. She really needed soap, scented or not, so she selected a thin bar, which in her pocket showed no more distinctly than a wallet.

And perfume. How nice it would be to dab perfume in the crooks of her arms, on her breasts. But, in this store at least, there was a woman behind the counter watching it. Regretfully, perfume was out.

Françoise decided to leave the store. She had actually reached the street when the man grabbed her. At first she thought he was making some kind of sexual assault. He had one arm across her breasts, and his other had a grip on her belt. She fought him but he was much too strong. Along the sidewalk, pedestrians stepped back to watch the struggle, which did not last long. The man dragged Françoise back into the store.

Five hours later Stack got a call from a court-appointed lawyer in Toulouse. He refused to take the call, not knowing what it was, and unwilling to get into a discussion in French with some lawyer he didn't know. He had the call switched to Aline, who a few minutes later appeared in his doorway.

"You'd better take this call. Françoise is in trouble in Toulouse. The lawyer speaks English."

Aline stood in his doorway listening.

Hanging up, Stack called past her to his secretary: "Get Saar in here." Stack added: "And get some money out of the safe. Bring me five thousand francs."

To Aline Stack said: "This is going to cost at least a thousand dollars. In addition to shoplifting, they have her on a drug charge. According to the lawyer the store manager will drop the charges for a thousand francs. An arrangement can be made with the police about the pills, the lawyer thinks, but he doesn't know how much it will cost."

Aline stared. He couldn't be sure, but it almost looked as if she approved of him for a change. "You have a heart after all, don't you?"

"She's part of my family."

"Family?"

"And she's just a kid. It isn't her fault that she was born into a world so screwed up she can't understand it."

"She isn't the only one who can't understand it."

Stack said: "Speak for yourself. I understand my world perfectly."

This time there was no mistaking Aline's warm smile. "Yes, superman," she said.

Françoise walked down the steps to the sidewalk. Behind her was the official building. Beside her stood Saar. Françoise breathed the free air.

"Where are you living?" demanded Saar.

Françoise said nothing. The expression she turned on him was inscrutable.

"We'll go by and get your things," asserted Saar. "He wants me to bring you back to the château."

Françoise gazed at him.

"You are some surly kid."

"I'll need money," Françoise said.

"How much?" demanded Saar suspiciously.

"I owe the rent. I owe money in the bakery, in the food store."

"How much will it come to?"

Françoise named the highest figure she dared.

"All right, let's go there. I'll pay out the money personally."

Françoise stared at him.

"What's the matter now?" Saar asked.

"Do you think I want to be humiliated by you? I'll pay them myself or I won't go back with you."

Saar considered this, then agreed. That was when Françoise knew she had him.

"Let's go do it now," Saar said. "I want to be on the road in an hour."

"I can't leave Toulouse until tomorrow."

"What?"

Françoise stared at him.

"Now see here—" Saar said. "If you think I'm going to cool my heels in a town like this over some little twat like you—"

"You don't have to wait for me," said Françoise. "I'll come tomorrow on the train."

She watched Saar's eyes. She saw that he was in a hurry to get back to Bordeaux.

"I'll need money for the train fare," said Françoise.

Saar telephoned Stack.

"I paid off the cops. I got her out of jail. But she won't come with me. She says she'll come tomorrow on the train."

"Absolutely not," said Stack. "Stay with her. Don't lose her."

"I've already lost her. It's too late. You don't know this kid. I gave her money to pay off some debts and she disappeared on me."

"Find her."

"How the hell am I supposed to find her? This is a big city."

Saar hung up feeling pleased with himself. He had followed Stack's instructions to the letter. He had paid out a good deal of Company money and he did not think New York would regard these bribes as legitimate business expense. To The Company Françoise was no one, an oversexed teenage twat Stack had probably been screwing. Saar had been enlisted by Johnston to send secret evaluation reports to New York. Saar had judged that Stack was weak in New York, and that Johnston was strong. A man who wanted to get ahead in The Company would ally himself to Johnston, not Stack. Especially since Stack would never know anything about the secret reports. In addition, Saar disliked Stack's autocratic ways. Stack behaved like a god, and he treated Saar like a flunky.

Saar's next report to Johnston would concern Françoise, and would make for racy reading indeed.

Françoise went back to the room on which she had paid no rent for two months. Her boy friend was asleep on top of the blankets, and this annoyed her. The guy was always sleeping. He was a tall bearded young man. She considered him handsome even though his smoldering black eyes were almost all she could see of his face. But she liked the beard. Recently she had decided that all men ought to wear beards. The beard was one of the things that differentiated men from women after all, and, especially in this age when men and women dressed alike, that was important. The beard was a secondary sexual characteristic, just like a girl's bosom.

Françoise sat on the bed looking down at the sleeping young man. A man without a full beard made no more sense than a woman without breasts. He was handsome. She considered him much older and more worldly than herself, for he was twenty-five. They had wonderful conversations together, and they went on trips together without ever leaving this room. He agreed with all her thoughts and feelings about life. He told her that anything she truly thought and believed was true for her, and that's all that counted. Talking to him was truly like talking to herself.

She shook him gently, and after a while he woke up. He had a way of waking up without moving. Only his eyes moved.

"Look," she said. "Money."

320

She fanned out the bills like playing cards.

He sat up. After a moment he took the money out of her hands and thrust it into the pocket of his jeans. This act disappointed her. It was her money, not his.

"Good girl," he said, squeezing her left breast. "For that you must have a reward."

For a moment she thought he was going to make love to her, but instead she saw his hand rummaging in the other pocket of his jeans. He came up with two round pills, one red, the other blue. He shook them together in his cupped hands, then held out two fists to her.

"You take one, I take the other," he explained.

"What are they?"

"How do I know? A guy gave them to me last night. He said they're great."

Françoise tapped the left fist. It opened and the red pill rolled down into her palm.

She was excited, eager to swallow it. Each time was like the first time. It was like feeling a boy's hand on your leg. Where would that hand go, and what would it do when it got there?

She popped the pill into her mouth and swallowed it. "Maybe we should both take the same pill," she suggested.

"No, different is better."

The reasoning behind this was not entirely clear to Françoise. "How can we go on a trip together if we take different pills?"

The young man had popped the other pill into his mouth. She watched him swallow it. "You'll see," he explained mysteriously. He lay back, waiting for the pill to take effect. Françoise, sitting on the edge of the bed, raked her fingers lovingly through his beard.

"And after that what will we do?" she asked.

"We'll go on a real trip together. We'll go to Africa."

"How will we get there?"

"Hitchhike."

Françoise began to visualize the trip. They would hitchhike down through Spain and take the ferry across to Tangier.

Her boy friend's eyes were closed now. "Tangier," he murmured. "Greatest place in the world."

Françoise wished he hadn't taken her money.

Françoise felt the pill begin to take effect. She wondered whether it would be an upper or a downer, or what it would be. What would it do to her? That was the excitement. Her mind began to expand, or so

321

she thought, and she could actually see the trip, the rides they would get, the country they would pass through, the ferry ride across to Africa, where she had never been.

It was going to be a grand trip. She raked her fingers through the beard of her boy friend and visualized Africa. She could see it clearly. It was beautiful. And of course any place was better than going back to Margaux and the vines. She lay down beside him and closed her eyes and went on a trip with him. Soon she was floating.

10

Hot, arid August. The grapes swelled on their stalks, pressing ever tighter against each other until it seemed they might burst their skins and bleed their juices all over the stony, sandy soil.

In his report mailed to New York September 1 Stack stated that the harvest was expected to begin on September 23. This was an approximation, but if the present splendid weather continued that would be the date. The Ban des Vendanges would be proclaimed at a banquet at Château Haut-Brion, whose turn it was to throw the traditional party. The ritual proclamation would be read, opening the harvest.

But the fine weather did not hold, and by September 10 it was raining hard every day. Temperatures dropped into the fifties, where they stayed. Each day of bad weather put the harvest back twenty-four hours. The Ban des Vendanges, however, would take place on schedule, as all preparations had been made.

By personal letter Stack had invited the chairman to the banquet and to watch the harvest start the next day, and the chairman had agreed to appear, a good sign. It would be his first visit to the château since that fiasco of a press conference.

But, when on the morning of September 23 The Company's executive jet touched down at Bordeaux airport, it was Johnston—not the chairman—who stepped out. Under his arm he was carrying two tennis rackets.

The banquet took place in one of Château Haut-Brion's great chais, which had been cleared of its rows of casks of aging wine. White table-cloths had been laid down over long trestle tables, and these gleamed like snowfields under their vast arrays of glasses—five glasses to each plate.

The banquet went well. Funny speeches were made. Fabulous old wines were drunk. As a finale, bottles of very old, very rare wine were auctioned off for charity.

The wine harvest was proclaimed open, though the grapes weren't ready.

During the banquet Johnston had, for the most part, kept his ears open and his mouth shut. He ate and drank sparingly. Most of those who spoke to him at the banquet found him charming.

Several executives from the Paris Profit Center had accompanied Johnston to Bordeaux, and the next morning all attended a conference in Stack's office. The principal topic was the scope of new French laws relating to foreign-owned businesses.

Johnston had brought a tennis racket to the conference. He kept punctuating sentences by waving the racket, one of whose strings was broken. When any other executive spoke, Johnston stared at, and sometimes fingered, his broken string. Two days previously Johnston's brother had been named head of the Securities and Exchange Commission.

It's clear now, Stack thought, that Johnston is the new power in The Company. Stack had spent years cultivating the chairman. It should have been Johnston.

"I want to try out your new tennis court, Charlie," Johnston interrupted.

"We can do that, Johnny. Just as soon as we finish here."

"Not unless I get this string fixed."

A group vice president representing a line of food oils began describing certain legal difficulties his division faced.

"What do you say, Charlie?" Johnston interrupted. "Get somebody to take this racket and get it restrung, will you?"

"You mean right now?"

"Better now than never, right Charlie?"

"There's nobody here in Margaux who can do that kind of work. We'll have to send it into Bordeaux. I thought I saw you with two tennis rackets."

"But this one is my favorite."

They were not discussing tennis rackets at all, Stack realized. Rather the subject was Johnston's rise to power. He was now powerful enough to interrupt conferences with nonsense about a tennis racket.

"I'll see to it," Stack said. Taking the racket from Johnston's hands Stack stepped out into his secretary's anteroom.

Behind Stack's back his office door opened and Johnston peered out. "—with gut, Charlie, not nylon."

"With gut," Stack said to his secretary. "Send someone into Bordeaux right away."

"Gut, monsieur?"

Stack had no idea what the word was in French. "Just have him tell the tennis pro gut. The pro will understand. Gut. G—U—T."

As the meeting proceeded, Johnston again interrupted the presentation of a group vice-president. "Those are nice trousers you got on," he said to Aline, who had been quietly taking notes in her corner. Johnston reached out and touched the cloth above her ankle. "Denim, is it? Nice material. Did you get that here?" He was practically fondling her leg.

Aline uncrossed her leg. Ankle and denim dropped out of Johnston's reach.

After lunch the conference continued.

Johnston interrupted the speaker. "Why don't you and I go into Bordeaux and have dinner together tonight?" he suddenly asked Aline.

Stack was shocked. How could the man ask such a thing in front of so many subordinates? Suppose she said no?

Then Stack realized, as Johnston must have, that Aline wouldn't dare say no. In private she might. In public she couldn't, for she worked for him.

Almost breathlessly, Stack awaited Aline's reply. Though shocked, she had recovered beautifully. Flashing a big smile, she said: "We'll have to talk about that later."

"Right you are," said Johnston, pleased with himself.

When the meeting finally ended all the executives cleared out of the smoky office, Stack included. Suddenly Stack realized that Aline and Johnston were still in there. Stack stepped back into his office to find that Johnston had Aline pinned in the angle of the corner and was talking to her in a low voice. It was the same scene Stack remembered from his party: Johnston had had that secretary, Vera, pinned in a corner exactly that way.

And that had concluded with a semen stain on Stack's bedspread.

324

As Johnston glanced around at Stack, Aline slipped out from under his arm.

Johnston seemed irritated by the interruption. "I was pursuing my dinner invitation," he said.

"Maybe tomorrow," Aline said. She seemed to glance gratefully at Stack.

It was a cold cloudy day. The group moved toward the chai. Stack walked with Aline, with Johnston trailing them.

Aline began talking to Stack in French: "You've got to save me from that awful man. He doesn't speak French, does he? You've got to help me."

"Just tell him no."

"I can't do that. I work for him, don't I?"

Stack began to laugh. "I suppose you do."

"I don't think it's funny."

"You're right," conceded Stack. "He's not a funny guy. Take one of the cars and drive over to St. Émilion. Check into the nice hotel there. I'll pay for it. I'll tell Johnston that you had to go over there to buy up some planting rights. I'll ring you up after he's gone and you can come home."

Aline's face brightened, and for a moment she gripped his forearm.

"There's a price," Stack said.

"There always is, isn't there?" Aline said bitterly.

"The price is this. On the night that you come home you have to go out to dinner with me."

Even as they gazed at each other, Johnston's footsteps on the gravel closed in on them.

"All right," Aline said in a low voice.

It was noon the next day before Johnston noticed she was gone. Stack was standing out in the vines, wearing a windbreaker, for it was another cold, windy day. Johnston came up.

"You have a nice setup here, Charlie."

"I like it," Stack admitted.

"Say, where's that girl Aline? I've been looking for her, and they say she's gone across the river."

"That's right. She went over to buy up some planting rights."

"I thought she and I had a dinner date tonight."

Stack held his hands up, palms outward. "I don't know anything about that."

"Who sent her over there?" Johnston demanded.

325

"Why, I did."

Johnston was furious. "She and I had a date tonight."

Grow up, will you, Stack felt like saying.

But instead he said: "I didn't know anything about that." Showing his most innocent grin Stack added: "Anyway, business before pleasure, right, Johnny?"

Johnston stood fuming. "I came over here to watch the start of the harvest," he said coldly. "So why haven't you started it?"

Stack could feel the wind against his windbreaker. "The weather turned bad. The grapes aren't ready."

"How do you know? They look ready to me."

"We take cuttings every day. We mash up a few grapes and test the juice. The instruments say that the acidity level and sugar level are not yet what they should be."

"In the meantime, all that money is lying out there in the open. Anything could happen to it."

"That's true," Stack conceded. Stack thought a moment and then said: "I was talking to my cellar master, Gorr, today. He said to me, 'The land gives us signals, but we can't always read what they are.' That sounds pretty pompous when I say it. But when he said it, it sounded like the wisdom of an old farmer."

"So when are you going to harvest?"

"When the grapes are ready."

After a time Johnston said: "I'd go stir crazy living here."

"You get used to it. Your whole interior clock seems to slow down. You get so you feel practically like a human being again."

"Don't get to like it too much," Johnston muttered.

The next morning Johnston abruptly left Bordeaux. He phoned for the executive jet to come in and get him, and it did. At the airport he said to Stack: "My time is too valuable to wait around here until you decide to start the harvest."

That day Stack drove down to the river bank, but could not get close to it. At the end of the road there should have been a turn-around and a dock, but both were under water. So was the last hundred yards of road. When he got out and advanced a short distance the road went gooey under his shoes. He could not get close to the river.

It was cold. It had been raining all day, but was not raining now.

The river looked twice as wide to him as it had ever looked before. Then he realized that most of the island in the middle was under water too. Rubbish floated by. It went by fast.

Beside the bank long poles had been driven into the mud to form berthing slips for skiffs. The last time Stack was down here the skiffs had lain canted on the mud. Now they floated up near the tops of the poles, which were peeled and whitened tree branches. If the river rose any more they'd float out over the top. There had been a derelict fishing trawler there in the mud too. Now it floated proudly high.

Stack watched the smooth brown river rushing past, and worried about his harvest. His hands were plunged into the pockets of his rain-coat. When should he begin to pick his grapes? They were not really ready yet. They wouldn't make a great wine if picked now. On the other hand Stack may have waited too long already. Any day the grapes could begin to rot on the vine.

Still, the weather could break this afternoon or tomorrow. A few days' sunshine could make all the difference. Even the sunshine of a single afternoon could bring the sugar content up half a degree.

Did he expect to find his answer in the river? He watched the brown water flow by.

Stack turned and gazed across at the empty château which he had once thought could be converted into a luxury hotel. If it were a hotel right now its gardens would be under water. The hotel guests wouldn't be able to leave the building. It would be difficult or impossible to get their cars out of the parking lot.

I'm glad I saw the river this high, Stack told himself. I'm glad I didn't recommend that château as a hotel.

But when was he to start the harvest? All the good work done all year long was worth nothing unless he could bring the grapes in healthy and at the optimum time.

The wind blew at him off the river. It was a cold maritime wind. It cut right through him. Stack drove back to the château and got out. Gorr came toward him, beret in his hands.

"What degree did you get today?" Stack asked.

"Ten degrees."

"Is that good?" Stack was operating from too little knowledge, too little experience. He had to believe what Gorr told him, and then to look around at what other owners were doing, and decide. Past statistics were of some help, not much. It was not like test marketing a product. You could be pretty sure of what would happen if the tests were good. Here you were making a product that would not be salable at all for three or four years and not at its peak until long after that. You were making judgments based on anywhere from five to fifty years from now. It was absurd.

"Ten and a half would be better," Gorr said.

Why didn't the man come right out and say what he meant?

"How much longer can we safely wait?"

"The land gives us signals but we can't always read what they are."

Stack felt like saying: you said that before. He thought the idea might come to Gorr of itself, but apparently it did not.

Stack walked out amid the vines and handled a few clusters of grapes. The grapes were firm. There was no rot yet that he could see or feel. Still, he didn't know what the signs of rot would be.

Stack called Gorr over. Gorr waded out to him through the vines. "Call up the oenological station in Bordeaux," Stack ordered. "See what sort of readings they're getting from other parts of the region. Find out how many of the châteaux have started the vendange, how many finished, and so on."

If anything went wrong with the harvest Stack would have to document all decisions he had made. He would have to document how many times he had called the weather bureau and what the reports were.

Stack decided to walk over to see the Count de Grenelle. He buttoned his collar and started walking, feeling the wind. There was a hedge separating the two properties. Stack found a gap and walked through. He walked up through the count's vines to the château.

He found the count talking to his cellar master in the chai. The count's degree readings were the same as Stack's—ten.

"Ten and a half would be better," the count said somberly.

"And eleven would be better still," said Stack.

"But I'm beginning to worry about rot. It could start any time, and go awfully fast."

"Or tomorrow could be the start of five days of glorious sunshine," Stack said. "And if we picked at the end of those five days we could make a glorious wine. They'd still be talking about it a hundred years from now."

The count gave a wry smile. "The weather bureau isn't too optimistic."

"I know."

The count said: "If you bring in healthy grapes, you can always make something."

328

"I wanted to make more than just something," Stack admitted. "We had the super hot, super dry summer we needed. Conditions were so perfect up until now. My hope was, I'm ashamed to say, to make a really great wine my first time."

The count laughed. "It's the hope of all of us every year."

Stack added: "And in my case I promised the board of directors a great wine."

"Surely they can't hold you to that. Everybody knows that in agriculture you're at the mercy of the weather."

"I'm not so sure my board of directors does. They don't think they're in agriculture, they think they're in the wine business, and they think they're going to make a fortune."

The count gave Stack a look.

Stack thought: What's happening to me here? Since when do I start blabbing my fears and insecurities to people I hardly know? What happened to iron-hard Charlie Stack?

The answer, Stack reflected, was that living close to the land seemed to have changed his values. A man could ask another man's advice here. A man could expose his fears and nightmares and not seem less manly, and his listener could not use the information to undermine, undersell, or otherwise betray him.

Under the vast sky of the Médoc different rules applied. No one could subvert the rain clouds, or start or stop a hailstorm just to put you out of business.

The count gazed up at low scudding clouds. "If I were you, I'd worry more about the weather than about my board of directors. Myself, I think I'd better be happy with what I have. I'm going to start bringing the grapes in tomorrow."

Stack stood with his friend discussing, like any Vermont farmer, the weather. There was a tension—and a pleasure—in talking about the weather, almost as much tension—and pleasure—as there was in the tasting of fine wine. And talking about the weather made it seem much less menacing.

Unknown to Charlie Stack, a second threat hung over Château Conderie. In Bordeaux, after brooding a month, Bozon had settled on a plot to ruin Charles Stack. He had hired men. He had disbursed sums. The plot was costly, but pleasure of any kind was costly, and revenge, Bozon had found, was usually the most expensive (but also the most satisfying) pleasure of all.

In addition, Bozon still needed Château Conderie as his flagship wine, and once Stack was gone he would be able to present his proposed agreement again.

The chairman phoned Stack from New York. "Got those grapes in, have you?"

"Not yet. We're still being held up by the weather."

Stack listened to a dollar's worth of transatlantic silence.

"Well, is that wise, Charlie? I mean, the other châteaux are all bringing in their grapes, I'm told. Some have nearly finished, as I understand it."

The spy, Stack assumed, was Saar. Saar reported directly to New York. After the harvest he would get rid of Saar, if New York did not protest, though New York, he knew, would only corrupt Saar's successor.

Stack began to explain to the chairman about the degré de baume. The sugar content of the grapes would be converted directly into alcohol.

But the chairman was not interested in details. Stack could feel his impatience through the wire. "Is it cold there?" the chairman interrupted. "Suppose you get a bad frost?"

On the subject of frost, Stack was pleased to note, the chairman was misinformed.

"No, the frost can't hurt us at this stage. The only thing that could hurt us would be hail or prolonged rainfall."

"Explain that to me, will you, Charlie."

Stack assumed the chairman was taping this conversation. Stack was about to give evidence against himself.

"Hail would knock the grapes off the vines. They'd all be lying there in the mud. Don't be alarmed. I'm talking about a freak storm. And if we had to pick in the rain, we'd get a great deal of rainwater in the grape juice. There would be rain clinging to the skin of every grape, and no way to separate it out. We'd end up with a wine that was to a greater or lesser degree watery." There, those were two of the major risks announced loud and clear in the culprit's own voice.

Stack did not mention rot. Grapes could turn gray and shrivel up almost to dust, like the rosy bosom of a girl turning into the empty dugs of a crone overnight.

Once rot started, Stack had been told, it moved very fast. There had been years when individual châteaux, delaying only a day or two later than their neighbors, had lost the entire crop. Was this about to happen to Charlie Stack?

On the line from New York, Stack felt the chairman's implicit challenge, and his own response. No freak storm would occur. Rot would not happen. Stack would wait for sunshine—and make a brilliant wine.

But how could he be so sure? Could Stack change the weather just by wanting to?

The chairman sounded mollified. "Well, it's your decision to make, Charlie. You're in charge over there. You're our boy on the scene. And, as I've said before, Charlie, a guy with a good success pattern I'll go along with."

Stack realized that the chairman was absolving himself of responsibility. He had exercised direct supervision. He had observed all the principles of the management textbooks, including giving final authority to the executive on the scene. If disaster now occurred the chairman could not be blamed. On the other hand the chairman could share in any success, having made the decision to trust Stack.

Shrewd, Stack thought. That's why he's chairman.

But Stack was shaken. "If prestige is our object," Stack said, as if seeking the chairman's support, "isn't it worth the slight extra risk to try to make the best wine of the year on our first try?"

The chairman, immediately perceiving Stack's insecurity, immediately pounced. "The only thing that bothers me, Charlie, is that everyone else is already bringing in their grapes. What do they know that we don't know?"

No, there could be no support from the chairman or anyone else.

Stack forced a confident laugh. "What do they know? Nothing, Warren. A bunch of peasants. It's the herd instinct at work again. One starts and they all feel they better start too. Security in numbers."

At the other end of the line there was silence. Then the chairman said: "Right you are, Charlie. Well, keep me informed."

When Stack had hung up, his forehead and also his upper lip were bathed with sweat. He got out a handkerchief and wiped his face.

Stack called a meeting in his office: Conderie, Saar, Aline, Gorr, and himself.

"If it were my decision, I'd pick," said Conderie.

"Why?"

"Why, old man? Because everyone else is picking, of course. It's no good going against the general consensus."

331

"And you, Aline?" inquired Stack.

Aline refused to look up from her notes. After a moment she said: "My father's got a point."

Straight up in the straightest chair in the room sat Gorr. In his lap he was turning his beret in both hands. He seemed to find it incomprehensible that a man like himself would be invited into such a conference and asked for advice, when he wanted only instructions.

Saar's opinion was the same as Conderie's, and for the same reason: most of the other châteaux had now started.

"That's just a follow-the-leader thing," Stack snapped. "One starts because the guy next door has started. It isn't each man determining that now is the time. They're all getting the same figures we're getting on their test cuttings. None of them knows anything more about the weather than we do."

"We've had the Spaniards here five days waiting to start," Saar pointed out. "They're costing us almost six hundred dollars a day in wages and food."

The migrant Spaniards would pick grapes for almost two months, starting with the southernmost regions of France and moving slowly north.

Dormitory space had been cleared in the chais, in garages and storerooms. Blankets had been brought out of storage. Meals were cooked in great cauldrons over wood stoves. There were about forty-five Spaniards of assorted ages and sexes, who consumed great quantities of soup, stew, bread and bad wine bought from a wholesaler in Bordeaux.

Because they were not working, the Spaniards were constantly in the way. They got on everybody's nerves, particularly Stack's. He saw them as a kind of permanent reproach to each day's decision not to pick yet.

Stack wished he could pay them off, save what they were costing, and get them out from underfoot. Unfortunately this was impossible. There would be no way to replace them later.

Stack realized that he had made his decision—again. Let the other châteaux bring in their grapes now. He would wait another day or two at least, and if the sun began to shine he might wait longer.

When the meeting broke, Stack went out and stood amid his grapes. The autumn colors were beginning to appear in the vines. There was red in the leaves now. The plump hidden grapes were purple and the stakes were blue from the sulfate sprays.

332

He heard footsteps behind him. It was Aline.

"To pick or not to pick," she said. "Is that what you're brooding about?"

"What do you really think?" he asked her.

"I would wait."

"Why didn't you say so in there?"

"Because it would have hurt my father's feelings."

"I would have liked some public support."

"So would my father," Aline informed him, "and he comes first."

Stack was silent.

"This is your spot out here, isn't it?" Aline commented.

"I find a curious kind of peace when I'm surrounded by grapes. Isn't that ridiculous? The whole year hinges on the next few days."

"You could bring the grapes in now and make a good enough wine. No one would criticize you."

"There's risk to waiting. I know that. But four more days of sunshine, even two—even one—and the quality will go up so much. When I'm an old man I'd like to drink a bottle of this year's wine and say, I made that wine, and feel proud. Does that sound strange to you?"

Aline stood close, though without actually touching him. "I hope you succeed," she said.

11

As dusk fell the Spaniards lined up in the courtyard to receive their wages, though they had not picked a grape as yet. The cauldrons were already steaming and they moved from Stack's paymaster to the trestle tables set up in the garage, and dinner was ladled out.

Afterward three Spaniards, two of whom were picking their teeth, strolled down into Margaux, where they made a phone call from the Savoie, speaking into the bar telephone in Spanish, presumably to one of Bozon's agents in Bordeaux. The barman later claimed that he had no idea what was said. The Spaniards then ambled back to the château.

All the families must have packed hurriedly, because when the two open trucks drove up an hour later the Spaniards were ready to climb aboard, bag and baggage. The trucks, having spent barely five minutes on château ground, drove back down the lane and were gone, the pickers with them. No one noticed except one of Stack's tractor drivers, who said he supposed the Spaniards were off to the cinema or the city en bloc.

The trucks drove straight north to the end of the Médoc peninsula with many of the Spaniards standing up in the backs of the trucks feeling the wind in their faces. Apparently the plan called for the Spaniards to cross the river on the last ferry, putting them out of Stack's reach until tomorrow at the earliest, but someone miscalculated, and when the truck had pulled up, the last ferry was just backing out of its slip.

Both trucks, as soon as the Spaniards had climbed down, immediately turned and drove away.

There was the threat of trouble, for lodging had been promised on the other side, and the Spaniards had no place to sleep. But the trucks were indubitably gone, and soon the Spaniards, with plenty of money in their pockets, calmed down, and camp was made in the forest under the trees. It had been a warm sunny day such as Stack had been hoping for, and the night was mild.

In any case the Spaniards were still on the Médoc side of the river, still in a group, until the next morning. Had he known, Stack probably could have gone there and induced them to come back to honor their contract with him—without them he had no way to get his grapes in. But of course until the next afternoon he had no idea they were gone. By then the Spaniards had crossed, made contact with another of Bozon's agents, and were on their way up into the Cognac to pick there. Cognac is a big place; there was no longer much chance of Stack's finding them.

Stack was in Bordeaux most of the day. Business meetings lasted until well after lunch, and he got back to the château with a briefcase full of papers to go over.

Instead he was greeted by an employee named Cordier, field boss of the pickers, who gave him the awful news. It came like a sock in the gut. His pickers were gone. He felt sickened. It had been another warm sunny day, too.

Although he had sensed the answer at once, Stack wasted two hours trying to find out exactly what had happened. Simultaneously he set

Cordier, Gorr, and Aline to trying to hunt down substitute pickers, but their many phone calls produced none. All the other châteaux were picking this week, none had pickers to spare, and there seemed to be no other idle migrants around. The surplus, if any, presumably had gone up to Cognac, where the picking always started a week or two later, to find work there.

Stack personally interrogated the Spanish kitchen girls. They had heard rumors, they said. Two Spanish-speaking Frenchmen had addressed the pickers a few days ago. There was talk of money; some rich señor from Bordeaux was supposed to be behind it. That was all they knew.

Someone had subverted Stack's pickers, and it seemed important to him to prove it was not some nearby, short-handed château. Once he knew that the Spaniards had been seen to cross the river, then he was certain who the culprit was. With certainty came a mindless rage.

The infuriated Stack sped toward Bordeaux, where he burst into Bozon's warehouse.

Bozon's concierge, phone in hand, attempted to stop him: "Monsieur Bozon is in the back supervising a delivery. Who shall I say is—"

But Stack was past him, hurrying toward the rear of the interconnected buildings. He passed through the cooperage, with its blazing forge and its blacksmith hammering on hoops; and through a dank vault where men were manhandling barrels up on top of other barrels. Stack was moving fast, fists balled, careful not to trip over the rails underfoot. Now he was moving down a long, narrow corridor. Overhead dim electric bulbs burned, dangling at the ends of wires. Bottles stacked on their sides from floor to ceiling formed the walls of this gloomy corridor, walls that seemed to press in on him. Though not aware of it, he was breathing hard, and the air he inhaled was sour, reflecting a century or two of spilled wine.

At the distant end of the catacomb of bottles a figure appeared, hurrying toward him, looming rapidly larger, now passing under a burning bulb so that Stack could see who it was.

Bozon.

Good.

In a narrow pool of light they confronted each other.

"Where are my pickers?" cried Stack.

He was conscious of Bozon's size. The man's shoulders nearly touched the bottles on either side.

"Pickers?" inquired Bozon, grinning.

335

Stack had come with some notion of forcing Bozon to tell where the pickers had gone. Once located they could be contacted and perhaps brought back.

"Pickers?" said Bozon again. "Oh, you mean *those* pickers." The shipper was overcome by gales of laughter. He was being rocked by mirth. The noise rang off the butt ends of 100,000 bottles of wine.

Stack grabbed the shipper by his shirt front and tie. "I want to know where they are, goddamn you."

The gales of laughter ceased, cut off as if by a light switch. With a powerful shrugging motion, Bozon threw Stack backward.

"Out," he shouted, "out of my place."

Here he came, advancing down the corridor, filling it, his big chest forming a third wall that bore down on Stack. There was no room to sidestep, and the movement of Bozon's body seemed inexorable. Stack found himself in the humiliating position of having to back away from the confrontation he himself had forced.

The speed of Bozon's advance increased. Stack had to back-pedal or meet him head on surrounded by bottles—the insubstantial walls seemed twice as insubstantial to Stack. This was no place to fight or even to argue—the walls would fall down on top of them.

Stack was stepping backward as if from fear. Bozon seemed an unreasoning force. One did not confront a madman, at least not here.

They were approaching the end of the corridor now, and in the vaulted room next door were employees of Bozon's. In a moment the man need only shout orders to have Stack chucked like ordure out onto the pavement.

So Stack stood his ground, hands out, trying to ward Bozon off.

There was no time to imagine what might happen next. Stack believed he was expecting a rain of punches, and that he was ready for them. He was a big man himself, and younger and in better shape, though outweighed by thirty pounds and no longer stimulated by rage.

But it was dark. The black bottle ends reflected no light at all, nor did the gluey mold that encrusted the ceiling. Stack never saw the first punch coming, a roundhouse right that came from out of the darkness somewhere—it caught Stack on the side of the head and brought on a paroxysm of blinking. It seemed to him amazing that Bozon could get so much power into such a punch in this cramped place.

Infuriated, Stack drove forward, shouldering into Bozon like a linebacker trying to knock an opponent down. Stack was trying to create enough space—and time—in which to calculate. He had not come here

336

to get into a fist fight. He had not lost his temper to this extent since college or even earlier. A fist fight under this warehouse in a dim corridor constructed of delicately balanced wine bottles was madness.

He was wearing a new tan suit, which would get ruined. Bozon's suit was no doubt expensive also. So far only Bozon's tie had suffered. It dangled outside his suitcoat and had been stretched to a foot's extra length.

Bozon came on swinging both fists. There was no room to dodge, and no light to track the punches in. The first whistled past Stack's head, the second numbed his shoulder. The third knocked Stack reeling into the bottles. A number came tumbling down. Perhaps one or more smashed, he had no time to check. He began to punch back, but nothing slowed Bozon down.

As Stack charged again, shoulder foremost, a punch struck him atop the skull. He was amazed at how accurately the bastard could punch— but Stack's shoulder found the soft midsection, and he felt Bozon go off balance, though not down, and he drove him backwards eight or ten yards along the corridor, until Bozon turned sideways, banging into bottles, some of which collapsed, while Stack slid off past him.

They stood punching each other. I can keep this up longer than he can, Stack thought, and caught Bozon with a right-hand wallop, best punch so far. Bozon's head snapped back into bottles. A cascade of bottles descended on top of him as he slid down into a sitting position, where he seemed to shake the dizziness away, while eying Stack.

There were bottles piled all around Bozon, and many must be broken, for the shipper's suit was soaked with what looked like blood but could only be wine.

With the neck of a broken bottle clasped in his fist, Bozon climbed to his feet and advanced on Stack.

Stack, eyes fixed on the jagged glass, retreated. He was trying to calculate, without looking, the length of the corridor behind him, while at the same time trying to gauge the shipper's rage or perhaps madness.

Backing down the corridor, Stack passed underneath one hanging light bulb and then, twenty yards further along, under a second.

Bozon stopped directly under a light. It painted his features with dark streaks of mascara.

Suddenly he began to laugh. He laughed uproariously.

The surprised Stack watched warily.

"This is absurd," cried Bozon suddenly. "We're fighting over a woman. You know that, don't you? We're not fighting over your pickers

337

or my deal. We're not fighting over the business of wine. We're fighting over that cow of an ex-wife of mine."

Stack decided this was no time to attempt to defend Aline from slander.

"You queered my deal with your company. I made off with your pickers. We're even. It's over." Bozon tossed the jagged bottleneck to one side.

"It's absurd, two grown men fighting over a cunt," he stated. "The world is full of cunts."

This was true, Stack thought. He was still wary, though less so.

"We'll call off our quarrel," said Bozon, offering his hand. "What do you say? I'll send you some of my men to help you get your grapes in."

Stack didn't want to shake hands with Bozon, fearing treachery, but there was no way past him without doing it and, as the shipper had said, a fist fight between two grown men made no sense at all.

Their hands met and clasped. Bozon threw one arm around Stack's shoulder. "Come up to my office and we'll drink a bottle of wine together, and we'll work it out about the pickers. Wine heals all quarrels, right? I have some quite good bottles in this rack here. Wait while I select one."

Bozon entered a kind of cell, and, when he had come out, locked the gate with a heavy rusty key. He handed the bottle to Stack, saying: "What do you think of this one?"

Stack, after reading the label, handed the bottle back.

The bottle caught Stack just above the nape of the neck. There may have been a second blow that slid off the top of his skull as he was falling —he wasn't sure. He did not go unconscious immediately. Instead, in a moment of absolute clarity he knew exactly what was happening, and cursed himself for a fool to get blindsided like that. His trust in himself both physically and mentally had been total, a misplaced conceit, for he had forgotten that this opponent, being without honor, could not be trusted at all. Stack's momentary lapse of concentration would cost him heavily—perhaps would cost him not only pain but the harvest and his career. He could even have his brain turned to mush.

He was in a gray area by then, his brain going rapidly fuzzy, though acute awareness returned for another second. He seemed to see the bottle raised again and again—perhaps it caught the glint of the light bulb burning above Bozon's head—so that Stack thought: Good God, I might be killed.

How many such blows could the human skull stand?

338

Then he was sliding downhill out of control. He seemed to be sliding and rolling down a vast sand dune, except that the dune was made entirely of empty wine bottles that clattered and rolled under him, though some broke and proved to be filled, for he could feel wine being poured on top of him, or perhaps it was a wave coming in from the sea.

Bozon, having stepped over Stack's body, had gone into the barrel room and fetched two workers. The three men peered down at Stack.

"Get this shit-sucking piece of slime out of here."

One workman lifted Stack under the arms, the other under the knees.

"Take him out the back onto the pavement and sit him against the wall."

They lugged Stack to the rear of the building, passing through the vatting room to the great amazement of several colleagues, and out through the steel doors.

Cars went by in the street but it was getting dark fast and there were no pedestrians.

"Drop him right there," ordered Bozon.

They set Stack down against the wall, but he fell over onto his side.

The two workmen stared down at him. "Is he dead?" one asked.

Bozon's rage was leaving him, and there were practical matters to be considered. "He attacked me," Bozon said. "I struck in self-defense. He's not dead. As you can see, he's still breathing."

One of the workmen leaned down and pressed his ear against Stack's chest. "I can hear his heart."

"Good. Now get back inside," Bozon ordered them.

He was still carrying the bottle with which he had slugged Stack. When the iron doors had clanged shut behind the workmen, Bozon struck the neck against the building wall. The neck broke off and fell to the pavement, where it shattered.

Bozon emptied the bottle over Stack's tan suit, then set it upright on the pavement next to Stack's face.

This was when Stack in his dim dream imagined that the sea was washing in over him now and was afraid he would drown. In terror he tried to sit up, or thought he did. Instead he passed into a deeper level of unconsciousness.

It was nearly quitting time for Bozon's work force. After counter-locking the iron doors with his own key and giving orders that his employees were to exit via the front, Bozon mounted to his apartment, where he bathed and changed into fresh linen and a new suit.

For an hour he sat in his office brooding, then went downstairs and through to the back and glanced out into the street.

Stack, either dead or still asleep, had not budged from the position in which he had been dropped.

Bozon went back to his office and brooded a bit more, then picked up his telephone and dialed the police.

"There's a drunk against the wall on the Cours Balguerie. He looks in pretty bad shape."

The police operator wanted his name, but Bozon hung up.

When Stack awoke shortly afterward, he could not remember where he was and he started to slip back into dreamland, but fought it. He knew he had a ringing headache and reeked of wine, and then he remembered going to see Bozon and the start of the fight. That was all.

Struggling to his feet, he pushed away from the wall, staggered and nearly fell down. It was at this moment that the police car drew up. The two cops watched him.

Stack was trying to sort out his brain. Bozon had defeated him in the fist fight, that much was clear, and some bottles must have got broken, for his suit was soaked with wine.

He eyed the two cops, who eyed him back. And now I stand a good chance of being arrested as a drunk, Stack reflected.

Because the cops made no move to get out of their car, Stack realized that if he could walk away the cops would let him. Pushing off from the wall, he strode as best he could down the sidewalk. After a moment he heard the police car start up and drive on.

Stack leaned against the wall again. Dizziness nearly overcame him, and tiny white stars flashed across the screen behind his eyeballs. He was hurt badly but did not believe it. Though Bozon had evidently kayoed him, the man was not a prizefighter—the punch could not have been that hard.

He had to find his car. He could remember parking it in front, a long hike from here, for the block was three hundred yards thick and pierced by very few side streets.

He bent forward and began to retch. Very little came up. The spasms racked him. When they stopped he started walking, though with frequent pauses to rest. Perhaps an hour elapsed before he reached his car. Cars passed by in the street without taking notice of him, and he crossed the paths of only two pedestrians, who glanced at him oddly but offered no assistance.

340

He drove slowly out of the city, for he felt as uncoordinated as if drunk, and if he was ever stopped the cops would take one sniff and lock him up.

He was too weak to feel much anger; he might or might not feel angry in the morning, but he knew absolutely that he would feel shame. What an ass he had made of himself. He was a sophisticated adult who had allowed himself to get sucked into a fist fight—which he then had lost decisively—all the while knowing full well that violence settled nothing, solved nothing, not ever. He had behaved like a fool.

He felt dizzy, weak, nauseated, his brain throbbed with needle points of pain, and he still had no pickers.

The château was dark.

After swallowing three aspirins he lay in a hot bath for a long time. Had Bozon knocked him out with one punch or several? Perhaps he had crashed backward into the bottles and knocked himself out when he hit the floor. That would explain his wine-soaked suit.

Putting on a bathrobe he carried his suit and underwear downstairs, where he balled it all up in a newspaper and buried it under that day's garbage in one of the cans outside.

The suit had cost him $210 in New York and he had worn it only twice. The pain of throwing away the suit was worse than the pain in his head.

He didn't want anyone to find the suit, or to ask questions he would be ashamed to answer.

The screen door slammed in the night, and he went up to his bedroom again.

There was a note on his bed from Aline. A tribe of gypsies had been found and brought in—they were camped down by the stream. They had picked last year for Château Angludet, where they had done a barely adequate job. In any case, they were the best that Aline, Cordier, and Gorr had managed to find after an all-day search.

Stack went to bed.

12

The rain had stopped. The sun seemed trying to come out. Stack walked down toward the stream where the gypsies were camped. He wanted to see what they looked like and try to judge their reliability.

There were several tents, a former school bus whose windows were painted over, two horse-drawn carts, and a thirty-year-old Cadillac. Stack passed between the bus and the Cadillac—and stepped into the middle of a knife fight.

Two men, knives extended, were circling each other inside a disordered circle formed by other gypsies. There were women who looked concerned and kids grinning with pleasure. A girl had her left breast out, and her baby had a mouthful of the breast. It was a rather big baby, perhaps two years old. The mother's attention was divided. She kept glancing from the baby's face to the knife fight.

One of the men lunged, blade flashing. Then the other lunged. There was a thrust that happened so fast Stack never saw it, but one man's sleeve was suddenly cut and blood spilled down his arm.

Stack jumped between them, calling out in French: "Enough!"

Now Stack was in the middle, knives circling round him, and he was in trouble with his French as he tried to bark out commands: "Stop. Drop your knives. Step back."

He had no experience with such idioms, but did have the habit of command. After a moment the gypsies obeyed. Knives went back into belts; one spat at the other, and turned away. The man who had been spat at hesitated, then hawked up spittle and blew it after his opponent. In the surrounding circle of gypsies there was a good deal of muttering.

Stack wondered what to do. He knew nothing about gypsies. Would the knife fight resume as soon as he left? Would there be a dead body here by morning?

Stack addressed himself to the oldest-looking gypsy, and they walked back to the man's tent together. Stack called the old man chief

—was that correct?—and learned that the fight was over a missing package of cigarettes. The younger of the two knife fighters had stolen the other man's cigarettes, a serious breach of honor. Gypsies stole only from outsiders, the chief said, or so Stack understood.

In front of the tent Stack and the old man sat on a bench which had once been a church pew. Other gypsies gathered around. Someone made a fire, and coffee was brewed and poured out into chipped cups. The one cup with the handle was passed to Stack, for this was their best cup, and he was guest of honor. Stack learned that some of the gypsies came from Hungary, and some were Spanish. Their French was difficult to understand.

Overhead the sun came out, an exultant moment to Stack, one which he tried to share with the chief, pointing at it repeatedly. The old man offered Stack more coffee.

Stack asked what would happen now between the two knife fighters. Nothing at all, he was told. The quarrel was over.

These gypsies, Stack reflected, behaved in the noblest sense more like animals than people. They lived off the land. They worked as little as possible. They enjoyed the sun and the moon, the wind, the beauty of the countryside. They moved around whenever they felt like it. When they fought it was the way deer fought. They locked horns. Their weapons clattered, and then, usually, both parties turned away before anyone was hurt.

These gypsies would be incapable of fighting their way up The Company's corporate career ladder. The idea made Stack smile. What would Johnston or the chairman think to know that these gypsies were, for this week at least, employed by The Company?

The old man was chief of the tribe because he was oldest. Being oldest made him wisest. He's so wise he thinks I'm French, Stack thought.

Still, it was nice to sit with gypsies sipping strong coffee, gossiping in a language strange to all of them about nothing much, while the afternoon warmed up and the precious sun moved on over the trees.

Later Stack walked in sunshine back toward the château, detouring so as to walk most of the way through his vines. The grapes were drying out fast.

When the next day was fine too, Stack's confidence expanded. He was almost exultant.

A phone call came from Johnston in Paris. "Say, Charlie, how's the weather there?"

Stack felt pleased to talk about the weather. "We've had beautiful sunshine here three of the last four days."

"That's great news. You've made all the right decisions so far, Charlie. So when are you bringing the wine in?"

Stack thought: They hound you and hound you and hound you. Everyone is pressured into making the most conservative move at all times. Big business takes no chances. None. There is no room for the calculated risk or the brilliant stroke.

Stack could hold out no longer against such pressure. "I've decided to start the picking tomorrow if the weather holds," he said.

"Change your mind, did you, Charlie? It's your decision to make. You're in charge there. I don't want to horn in on your decision."

"Not at all. It's time. By tomorrow the grapes will have had three extra days of sunshine. We might wait another day or two more, but I don't think it's worth the risk."

"I agree with you there, Charlie. Say, Charlie, somebody told me you had hired a bunch of gypsies to do the picking."

And who could have told you that, Stack asked himself disgustedly.

"Well, is that wise? Gypsies? I mean—"

"Gypsies can cut grapes about as well as anybody," Stack said dryly. "It isn't something you need a college education for."

"But are they dependable, Charlie?"

"We'll soon see, won't we?"

Johnston was merely informing him that the gypsies were his responsibility. If the harvest failed, the gypsies were one more decision Stack could be blamed for.

How vulnerable I am, Stack thought. I should have begun picking the goddamn grapes two weeks ago like most other châteaux, and delivered them a poor or quite ordinary wine. They would have voted me a raise for it. As far as the taste of the wine goes, not one of them would have known the difference.

"Look," Stack said, "I thought the chairman agreed that it was worth delaying the harvest and trying for an especially fine wine our first year."

"The chairman said that, Charlie? I think he just said it was your decision to make, Charlie, my feelings exactly. And if it's the right decision we're with you one hundred percent."

"I see."

"But, if it's just going to be a poor or ordinary year for everybody else, we're not going to be able to charge high prices for our wine,

344

Charlie. Nobody's going to believe our wine is that different from anyone else's. So what's the point of the extra risk?"

They had been all over this argument. "But we're in a position to command super publicity for our wine and therefore sell it for a high price."

"You know as well as I do, Charlie, that you can't 'command' publicity. You can take some journalist to dinner or what have you, but you can't make them write the piece. A case in point would be that fiasco of a press conference you invited the chairman to when we took over the château. The *Times* didn't run a word, you'll recall."

Stack was silent.

"Well, I just called up to wish you luck, Charlie."

Stack, hanging up, warned himself not to be unreasonable. See it from their point of view. At current prices there's something like two million bucks lying out there in those fields exposed to the weather. These are just hard-nosed businessmen. The concept is too strong for them. They can't bear it. They'd feel better if the place was surrounded by armed guards. All that money. It drives them crazy.

Stack thought: It drives me crazy too.

He went outside and got into his car. The top down, wearing only a sweater, he drove slowly down the dirt road to the highway and then into Margaux, to see what other owners were doing. There were vines along both sides of the road. About two fields out of every three looked picked. He drove on through the village and came out the other side. Nearly everybody had at least half of their grapes in, he judged. Some would already have made most of this year's poor wine. But he had held off.

Had he done the right thing? We'll soon know, he told himself.

In the morning he awakened with daylight and stepped to the window to peer out. There were some clouds overhead, but the sun was coming up loud and clear.

When he went out of the château, it was so cold that he could see his breath, and when he went out through the gate he saw mist rising from fields as if from the surface of a lake.

He went to find Gorr.

"We have to give the dew a chance to burn off," the old man explained, nodding his head sagely. "It will warm up, don't worry."

"How many days will the harvest take?" Stack had asked this question twenty times already, and the answer, like all of Gorr's answers, never changed.

"About twelve days, if they pick well," Gorr responded.

"Do you think they'll pick well?"

"Well, they're gypsies."

"You're the one who said we should hire them."

"Well, the Spaniards left. We didn't have much choice after that."

Stack ate his breakfast standing up in the kitchen, then hurried down to the gypsy encampment. It seemed to him that there were fewer people there than two days before.

The old chief told him that one of the tribes had decided to drive on south yesterday evening.

Seven pickers had decamped. How to compensate?

Stack, though edgy and tense, forced himself to sit with the old man, sipping the muddy black coffee, for he had an idea to propose to the tribe. After the old man had called over two of the family heads, Stack suggested that the two families form two teams. Stack would put up a prize. Whichever team picked the most grapes today would get the prize.

The gypsies didn't seem to know what he was talking about. Stack blamed his own halting French and went through the plan again. Competition. A spirit of fun. Prize money. Extra money. Money.

The gypsies still didn't understand.

Stack felt his nerves beginning to crack. He took a hundred-franc note out of his billfold and waved it at them, explaining his plan again. But the gypsies seemed unenthusiastic.

It took about thirty minutes more before the gypsies had formed into a group and were ready to follow him up to the château. Stack had explained his prize-money plan to Gorr, who had approved it: "That will make them work fast."

Now Stack addressed all the gypsies, explaining that he was putting up a prize of one hundred francs to whichever of the two families picked the most grapes today.

Five different species of vines grew on château property. The two principal ones were Merlot and Cabernet Sauvignon. The Merlot, which comprised about thirty percent of the finished blend, always ripened first and was picked first. The Cabernet ripened last and was picked last. About sixty percent of the blend would be Cabernet Sauvignon. The remaining three species fitted into the blend in small amounts, like single voices in a massed choir.

It was Stack's hope that half of the Merlot could be picked today. If he had had college boys picking it could have been done easily. Put up a prize for college kids, and they'd scramble through the vines at breakneck speed. College kids would go for the game aspect of it, and the extra money. Stack reviewed his decision to hire the gypsies. He had had no choice, had he?

Had he?

All day Stack moved among the pickers, urging them to pick faster, joking with them as much as he could, exhorting them always. He stripped his kitchen staff, and sent them out into the fields to pick. At midday he went into the chai, where six men were engaged in dealing with the loads of grapes as they were brought up the ramp and dumped. Stack left three men to cope with the grapes, and sent the other three out into the fields to pick. They went grumbling, but they went.

The gypsies seemed to do a great deal of lounging against the wagon. There were always more gypsies standing up amid the rows of vines than bent over with their clippers. By five o'clock in the afternoon the gypsies wanted to stop for the day. Stack told them they had agreed to work eight hours a day and must do so. Stack visited first one field, then the other, making sure they did go on working.

At 6 P.M. the gypsies moved to the road and tossed their cutters up into the wagon. Stack appeared. There was still an hour of daylight. He'd give each man, woman, and child ten francs extra for another hour's work, he said.

A few of the gypsies seemed tempted. The rest were not. All now began to straggle down to their encampment.

Stack went inside the chai, where Gorr was making notations in a notebook.

"How much did we get in?"

"Not bad, not bad."

"How much, goddamn it?"

The old cellar master looked at him, surprised. The answer was about seven percent of the total.

At that rate it would take another twelve or thirteen days to get the grapes in, and Stack suddenly feared he didn't have that much time.

But he went into the office and sent a telex message to New York: First day's harvest a success.

The second day's picking was a duplicate of the first. During the succeeding two days the weather stayed sunny but turned cold. By the time the gypsies tossed their cutters into the wagon on the fourth night all of the Merlot had been picked. The château staff had brought in most of the three lesser species of grapes.

347

That left the Cabernet Sauvignon, the biggest and most important portion of the crop. Stack was standing in front of the chais in the bronze light, fists jammed into his ski jacket, when Gorr came up grinning. The cellar master had just taken a cutting of the Cabernet Sauvignon and tested it. He reported to Stack that acidity and sugar content were exactly where he wanted them. In addition, fermentation had started in vats one through four.

"If the weather holds, we're going to make a great wine," he said enthusiastically.

Stack nodded.

The old man stood in front of him, grinning and nodding.

Stack thought: If the weather holds.

"What does the weather bureau say?"

"You know how they are. Always wrong."

So the weather forecast was bad.

Stack said: "Do you hear anything from your daughter?"

The old man's grin disappeared. "I have no daughter."

All right, Stack thought, if that's the way you want it. He turned and went into the château.

Aline was coming down the marble staircase. "Stop worrying," she said.

"How can you tell I'm worrying?"

"You can't worry about every day of every harvest."

"Yes, I can."

Aline began to laugh. After a moment Stack laughed too.

"Would you like me to make you a drink?" she asked.

Stack said suddenly: "I'd like you to come with me to Bordeaux. We'll have dinner in a restaurant. Maybe that way I can stop worrying."

She hesitated.

"You owe me a dinner for saving you from Johnston."

"So I do."

He put his arm around her and gave her a squeeze. To his surprise she did not seem to mind. Instead she turned on him a half-sheepish smile.

In Bordeaux Stack parked the car and they strolled through streets to the restaurant. It was a cold night. Tables were out in front of the cafés, but no one was sitting at them.

Stack was beginning to feel relaxed. Aline, whose arm he held, seemed relaxed too. Neither suspected that disaster was now less than three hours ahead.

348

13

Dupont had been summoned to a high-level conference at City Hall. Inspector Dompierre had telephoned personally.

"Can you come over here please, Dupont."

Please? That was a surprise. "Yes, sir," said Dupont.

"Right away, Dupont, please."

Dupont walked into a crowded conference room. The mayor was there. Everybody was there. They stood up and applauded as he came through the door. Him. Alexandre Dupont.

Dupont was flabbergasted. Seeking an explanation he glanced at Dompierre, the only face in the room not beaming.

The commander of the Fraud Brigade, down from Paris, moved forward to shake Dupont's hand.

Dupont searched face after high-ranking face for an explanation. All were grinning, waiting to shake his hand: the prefect, representatives from Interior and Agriculture from Paris, a general of gendarmes, the superintendent of police, the chief of customs—all were grinning at him.

Dompierre, Dupont realized, looked green with envy. "You were right after all, Dupont," said Inspector Dompierre.

When the conference resumed Dupont began to grasp what had happened. A Spanish trawler had left Santander loaded down with sugar. Spanish Customs, alerted for such shipments, had informed French customs. A gendarmerie helicopter had picked up the trawler as it closed the French coast. Once it entered the estuary of the Gironde, a customs launch had boarded it. And found the sugar.

The trawler captain was still being interrogated. But he had already divulged the rendezvous point, an abandoned dock near Blaye. Spanish-speaking French customs police were even now driving the trawler upriver toward that rendezvous point.

The discovery of the clandestine sugar was the first solid proof that

Dupont's wine-fraud ring actually existed, and a number of men around the table, Dupont understood, had decided they wanted to get a look at Dupont.

They didn't want anything from him, Dupont realized. They just wanted him to stand there by the door while they went on with their conference. From time to time they looked up, admiring him, as if he were a nude girl on a table during an art class.

He was acutely embarrassed.

"What happens next?" someone asked. Dupont wanted to hear the answer too. Could he go now, or must he stand there?

Suddenly Dompierre said: "Again congratulations. That will be all, Dupont."

"Yes, sir."

The mayor growled: "Let him stay if he wants to stay."

"Of course, sir," said Dompierre, flustered. "Do you want to stay, Dupont?"

But Dupont wanted only to get out of there. "No thank you, sir."

"Take a seat, Dupont," suggested the mayor. Surrounded by high-ranking police types, the mayor may have wanted the modest Dupont for support. "It won't hurt to get another man's opinion," the mayor said.

But, in a gathering as august as this, Dupont had no intention of saying a word. Instead he listened to men he considered his betters while decisions were made. The trawler would unload on schedule. According to the Spanish captain the cargo was always transferred in the dark from trawler to truck. The captain was then handed money which he counted by flashlight. He had no idea as to the identity of the men who met his boat or where they went with the cargo.

All the dignitaries were leaning over the conference table now. Dupont watched them pore over a topographical map of the river banks. The site of the drop was caressed by fingertips, and voices began to whisper.

It was decided to make no arrests at the drop zone. The truck was to be allowed to proceed to its destination. The general of gendarmes explained the principle of surveillance grids. The grids—cars manned by gendarmes—would be set in place. The truck would enter the grid. Presently it would either enter or not enter a second, interior grid. The third grid surrounded Château Cracheau, the supposed destination. That grid also the truck would either enter or not enter. In any case,

350

the approximate location of the truck could be known at all times. The truck could not escape.

Still, no arrests would be made. The gang was to be given enough time to concoct the brew. Evidence would be needed in court. The best evidence was the fermenting brew, not contraband sugar.

Up to now Dupont had not heard Bozon's name mentioned once. Was the shipper so big no one dared move against him? Dupont was only a minor government functionary and well used to according special privilege to the great and near great. Nonetheless his dismay now approached moral outrage.

"Has no further evidence turned up against—" every eye in the room turned Dupont's way. His voice broke and he had to swallow— "against this fellow Bozon?" He told himself he had not meant to speak, and now that the words were out he felt not pride but fear. What would these men do to him?

A number of furtive glances swept around the table.

But the name had been mentioned. It could no longer be ignored. A buzz of voices, some overlapping, announced doubt that a merchant as illustrious and as rich as Bozon could be involved in this. Why should a man that rich risk all in a scheme certain to be uncovered by the authorities, meaning themselves? That the scheme had been discovered at all was due only to luck, and to the persistence of the lowly Dupont, but as always, once a conspiracy unraveled, officials congratulated themselves on the inevitability of its unraveling, given the intelligence and foresight which men such as themselves had always been ready to bring against it.

The mayor said: "There may in fact be higher-ups that we don't yet know about, not necessarily Bozon, of course. If one or more of these higher-ups could be tricked into giving away his own involvement, fine. Arrest him. Otherwise arrests seem out of the question, given the delicacy of this matter. Gentlemen, this city exists by and for wine, and let's not forget it."

The prefect spoke next: "I suggest limiting our arrests to those men we find in proximity to the false wine when we raid Château Cracheau."

"The wiretaps on Bozon have shown nothing so far," added the mayor. "This is a very delicate matter, I repeat."

"If this fellow Bozon is involved," said the gendarme general, who felt as outraged as Dupont but was constrained by his stars to hide it, "and I don't believe for a minute he is, it would be nice to scoop him up too. If only we could grab him at the château. But I suppose," the general concluded glumly, "he'd be too smart to put himself close to hard evidence."

Dupont heard himself say: "Suppose there was some way to make him go there?"

The gaze of Inspector Dompierre was fixed on Dupont. Dompierre looked incredulous. Dompierre could not believe his ears. The mayor wanted Bozon left alone. Little Dupont was defying the mayor.

The other men stared at one another around the table. No one spoke.

"If I may, sir," suggested Dupont hurriedly, "suppose someone went to him. Suppose someone showed him a photo of this Italian, asking Bozon, for instance, if he had seen or heard of such a man in the course of his business. Perhaps he might—"

My suggestion must indeed sound idiotic, thought Dupont. He could not finish his sentence. He went mute.

The general of gendarmes looked around the table from one officer to another, but avoiding the politicians. "Well," he said. "Well, is that a good idea, or not?"

The commanding officer of customs cleared his throat. He too refused to glance toward the mayor or prefect. "It might work. It might have a chance."

The general of gendarmes said: "My feelings exactly."

Inspector Dompierre now clapped Dupont on the shoulder. "Well done, Dupont."

The mayor's lips, Dupont noted, were pressed tight together.

The Fraud Brigade commander from Paris said: "The next question is, who goes to see Bozon?"

Dupont hoped they would send someone with plenty of rank.

"What about Dupont, here?" asked the general of gendarmes.

There was a general murmur of assent around the table.

"Why not?"

"It's his idea after all."

"Do you think you can pull it off, Dupont?" said Dompierre.

Dupont glanced up, intending to excuse himself. It was too big a job for a man like him, but he looked up into a round of smiling faces —except for the politicians—and he could not get the words out in time.

"It's settled then," said the general of gendarmes. "Dupont's visit may provoke something over the wiretaps. Or Bozon might go out to the château directly. If he's involved, that is. The surveillance teams will not follow him. He either goes there, or he goes nowhere that interests us. We'll know when he enters the grid several kilometers from the château. If he does go to the château, we arrest him. Any questions?"

14

Aline and Stack strolled through city streets, peering into shop windows that were brightly lit. They passed a bar with an oyster stand out front, where two men wearing berets and rubber aprons were opening oysters out of boxes. The men wore rubber gloves with their fingers sticking through, and worked deftly with knives. They were arranging opened oysters around the perimeter of metal trays with seaweed on them. In a moment a waiter would come out of the bar to carry the trays inside.

Stack and Aline came out onto the boulevard. Across was the opera with its rows of Grecian columns, looking like a massive Greek temple. It was built, Aline told Stack proudly, in the same style as the opera in Paris, and was almost as gorgeous. Ahead the Maison du Vin loomed up, the lights out in all its offices, but its great neon letters spelling out the single product on which the economy of this beautiful little city was based.

One entered the restaurant Dubern through what was, in effect, one of the world's most fabulous delicatessens. Stack and Aline were immediately surrounded by hors d'oeuvres, by hanging sausages, by pyramids of cold cooked game birds, by raw hams on boards, by pheasants in gorgeous plumage. There were filets of smoked salmon and pieces of smoked eel and rows and rows of delicacies in dishes: diced beets, marinated mushrooms, tiny salted shrimp, mussels swimming in sauces, hearts of palms. Then came baskets of raw vegetables: carrots and celery, stalks of onions and scallions standing upright, artichokes, radishes, green peppers, tomatoes all jammed in.

The building itself had once been someone's mansion. Stack and

Aline went up a wide carpeted staircase. A maître d'hôtel took their coats, and they were led into one of the elegant dining rooms. The tablecloths hung nearly to the floor, and the silverware was heavy. Although the room was big, there were only about ten tables. No table was close enough to any other for conversations to be overheard. Menus were brought that were bound in leather, as was the wine list.

After glancing around the room Aline said: "Do you know something? I know everyone in this room at least by sight."

Stack smiled. "I think that's very nice."

"Nice?"

"To belong to a place so totally that you know nearly everyone, and nearly everyone knows you."

"Well, it can be a little putting-off at times, you know. For instance, the fact that I'm here with you tonight can be the talk of Bordeaux tomorrow."

The wine list contained several hundred different château-bottled wines.

"That's so that any owner can bring guests in here and order his own wine," Aline commented. "It's a matter of prestige. The place has to carry nearly every wine."

They started off with cèpes à la bordelaise. The big autumn mushrooms of the local forests were sliced and cooked in olive oil. After that came another of the local specialties, mussels and baby crabs. The mussels had partially devoured the baby crabs but had been caught and cooked before digesting them completely. The mussels and crabs were served in a kind of soup made from white wine, garlic, parsley, fresh tomatoes, and tender diced carrots. For wine Stack ordered a white 1966 Château Haut Brion, which Stack had come to know as a luscious, fat wine. After he so described it to Aline he grinned sheepishly: "I'm beginning to talk about these wines like everybody else."

But he held the goblet up to the light, admiring the most golden of all the white wines he knew about. The French were right. There was pleasure to the way certain wines caught the light. The French bragged that a Frenchman ate first with his eyes, and Stack realized that he himself did too now, and that eating and drinking had never been this much fun before.

15

Preceded by a phone call, Dupont had entered Bozon's warehouse on the Quai des Chartrons.

The building's narrow frontage was as shabby as waterfront buildings everywhere in the world. The entrance corridor was shabby. There was a concierge sitting in a glass booth beside the door, and from the doorway what appeared to be narrow-gauge railroad tracks ran straight backward down the narrow hall and under the wooden doors which closed off the warehouse proper. These were tracks down which, in the old days, wine casks used to be rolled out of the building, across the street, and onto the ships. Nowadays barrels went out the back on trucks. The idea of anyone rolling a cask across the Quai des Chartrons through the speeding traffic was preposterous.

Beside the rails a narrow shabby staircase mounted to the offices above.

Bozon met him on the third-floor landing and led him into an office whose big windows looked out over the docks and the river. Drapes hung on either side, and there was a Persian rug on the parquet floor. Bozon's desk was set so that it commanded a view both of the river and the door, and a number of armchairs stood about. On the walls were framed testimonials from wine societies. On an antique table stood ten or a dozen miniature wine bottles bearing gummed labels marked by identifying numbers in ink. There were crystal wine goblets on this table too, clean ones upside down, others stained from recent use.

"Could I offer you a glass of wine?" Bozon asked, moving to the table behind his desk.

Dupont, uncomfortable, not knowing quite how to proceed, nodded assent, and Bozon poured a goblet one-third full, and handed it over. The full-sized bottle, Dupont noted, bore only a gummed label and identifying number in ink.

"This is just an ordinary little wine," Bozon said conversationally.

"It's entitled to the appellation Bordeaux only."

Dupont, not knowing what else to do, sipped it. He wondered if he were drinking real wine or fake. It tasted all right to him. But people in various parts of the world at that very moment were drinking ox blood and rat poison thinking they were drinking wine. To serve such a concoction to his guests, particularly official guests representing the Fraud Brigade, was perhaps just the thing to appeal to Bozon's sense of humor.

Bozon was watching him with a pleasant smile. "What do you think of it?" he asked.

Dupont stared into the glass. "I am hardly an expert on wine, monsieur."

"No, no. We're none of us experts. It's a matter of taste. Your opinion is very valuable to me."

Dupont, half convinced, took another sip of wine.

"There's quite a lot of this available," Bozon said conversationally. "I'm thinking of making a major investment—mostly for the foreign market, of course."

The two men nodded at each other.

Bozon opened a notebook on his desk, consulting prices. "The wine you're drinking now would sell for about eight francs in France. Actually, I think most of it would be exported. The French are great wine drinkers, but not in that price range as a rule."

Again they nodded at each other. Bozon, Dupont noted, seemed completely at ease. But surely, Dupont thought, he must be asking himself why I'm here.

"So I'd be very interested to hear what you think of this wine," Bozon said. "Tell me very frankly."

"I'm really not an expert, monsieur," Dupont said into Bozon's smile.

Bozon grinned hugely: "Oh, reserving judgment, are you?"

Dupont began to wonder how to move the conversation in the proper direction. He wanted to alarm Bozon, but not too much. He wanted to drop a few hints, then leave. He wanted to insinuate, not convince. All depended upon his manner as much as his words, and he had been unable to work out a plan in advance.

"But surely you didn't come up here to taste my wine," Bozon said conversationally. "What can I do for you?"

Dupont set his briefcase down on Bozon's desk and unzipped it. Taking out a folder, he began to leaf through photos. He handed one

356

across the desk to Bozon. "Have you ever seen this man?"

Bozon studied the photo, shook his head, and handed it back. "This one?"

Again Bozon studied the photo, shook his head, and handed it back.

"How about this one?" asked Alexandre Dupont, handing the shipper a photo of the Italian wine swindler.

Bozon stared at the photo.

Alexandre Dupont, watching closely, thought he discerned a tightening of the brows. For an instant the skin on Bozon's skull seemed to become tighter. Then it was gone. If Dupont had not been looking closely, he would not have seen it at all, and a moment later he was not sure he had seen it.

Bozon studied the photo, shook his head, and handed it back.

The phone rang.

Bozon put his hand over the receiver and said to Dupont: "Excuse me, but it's New York calling, I'll only be a moment."

At the window Dupont looked out over the docks and the river. It was dusk now. The Spanish trawler, chugging upriver, was still several hours from the drop zone.

Below on the quai traffic had begun to thin out. Night lights were burning on a few of the cargo ships that snuggled against the quai. In the early days of the wine trade, Dupont reflected, the merchants were all foreigners, and all Protestants too. They came here from England, Ireland, Denmark, Holland, Germany. After a generation or two all had acquired French nationality, but they stayed Protestant, and they stayed confined to their own quarter here close to the Quai des Chartrons. They were referred to as Les Chartrons, and were forced by the Catholic elite to live outside the city walls. They were allowed to enter the city only between sunup and sundown. They had lived in fact in a ghetto. In recent years their social status had shifted somewhat, though not entirely, as some of them bought châteaux themselves and moved into the country, sometimes even adding their own Protestant name to the proud name of some great French wine. But the class difference was still there. Class differences died hard in Europe, and especially in France, and the descendants of the original Chartrons were unacceptable to many of the old Catholic families still.

And why be so surprised? Dupont reflected. If the cellar masters and régisseurs are of a lower social order and must not mix, then it is easy to believe that the Chartrons are not good enough and must not mix either.

357

Édouard Bozon, talking apparently calmly to New York behind Dupont's back, was a Chartron. His ancestors had come from Holland or some such place two hundred or more years ago, but he was a Chartron still.

Dupont attempted to eavesdrop on the phone conversation, but it was in English. The timbre of Bozon's voice contained no flaw Dupont could detect. Bozon was agreeing to ship somebody a great quantity of wine. At the window Dupont bowed his head. Real wine? How could such a man get involved in something like this? His family had been in the wine trade here for hundreds of years. He himself was rich.

How? Why?

Dupont didn't understand it, and he was filled with doubts. Perhaps somewhere he had made a terrible mistake. Certainly if Bozon was involved, he should have had more of a reaction than that to the photo of the Italian swindler.

Bozon hung up the phone, and came around in front of the desk. He was beaming.

"It's good news?" inquired Dupont.

"Yes, very good news," said Bozon. "Business really is excellent these days. If things go on this way, we all stand a chance of becoming very rich."

"Except those of us who work for the government," observed Dupont.

Bozon clapped him on the back in a friendly way. "With your experience, my good friend, I'm sure there would be a place for you in the wine trade if you wanted one."

Behind his desk again, Bozon remarked: "I'm sorry I couldn't help you identify those men. Who are they, anyway?"

Dupont pushed the first photo across the desk. "This man is an agent of the Fraud Brigade." Dupont pushed the second photo across, covering the first. "This man is an army officer convicted of murder, currently doing time in the Santé prison."

"And that third chap?" inquired Bozon easily.

Dupont pushed this photo across. "His name is del Greco. He was convicted in Italy of concocting wine out of sugar, water, dregs, and noxious chemicals, ox blood for instance."

Bozon began to laugh. Dupont, watching closely, thought that the laughter sounded genuine and his heart sank.

"Ah, those Italians," Bozon said. "Life is a game to them. I bet the fellow did it just for a laugh. I'll bet he expected, if he got caught, that

358

everyone would applaud his ingenuity. Those Italians are something, aren't they?"

Dupont watched him.

"That reminds me of a joke about Italians," Bozon began. He told the joke straight through without a break in his voice, and when he came to the punch line began to giggle.

Dupont laughed politely. Dupont was no longer sure of himself at all. Bozon was a big imposing man, big enough to be a heavyweight prize fighter. He had piercing eyes and a big jaw, and gorgeous teeth when he laughed. He had been educated in England, Dupont knew, and spoke at least two languages. He was rich.

Dupont's misgivings approached fear. If Dupont was mistaken, what might not Bozon arrange to have done to him? Forced early retirement was almost the best that he could hope for.

"So the first two photos were control photos," observed Bozon. "That Italian is the one you're interested in. So why come to me?"

"Have you ever seen this man?"

"How could I? He's in jail in Italy."

"I didn't say he was in jail. He's out now."

"I haven't been to Italy in four or five years."

"We have reason to believe that he's in France."

"Information from an informant, I suppose."

Dupont, watching Bozon carefully, nodded.

"You have information that he's operating here in the Bordeaux area, don't you?" said Bozon. "That's why you're here."

"Have you ever seen him?"

Bozon reached for the photo again, and studied it for a long time. Dupont noted no change whatever in the shipper's facial expression.

"Well, I may have, of course. I go all over this area on buying expeditions. It's possible I may have seen him. I'm racking my brains trying to decide if I've ever seen him, but, sorry to say, nothing rings a bell."

"Nothing?"

Bozon shook his head. "I wish I could help. Something like that is a terrible thing for the wine industry. I mean, if something like that ever got out—you say he's been sighted here in Bordeaux, or he's known to be operating here in Bordeaux?"

"I was just asked to show you the picture, monsieur."

Bozon nodded. "Yes, of course, you're here to get information, not give information. Well, sorry I can't be of any help. If anything comes

359

to mind I'll call you. Let me note down your telephone number."

As Bozon showed Agent Dupont to the door, the shipper said: "You can rely on my absolute silence in this matter."

Since Dupont had not asked for such silence, this statement raised in him a momentary glimmer of hope. But, as he descended the dark narrow staircase, as he stepped carefully over the rails so as not to break a leg, Dupont was miserable. If that was a performance upstairs, it was a splendid one.

He drove back to City Hall and entered the conference room. At least the politicians were gone; only the policemen remained. "Nothing," Dupont reported glumly. He asked hurriedly: "Has anything come over the wiretaps?"

Nothing had. If Bozon was guilty, Dupont thought, surely he would have telephoned a warning to somebody.

"What do we do now?" he asked.

"We wait," said the general of gendarmes.

"If there is a swindle going on," Dupont said hopefully, "then there's a forger involved. There has to be. They can't move the stuff without acquits. It would be too dangerous. Someone is providing them with phony acquits. Couldn't we round up every known forger in the area?"

The general of gendarmes jotted something down. "I'll look into that," he said. He began whispering to one of his aides, who then left the room. The rest of them sat there, waiting.

16

Édouard Bozon at the window saw the Fraud Brigade agent come out onto the sidewalk, step into a car, and drive away. Turning off the light in his office, Bozon went upstairs one flight to his sumptuous apartment, crossed to the bathroom, knelt in front of the bowl and began to vomit. Convulsions racked him. When at last they stopped he paced his bedroom trying to think, but no thoughts came. Once he stepped to the telephone and lifted it. But the idea of wiretaps came to him just in time, and he dropped the receiver back fast.

He must have paced an hour or more before thoughts began to arrive in an orderly manner. In his head he went over his original plan. He could see nothing that would link him legally to the crime. The false wine already made and bottled was gone from this warehouse, distributed to various parts of the world. The papers covering this wine would withstand all but the most intense scrutiny; even then there would be doubts. At worst it would appear that he himself had been duped into buying the wine. A jury, he was confident, could never be convinced into believing otherwise. The forger lived close to Bayonne, almost two-hundred kilometers away, and was known only to himself. No one could give the forger away. The forger, even if caught, knew little. He had prepared official forms bearing official stamps, but the information on these forms had been typed in later. The forger had no idea of the scope or detail of the scheme. Since he had a long record of convictions, his unsupported testimony against a man of Bozon's stature would convince no one. Bozon's contact in Spain knew Bozon under another name. The trawler captain who sailed the dregs and sugar into France had no idea whom he was delivering them to. He delivered to a spot and was paid in cash by a man he did not know. That left only two evidentiary links to Bozon, the Italian and Claude Maurice, for Château Cracheau itself could be traced no further back than the nonexistent Monsieur Aubervilliers.

The only vulnerable links were those two men.

Bozon decided he must go to Château Cracheau. Although there was a chance that the police were watching the place, and that he could be caught there, this seemed a lesser risk than to do nothing. He couldn't risk phoning the two men, and he could not be sure they would obey telephoned instructions anyway. They would want money. He would have to go.

Crossing to his wall safe, he dialed the combination, reached in and withdrew sheaves of hundred-franc notes. After hesitating a moment, he also withdrew his revolver.

Now that he was committed to action, Bozon began to feel more confident. He went downstairs and strode between the rails toward the rear of his building, sniffing as he walked the dank mold that coated the walls and vaulted ceilings.

Unlocking the back door, Bozon stepped out into the night. From his driveway, he glanced apparently casually up and down the street.

He could discern no man obviously standing surveillance on this exit. Across the street were shops with people in them, and a few cars moved by.

There was no team of agents keeping vigil, Bozon decided, and if a single detective was in fact watching for him, the man was in for a surprise.

Ignoring his Mercedes, which was parked at the curb, Bozon crossed the street and entered the apartment building opposite, opening the door with the necessary key. He walked straight through the building and out the back, where he was stopped by an iron gate. The gate was in a fence surrounding the garden belonging to still another apartment building, which faced onto the street beyond. Bozon, using his keys, locking each gate after him, crossed this garden and went through the other building and out onto a residential street, where he looked up and down but saw no one. Parked at the curb was a car rented in the name of the nonexistent Aubervilliers. Bozon unlocked this car and drove away, watching the mirror closely.

But no one followed. He kept to empty streets as long as he could, and still no one followed.

Behind him, the detective staked out in a store phoned in: "He's just entered the building across the street."

"Remain on post. Let us know when he returns."

Bozon drove out of the city. After he had crossed the river and was deep into the wine country on the other side, he began to turn almost aimlessly up and down empty country roads, watching his mirror closely. No one followed. Nor did he notice any suspiciously parked police cars. He was ready at any moment to turn back, but as time passed he began to feel exultant.

As he drove, Bozon replayed in his head his interview with the Fraud Brigade agent, and he became convinced that the man knew nothing specific. Probably all merchants and brokers were being interviewed. Some kind of tip had come in, probably from Italy, and the authorities had to check it out, whether they believed in it or not. In a day or two they would become discouraged and go on to something else.

Probably there was no need even to liquidate the Château Cracheau business.

Nonetheless, Bozon's stupendous excitement at the first successful brew had been succeeded by tonight's convulsive vomiting. He wanted no more of this scheme. The thrill was over and the money not impor-

362

tant, so why continue? It was too risky. The business would be liquidated tonight. He would walk away from Château Cracheau. Let the weeds and the bush have it. It was not worth further risk, and as far as profit and loss went, it had already paid for itself several times over.

And so Bozon entered the surveillance grid. He was still watching his mirror, driving slowly, spotting nothing whatever tailing him. But as he swung onto the dirt road that led past Château Cracheau two gendarmes secreted in the trees radioed this information to Bordeaux.

"A car just turned in."

"Stay on post; notify us of any further traffic."

Agents at the opposite side of the grid were notified of the make and description of the car, but presently radioed that the car had not come out. "There's no sign of it."

In the conference room in Bordeaux, the general of gendarmes said: "Let's move."

Dupont felt acute distress. He felt they had waited too long already, and they were too far away.

Dupont touched the sleeve of Inspector Dompierre. "Would it be possible, I mean, could I come too?"

The general of gendarmes looked up sharply. "Of course, Dupont. Come along."

Two kilometers away from the château Bozon sat parked in the dark. He waited there thirty minutes, but nothing came by. Starting up his car, he drove on to the château and turned into the yard. As he climbed out his heart began to race. He was in terrible danger now, and knew it.

At this moment Alexandre Dupont was sitting inside a minibus stamped GENDARMERIE NATIONALE which was blocked in traffic on the far side of the suspension bridge spanning the river. There had been an accident ahead. Dupont, craning his neck, could see dome lights turning up there. What looked like flashlights moved about. There must be gendarmes on the scene. They appeared to be moving the traffic forward one car at a time.

Dupont fretted, for the minibus was still more than twenty kilometers from Château Cracheau. Dupont sat in the last of four ranks of seats, sandwiched in between the burly Inspector Dompierre and a customs official. The gendarme general was in the front seat and Dupont heard him from time to time conferring with other units by radio in police code. There was no urgency in any of the voices, and no squads had yet been moved up close to the château. The general of gendarmes seemed to be taking this affair lightly, perhaps because no violence was involved, or likely to become involved, whereas Dupont was worried about tonight's arrests—or lack of arrests—causing the collapse of the wine industry, one of the first industries of France.

The minibus had begun to creep by the wreck. Gendarmes with flashlights were waving the cars through. Dupont murmured to Inspector Dompierre beside him: "Could we put the siren on now? We're still so far away."

"Quiet, Dupont."

"Excuse me, inspector, but—"

"The general knows what he's doing."

Dupont, who was not so sure of this, could say no more.

Instead he sat there squirming. He judged he knew the countryside better than anyone else, and a possible escape route had occurred to him. The malefactors could cut straight across through the vineyards and come out on another road on the other side. If they happened to have a car there they could be outside the grid before any raid began. However, to call this information to a general of gendarmes across rows of intervening high-ranking officers seemed to Dupont presumptuous. So he said nothing.

"Stop squirming, Dupont," Inspector Dompierre ordered.

From outside the chai no light showed. Using the prearranged signal, Bozon rapped on the door and was admitted. The door was quickly barred again, and the lights went back on.

Bozon, blinking from the bright light, found himself looking into the grinning faces of Claude Maurice and the Italian.

"We didn't expect you," said Maurice, "but we're glad you're here, aren't we, Emilio? Look at this."

As they were designed to do, the two stainless-steel vats had been swung aside on their secret pivots. Bozon stared down into a portion of the concrete vats underneath. The two vats were about three-quarters full of bubbling, fermenting red liquid.

"What's this?" demanded Bozon. "The new shipment is not supposed to come in until tonight."

"We had enough for an extra brew. Emilio wanted to experiment."

Emilio in his curious accent said: "I change something. Is same dregs as last batch, used twice. I find chemical that practically dissolves them. And the wine—the wine is better than ever. Is real nectar this time. Wait till you taste."

364

"I just chucked the rat poison in," Maurice said. "It'll stop fermenting any minute."

"Yes, well, just open the faucet and run that stuff out fast."

"What's the matter?"

"The cops are looking for Emilio."

When Bozon had explained, Claude Maurice snorted contemptuously. "You've just got the wind up. You're scared. They may be looking for him, but they don't know where to look. If they did, there would be signs."

"Run the stuff out," Bozon ordered. But there was just a shade of panic in his voice. Already he suspected he would not be obeyed.

"We can't just run the stuff out," protested Maurice. "That rat poison would kill the vegetation for a hundred yards around."

Bozon, trying to control his voice, said forcefully: "Listen to me, both of you. We're liquidating this operation tonight. In ten minutes this place will be empty. The vats will be empty, and the house will be empty. I don't want so much as a sock left behind. I'm taking no chances."

"Wait a minute," Maurice protested. "We've got a good thing going here. I've worked hard, Emilio's worked hard. You can't just close us down."

"Yes, I can," said Bozon. "As of this minute you're closed down."

The Italian looked from one Frenchman to another, a puzzled expression on his face.

Maurice asked: "What about tonight's shipment?"

"To hell with tonight's shipment. Let those Spaniards unload the stuff in the trees. What do we care?" Bozon looked into the hard face of Claude Maurice, and found himself pleading. "It isn't worth the risk. They're closer than you think. It doesn't make sense to go on with it. We've made a nice profit. Let's be satisfied. Once we're away from here we're absolutely safe. For as long as we stay here all three of us are in danger."

Bozon's voice had risen high, for suddenly he was focused on the risk to himself if he got caught here next to the bubbling evidence. "I say we close down now. Open that drain, Emilio."

"Don't do it, Emilio."

"You heard me, Emilio."

The baffled Italian glanced from one to the other.

The vats had been designed for quick voiding via a single big drain, which exited part way down the hill. Bozon lunged toward the drain control—the wheel was six inches or more in diameter and below floor level, so that he had to crouch as he began turning it. Claude Maurice tried to pull Bozon away from the wheel, failed, and swung a blow which caught Bozon in the side of the head, knocking him flat. Bozon sprang to his feet, furious, and the fear came on strong.

"Believe me, it's got to be done," Bozon cried. "For all we know the police will be here within a few minutes. You can go to jail if you want to, but I have no intention of joining you there. Now get out of the way."

"No."

They glared at each other. The only sound was the hum and buzz of the fermenting "wine." It sounded like the buzzing of bees, and it had been gradually slowing down during the last several minutes.

"I've brought money," cried Bozon.

Maurice became less truculent. "How much?"

"Enough to cover your expenses for the next few months." Bozon withdrew the sheaf of bank notes from his breast pocket and waved it in the air.

"How much?"

"Fifty thousand francs. Half for you, half for Emilio."

"Not enough."

"Oh, yes, you can go a long way on that."

"Are you kidding me?" Maurice gestured at the open vat beside their feet. "There's more than that bubbling around in that vat right now. Not to mention the money we could make with what's coming in tonight. You just want us out of here so you can keep the profit for yourself."

"I want to empty that vat into the ground. Doesn't that prove I have no ulterior motives?"

Maurice thought a moment. "Let me count the money."

Bozon handed it over, and Maurice thumbed rapidly through the notes. "You chiseler," he shouted. "There's only thirty-five thousand there."

It occurred to Bozon that he had made a mistake. He should have brought extra money in case he needed it.

"I'll make a deal with you," Maurice proposed. "You want to close down, right? Okay, we'll close down. All you have to do is bring us two hundred fifty thousand francs. You hand us the money, we'll close down and disappear."

He means it, Bozon realized with sudden horror. He means to

366

blackmail me. "I couldn't get that much money ready for two or three days."

"We'll wait. In the meantime, we'll bottle this brew."

"Two days might be too late."

"We've risked it this long, we'll risk it two more days."

Abruptly Bozon turned to the Italian: "How about you, Emilio? You've served time already. Do you want to go back?"

But the Italian's French was weak, and the argument was vague to him. All he knew was that he didn't trust wine merchants. In Italy he had gone to jail, and the merchants had not.

"What you ask me," said the Italian, "is who I trust? I trust you, or I trust Claude. You ask me, I tell you. I trust Claude. You want to close us up, you bring more money."

A lifetime of sharp dealing, Bozon realized, was no help to him now. The moment called for force. In a profit-and-loss situation, a businessman did what he had to do to survive.

From his pocket Bozon withdrew the revolver.

17

Aline and Stack left the restaurant. As they came outside into the street, the night seemed bitterly cold, and a sharp wind was blowing.

The storm hit as they approached the village of Ludon. In ten minutes they would have been home. Being with Aline tonight had soothed Stack; tonight it had seemed possible to believe not so much in the rich good life as in the sanity and order of life, and that the simplest pleasures, to eat, to drink, to make something grow, were really the biggest ones.

The storm struck hesitantly. There was a pinging on the hood of the car and a kind of rasping noise on the canvas top—as if someone were rubbing it with sandpaper.

"Hail," muttered Aline.

Stack heard her sharp intake of breath.

At first he didn't understand. He looked out over the hood, which had become lightly dusted with tiny crystals of snow. Other tiny crystals struck the windshield and instantly dissolved. Stack thought this the equivalent of driving through a bank of fog. In a moment he would come out the other side.

He in no way related this to his vulnerable vines, to the hundreds of thousands of dollars' worth of grapes still to be picked. Aline sat beside him, mute, terrified, and he did not even notice.

The individual grains fell against the car for about a minute, while Stack's headlights probed on homeward. Then the first minute ended. It was like a signal. Abruptly the individual grains turned to crystals the size and weight of rock salt. The car was being pelted by them. The windshield blades swept them into the corners of the glass, where they coagulated. This was hail such as Stack was used to, but he was still not unduly alarmed.

However, he became conscious of Aline crouching in her seat.

"What's the matter with you?"

"Hail."

Though he had heard of hail destroying grapes Stack had supposed there was no danger unless it hailed for hours. His principal emotion right now was impatience. He did not want to let go of the contented glow that the evening had given him so far. He wanted to get home, perhaps sip another cognac with Aline, perhaps—who knew—even kiss her goodnight. A kiss would be nice. Peering out at the falling hail, he was even amused to entertain such a mild ambition.

He had worried about his vines all day. He did not want to worry about them again until tomorrow. Light hail like this could not hurt his vines.

But the hail was pelting the car now. The wipers were working hard. The hail was becoming packed into the corners, interfering with the blades.

Next to him Aline muttered: "Please God, no."

It was as if she were praying. Despite himself, Stack began to be alarmed. She had lived here all her life, and perhaps knew something he didn't. But his contented mind moved slowly, and he could not figure out what was about to happen.

"Oh God, we're driving right into it," Aline muttered.

They were moving through a forest and the trees were close on both sides. To Stack it seemed that the storm was thinning. The drumming on the canvas roof sounded less relentless. His headlights seemed to reach further down the road. Contentment returned. He accelerated. Five minutes more and they would be home. He would make a fire, they would enjoy a cognac while staring at the flames.

Hail such as they had just come through could do no serious damage, whatever Aline might think. There were layers and layers of leaves covering every cluster of grapes. The leaves overlapped like fish scales. In most cases you could not even see the grapes till you got up close and parted the leaves.

Suddenly what looked like moth balls were bouncing and rolling in the road, first a dozen of them, then a hundred, then suddenly thousands. They rolled downhill from the crown of the road. The crown of the road was always empty, and there were always a million mothballs bouncing high and then rolling away. The headlights showed it all to him. Stack was incredulous. He could not believe his eyes.

"Oh, this country," Aline muttered, "Oh, this bloody country."

The hail drummed on the car. Stack's first thought was for his paint job. The hail felt as heavy as stone. It would leave dents. It might crack the windshield. It could pierce the canvas top. He pulled off the shoulder under a tree.

The hailstones still drummed on the car.

"They're as big as pigeons' eggs," Aline muttered.

Stack had never seen pigeons' eggs—or hailstones like this. In his headlights they bounded onto the road like ping-pong balls. On the car they sounded like the drums preceding a court-martial—his own. His momentary awe at the force and majesty of such a storm turned to fear —fear for his vines. The prisoner, himself, had been brought to justice. He felt as helpless as a man must feel tied to a post, blindfolded, waiting for the bullets.

He had heard of hailstorms that destroyed vineyards, and had tried to decide what such hail must be like, but had not come close. Because now, seeing such hail for the first time, he recognized it instantly, the way a man must recognize death when it touches him on the shoulder: so this is what all the talk has been about. Out through the windshield he stared aghast at the giant hailstones bounding in the road in the headlights.

Beside him in the dark Aline seemed close to tears.

"Perhaps it missed us, our land," said Stack numbly.

She only shook her head.

The hailstorm lasted only ten minutes. The hail fell at full force and then stopped. It never diminished. There was no final trickle. It simply stopped. The great dump truck in the sky was empty.

Stack and Aline sped along the crown of the road, which was virtually dry. They sped along between what looked like snowbanks lining both sides of the road.

When they came out of the forest the sky looked vast, and was suddenly full of stars. Stack kept hoping that the snowbanks would disappear, but they did not. He sped through Cantenac, turned off the highway, and then off the secondary road onto the dirt road leading up toward the château at the top of the slope. The vines to either side of this road were planted in Merlot and had been picked. But what he could see in his headlights frightened him. The troughs between the rows were full of snow. The vines looked the way they looked in midwinter, just before they were pruned back. Stripped of leaves. Long skinny stalks. Each plant a candelabra of stalks.

He went under the arch, skidded on the gravel, rounded the turn in front of the château, and sped out under the other arch onto the dirt lane behind the chais. Two hundred yards further on there was another turn-around amid the vines. He aimed the car diagonally so that the headlights shone out over these unpicked vines, stopped, and sprang out.

This field slanted downhill toward the highway. It was planted in Cabernet Sauvignon.

The gullies between the rows were filled with hailstones. It looked as if somebody had emptied an enormous number of ice trays out into the troughs, which were heaped white. Stack waded between two rows of vines. The headlights showed him not enough of the heartbreaking scene—or else too much.

He had hoped these unpicked vines might have withstood the storm better than the Merlot. The coverings of leaves would have rested upon plump clusters of grapes. The grapes might have supported the roof of leaves. The roof of leaves might have protected the grapes from the battering of the hail. As he had crossed in front of the château this had been Stack's last and only hope.

The vines were devastated. There was almost nothing left to pick on any of the plants. A few leaves hung here and there, a few forlorn stalks. Some were stripped clean. Some still bore five or six grapes. Some grapes still attached to the stalks were split open, oozing their life's blood down onto the heaps of hailstones.

Stack shuffled along the row, hoping for better news at the other end. There was no better news anywhere. When he reached the edge

370

of this field he stared up at the sky and wanted to cry.

He became conscious that Aline had followed and was standing a few paces behind him.

"Bloody, bloody, bloody country," Aline muttered. Her hands were jammed into her pockets and he saw there were tears in her eyes.

"It's not the country's fault," Stack said. "It's mine. I waited too long."

Aline came forward and embraced him. He felt her hot face on one cheek. They stood up to their ankles in hailstones between two rows of vines, and the cold wind stung Stack's other cheek.

"I—I just don't understand how ten minutes of hail could have done this much damage."

"They never last longer than ten minutes. They wipe out a year's work in ten minutes."

Stack said: "I never realized who my real enemy was in this thing. I thought it was Johnston. And all the time it was God."

They became conscious of a man with a flashlight wading toward them. It was Gorr. As he came up he doffed his beret.

"Some of the other fields are not quite as bad as this," Gorr said hopefully.

Stack said nothing. The night felt bitterly cold.

"The electricity's out," Gorr noted.

Stack glanced around him. There were still grapes to be harvested in this field. Not many but some, and other fields were less badly devastated, Gorr had said. There was still hope then. The remaining grapes could be harvested. The disaster could be mitigated. He would not give up. He began making decisions.

"How many men could we get out here right now?" Stack demanded.

"Right now?"

"You heard me."

Gorr considered. "Maybe fifteen of our people."

"What about the gypsies?"

Gorr looked doubtful. "I could ask them, of course."

This was Gorr's way of saying: Not if I know my gypsies.

"We'll pick all night," said Stack. "And if there are any grapes left on the vines by morning, we'll pick all day. Rouse the men."

They waded back to Stack's car. Stack did not remember how contented he had felt only a few minutes ago. Though it was nearly midnight, he was not tired. He wanted to work. He wanted to fight back.

371

"It will be cold," Stack said. "Warn the men to bundle up and to wear gloves. Get some of the older women to make hot coffee and hot soup."

Beside him in the car, Gorr looked unhappy. The wine harvest was supposed to be a leisurely affair. It was accompanied by good eating, good drinking, by laughter and song.

There was no conviviality in what Stack planned. This was not a harvest any more. It had become a kind of willful defiance of nature itself.

Stack was reassigning his personnel in his head. Instead of one porter for every four rows, he would assign one for every ten.

But was it wise, he asked himself, to work all night. Perhaps they could pick more efficiently if he waited till morning.

But the hailstorm might come back before morning. Or some other storm. Stack felt helpless, the way villagers must have felt centuries ago knowing they were in the path of Barbarians or the plague. Man for all his courage was puny. At any time some mindless force could swoop down and destroy him.

"We can't set up floodlights," Gorr said mildly. "The electricity's out."

"Park all the cars and trucks on the edge of the fields with the headlights on."

Stack in his room pulled on boots, corduroy pants, a windbreaker, a ski cap that pulled down over his ears, and gloves that had gripped poles on snowy mountain tops. Designed for one of the most esoteric of human tasks, they would do fine for one of life's most basic.

Stack went down the steps and out to his car. At the gypsy encampment he began banging on the walls of the trailers.

Two or three sleepy-eyed men stuck their heads out. The old chief came out and began arranging twigs above the remnants of last night's campfire. Flames began to lick up through the twigs. The metal coffeepot, its wooden handle long since burned away, stood on old coals amid the burning twigs.

"Let's have some coffee," Stack agreed, trying to check his impatience.

These people did not work for The Company. They were a different kind of people. He would have to convince them, if he could, to work all night. It would take time.

At one point he counted ten men sitting around the fire warming

372

their hands, but one by one they began to go back into their tents or trailers.

Three of the gypsies were willing to work all night. It was hopeless to try to attract more. Though he had promised double pay, money meant nothing to these people. The three who followed Stack's car up the road would work for reasons of their own. Because they liked Stack, perhaps. Because they wanted to show off or punish their wives, or perhaps because they hoped to find something to steal.

He didn't care what their motives were, only that they help him get his grapes in.

18

Though the revolver felt puny in his big hand, Bozon's voice was hard. "If either of you moves a muscle, I fire."

Both of them, he noted, stared at the barrel of the gun, four eyes fixed on a miniature fifth eye. Maurice's hand clutched thirty-five thousand francs.

"I give orders here. I'm opening that drain. Then we're going up to the house and clearing out. We're going up over the hillside and down the other side where the truck is, and we're going out onto the big road, and you two can spell each other driving—all night. I'll sit behind you and make sure you drive away from Bordeaux. Is that understood?"

Neither spoke. The Italian stared at the gun barrel, Maurice at Bozon's face. Maurice's hard eyes showed hatred, or perhaps contempt, but Bozon had begun to feel confident. He had managed to turn the business deal to his own advantage.

"Don't move," he cautioned again, and reached for the faucet handle. The wheel was just below the level of the floor, and with his eyes fixed on two dangerous men he could not find it. As soon as the vats had drained out, Maurice and the Italian would willingly leave the château,

Bozon was sure. There would be no reason not to. So Bozon's first job was to open that drain, but his groping hand could not find it. It was perhaps lower than he thought, so he sat on his heels, and groped again —and found it.

He managed to give the wheel half a turn—there was the noise of the brew beginning to gurgle out. All this time Bozon had been watching principally Claude Maurice—that's where the danger was, if any. His eyes had flicked from the wheel to Maurice, and back to the wheel again, and he was trying to turn it one-handed while bent sideways and squatting on his heels, while holding a gun on two men, and suddenly the Italian with a cry of rage leaped on him.

Bozon might have shot the Italian. There was perhaps time, and the range was point blank. But Bozon had not made up his mind to shoot anybody. A businessman, once he accepted a risk, must accept its inevitable conclusion too, but Bozon had made no such decision. The Italian came flying at him, Bozon hesitated, and then it was too late.

The Italian sent him flying. Bozon's left hand was entangled in the spokes of the wheel, and he felt a searing pain as one of his fingers broke. This, or perhaps just the force of the Italian's charge, caused him to drop the revolver.

The Italian was wearing farm coveralls and heavy boots. Bozon was impeccably dressed in a double-breasted blue suit and red knit tie, a tall, handsome man, with a big jaw, black moustache, and big white teeth. The Italian and Bozon grappled with each other. Bozon, being much the bigger, was able both to struggle with the Italian and to grab up the revolver, which he brought up to use as a club. But the Italian got his hand on the barrel, trying to wrench it away from Bozon.

The gun fired.

Bozon went reeling across the floor. He did not know he had been shot, just that he had lost his balance. He saw the gun in the air, halfway between his hand and the floor, stuck there, and he lunged for it but missed, for he was already reeling in a different direction, trying to catch his balance.

His concentration shifted. He noticed the hole in the floor ahead, and, although he told himself he must avoid that at all costs, saw he wasn't going to.

I'm going for a swim, he thought; how ironic.

Immediately he struggled to change direction lest he both ruin his suit and appear ridiculous. He could afford many suits, but could not afford to appear less than the powerful, ruthless man he indubitably was, for he still had to alter the conduct of these men, and if they should see him in a comic light, it would be impossible.

He still didn't know he had been shot. He did know that suddenly he had stepped out on top of the wine, and that it was not going to support him. He saw his shoe go into it, an act as repugnant as stepping in dog shit on a pavement. The wine came up over his cuff to his shin. Only his right pants leg was ruined so far and he was struggling to keep the other shoe high and therefore clear. He would find a solution to all this yet, though it would take a few moments' concentration.

He plunged into the vat of fermenting brew.

There had been the stupendous detonation of the shot, followed by the noise of Bozon's shoes slapping the floor as, fighting for balance, he strode toward the hole. And lastly, following an instant of absolute silence, came the tremendous splash thrown up by the wine merchant's final belly whopper. It was almost funny.

Bozon, lurching across the room, had worn an expression of gaping incredulity. Maurice had gaped incredulously too as Bozon disappeared from sight. Choking back laughter, Maurice ran to the hole, thinking: He's going to be awful mad.

Meanwhile, the Italian had lunged for the drain wheel. On one knee, he was cranking the drain shut with both hands.

"Got to save the wine," cried the Italian, cranking vigorously.

Bozon, who lay face down in the brew, realized vaguely that he could not move, but this did not matter for he no longer wanted to, even to breathe. Then for a heartbeat longer he struggled to stay alive. It was outrageous that this could be happening to a man as powerful as himself. Reality was refusing to conform to the importance of his image. In a moment he would rise up and make it.

Maurice was staring down into the hole, mouth agape. It had just dawned on him that Bozon was not going to start swimming.

"Jesus Christ," muttered Maurice. "Christ Jesus. Oh, Jesus. Oh, Christ."

The vats had ceased their loud escaping gurgle. The Italian breathed: "Thank God."

"You shot him," Maurice pointed out.

The Italian shrugged. "Well, it was him or the wine."

Directly under the overhead light, Édouard Bozon, former wine merchant, floated on his face in the floating morass of the still-fermenting brew. The surface seethed around him. It looked like he was being nibbled by tiny fishes.

"He's moving," cried Maurice.

"No, he's not," explained the Italian proudly. "That's my wine moving. It's the best I ever made."

Having stooped to recover Bozon's gun, the Italian suddenly pitched it into the brew. There was a splash and it disappeared.

"What did you do that for?" demanded Maurice.

"That gun is his gun," explained the Italian.

Maurice thought that the Italian, like all artists, was a little crazy. The gun was important, and they should have decided what to do with it. Maurice peered down at the brew. The gun was gone.

"You picked a good place for it," Maurice muttered sarcastically, "it may even melt. Let's get out of here."

In the farmhouse each rapidly packed a small bag. Maurice collected all receipts and papers and burned them in the stove. With a damp cloth he spent about ten minutes rubbing possible fingerprints off every surface he could think of. There were very few dishes in the place, and he went over all of them. The Italian, who appeared to have gone into a state of shock, watched him.

"I hate to walk away from my wine," the Italian said dreamily. "It's the best I ever made."

"You can't sell it with him floating in it," answered Maurice.

"You can't tell about wine. He might even improve it."

"The customers wouldn't like the idea of him floating in it, though."

"How would they know?"

"Christ, let's go," cried Maurice. He wished he had more money. He should have robbed the floating Bozon. But it was too late now.

They went up the dirt lane between rows of vines, past the fruit trees in whose shade old man Cracheau used to sit, over the hill and down the other side. At the edge of the property their truck was parked. The night was still clear, for the hailstorm had not yet crossed the river.

Maurice got in behind the wheel. The truck started right up, and they drove out of there.

Behind them in the moonlight the ghost of Bozon hovered over the château, maintaining: I was an important man. You can't make jokes about me just because I didn't get a curtain speech. In my way I reached for glory, and so glory, not levity, is what you must give me.

No one knew it yet, but glory was exactly what Bozon would presently be accorded.

376

19

The general of gendarmes, exercising great care, brought his two squads in simultaneously from either end of the road. When they were close, he had them fan out so as to surround the farmhouse and the chai. A truck then turned into the driveway and fixed the buildings in its spotlight. The general got on a bullhorn and ordered: "You're surrounded. Come out with your hands up."

A long silence followed.

Dupont had been trying to get the general alone. "Excuse me, mon général," he said. "There is a dirt road on the other side of the property. It is possible they escaped via there. We waited so long before closing in."

The general turned to smile at Dupont. "Don't worry, we'll get them."

But he stepped immediately to the command van and radioed orders to other units.

Dupont watched a dozen law-enforcement officials approach the buildings. Some entered the farmhouse, and lights went on inside.

A man called from the doorway: "No one's here."

Attempts were being made to open the door to the chai, but it would not budge. At length the shutters were pried back and entry forced via a window. From inside, the big doors were opened. To Dupont the interior of the chai looked exactly as he remembered it, except that bright lights were now shining. There were stacks of new bottles against one wall, and the bottling machine, all its wires and tubes tucked into its mouths, stood in a corner. There were burlap sacks against one wall. These contained, it would later be determined by chemical analysis, dried ox blood. Boxes of other chemicals stood on shelves.

The two stainless-steel vats seemed firmly anchored to the concrete floor.

"Empty, by god," said the general of gendarmes, who had climbed a ladder to peer down inside.

"If this is a wild-goose chase," said Inspector Dompierre to Dupont, "you're in trouble."

"The vats," said Dupont.

"We can all see the vats, Dupont."

"The cement vats are under the floor." Dupont was nosing about. "These steel vats must swing back somehow," he said.

A customs captain came over to help him. The captain found the toggle, and in a moment he and Dupont leaned against one of the vats and it began slowly to swing to one side. The toggle on the second vat was found more easily, and it too was pushed back. The captain drew up the floor panel, and all stared down into the vats.

Bozon still floated on the top of the chapeau.

"Well, well," said the general of gendarmes. "Well, well, well."

The captain poked the body with his stick and the face turned to the side like a swimmer breathing.

"That's him," said Dupont soberly. Dupont's business was fraud, not murder. He had never seen a murdered corpse before, much less one floating in what seemed to be wine. Dupont was offended. To Dupont wine was sacred. Great irreverence had been done to wine here tonight.

Suddenly Inspector Dompierre began to vomit. The contents of his stomach spilled out. He had leaned forward over the hole. His dinner struck Bozon's pants leg and added itself to the brew.

Men turned away in disgust.

"That stuff will really be tasty now," muttered the general of gendarmes.

Dompierre had straightened up and was wiping his chin with a handkerchief.

"We could bottle it, see if it improves with age," the general said.

Dupont, whose emotion had gone over into hysteria, was laughing.

"Don't be funny, Dupont," said Dompierre.

The general of gendarmes began giving orders in a cheerful voice, for the corpse in the vat had given him confidence. White-collar crime scared him—that type of crook always had more influence than the poor cop, and could get the cop in trouble—and political crime was even worse. But crimes of violence he understood perfectly. He judged that the fugitives had no more than twenty minutes' headstart. He would run them down within an hour.

378

Suddenly he felt little Dupont tugging at his sleeve. "What is it, Dupont?"

"Mon général, I've checked through the cars outside and there is a truck missing." Dupont opened his notebook and produced the license numbers off the truck he had spotted delivering wine to Bozon's warehouse, and which had later proved to have been rented by the Italian. "There's a dirt road on the other side of the hill. The truck could have been parked there, and if it went out that road it could only head north or south on departmental route 276."

To Dupont's relief, the general walked down to the command truck and radioed this information to all units.

About an hour later the general received word by radio that Maurice and the Italian had been captured at a roadblock and had surrendered with no resistance. The murder weapon had not been found.

"Don't worry, we'll find it," the general said confidently, and ordered up two hundred more gendarmes. An hour later he set all two hundred combing the vines by flashlight, looking for a pistol. By that time it was raining hard, though no hail ever fell that night on that side of the river. The general's final order was that all units should be kept on duty at Château Cracheau until further notice; for not a word of this operation could be allowed to leak out until he had had a chance to talk it over with the politicians.

As the dawn came up the two hundred gendarmes, abandoned by their leaders, sat in their buses in sodden uniforms, waiting for permission to return to their barracks. Rubbing steam off the bus windows, some of them watched with dull eyes as the medical examiner's ambulance made off with the body of the wine merchant. According to one rumor which swept the buses, the gendarmes would be kept there all day as punishment for not finding the murder weapon. According to another, they were being held incommunicado because in reality the dead wine merchant was not a wine merchant at all, but a German spy.

20

Stack, after investing nearly half an hour with the gypsies, had brought only three more workers into the vineyard.

They worked all night, eighteen men including Stack, five women including Aline, two teenage boys. The night stayed cold and clear with a biting wind, and the hailstones heaped between the rows of vines did not appear to melt. The work was illuminated by the headlights of two trucks and four cars, including Stack's Ferrari, and by the stars. One of the trucks ran out of gas and no one noticed until its headlights began to go dim. The moon began to rise. It was nearly full. It threw a creamy light on the vines and the bent pickers, but then the sky began to cloud over.

"We must hurry," Stack urged, moving among his pickers.

The baskets were dumped into the hotte of a single porter, and when it was full he moved to the untended cart behind the tractor, climbed the ladder, and dumped grapes and stalks over his shoulder into the cart. Slowly the cart filled up. The headlights showed its color to be mostly green from stems rather than purple from grapes.

Three times in the course of the night two old women in long overcoats, scarves tied around their heads and ears, staggered along the lane carrying between them a cauldron of soup. The soup was hot, of course, but it was also delicious, Stack realized vaguely, a thick French vegetable soup made with fresh carrots, fresh tomatoes, leeks, potatoes, and lots of butter.

Another time the women came out with pitchers of coffee. Apparently they were working by candlelight, boiling up cauldrons of soup and coffee over the wood stove. There was still no electricity, they reported.

Back in the chai stalks and grapes piled up in the bin. Soon the bin was nearly overflowing, for there was no electricity to destem the grapes and push them up through the hoses into the vats.

380

As soon as the sun peeped above the horizon the three gypsies refused to go back into the vines. Stack argued with them, but it did no good. Stack threatened them about the money he owed. They shrugged and left anyway.

With the sunlight the headlights could be turned off. At first Stack missed the noise of the engines. No birds sang. The dawn seemed incredibly still.

By nine o'clock in the morning they were still picking, but in the chai the grapes and stalks had begun to overflow the bin. There were still a number of wooden douils that could be filled and Stack ordered these placed on the cart and carried out into the fields.

Stack still worked feverishly but all the others flagged. Their movements had become sluggish and inaccurate. He saw pickers tilt their baskets toward the hotte—and miss it completely. Then porter and picker would kneel to recover what they could from amid the now melting hailstones.

The pickers were beginning to complain, first among themselves, then to Gorr, and finally Gorr came to Stack.

"They're too tired. They want to stop."

Stack addressed them. He begged them to keep going just a little longer. Just fill the cart one last time, then they could stop. Something about his own desire, or his feverish eyes communicated itself to them. They nodded and went back into the vines. When the cart was full, Stack himself mounted the tractor and dragged it back into the courtyard, while the pickers trooped off to bed. Stack looked into the chai. Now is the time to start the machines, he thought, get all this stuff up into the vats, but though he pushed several switches no machine started, and no lights came on. Aline stood in the doorway watching him while he dialed the electric company, but their phone rang busy, so he called the village curé, to whom he had given six bottles of wine last Christmas.

The priest said that lines were down all over the Médoc. The lights might not come on until tonight or even later.

It wasn't the lights Stack needed, but the machines. He looked around at all the grapes that had been picked: full bin, full cart, fifteen or more full douils. The grapes had to be torn off their stems and pumped up into the vats, and it would have to be done by hand, and he had no energy left, no manpower left.

Stack's hands and clothes were stained purple, and when he noticed this he could not at first comprehend how it had happened or what

381

it meant. His mind felt wooden. When would the electricity come on? If the work had to be done by hand, who could do it? Who had any strength left? How soon could it start? Were there winches to lift the douils up over the vats and dump them? He stumbled into his office to think about all this, dropping into the leather chair behind his desk.

He became conscious of Aline standing in the doorway.

"Go get some sleep," he urged her.

"You have to sleep too."

"There's no time for that."

"You can't do any more. There's no one left to help you."

"Maybe I can get one or two of the gypsies."

"They're all gone."

"What? All of them?"

"Didn't you see their bus and carts going along the highway while we were picking?"

His mind wasn't working properly. "What bus?"

"The bus with the smokestack in the roof. It must have been about nine o'clock. I went down to the camp. They're all gone."

He would have to work this out. In a minute he would start working it out. He had a terrific need to close his eyes for a moment, but could not do this with Aline in the room. Why didn't she go?

"Go get some sleep."

"You too."

"All right," he told her.

"Promise?"

"Promise," he lied.

He had to go into the chai, work out what could be done, what hand-operated gear was available, how many men he would need, decide when to start. He had to go out into the other parts of the vineyards, see what grapes were left, if any, work out a way to pick them swiftly. It was possible the storm had spared whole fields out on the extremities of his property. He hadn't even looked yet—and that sometimes happened. These hailstorms, someone had told him during the night, cut swaths through vineyards. They cut swaths through the whole Médoc, sparing some places and not others for no reason. If some of his fields had been spared, and if the weather held, and if he could find pickers, there might be more grapes to bring in. He was not defeated yet. He would not give up.

If he could make just one bottle of great wine against such odds, would this not be the greatest triumph of his life?

Aline was gone. He would get up and go back to work, but first he would let his eyes close.

His mind was getting fuzzy. It was floating around words like triumph. It could not concentrate on hard facts. Decision eluded him. He would just rest his eyes another moment.

He fell asleep.

In Bordeaux the mayor was trying to set up the conference that would decide what to do. The mayor was on the phone in his office, and the prefect of the Gironde department was on the phone to Paris in a spare office across the hall.

"What about my men?" asked the general of gendarmes.

"Find an empty barracks somewhere that will hold all of them. I want them isolated until Bozon is under the ground. I don't want them talking to anyone. Hold the other people who were with you too, customs, Fraud Brigade and the rest."

"They're all dispersed."

"What?"

"I had no authority to hold them."

"You don't seem to realize what a crisis this is."

"Indeed I do. A man has been murdered, but we've got the perpetrators locked up."

"The murder is nothing, man. The entire wine business is at stake here."

"Yes, sir." The mayor had no authority over the general, but with politicians it was always better to pretend they did. "What do you want me to do?"

"Round up all those men and seal their lips. I don't care how you do it. Then rejoin your men. You're quarantined too."

"Do you really think that's necessary, sir?" asked the general stiffly.

"Yes."

The mayor wanted the conference held within hours, and Bozon stuffed under the ground almost at once, but the prefect came in with instructions from Paris: The ministers of agriculture and interior would attend the conference. All decisions would be held until they got there.

"When will that be?" demanded the mayor.

"Probably tomorrow."

"Jesus, this whole thing could explode by tomorrow, don't they know that?"

"I'm only telling you what they told me."

21

The telephone bell awakened Stack. Where was his secretary? Why didn't his secretary answer? It must be Saturday or Sunday, for no secretary was there. Stack grabbed up the phone.

It was Johnston calling from Paris.

Stack felt as if he were ten feet underwater, staring upward at the sun, swimming hard.

"I hear you've had some trouble down there. Trouble with the harvest."

Stack's mind broke the surface. He seemed to shake water out of his ears and eyes, and to take a deep breath. If it was Saturday or Sunday, then Saar wasn't around either, and Saar was Johnston's spy, wasn't he? So how did Johnston know?

"We've been hailed. We've worked all night getting in what we could."

Johnston's voice was cool. "Damage pretty severe, was it, Charlie?"

"It didn't do us any good."

"I've got to call the chairman in New York. What do I tell him, Charlie boy?"

"Tell him we've been hit by a severe hailstorm. I'll report on the damage as soon as I know what it is."

"Gypsies working out all right, are they, Charlie?"

"Fine."

Stack realized that his nose and ears were cold. His hands too. That meant the heat hadn't come back on. The electricity was still out.

"It was quite a storm," Stack said. "Every château in the area has been hit, I believe."

"But they would have suffered less than us, wouldn't they? Most of them had most of their grapes in already, as I understand it. Is that right, Charlie?"

"If you don't mind, I've got to get back to work," Stack told John-

384

ston. "Tell the chairman I'll make my report as soon as I can."

When he had hung up, Aline, looking tousled-headed and sleepy-eyed, was standing in the doorway.

She must have slept in the chair in her office, Stack thought. He was strangely touched. Stack rubbed the bristles on his face. He would give the men another hour's sleep, except for Gorr, whom he would need at once.

Sending Aline to fetch the cellar master, he went out to his car and drove to the furthermost corner of his property, where he found rows of vines that had not been touched at all. But elsewhere it was as if somebody had gone to work with a scythe.

Fifteen minutes later, Stack had come to the conclusion that it might be possible to save as much as 50 percent of the crop. If he could save that much, then at the same time he might possibly save his job.

If the weather held, if he could get the surviving grapes in fast—

But he had no pickers. Worse than that, for the moment he had no receptacles to put more grapes in. The first job was to empty out the bin, the douils, the cart. The grapes collected last night had to be pumped up into the vats first—by hand, if the electricity stayed out, a backbreaking job.

When he got back to the chai Aline and Gorr stood waiting.

To Aline, Stack said: "Get the kitchen girls to make up soup, coffee, food for every man, woman, and child on this place who can be put out into the vines. Get somebody to contact all of our people. Tell them they're to be in the vineyards at three-thirty."

He watched Aline as she hurried toward the château, then turned to Gorr. "You and I have less than one hour to empty some of the receptacles into the vats."

Gorr suggested they wait for the electricity to come back on. "With only two of us, monsieur—"

Just then Saar, dressed in a gray suit, gleaming black shoes, and a silk tie, came into the courtyard.

You goddamn spy, Stack thought, eying Saar.

"You're one of the most devoted employees this company has, wouldn't you say?" Stack called out.

Saar, after looking into the chai at the mounds of grapes, answered: "I would hope to be considered in that manner."

"I imagine you'd do just about anything to help The Company out of a tight spot."

"Just about anything."

"Right. The Company has never needed you more than it needs you today. You and Gorr and I are going to get those grapes up into the vats."

Saar began to protest that he was a lawyer, an office man. He knew nothing about grapes. He wasn't dressed for it. He would ruin his clothes.

"Johnston just called from Paris. Somebody told him we're in trouble here, and he wants me to use any means I deem necessary to save the crop."

Stack grabbed the lawyer and led him into the chai, where the twenty-four oak vats stood with rims fourteen feet above the floor. The first four had been filled during the first days of the harvest, and the buzzing of their fermentation was faintly audible inside the chai. Fermentation had not yet started in four other full ones. When Stack had thrown back the great iron doors in the wall, sunlight fell in on the bin piled high with last night's grapes. The bin measured about twelve feet square and three feet deep, but could take no more. The juice had run forth from millions of broken grapes and was ready to overflow. Outside in the sunlight waited last night's final cartload of grapes. About fifteen oak douils, each containing a hundred gallons, stood in the center of the floor. They were like enormous buckets. They could be raised by winch above the rims of the vats and upended.

Stack, Gorr, and the lawyer began rigging such a winch, lashing it to a rafter above vat number nine. Then, with Saar hauling and Stack guiding, the first douil went over the rim of the vat, and Gorr on a ladder upended it. There was a satisfying splash as its contents struck the floor of the vat.

Gorr called down: "There are an awful lot of stems in there in proportion to the number of grapes."

In the old days, grapes and stems both went into the vat. Most great wines were undrinkable for up to ten years. Then it was discovered that if the stems were torn off first the wines would contain less tannin, would be softer, would become drinkable in three or four years.

Now Stack was being forced by circumstances to make wine in the old way, to empty all the douils at once, stems and all.

"As soon as the electricity comes back on, we'll run what's left through the stemming machine. But we've got to have some receptacles ready for the men to fill as soon as they come to work."

I must be awfully tired still, Stack told himself. No competent executive explained his actions to people like Saar or Gorr.

386

Soon the men straggled in.

The contents of the douils were still slapping down hard on the bare board floor of the vat—unwelcome noise to Stack, for it meant that the floor was not yet awash. Stack, listening hard as the next load was dumped, began to despair of ever filling the vat, for the douils were minuscule compared to it.

It soon became clear that they were not going to be able to empty douils fast enough to keep up with the pickers. They were going to have to find a way to pump out the bin, and after that the dump cart in the yard, but the hand pump, Gorr warned, would clog on the stems. They tried it, and it did.

Stack talked it over with Gorr. How long had they had the stemming machine? What did they do before they got one?

Years ago, Gorr replied, the grapes were dumped out on a cross-hatched table and rubbed back and forth until they had detached themselves from the stems and fallen through to the bin underneath.

Was that table still around anywhere?

Gorr remembered that it was, and led Stack to it. They found it clotted with cobwebs.

It would have to be scrubbed off first, and Stack set Gorr to doing this while he himself went into the fields to gather men and women to work at destemming the grapes. There was no point picking any more grapes till they had dealt with what were already in the chai.

And so the laborious work began. The table was set up in the bin. Men stood in the bin up to the shins of their rubber boots in running grape juice and stirred the grapes through the cross-hatched slats, and then swept armloads of stems over the side onto the floor. The destemmed grapes began to be sucked into the hand pump.

Little by little the bin was cleared and more grapes could be brought in. When night fell a truck was set up in the yard to throw its headlights through the open doors. Stack and Aline worked opposite each other at the trestle table. There were five people working around the table, three men working the pump, and two others pitchforking loads of grapes onto the table. The rest of the people were out in the vineyards gathering more grapes.

The night was cold. Stack saw his breath rise into the glare thrown by the headlights of the truck.

At last the bin was empty, the dump cart too. The workers had emptied all the douils as well. It was 10 P.M. Stack begged them all to go out into the fields and, by the light of headlights again, to fill the

387

dump cart one last time. They could do it by midnight if they all worked fast, he pleaded. He asked for volunteers. All of the men agreed to go on working, but decided that their wives had to be relieved.

Aline and one of the women from the kitchen came in with more soup. Men and women sat on the low wall of the bin and drank soup from bowls. Stack had decided to give the men fifteen minutes to drink their soup, but this time elapsed and he realized he must give them more. They were too tired.

At length he herded them out into the vines. Cars and trucks were adjusted to throw headlights down new rows, and the pickers started forward, clipping. The night was terribly cold. In the sky above Stack could see neither stars nor moon, and the wind blew. He moved down his row of vines, feeling for the clusters of grapes, clipping regularly, and his eyes felt clotted, and his back felt fixed into a permanent stoop. His fingers and toes felt icy.

At last the cart was full, and the tractor dragged it back to the chai, where Stack bade his men goodnight, and watched them shuffle off.

He should go to sleep himself, he knew, but the dump cart stood outside the open steel doors, and it was full, and rain or more hail could fall, so he climbed up on top of the grapes in his rubber boots, and began pitchforking loads of grapes and stems down onto the trestle table. Jumping down into the bin, he began rubbing clusters of grapes along the top of the table. The table rasped the grapes off the stems, or broke them off, and the grapes fell through onto the tops of his boots, and he kept going until nothing was left but stems.

Now the wind blew against his face, for he was standing atop the cartload of grapes again, forking a second load—or was it a third—down onto the table.

Now he stood at the table, rasping grapes through slats with frozen hands.

Aline stood opposite him, also rasping grapes. Where had she come from? He was so tired he imagined he might be dreaming. He rubbed on. After what seemed hours, miraculously, the table top was empty.

"You should get some sleep."

"As soon as I empty the cart," said Stack, who hardly realized why he was still working, though these were the Cabernet Sauvignon grapes, the most important proportion of the eventual wine. Without them there could be no wine worthy of the château's label. With them perhaps he could still make a quantity of splendid bottles. They would be his bottles, his wine. That was important. He tried to explain it to

388

Aline, or perhaps only thought he did.

"I'll go up to the château and make you some coffee," she said.

Climbing up onto the dump cart, he pitchforked more grapes down, rubbed until there were no grapes left, swept away stalks, climbed up onto the cart again and pitchforked down a new load.

Aline came with coffee. Her face was concerned. She was watching him closely.

He grinned at her over the cup. "Don't look at me like that. I'll be all right."

Later the floor was littered with grapeless stalks, and the bin was half full of grapes and juice, but the cart was empty at last. For hours Stack had been wading in grapes and juice in his often-muddy boots, but that didn't matter, he told himself; juice transforming itself into wine would also purify itself, a miracle as miraculous as the transubstantiation. His only duty as a man was to labor in the vineyard.

It was all getting foggy in his head.

Now to pump it all up into the vats. He rigged up the hand pump and worked the handle up, down, up, down. Once his hand slipped off and his body pitched forward so that he struck his forehead on the base of the pump. It woke him up, and he went on pumping.

"Let me work it for a while," said Aline. He let her. Her arms worked the pump handle while he wondered what she was doing there. Was she in love with him, or only with the wine?

"My turn again."

He pumped on, monotonously, relentlessly. He had to pump juice, pulp and skins fourteen feet into the air so that they would pour out into the vat, had to keep pumping hard.

The pump sucked air. It was over. He could do no more tonight.

He sat down on the low wall of the bin and put his face in his hands.

Aline was still there. "You're exhausted," she said.

She led him into the offices, where he sank down into the first chair he came to. He was sitting at his secretary's desk. It must be after midnight now, already Sunday. His secretary would not come in for another eight or nine hours. No, that wasn't right. Another eight or nine hours plus a full day. The mathematics of it was too much for him. He didn't know when his secretary . . .

The room was cold. His nose and cheeks ached from the cold, and so did his hands. He plunged his hands into the pockets of his jacket. He felt amazed to be sitting at his secretary's desk. An executive shouldn't do that.

389

Aline said: "We have to go across the courtyard into the château, and up the stairs, and then you have to go to bed."

On the desk between them a kerosene lantern burned. Aline's face looked as cold as his felt. But he was worried about his wine. She should understand that he could not go to bed now.

In "difficult" years, Gorr had told him, Gorr slept with the wine until the fermentation was complete. "I would rather go without sleep those few nights," Gorr had explained, "than go without sleep all the rest of the year because the wine was ruined."

If temperature was essential to the making of wine, and if the electricity was out, and if there was no heat, and if cold might kill the fermentation, then who knew what might be happening to his wine right now?

Gathering cushions under his arm, Stack returned to the chai, where he laid the cushions against a wall, planning to doze as close as possible to his wine. Even as he arranged his cushions it seemed to him that the noise of the fermentation had diminished, half the buzzing bees were dead or something, the fermentation was slowing down from the cold.

"Stop following me around," he shouted at Aline. "Go to bed. Leave me alone."

He shined his flashlight on the walls of the vats. "It's slowing down. Can't you hear it?"

If the fermentation stopped his wine would be ruined.

Stack felt tears in his eyes. It's just the exhaustion, he told himself. I can't face the idea of any more work.

He sprang to his feet. "We've got to get some heat into this chai."

He peered the length of the gloomy chai, where storm lanterns burned in several places. He remembered two butane gas heaters in one of the storerooms. Aline followed him out into the night. The storeroom door was closed with a hasp and padlock. With a length of pipe lying in the dirt, Stack ripped the hasp out of the door and shone his beam inside.

"There they are."

He manhandled one out into the yard, then the other. They rolled on casters—badly. He pushed one ahead of him, but it wouldn't roll and he had to pick it up, then come back for the other.

But the chai seemed vast to him, and so cold that the two heaters now burning would do little good.

For controlling the temperature of fermenting wine there was an arrangement of copper coils. The wine could be electrically heated or chilled while being pumped through them and back into the vat. Stack conceived the idea of ripping the coils loose from the contraption and heating them over a charcoal brazier, like links of gigantic hot dogs. Then he would only have to pump thousands of gallons of wine from each vat through the coils and back into the vat.

In the field kitchen he found the brazier he wanted, lugged it into the chai and went back to fetch charcoal.

While Aline set fire to the charcoal, Stack began to arrange the pump and hoses he needed. One hose would have to go up over the top of the vat. He climbed a ladder, dragging the hose. The vat was nearly full. He shined his flashlight down on the mess inside. It was hardly bubbling at all as he fixed the hose in place.

Suddenly he became aware of silence. "Listen," he cried.

Fermentation had ceased. There was no sound. It was as sudden and startling as if the sea had suddenly stopped beating against the beach. Something which ought to be happening wasn't happening any longer.

"It's over," said Aline numbly.

"I'll get it started again," shouted Stack.

If he could just empty that entire enormous vat through the coils and pump it back in again—

How many hundreds of gallons?

Not hundreds, thousands. Thousands of gallons to pump through that coil.

He opened the faucet and began pumping. Up down, up down, up down . . .

When it seemed that his arm would break off, Aline spelled him. Up down, up down, up down—

The linked hot dogs glowed red hot. He pumped for what seemed hours more, until at last the wine began bubbling again. The buzzing fermentation had resumed in vat number one.

"But there are more vats—"

The exhausted Aline said: "You don't have to worry about that. If we can just keep this one going, it will set the others off."

He was too tired to believe her.

"The fermentation spreads from vat to vat and no one knows how," Aline said. "It's spontaneous. It jumps across in some way as a fire would."

So Stack went on pumping juice. The faint buzzing got louder, steadier.

Suddenly it jumped across into vat number two. Stack ran up the ladder to make sure. From up there he began to yell with delight.

Under his ski jacket he was bathed in sweat and his arms were so sore he could barely lift them. But in his sudden elation fatigue momentarily left him. Jumping down, he hugged Aline, and then he kissed her hard.

It was as if he had experienced divine revelation, or as if his brain suddenly exploded, but at that exact moment all the lights came back on.

Stack started laughing. "This is too goddamn biblical to be believed," he chortled.

Vat number three began bubbling again. Vat number four started up.

Stack's watch showed that it was 4:30 A.M.

"Let's wait another half hour. I don't mind, do you?"

They sat on the wall of the empty bin sipping coffee, listening to the faint music of the vats.

"You've saved the harvest," she told him.

"Maybe part of it."

"Next year—" she began.

But for him there would be no next year in the wine country. Despite his fatigue, or perhaps because of it, he saw the future quite clearly. He would be brought back to New York to an office job somewhere, and he did not want to go. He wanted to stay on the land. He had come back to the land without even realizing it, and the land seemed to have recaptured part of his soul.

He set his cup down. "Will you do me a favor?" he asked Aline. "Will you go down and rout Gorr out of bed and bring him up here so we can get some sleep? While you're doing that I want to check the temperatures in the vats, and I guess I want to climb up on the ladder and look down on the wine we worked all night to save."

He did this. My wine, he thought, looking down.

The dawn would be up soon. The radiator heat was coming up already. By midday perhaps there would be problems caused by the wine fermenting too hot. Gorr could cope with all that. Gorr and the other men.

When Gorr came in looking sheepish, Stack handed out instructions.

Gorr said: "It's raining out."

392

Stack knew what this meant even before he asked. The harvest was over.

"What grapes are left will rot very fast now," Gorr said. "Grapes don't like abrupt changes of temperature. And, besides that, for the most part they've been bruised by the hail."

Perhaps Stack even found satisfaction in the somber news. Every grape it was humanly possible to save Stack had saved. No man could win against nature, though individual men sometimes attained nobility trying. Stack felt defeated and swollen with pride both. He felt one with mankind down through the ages. He had struggled against nature itself, the true test of a man, not against plots hatched in a company cloak-room. To struggle against the intractability of the soil and the inevitability of the storms was what made a man a man.

Was this even true? Perhaps it was nonsense. He was so tired.

Aline had not come back. Stack went outside into the slow rain and plodded across to the château and up to his bedroom. His outer clothes were stained purple, and his socks and underwear were soaked with sweat and grape juice and clung to his body. He peeled them off, pushed them into the clothes hamper, and stepped into a hot shower. He stood under it with his eyes closed until it began to run cool. After drying himself off, he combed his hair, and stepped out into his bedroom.

Aline in a bathrobe was standing beside his bed. He could see her nightgown below her bathrobe. She must have just washed her hair, for it was wrapped in a towel.

She said: "I knocked on your door. There was no answer. So I came in. I just—wanted to say goodnight to you."

"You don't have to apologize."

Stack realized that he wanted to step forward and embrace her. But he was afraid to. He should put some clothes on first, but was afraid that if he moved at all she might run away.

They watched each other.

There is a curious intimacy between us, Stack thought. We can stand like this, she in her bathrobe, me as I am, and both of us are tense for various reasons, but we're not embarrassed, are we?

"You say you wanted to say goodnight to me."

"Yes."

"Would you kiss me goodnight too?"

"Yes," she said, but didn't move.

"Would you like me to put some clothes on?"

When she made no answer, he smirked at her. After a moment, she smirked back and, stepping forward, embraced him.

Holding her tight, he said into her cheek: "Will you come to bed with me now?"

When she didn't answer, he began nibbling her ear. He nibbled until she started to laugh, and with her laughter he realized he had nothing further to fear, so he began to kiss her fleshy lips, which, after a moment, opened under his. He pulled the towel off her hair, first act in the drama of undressing her completely.

In bed, with the early-morning light coming into the room, he said: "You've got the most marvelous bosom to feel I've ever felt."

A little later she asked shyly: "Do I respond as well as—as other women you've known?"

It was something a much younger girl might have asked, and Stack, filled with tenderness for her, drawing a line with his forefinger from her throat down to her navel, said: "Your response is on a par with your bosom. It's—marvelous."

His tickling forefinger made her giggle.

Stack, terribly drowsy, reclined against the headboard, feeling the whole length of her against him. He wanted to fall asleep and then wake up and start a new life. But first something had to be settled between them.

He said to her: "I'm finished here, you know that."

"Maybe not."

"You know them, you know how they are."

"It was a freak storm."

"In the American corporate world, freak storms count against you too."

"Hush," she told him. "We can talk about that when we wake up."

"No. I want to talk about it now. You see, I don't want to go back to New York. I want to stay here in the Médoc, and maybe I can stay, if you'll help me. I have some money, and I know people who have money. I want to buy a small château and build it into something."

Was he so sure he could live in this remote place, without the tension, without the constant warfare inside The Company? He didn't know.

Had his personality been so abraded that the life man was apparently made to live—life on the land—had become impossible for him? Had he become so used to forcing the world to obey his will that he was

394

now incapable of waiting—merely waiting—while the land gave forth its fruit at its own speed?

He didn't know these answers. He only knew that he wanted to stay on the land.

"I hope it works out for you," Aline said. There was a sadness in her voice and he perceived her feelings. Even in a moment as intimate as this one, he seemed to be making plans that did not include her.

"A foreigner can't buy a vineyard here any more, you know," Stack told her. "I'd have to go into partnership with a French citizen—" then he added— "or marry one."

He had no idea how this would sound to her.

"If you would marry me," he told her, "we could buy some run-down place and bring it back together. We could work the land. We could live off the land."

Such a life should be enough for a man and a woman, Stack thought. But would it be enough for him? And for her? He was offering her his life, which was no small thing, but he was too embarrassed about the offer to make it directly.

"We could keep a small car," Aline said, "and in the years when the harvest was good perhaps we could drive down into Spain—"

He was so terribly drowsy. She pulled his head over against her breast. "Go to sleep," she told him. "When we wake up I'll cook us a nice meal. You can go down into the cellar and bring up some find old bottle, and probably we'll both get a little high."

Food and wine and love and sleep, Stack thought. That was all a man had ever needed with which to face the future. Food and wine and love and sleep—plus a little hope. Which was what wine was for. With wine there was always hope.

22

Paul Conderie in his Paris apartment received two phone calls. The first was from his daughter. The vines had been hailed; they had managed to save what grapes they could.

"Your place was here," she reproached him. "We needed you here."

"A business matter kept me in Paris, my dear."

When he had hung up Conderie felt exceptionally exuberant. The conglomerate that had humiliated him would lose money. Good. The Americans would have to learn that to make something grow required love and time, not conferences and reports. The vines were not machines. The Château Conderie was not a factory.

Unfortunately, since all his friends believed he still controlled the place, Conderie would not be able to share his pleasure with anyone. Though feeling splendid, he would have to show a long face whenever the glorious hailstorm was mentioned. Friends would offer sympathy to a man who wanted to laugh out loud. Such a bore, Conderie thought.

The second phone call was from a member of his club, who reported that Bozon was dead. The news was all over Bordeaux. A terrible scandal was probably about to erupt, though the authorities were trying to hush it up. There was talk of a hero's funeral for Bozon, if they could hush up the fact that apparently he had concocted wine out of chemicals. The police were closing in even now on other leaders of the gang.

"Other—leaders of the gang," Conderie choked.

"You don't sound so hot."

"I just received bad news about my vines."

"Some of the biggest names in Bordeaux are supposed to be involved. Will you come down for the funeral?"

"Of course," Conderie managed to say.

When he had hung up Conderie imagined himself in handcuffs or, worse, sitting in a jail cell garbed in rough denim clothes. The Conderie family name had been left to him in precious trust, but he had lost all its possessions and brought it to this ultimate disgrace, and, alone in his apartment, Conderie considered killing himself.

However, this idea proved so unattractive that he phoned up his travel agent and ordered himself put on the first plane to London. "Business calls me there," he told the agent cheerfully.

While waiting for confirmation he brooded. He brooded about his daughter, who obviously had not yet heard of the death of her former husband, and who would need him at her side once she did; and he brooded about the funeral. He knew what type it would be. All Bordeaux would be there, and should he fail to lead his daughter into the church in the first line of mourners this would be remarked upon by people whose good opinion he valued. His place, obviously, was at the funeral. Also, his absence might attract the attention of the police.

There was always the possibility that the police were not after Paul Conderie at all. Or that, in an effort to hush up the scandal, they would overlook him. He was not a bad man, he told himself, and had done his duty to the best of his ability most of his life.

Duty called him back to Bordeaux. His place was there. Bowing his head, he dialed the phone again. "Route me via Bordeaux," he told his travel agent.

Later, peering out the porthole at the uprushing wine capital of the world, Conderie was ashen. He fully expected to be arrested as he walked up the ramp. He was only dimly aware that, in returning to Bordeaux at all he was performing the bravest act of his life.

The conference began at noon in the mayor's office, and the general of gendarmes was not invited. Present were politicians only: the mayor, the prefect of the Gironde department, and four cabinet ministers from Paris. The politicians were in unanimous agreement and the meeting lasted only an hour.

The lid would be kept on, and as much blame as possible laid on the Italian. Italy had been gaining on France in world-wide wine sales. This would dump them back where they belonged.

All law-enforcement officers involved would be rewarded—and then immediately shipped far away. Bozon would be converted into a hero and buried with full military honors.

"Just so long as we get him under the ground fast. Any relatives?"

"Some cousins, an ex-wife. I see no problem."

"Fine. We bury him tomorrow."

"What about accomplices?"

"If there are accomplices we don't want to know about it. The investigation ends at once."

The press could be controlled. This was France, not the United States. The mayor, partial owner of the Bordeaux paper, would accord a single interview to the *Étoile*'s wine columnist, Fernand Front, who would not dare ask any probing questions. No other interview would be accorded anyone.

Presently this decision was amended. The mayor would dictate Front's article to the mayor's secretary. Front would be called in and handed the completed text. He would need only to put his own name on it. He would be flattered.

Someone said: "And it should improve the prose content of the paper, too."

They all laughed.

By ten after one they had thrashed out an official communiqué: a band of Italian wine swindlers had sought to infiltrate the French wine industry, using their well-known unsavory methods. The famous and noble wine merchant Édouard Bozon had become suspicious, had alerted the Fraud Brigade and the gendarmerie, and had led the raid on the suspects' laboratory. It was the heroic Bozon's own idea that he should enter first. He did so and was killed, giving his life for France. The good work of the following officers and functionaries was to be commended most highly.

That evening Bozon lay in state in city hall, and the next morning half the population of Bordeaux saw him to his grave. A bugler played taps, and a squad of gendarmes fired a farewell volley into the sky.

Paul Conderie, terrified that he had waited too long already, sped from the funeral to the airport. But the plane to London was late and he was obliged to wait for it. He was extremely nervous, but trying to hide it. In the airport he saw a cop behind every potted plant. He expected a tap on the shoulder any moment. He expected to be grabbed as he went through the boarding gate.

"A very interesting business opportunity awaits me in London," he told his daughter as she kissed him goodbye. He licked his lips nervously and studied two security policemen who stood at the boarding gate checking tickets. He would have to stride past them.

"Let me know if anyone asks for me in my absence," said Conderie.

Taking a deep breath, he released his daughter, shook hands with

Stack, and approached the boarding gate.

The two policemen verified his boarding card and waved him through.

Conderie nearly fainted with relief. Though his knees barely supported him, he forced himself to turn to wave cheerfully to Aline. A moment later he walked out toward the plane, and his step seemed to lengthen with each stride.

On the way back to the château, Stack said to Aline: "How do you feel?"

"About the funeral? Not sad, if that's what you mean." In fact, she felt almost glad. Did this make her a monster? It was as if she had committed an obscene act, and the only witness was dead. It was as if she were guilty of a crime on which the statute of limitations had just run out. It was almost as if, now, she could have her innocence back.

Once she had been a bride, but the bridegroom had been dead inside and soon the bride had gone dead inside too.

She began to cry.

"See," said Stack, "you do care. You're weeping for him."

"No, it's myself I'm weeping for." She wiped her eyes and was angry at Stack. Men never understood anything, did they?

A moment later, feeling contrite, she leaned over and embraced Stack's arm. In response he gave her thigh, familiar terrain now, an affectionate squeeze. Smiling out over the windshield, he drove on.

Within a week the general of gendarmes had been given an extra star. His new assignment: command of the forces of public order in the overseas departments, with headquarters on the distant island of Martinique. The customs chief was promoted and transferred to the Belgian frontier. Inspector Dompierre was promoted two ranks and awarded the highest medal for which he was eligible. He was transferred to Paris.

There were other promotions and transfers, but at first Dupont seemed to have been overlooked. He did not mind. He had never expected official recognition, and in any case he did not want to leave his beloved Bordeaux. About a week later, someone must have noticed the oversight, for he was notified that he would be awarded a minor medal, and he would also be named a chevalier in the Legion of Honor. Henceforth he would be eligible to wear a rosette in his buttonhole. He rushed right home to his small flat, where his wife was cooking up a soup, and grabbed her, crying: "You'll never believe this, but I've just been named to the Legion of Honor." They stood in the small kitchen, weeping with joy in each other's arms. Later, to celebrate, they went around the corner to their favorite bistro to have dinner, and all the patrons of the place came by to shake the beaming Dupont's hand.